RULE
BREAKER

RULE
BREAKER

LORA LEIGH

BERKLEY BOOKS, NEW YORK

THE BERKLEY PUBLISHING GROUP
Published by the Penguin Group
Penguin Group (USA) LLC
375 Hudson Street, New York, New York 10014

USA • Canada • UK • Ireland • Australia • New Zealand • India • South Africa • China

penguin.com

A Penguin Random House Company

RULE BREAKER

This book is an original publication of The Berkley Publishing Group.

Library of Congress Cataloging-in-Publication Data

Leigh, Lora.
Rule Breaker : a novel of the Breeds / Lora Leigh.
pages cm. — (Breed ; 13)
ISBN 978-0-425-26545-1 (hardback)
1. Genetic engineering—Fiction.   2. Paranormal romance stories.   3. Erotic fiction.   I. Title.
PS3612.E357R85   2014   2013047384
813'.6—dc23

FIRST EDITION: February 2014

PRINTED IN THE UNITED STATES OF AMERICA

10   9   8   7   6   5   4   3   2   1

Cover illustration by Rita Frangie.
Cover design by S. Miroque.

For the self-proclaimed Sluts at the optometrist's office, UO.

Thanks for the wonderful conversation on books, tight male butts and hijacking room keys. You know the doctor's office is a good one when you leave laughing and ready to write.

And to you, the readers, for loving the Breeds.

Thank you for the e-mails, the encouragement and the continual push for more in the series. I hope you continue to enjoy the books, and keep demanding more.

⋆ T H E   W O R L D ⋆
⊙ F   T H E   B R E E D S

They're not shifters or werewolves.

They are experiments in genetic engineering. Created to be super soldiers and the advanced lab rats needed to research new drug therapies for the human population.

They weren't created to be free.

They weren't even created to live.

They existed to serve the men and women who created them, tortured them, filled them with rage and a hunger for freedom.

Now they're free, they're living and they're setting the world, and their mates, on fire.

───────────

For a glossary of Breed terms, please flip to the back of the book.

RULE
BREAKER

✦ P R O L O G U E ✦

GYPSY RUM MCQUADE, AGE FIFTEEN

Gypsy stared at the file her Coyote abductors had possessed. Stained by dirty fingers, the edges wrinkled, pictures half sticking out of it. The file lay on the wood box in front of the rough pallet of sleeping bags she sat on, its very presence a testament that what had happened had not been a mistake.

Atop the pictures sticking out of the manila file was the most loathsome. The weak link, they had called her. The one their contact had assured them would do something stupid enough to allow her to be caught.

It was a picture of her.

A picture of her, then one of her brother, Mark.

Laughing Mark, with his dark green eyes, light brown hair and ever-ready smile.

His picture was beneath hers, along with pictures of her sister, Kandy Sweet, and her parents, Hansel and Greta McQuade. Thank God they were out of town, out of reach . . . out of danger. Now she wished she had gone with them, wished she had begged her parents to take her with them rather than staying behind because of that damned party.

Her abductor, Grody, had snickered and told her that she was known to be her brother's only weakness. Poor Mark, he'd sighed. To have such a liability must be a terrible curse.

She wouldn't have been such a liability if she had just gone with her parents as they had asked.

"Gypsy?" A Breed, taller than the others who now filled the cavern, spoke her name softly.

Jonas.

He was Jonas Wyatt.

He was the director of the Bureau of Breed Affairs.

He and his Breeds had saved her.

In those seconds just before the Coyote would have raped her, she had seen the Breed who had come in with him and fired the shot that killed Grody as other Breeds fired on Grody's companions.

But they hadn't arrived in time to save Mark.

She stared up at Jonas, her eyes sore, her throat raw from screaming.

Her face hurt where the Coyote had hit her, and the rest of her body was bruised and aching, but none of it compared to how bad it hurt inside her heart. There was no agony that could come close to the agony of losing the one person in the world who had loved Gypsy Rum McQuade, just because she was Gypsy Rum McQuade.

Gypsy knew she should thank Jonas and his Breeds for coming when they did, but at that moment, all she wanted to do was hate him for not being there sooner.

She couldn't hate him, though.

She had seen the grief, the pain in his eyes as he and the other Breeds had torn the dead Coyotes from where they had fallen around her.

At least she was covered now.

The Breed who had killed the Coyote preparing to rape her had been there when the dead Breed had been dragged from her. He'd obviously stripped off his T-shirt quickly. He was bare chested beneath his tactical vest, the black shirt normally worn with the mission uniform in his hand. He'd shoved it into a female Breed's hands and ordered her harshly to get it on her as his mesmerizing gaze had touched hers, the blue spreading across his eyes, filling even the whites for the briefest second before they were normal once again.

Or perhaps she had just imagined the completely blue orbs. She wished she had just imagined the rest of the night.

The shirt was way too big for her, but it covered her. And it was warm, warm enough that her teeth weren't chattering anymore. The scent that clung to it wrapped around her, and it comforted her. She wouldn't have thought anything could comfort her now, let alone a long black T-shirt with the Bureau of Breed Affairs insignia on the left breast that smelled a little bit like chocolate and peppermint.

It was like invisible arms wrapped around her, and she imagined it was all that kept her from just drifting away and not existing anymore.

The warmth of the shirt, the softness of it, enclosed her. Like a wall around her. A shield that kept away the world.

At least for now.

Maybe, in this shield, she thought, she could find a way to just slip back to that time when the nightmares didn't exist anymore.

"I want to go home." She hadn't meant to say the words. They seemed such a travesty. But maybe, there she could find a way to make it better.

She wanted to find a way to make this night not exist and to bring her brother's laughter back.

She wanted to just go to sleep and not have to ever wake up again. Maybe then, she could just dream. She could dream of what life was like before she'd slipped out of the house to go to a party that didn't really matter.

Distantly, in some unfocused part of her mind, she wondered if that was how these Breeds had felt when they were held captive? Tortured?

God, how had they kept fighting? Kept trying to survive?

Had they just found a place in their heads where the pain hadn't happened yet? Could she do that too?

"You can go home soon, Gypsy. A heli-jet's picking your parents up now," Jonas assured her.

The news jerked her out of her numbness for a moment. She flinched at the surge of agony that pierced her soul.

Oh God, how was she going to face her parents?

The fact that they were coming wasn't of any comfort to her. They would come here to get her.

They would see Mark's body in the dirt outside the cavern.

They would see the blood that had soaked into the ground and stained the hands of the huge Coyote Breed who had killed him.

The blood that had been smeared over her face and breasts as the Coyote's laughter shredded her soul.

Those Coyotes were all dead now, she reminded herself desperately. They couldn't come back. They couldn't hurt anyone anymore.

It wasn't enough compensation for the loss of her brother, though.

Nothing she could ever do would make up for the mistake she had made.

She heard Jonas's heavy sigh a few seconds before he picked up the file she'd been focused on, then sat on the box and stared at where she sat— where the Coyote had been killed.

Turning her head away from him, she tried to ignore him.

She tried, tried so hard to just wish it all away.

Tightening her arms around her knees, she huddled closer to the wall, wishing she could cry.

If she could cry, maybe her chest would stop hurting so bad.

Mark always told her that sometimes, only tears could heal the heart and soul. He would tell her to cry whenever she needed to; that way, she would always be sweet and innocent and he would always try to find a way to make the tears all better.

Maybe if she started screaming and crying, if she begged God hard enough, loud enough, then it would all just be some horrible nightmare.

Oh God, she just wanted it to stop hurting. It was like an iron band tightening around her heart and her ribs, constricting her breathing and making it hard for her heart to beat.

Maybe her heart would just stop beating. Hope flared inside her for a second.

Maybe someone would have mercy on her and kill her as well.

She was trying so hard to be brave, as Mark had told her to be, even though he'd told her for so many years that it was his job to be brave, and her job to cry and be sweet.

But now he wanted her to be brave. He'd told her not to cry.

It was the last thing he'd asked her to do.

"Gypsy, I need to ask you some questions," Jonas told her gently, watching her with a heavy sympathy that sickened her.

She didn't deserve his sympathy.

She didn't deserve anyone's forgiveness.

Least of all this Breed's.

Or her parents'.

Even Mark's.

"It was my fault," she told Jonas, staring into the back of the shadowed cavern now, her gaze unfocused, her need to escape threatening to over-whelm her. "It's all my fault."

"No, sweetheart, it wasn't your fault." From the corner of her eyes she could see him wiping his hand over his head, the short strands of his black hair gleaming in the low light of the cave. "None of this was your fault."

Oh, but how very wrong he was. It was all her fault.

She was childish, and her temper had done far more than just get her in trouble this time. This time, it had destroyed the person she loved more than anything.

"I wanted to go to the party," she tried to explain, but even to her own ears, the excuse was so stupid. So immature.

Why had that party been so important?

"Gypsy, what happened here wasn't your fault." His deep voice was rough, and she bet he managed to convince a whole lot of people of a whole lot of lies.

But he couldn't convince her of that lie.

"I slipped out of the house. My friend Khileen was picking me up. She lives in the desert." Khileen Langer was from England.

She and her family were staying in New Mexico on her stepfather's desert estate, where they were visiting for the summer. She liked Khileen. Liked the way the other girl was always laughing and daring her to have fun. To not be so serious.

She couldn't ever let anyone convince her of that again.

"There was this party," she continued, forcing herself to speak. "And a band and everything that some college boys were having in the desert. I just wanted to go see my friends, and the band."

And maybe drink a little.

Maybe flirt with some of the boys from school.

"So you left for the party?" he asked her.

Her breathing hitched and she shuddered.

It was like her soul was crying, but she couldn't cry herself because Mark had asked her not to.

"He was angry at me for some reason." Her fists clenched in the material of the shirt as her lips trembled and she hugged her knees closer to her breasts. "We had a deal." She rocked against the agony burning brighter inside her. "I would always tell him if I was going to a party and he would make sure he was there, so he could . . ." The whimper that escaped her surprised her. "So he could make sure I didn't get in trouble or get hurt."

"But you didn't tell him you were going?" he asked then.

Gypsy frowned. "I did. I tried, but he yelled at me." Why had Mark yelled at her? "He told me to just go away, that I was irritating him." She stared into the darkness intently. Why hadn't Mark ever told her that she irritated him? She would have tried to stop. She really would have. "Mark has never yelled at me before."

He had always loved her, always been patient with her.

"Were you aware your brother was in trouble?" he asked her then. "Did he tell you there were Coyotes searching for him? That the Genetics Council had identified him and sent a team to ensure that he couldn't steal the information he was hacking into anymore? That they were looking for him tonight?"

She turned to him slowly, blinking back in confusion. "I swear I didn't know. Mark was just acting so weird. He wanted me to stay in my bedroom and he wouldn't talk to me. He was being sharp and didn't want to be bothered. And he wouldn't listen to me when I tried to tell him I just wanted to go to the party. He wouldn't let me tell him anything."

She was going to throw up. She didn't want to move. She didn't want to have to find a place to throw up in privacy. Mark hadn't acted frightened or scared or worried. He'd been very, very angry, though, and he was snapping at her whenever he caught her out of her bedroom and ordering her back into it.

He'd hurt her feelings and made her angry at him. She'd decided to just go without telling him. He wasn't talking to her, why should she talk to him?

"Then how could you have known what would happen?" he asked, and the question sounded reasonable, but she knew it didn't matter.

She shook her head in confusion again before laying it against the rough stone wall beside her head. Mark had no doubt come to try to save her as soon as the Coyote had managed to get hold of him.

He'd have come straight to the desert, knowing he was going to die. He would have known he couldn't save her, or himself.

He should have just saved himself.

"Is Khileen okay?" she asked the Breed who still watched her thoughtfully. "She was so scared. She got away, though. When that Coyote pulled me out of the car, she was trying to get it back into gear after they forced us to stop. She's not used to a manual shift yet."

Her friend had managed to save herself, but she hadn't been able to do so before the Coyote had forced Gypsy out of the little sports car her friend had picked her up in.

She didn't blame Khileen.

She was thankful her friend had gotten away. It was bad enough that Gypsy had gotten her own brother killed. If she had gotten Lobo Reever's stepdaughter killed, then Jessica Reever, her mother's best friend, would never have forgiven her mother.

Her mom would need her friend when she realized what Gypsy had done.

"Khi's fine," he promised her. "If it hadn't been for her, we would have never known where to find you. We were at her stepfather's ranch trying to find your brother when she made the call to him."

Gypsy remembered her friend had said that her mother and stepfather had some kind of Breed company. A delegation from the Breed community or something.

Oh God, what was she going to do? Her parents were coming, and they didn't like putting up with her anyway. How many times had her mother laughingly told Mark how easy it would be to just get a babysitter when she was little? Or how easily she could just stay by herself after she turned thirteen?

They had wanted Mark to do stuff with them. Things that they said Gypsy wouldn't adapt well to. How could her sister adapt but Gypsy couldn't, she'd wondered.

This was why, she reminded herself cruelly. Because she was stupid and she did bad things.

How was she going to tell her parents what she had done this time? How was she ever going to explain to Kandy how selfish she had been?

That she'd sneaked out to go to a party when Mark was in such danger?

Her parents were going to hate her.

Mark was their only son, and though they often said they loved all their children, it was Mark they were best friends with. He was the one they had so much pride in.

Because he was strong and smart and never lied or sneaked out of the house. But whenever Gypsy did, he was always there, watching her, protecting her.

He wouldn't be there anymore.

All the security she had ever known in her life was gone now.

"I want to die." She wanted to close her eyes and just go away. "I wish they had just killed me first."

If they had killed her, then she wouldn't have to face what she had done. And she wouldn't have to live her life without Mark in it.

"Look at me, Gypsy." The demand in his voice was impossible to deny, but she was so tired that turning her head to meet his gaze seemed to take forever.

The gentleness in his expression, the sympathy and regret that filled those silvery eyes, urged her to believe him, commanded her to obey him.

"You can't die, Gypsy, you have a far too interesting future ahead of you," he said, glancing to her side for the briefest second before focusing on her once again.

An interesting future? No, there was no interesting future. There would always be the memory of the horrible mistake she had made.

"I don't want an interesting future," she answered him mechanically, stepping eagerly into the strange, unemotional shell she could feel beginning to wrap around her. "I just want Mark to come back."

Yes, she opened herself to that heavy weight, urged it to cover her quickly, to dim the agony resonating through her soul, just a little bit.

Jonas grimaced, rubbing at the side of his neck in a gesture of helplessness that she was certain was a completely alien feeling for someone so strong.

"Your brother was one of our best informants," he finally told her, and though she hadn't known that, she wasn't surprised. Mark had so admired the Breeds and all they had been forced to do to survive. "He was a high-level hacker who had found a way into their computers and was feeding us information on hidden labs and the identities of the Council's scientists and managing to steal dozens of their top-secret files," he continued as she watched him. "He refused to let us protect him. He refused to even let us know who he was. We were here because we had tracked him this far, unaware that the Council had managed to do the same so quickly. They would have found him whether you had slipped out of the house or not. The fact that you had slipped out and were with Khi is all that saved you, honey. No one could have saved your brother."

He was wrong.

Mark was smart.

If it hadn't been for her stupidity, he would have found a way to save himself.

She shook her head. "He was going to leave. I heard him on the phone the last time I tried to talk to him. He was telling someone he'd meet them in a few hours. He had to finish something." If she hadn't left the house—

If the party hadn't seemed so important at the time, her brother would still be alive.

She was only barely aware of Jonas rising to his feet and moving away from her. Seconds later she could hear the sound of his voice as he spoke to someone.

She was shaking as she fought to push back the memory of her brother's death. How he'd stared at her, his dark eyes bleak and filled with hopelessness. And helplessness, as he told her how sorry he was.

He was sorry? Why had he been sorry? It had been her fault.

The Coyote had laughed at him. Standing behind her brother, that big knife against Mark's throat, he'd laughed at Mark, then told him what they were going to do to her after he was dead.

She had begged them not to hurt Mark. She didn't care if they killed her. She didn't care, as long as they just let him go.

"Don't cry, Gypsy," he told her as that Coyote, Grody, had laughed at him. "Don't cry, and be brave, Peanut. Do you hear me? Don't cry. Be brave, Peanut."

She had heard him, but still, she had watched that knife bring blood and she had screamed. Screamed and begged, Please don't hurt him.

The knife had bitten into Mark's throat, blood welling at the side of his neck, and then there was a long, bright red line of dark scarlet that began to flow with sickening speed as the Coyote released his body. Mark had fallen to the ground as though in slow motion, boneless, his gaze locked with hers, dimming, then finally staring back at her with a blank look of sorrow.

She jerked, her eyes flying open as she realized she had let them close.

She just wanted to go to sleep.

She wanted to sleep for a very, very long time. Long enough that maybe her mom and dad would forgive her. Maybe her baby sister, who loved Mark just as much as Gypsy did, wouldn't hate her forever.

But every time she closed her eyes she could see that moment when Mark had died. That second when his blood had spilled down the front of his white shirt.

"Your parents will be here soon." Jonas spoke from beside her once again. "My team has just loaded them into the heli-jet."

They would be here soon.

They would be so angry with her.

Oh God, what if they didn't let her go home? What if they didn't even want her anymore?

"They'll hate me. Momma and Daddy will never forgive me for this," she told herself, unaware she was speaking aloud, that her words were breaking the heart of the new director of the Bureau of Breed Affairs. "They won't even want me to come home now. How could they ever want to live with me after this?"

Where would she go?

She was only fifteen, and no one would want the girl who had helped Coyotes murder her brother. Because everyone loved Mark.

He was everyone's best friend.

How could anyone ever love the awful person who had enabled those filthy animals to kill him?

"How could they ever want me to be home?" she whispered again, laying her head against the wall beside her and staring into the darkness once again.

Maybe if she was very, very still, if she tried hard enough, she could just disappear into that darkness and never have to exist ever again.

"I promise you, Gypsy, your parents won't blame you," he lied to her again. "But if that ever happens, I swear to you I'll make sure you're taken care of. Do you hear me, sweetheart? You have only to contact me, I'll never desert you."

She heard the words and he probably meant them. But he was so brave, and just like that Breed with those bright, bright blue eyes who had shot the Coyote, Grody, he was strong, and he knew how to protect everyone.

Even stupid, weak little girls who didn't know how to stay home instead of risking everyone they loved.

She didn't deserve his protection.

She didn't deserve anyone's protection.

◆ ◆ ◆

Jonas eased back to his seat on the crate and watched her sadly.

"They love Mark so much, just like I do. And I got him killed. It was my fault that the Breed used that knife—"

She broke off, shaking so hard he wondered how she was remaining in one place.

Rising, Jonas moved far enough from her that he could get the reports he knew were coming in.

He wondered if the shock would build in this child until she had her wish and she just went to sleep forever.

Hell, he'd grieve himself if this brave, broken little girl ceased to exist.

And should that happen, at least one Breed would surely suffer for it.

This grieving child would be far more to the Breed society than even she imagined if his hunch was correct.

Jonas turned and met one of the independent contractors who often fought alongside the Breeds, waiting for his report.

"Mercury just called from the McQuade residence," Simon Quatres reported. "Rogue Breeds hit McQuade's house at the same time this group ran Khileen's car off the road. Mercury and his men found video and audio devices in his room and at his workstation in the living room. Grody and his men knew who they were coming for, and where he was. Nothing could have kept this from happening. And if she had been in the house, we'd have never found out in time to get to her."

A low, all-but-silent little whimper reached his sharp ears then. A cry he was certain the girl was unaware she had even made.

"Where's that fucking doctor?" he questioned Lawe as the enforcer moved quickly toward him. "That kid's going to die of grief if he doesn't get here soon and give her something."

"They make drugs to cure grief now, boss?" Simon asked, his voice low and resonating with the same aching regret they all felt for her pain. "Can I have some?"

"Lobo's having the doctor flown in now," Lawe Justice assured him. "He should be here within the next five minutes. Rule's been outside coordinating our people and taking care of her brother. Reever's men are taking care of disposing of the Council's rogue Coyotes. One of them is still alive, though," he said, his voice lowered to carry no farther. "The guard who was at the front of the cave. Swears he's the one who contacted us and led us here after they took the McQuade girl."

Jonas's eyes narrowed. "How did he survive?" He knew that damned Coyote had taken a laser blast to his chest.

"Reinforced laser-resistant Kevlar," Lawe answered. "Seems he wasn't into suicide tonight, were his words I believe. Swears he has video and that he tried to delay McQuade's death and says you'll know him. Grody wasn't just here for the Council either, according to this Coyote. He was paid by a human to make certain McQuade and his sister both died tonight."

"And he has video?" Jonas mused.

Lawe gave a sharp, brief nod.

"What's his name?"

"Goes by Loki," Lawe answered. "But his brother, a full brother, is one of the Council's best trackers and assassins, Farce."

Jonas's lips curled at the name. "He's not their best, he's their luckiest." Then he sighed. "Damn, I didn't know Loki was in the area, though."

"You know him?" Lawe questioned, his eyes narrowing.

He knew him, Jonas thought with a sigh, and he should have known to expect him here.

"He's one of ours," Jonas confirmed. "As damnedably stubborn and hardheaded as he is, he's one of ours."

Lawe's eyes widened. "Rule's beating the fuck out of one of ours, then . . ."

Lawe turned and rushed from the cavern, motioning to several of the enforcers guarding the entrance as he moved to rescue the young trouble magnet, Loki, from Rule Breaker's clutches.

As the Breed rushed from him, several others following behind, Jonas watched as a young female moved toward him. With her short black hair and emerald green eyes, the Irish blood was damned close to the surface. As were her Breed genetics.

"Mr. McQuade is demanding to speak to you ASAP. He and his wife are en route for arrival in one hour, sir," Moira O'Malley, a young Breed just out of the labs she was confined in, faced him coolly with the information.

Jonas shook his head. "Contact Pride Leader Lyons and have him inform the McQuades that I'll answer what questions I can when they arrive."

There would be time enough for questions once the heli-jet landed. For now, he had other things to do now that he knew Gypsy McQuade's fate was tied to the Breeds.

Moving back to her, he watched the ghostly form that had begun advancing from the entrance of the cave earlier.

Wary, suspicious, it watched Jonas warningly, a savage snarl curling its lip.

He wouldn't have expected it, but that misty image of the lion prowled slowly, carefully to the girl until the huge beast settled protectively at her side to rub its huge head against her much smaller one.

A psychic connection, he thought in wonder, a manifestation of the creature's ability to sense far more than the man who carried it within him.

It blinked back at him, those eyes locking with his, and he knew. He knew in that moment, staring into the beast's eyes, exactly who this psychic creature was a part of, and felt a warning chill race up his spine.

The lion snarled at him silently, warning him to keep his thoughts to himself.

Jonas was curious just how strong the animal inside that Breed was now, and how long the man would wait once Gypsy matured before he was forced to face who and what she was to him.

He refused to allow that curiosity to influence any decisions he would make, though. If she was destined to eventually be the mate that Breed swore he would never have, then that was what she would be. If not, then forcing him to acknowledge who she was would only change the destiny evolving around her.

Either way, Jonas was responsible for ensuring that she survived here and now. Nothing less and nothing more. That didn't mean he wouldn't do a hell of a lot more, if possible, to make this tragedy easier for her.

Though God help him, how he wanted to ensure that neither she nor another child suffered the depravity that the Council practiced ever again.

Shaking his head, he moved to another female Breed rushing to him, heavy blankets cradled in her arms as she returned from the heli-jet they'd used to fly into the area. It had just landed again after making a run to the Reever estate.

"Enforcer Breaker asked that I tell you he's sending the dead Coyotes to the Reever estate until you can examine them and decide what do with them. Enforcer Justice has your contact secured outside and awaiting your orders, sir," the Jaguar female enforcer stated as she moved to Gypsy.

Jonas wasn't surprised that Rule had taken command while Jonas sat with the girl and tried to figure out what had happened in this desolate place.

He was surprised that Rule had broken protocol and decided to beat one lone, living Coyote within an inch of his life rather than saving him for interrogation, though.

Rule Breaker, despite his amusing choice of a name, this single, understandable mistake where Loki was concerned, was turning into one of his most intuitive leaders. His brother, Lawe Justice, though, was quickly becoming his right hand.

A female enforcer crouched before Gypsy and eased the blankets in place around the girl huddling on the makeshift bed. Gypsy's arms were wrapped around her scratched, bruised legs as her forehead rested on her knees. She was shaking so damned hard he was surprised her teeth weren't chattering.

He sensed the tears, the screams trapped within her. Sensed the agony burning like a fiery ball of pain that buried itself in her heart the second she was forced to watch the Coyote slice her brother's throat.

The debt the Breed community owed her brother was too great not to ensure that if his sister ever needed the Bureau or the Breeds, they would be there for her.

For now, though, all he could do was try to make her warm and comfortable and await the family flying out to her. A loving family, he hoped.

Parents who would try to help her repair the wounds this night would leave on her gentle heart.

As he watched her, watched the ghostly lion sheltering her, he had a feeling nothing could repair Gypsy's wounds, and he was afraid of what her parents' arrival might bring, regarding their acceptance of her.

Son of a bitch, he wished he'd gotten there sooner.

Wished he'd had Mark McQuade's location ahead of the Coyotes who had killed him.

As he watched Gypsy McQuade, he realized just how heavily the regret that he hadn't been fast enough lay inside him.

It was a futile wish, because it was now something he couldn't change. Jonas didn't dwell on things that couldn't be changed.

He moved on to things that could be.

And though it was the hardest thing he'd done in his life, he turned his back on her after giving the female enforcer a silent order to stay by her side.

This night was over.

He hadn't been fast enough, he hadn't tracked McQuade in time. When he returned to the Bureau, he'd ensure that all their equipment was updated with the best the government and the corporations ordered to provide for the Breeds could pay for.

The next time, he'd be ahead of the Genetics Council's lapdogs.

The next time, he wouldn't face the fact that he'd failed in the shattered eyes of a girl who would never forget the nightmare of her brother's death or her own near rape.

The next time—

Jonas sighed as he walked out of the cavern. God help him, he didn't want there to be a next time.

· CHAPTER I ·

NINE YEARS LATER

She was his fix and he'd been long months without his fix.

Too long.

This time, she would know he was there. He'd waited. For six years, since the night she'd shown up at her eighteenth birthday party dressed in leather and dancing like a seductress, he'd waited.

He'd been there every year for her birthday since the night her brother had died nine years before. Actually, he made certain he was there every few months just to check up on her, but the night of her birthday, he made damned sure he was there. Not to bring a present; he never did. Just to make certain she was safe, that she was taken care of and that she wasn't living on the streets, as it was reported her mother often threatened to send her.

The hell of that night, over nine years before, still haunted her.

Hell, it still haunted everyone who had been there. But Gypsy had paid more than anyone else. And she was still paying.

Staring across the bar, his gaze caressing the gentle lines of her face, he willed her to sense the caress. To sense his presence. To feel the hunger that had begun growing since the night she'd turned eighteen, the night she'd entranced him with the grace and erotic promise in her absorbed face as she'd given herself to the music.

Standing across the large room, the gyrating mass of dancers between them, her head turned slowly, her gaze seeking the sensation of whoever watched her. When her eyes met his, he watched the transformation.

Green eyes darkened, dilated. Arousal flushed her sun-kissed face as a sudden, vulnerable pain flashed across her expression. It was gone just as quickly, to be replaced by a hint of uncertainty, of want and hunger that he knew she believed she could never appease. Not if she intended to continue to pursue the shadowed course her life had followed for the past nine years, since the night she had lost the one person who held her uppermost in his life.

Most young women were raised knowing that their mother, father, even both, were there to protect her. That one or the other would ensure she was cared for. For Gypsy, that one person, that parent who had loved her above all others, had been her older brother. The brother who had died in the desert, drawn there by the Coyotes who had taken his sister, who had threatened to destroy her in ways Mark McQuade couldn't have imagined unless he took her place.

Surely the brother knew neither of them would escape? What had made him go into that desert believing his sister would return from it unscathed?

Whatever the reason, Mark had died and Gypsy had spent the past nine years trying to atone for a death she hadn't been the cause of. A death she was told repeatedly had been her fault.

The time for Gypsy to pay for sins that were not her own was over, he decided. Just as it was time to draw free of the past, to save one fragile infant's life and ease the hell a friend and his mate were enduring.

In that moment, as her gaze touched his, as he watched the heat and the hunger rising inside her, he made her a silent promise.

Soon, very soon, the games of the past nine years would be over and he'd ensure the shadows that lurked about her would come to light. While he was at it, he'd appease a hunger he was entirely certain was not, could not be, Mating Heat.

Because Mating Heat couldn't be allowed.

Rule Breaker, Investigative Commander of the Bureau of Breed Affairs, refused to allow himself a mate.

He refused to allow any woman to die beneath the cold, merciless blade of scientists determined to learn the secrets of a mating that nature was still determined to play with . . .

He shook the thought away. Before he could move to possess what he'd waited for for six years, he first had secrets to reveal, a game to end and a Bengal Breed to slowly draw into the fold of the Bureau of Breed Affairs. Years of searching for the Breed called Gideon, and he'd finally arrived in the one place Rule had been pushing him to.

The danger Jonas's daughter faced and the hell of a past research project, would see the end of its secrets. He would either see the brutal truths hidden among four victims of that horrible project revealed, or the possible death of an innocent child and the slow destruction of a man he respected above all others but his brother.

It would end here, he promised.

But what would happen to him, who or what he would have to fight for, once it was over . . .

Two months later

Jonas stared down at his sleeping daughter, his hands clasped together as his wrists rested on the rail of her crib. For the moment, he could almost convince himself that she was going to be fine.

Almost.

Rage festered inside him. His daughter was being killed right before his eyes, and no matter how hard he tried, he couldn't stop the serum she had been given seven months previously from doing as the scientists predicted: It was killing her.

Just as it had killed its creator, Phillip Brandenmore, weeks after he'd injected Amber.

It had rotted his brain from the inside out, killing him slowly, painfully.

God help him, he couldn't allow that to happen to Amber. It would destroy her mother, his mate.

It would destroy him.

Pulling back from the crib, his arms dropping to his sides, he gazed around the room, not for the first time, searching for some shadow, a spirit, something, some sign of a presence that could answer his questions.

Fairies, Cassie Sinclair called them. Jonas knew them to be spirits, psychic remnants or broken dreams.

And no such spirit or remnant, psychic or otherwise, walked his daughter's path.

Yet.

That didn't mean she had none.

It didn't mean she had no future.

It simply meant she was far too young to have drawn one to her yet.

Either way, that didn't mean he wouldn't keep fighting for her life.

The answers were here, in Window Rock, Arizona, waiting to be un-buried, while other secrets were waiting on the day they *could* be buried.

He didn't see the things Cassie saw and he didn't see those vague im-ages near as often. But he knew enough to know that the ancient Navajo ritual that had played out in this desert nine years before, three years after the escape of four incredibly gifted creations, would reveal the secret he needed to save Amber.

The question was whether he would uncover the truth in time.

Jonas knew he'd searched every area he could think of. He'd gone over every memory, no matter how unfocused or uncertain, that Liza Johnson had of her previous life as Honor Roberts. He'd especially probed at the hazy, scattered memories of the ritual itself that she remembered. The an-cient power that transferred the consciousness of two dying girls into Honor Roberts's and Fawn Corrigan's bodies wasn't as easy to decipher as he'd hoped, even with the help of the guides that sometimes came to him.

The spirits of Honor and Fawn had somehow been put to sleep until the time of the awakening, as it was called. Cassie assured him they were awake now, though, and working quite well with those of the spirits of Claire and Liza when they'd chided her for attempting to interfere.

A recent attack on Liza had revealed the partial memories that now allowed Jonas to piece together some of the missing clues they needed to crack the code that hid the information on the serum Amber had been injected with.

Just some of the pieces. Still, the formula and various notes of the years that the serum had been used on Honor and Fawn had yet to be decoded.

Claire Martinez, the young woman who inhabited Fawn Corrigan's body, had accepted the fact that she wasn't who she believed she was. Ac-cepting and awakening were two different things, though. And the secrets the girl was hiding were beginning to bother him. How the hell was he supposed to stand aside and let her continue to search for a way to honor-ably kill herself?

Son of a bitch, why couldn't he just fucking walk away from everyone else's problems and just focus on his own. On his daughter. On his mate.

Because it was all tied together, he admitted.

Woven so closely together that to abandon one would be to abandon the child his heart had taken as his own. And that meant doing what he could to bring Fawn Corrigan, or Claire Martinez as she was now called, along a path that would bring her face-to-face with the Breed sworn to kill her.

Claire had revealed nightmares and some scattered pieces of memories from Fawn's years in the labs as well. But there were still so many missing pieces and so little time.

Before he could draw the Bengal Judd and the feral Bengal Gideon out, the girls would have to reach inside themselves and find the spirits that slept within them. Liza and Claire would have to accept that the reprieve they had been given from death was at an end, and the parts of Honor and Fawn that still slept would have to accept that it was once again time to face their lives and truly awake.

This had to be finished.

Moving from Amber's bedroom into the main room of the hotel suite, Jonas strode to the desk that sat at the far wall and took his seat. Activating the holo-board of his computer, he laid his palm against the biometric scanner on the top of the desk and waited for the screen to appear.

When the holographic panel came up, he pulled up several files as he checked the time.

He had five minutes before the meeting he'd called with the newly promoted Investigative Commander, Rule Breaker.

The investigative field of the Bureau of Breed Affairs was growing quickly, requiring Jonas to put his best enforcers into key positions now available.

And into the investigations of crimes against Breeds and Breed Law.

Though soon, Jonas suspected, Rule would be heading the new offices in New Mexico as division director rather than continuing on to another assignment after completing this one.

That knowledge had reminded him of a silent promise he'd made to himself nine years ago as he flew away from the area, and to the broken child who had been left to the care of her family. A family tragically wounded by the death of the young man they had all treasured.

Arranging Rule's life was something Jonas had sworn to Rule he wouldn't do.

Hell, he'd even crossed his fingers, just in case, as he'd made that promise.

Maneuvering Seth Lawrence and Dane Vanderale, two of the Breeds' greatest benefactors, into doing his dirty work for him had required a bit more finesse. If they had even had a distant thought or suspicion regarding his actions, they would have created a Breed Town Crier just to announce it to every Breed far and wide.

Especially Rule.

Narcs.

That was what they were.

The old-fashioned term flashed into his mind.

They were nothing but damned narcs, both of them. If they weren't extremely careful, he'd show them exactly why they should be very wary. Because Jonas knew things of their futures that neither man could ever imagine.

So far, he was playing nice.

But the day was swiftly approaching for one of them that nice would be a thing of a past.

It was just a matter of time before he learned how to cure his daughter. He could then focus on restructuring the Bureau of Breed Affairs. Once that was completed, Jonas, Callan and Wolfe could rest assured that their vision of the Breeds' future could continue should anything happen to one, or all, of them.

Then Jonas intended to show his legitimate half brother, Dane Vanderale, exactly why Breeds and humans alike feared him to the extent they did.

He was just completing the final additions to each file that he'd put together when the door to the suite opened and the Lion Breed on duty, Flint McCain, stepped inside.

"Commander Breaker's here, sir," he announced.

Jonas nodded back at him firmly. "Let him in."

Stepping aside, Flint nodded to Rule as he strode into the suite, his neon blue eyes flickering with amusement at Flint as the other Breed lifted his lip into a subtle snarl.

Rule had put his time in guarding many of Jonas's doors over the past ten years. Jonas didn't begrudge him a second to torment Flint now.

"Jonas." Rule stepped to the desk, the years they had worked together pretty much obliterating protocol at this point. "How's Amber doing this morning?"

It was no secret she'd been deteriorating rapidly in the weeks since the attack on Liza. For some reason the unknown hormone Brandenmore had injected her with had suddenly increased overnight within her little body, after leveling for several weeks.

They'd had hope for a while, that she was fighting off the effects, only to watch her descend again into that world of pain and confusion.

"She's resting this afternoon," he answered. "Have a seat, Rule, I have something to talk to you about."

Rule sat down in one of the comfortable chairs facing the desk, his back straight, feet planted firmly on the floor. Dressed in the Bureau's black mission uniform—the insignia of his Breed placement, a snarling lion, on one shoulder, his commander's bars gracing the other—he looked like the expertly honed killing machine he was created to be.

Shoulder-length black hair was pulled back and secured at his nape; neon blue eyes surrounded by heavy black lashes and fierce, sharply defined features made him popular among the female sex, while the corded strength of his body and exacting control made him an excellent commander among his peers.

Pressing the command button to send the files to Rule's e-pad before deactivating the computer and sitting back in his chair, Jonas watched the Breed silently for long moments.

Rule didn't even look at the electronic pad he carried on a holster at his thigh. He just waited, perhaps not patiently, but silently.

"Have you been able to find any information on the Unknown yet?" he asked Rule then, watching intently as the Breed gave a negative shake of his head.

"Nothing more than the fairy tale," he finally answered. "Each generation, six warriors are chosen to protect the heart of the Navajo. No one knows what the heart is, though. They're gifted with ancient powers and

secrets that will aid them in hiding and protecting what's most important
to the People. That's it. What about your contacts? Have they come back
with anything yet?"

Jonas shook his head.

"Any suspects yet as to their contact?" Jonas asked, tapping one finger
against the arm of his chair as he watched Rule thoughtfully.

Rule shook his head again. "Nothing yet. And we won't have, until
someone actually admits to believing they're real." He frowned then. "It
would have been nice if the message you received about them had been a
bit more forthcoming."

A grimace tightened Jonas's features. "A name would have been really
nice," he agreed before leaning forward and bracing his arms on the desk
once again. "I just sent the files you'll need for your upcoming mission
to your e-pad." Jonas nodded to the device, though Rule made no move to
remove it. "Several hours after the assailants busted into the windows of
Liza's suite last month, she experienced a flashback to the ritual that hid an
additional presence within her own body. In that flashback, she saw six
painted warriors—the Unknown, she remembered Orrin Martinez calling
them. They told her they would protect her and Claire, as well as the one
who watched from afar and the one who would follow when the time was
right."

"Judd and Gideon," Rule murmured as he propped an ankle on his knee
before leaning his elbow on the arm of the chair and narrowing his gaze
thoughtfully. "We know Gideon's already here, and I've managed to find a
few leads on a Breed who arrived twelve years ago, only to disappear a few
days after Liza and Claire's accident."

Jonas clenched his teeth as he fought for patience. Dammit, he wouldn't
have to play these fucking infernal games if everyone would just stop trying to evade fate and the fact that he knew what the hell he was doing.

He breathed in deeply. "When we were here nine years ago, we were
originally searching for a transmission we traced to a young man, Mark
McQuade. He was an exceptional hacker, and for a number of years he fed
us information and files that he stole from the Council's secure computers.
Files so top secret that if they were released at the time, they would have
destroyed some of the world's top leaders. We used them to blackmail those

leaders instead." Jonas smiled mercilessly. "Some enemies are better used than destroyed."

It was a philosophy he knew Rule agreed with. Still.

"I knew we were searching for a hacker when we first arrived," Rule stated. "He was killed by Coyotes that night before we could reach him and his sister, though."

Rule was going to continue to play the charade, Jonas thought.

As though he weren't well aware that the Breed had made several trips a year to the area to check up on the girl since that night.

"Yes, he was," Jonas sighed. "He was killed trying to protect her when the Coyotes found her first."

Here it was.

Jonas pushed back a flare of satisfaction, knowing it was far too soon to feel any triumph. Only when Gideon faced him with the answers he needed, and Amber's cure, would he allow that triumph free.

But here, finally, was one of the final steps to ensuring it.

"Gypsy McQuade." Rule sat back in his chair somberly, though Jonas wasn't unaware of the phantom form of the natural lion that eased slowly into view until it sat beside Rule, watching Jonas suspiciously, powerful teeth prominently displayed.

Jonas had no intention of warning Rule that his mate awaited. Hell, if the Breed hadn't figured that out, then he deserved whatever he got.

Hell no, Jonas wanted the man who had betrayed Mark McQuade and his sister Gypsy.

He knew who it was.

He knew he had no proof.

But he knew how to pull that information from the darkness into the light. That was his strength and he would use it exactingly.

"What do you know about Gypsy McQuade?" Jonas asked, as though he had no idea that Rule likely knew far more than he would ever let on.

"Not a lot," Rule answered without so much as a flicker of the eye or the slightest scent of a lie. "Dane and I have run into her fairly often at many of the nightspots and parties used by our contacts to pass information to us. She's a regular at the clubs and bars, both legal and underground, and has been for years as I understand it. She likes to party, though she doesn't mess with the drugs and never drinks more than she can handle. She's actually become very good friends with the Coyote females from the Delgado pack, Ashley, Emma and Sharone. Surprisingly, her friendship with Khileen slowly faded, though they still seem to get along well whenever they see each other. I would think you know more than I've pulled, considering her friendship with your mate and child."

Jonas snorted. "As you probably already know, then, she's amazingly reticent about discussing her own life."

Rule nodded.

"Her brother was an exceptional hacker," Jonas sighed, continuing to ignore the reference to Gypsy's friendship with his family. "The Breed community still owes him a hell of a debt. Because of that debt, I've ensured she's always had friends to turn to. Not that she's taken advantage of it. She's as distrustful as her brother was." Jonas frowned; surely Gypsy had managed to cry out all that guilt and pain by now. "Gypsy was convinced she was the reason her brother was killed." He breathed out roughly. "Her file is on your e-pad, as well as my notes and observations, along with Liza's, Claire's and Terran Martinez's. Along with her file are the ones on her sister, Kandy Sweet McQuade, as well as Mark's former fiancée, an assistant DA in Window Rock, Theodora Lacey. They're the short list of contacts the Unknown are suspected of using to learn our movements in the area, as well as the rogue Breeds the Council sends out. The Unknown are suspected to be directly responsible for our inability to locate or capture Gideon, and we suspect they also know Judd's location. Find just one of them, Judd or Gideon, and we'll have what we need to pull both of them in and finish this. Barring that, identify just one of the Unknown, and we achieve the same result. And if we're very lucky, maybe I can learn who betrayed Gypsy's brother and destroyed that kid's life in the course of the investigation."

And Jonas could officially give Rule leave to run an investigation that he'd been running under the radar for far too long.

The search for the person or persons responsible for revealing Mark McQuade's activities to the Council Coyotes searching for him nine years ago.

Because as sure as that Breed was playing one of the most intricate manipulations Jonas had ever seen—outside his own, if Rule wasn't extremely careful—then he was going to get his ass burned if he was revealed to be doing so.

◆   ◆   ◆

Rule stared back at Jonas for long silent moments before pulling the electronic pad from the holster he wore at the side of his thigh. He activated it and pulled up the files Jonas had sent. He scanned each one quickly while giving the appearance of patiently reading.

Hell, he knew this file like he knew his own life.

Probably better.

How the hell had Gypsy become suspected of working with the Unknown?

He was going to end up kicking someone's ass for letting this happen. Years of maneuvering, watching her pretty butt, and protecting men—both human and Breeds—Jonas would give his canines for, could come to a quick and painful end for not just himself, but Gypsy as well.

He knew each of the other young women in the file, though he'd taken little interest in them over the years. He had no reason to.

Kandy Sweet McQuade—someone should have shot her father for that name—ran her parents' candy and gift store, while Hansel and Greta Mc-Quade, along with Gypsy when needed, and their deceased son's best friend, Jason Harte, ran a small but successful personal image building business.

Two sisters and the ex-fiancée of a dead man suspected to be working with a group so covert that, until now, they were only regarded as a damned fairytale. They should have stayed a fairytale. Someone was dropping the ball here, and they damned well better pick it back up before he began kicking assess.

The Unknowns contact, code name Whisper, was suspected to have begun working with the group between nine and ten years before, during the year after Mark McQuade died she was directly responsible for contacting the Unknown in time to keep the rogue Coyotes from moving in on the location where Honor, Fawn and Judd were hiding three years after they escaped the plans the Genetics Council had for them. Had it not been for Whisper, they would have been taken.

Eyewitness reports in New Mexico at the time described a small group of Native Americans disguised in war paint and battling a team of Coyotes as two others sped away with two teenage girls and a young adult male. And they were never seen in the area again.

Trails had been laid leading from New Mexico. There had been sightings in Venezuela, but neither Council nor Breed forces had ever gotten close enough to actually have a chance of capturing them.

Nine years of covering trails, manipulating truths and laying in lies— If he wasn't careful, Jonas would unravel it all before he could ensure Gypsy's safety.

He needed to assure Jonas of the ridiculousness of even imagining that Gypsy was involved with a group as well hidden and undetectable as the Unknown, if they existed.

Jonas had to be convinced he was wrong about this—wrong, or Rule had to uncover the fact that the other Breed was up to one of his fucking matchmaking games.

"You're certain about this list?" Rule finally looked up, finding no clear reason or even strong suspicion in the files for Gypsy to have been tagged as the suspected "Whisper" spy.

Jonas had no proof that Gypsy was involved in anything. And if Jonas didn't have proof, then there was no proof to be found. That was all that kept Rule from immediately having Gypsy taken and hidden so deep, so fast that finding her would require more resources than Jonas could pull together at the moment.

The Bureau couldn't use what they couldn't prove, or at least insinuate very well, Jonas always claimed. Rule would make certain Jonas had no chance to "use" Gypsy.

"Why? Aren't you?" Jonas closed the computer down and leaned back in his chair again, absently gripping a pen between his hands and idly manipulating it between his fingers as he watched Rule.

Rule ignored the distracting tactic even as he hid a knowing smile.

"Gypsy doesn't fit the profile such a contact would have," he explained patiently. "She's too friendly, and too interested in being a woman to worry about being a spy."

Fuck.

Jonas wasn't buying that one despite the fact that Rule knew it was a damned good argument.

"Rule." Jonas leaned forward in his chair, laid the pen on the desk and clasped his hands on top of it. "Even after her brother's death and her belief that she caused it by slipping out to that party, Gypsy still attended every party she could make. She was there when the Coyote soldier that led that group after Honor, Fawn and Judd met with one of his spies in the area. She was part of the group that soldier partied with that night despite her tender age. The next day, that spy was found just outside town, his tongue cut out and his throat slashed, with a note to the Council pinned to his shirt, stating, *resigning for reasons of permanent death and dismemberment.*

"Gypsy socializes with a high number of suspected Genetics Council members who live in the area, their contacts and employees. She's friends with purists, rogue Breeds and tribal law enforcement members. She has all the contacts needed to do the job."

Rule had to give whoever had penned that contact's resignation kudos for being efficient as well as amusing. He was actually rather impressed with the wording of it.

That didn't mean he didn't have an argument ready for Jonas.

"The list of young women who attended the party that night and are still attending such parties is a large one. There are several candidates I would have looked at first," Rule pointed out before allowing suspicion to narrow his eyes, hoping distraction would work where debate wasn't. "Who created this list anyway?"

Jonas acknowledged his point, as well as his suspicion, with a mocking tilt of his head. Rule knew Jonas would be well aware of why he suspected a setup. There were far too many Breeds who called Jonas the Mate Matcher.

He schemed, connived and manipulated Breeds until he had them aligned perfectly with their mates. Then he made damned certain those Breeds couldn't and wouldn't attempt to walk away.

"I had independent sources from within the Bureau as well as connected to the Navajo Council compile that list, from over a dozen suspects. Individually, then as a group, they weeded out each suspect and cleared them of suspicion, with the exception of six. Of those six, Gypsy was the only one they were unable to clear.

Rule turned his attention back to the file.

Rule knew the group Jonas had assigned that task to. Liza Johnson, daughter of the Navajo president's head of security, and her mate, Stygian Black. Isabelle Martinez, niece to the president and daughter of the nation's legal council. Malachi Morgan, Isabelle's Coyote Breed mate. Terran Martinez, Isabelle's father and said legal council. Dane Vanderale, Jonas's half brother and a hybrid Breed so well disguised by his far-too-influential father to ever be suspected of being a Breed. And one of the Coyote Breeds' most dangerous members, Dog.

Both Isabelle's and Liza's mated status to Breeds and their history in the area made them the perfect choices to compile the final list, as did their mates and Isabelle's father, Terran. Still, it smacked of a manipulation.

And it stank of danger running headlong in Gypsy's direction.

Pinching the bridge of his nose, Rule pretended to continue to read while he cursed inwardly at whatever trick or sleight of hand had been used to put Gypsy on that list. Whichever it was, it ended with Gypsy smack under the director's regard.

The last place Rule wanted her to be.

For both their sakes.

"You've been in her company more than once, so I'll assume there's no chance of a mating?" Jonas all but sneered.

"Lucky for you," Rule agreed, never taking his attention from the file.

Rule flat refused any missions Jonas had a hand in that involved a woman. Luckily for Jonas, Rule had actually spent quite a bit of time in Gypsy's company in the past couple of months since coming to Window Rock, and had been around her many times in the past years as he checked up on her.

"You know, you take that district directorship position out here, and Dane and Seth will cut that clause that gives you permission to run away should you suspect a mate, right out of that contract."

Rule didn't look up once and was quite proud of the fact that he hid his smirk. "The one concerning you and any assignment regarding a female, Breed or human, will stay. I've already discussed the particulars with them."

Jonas growled, an irritated sound. "That's ridiculous."

Rule lifted his gaze slowly. "So says the Breed they call the Mate Matcher."

Jonas glared back at him, his silver gaze swirling with ire. Rule opted to distract the director at that point rather than continue what was sure to turn into a less than friendly debate.

"Jonas, why are you so convinced the Unknown actually exist?" Rule asked before Jonas could deny the charge. Or worse, admit to it. "I've been searching for weeks now, and there's not so much as a hint of the Unknown being anything but a fairy tale, let alone finding any ties to any of your suspects. Tell me what the fuck is going on here or find someone else to play games with because I don't have time for this shit."

"Orrin Martinez," Jonas finally answered, his jaw tightening at Rule's demand. "When I mentioned the Unknown to him, the scent of fear was unmistakable. As was the scent of desperation as he attempted to convince me that the Unknown were just as you said, a fairy tale. They exist, Rule, I promise you. And they were the same group that hid Judd, Honor and Claire, and countless other Breeds that made it to the Navajo Nation over the decades."

Rule rubbed at the back of his neck, considering the information. "Are we sure we can trust that response, though?"

Orrin should have been Jonas's grandfather rather than Rule's and Lawe's. The man was just as manipulating and just as calculating as Jonas could be.

"The truth was in his eyes, and his scent," Jonas growled before his gaze turned intent, somber. "Rule, I need you on this. I don't want you going off half-cocked because you think someone might be your mate," Jonas stated, his voice echoing with concern now. "This is Amber's life. Liza's memories of her life as Honor Roberts are still too scattered and broken to help much further. Claire's have returned in even smaller portions, and we have no idea how to find Judd and Gideon. Without the information they hold about those experiments and the key to Brandenmore's encrypted files, Amber doesn't have a chance of surviving this."

Rule deactivated the e-pad and returned it to the padded pocket he stored it in before staring back at the director. "I never go off half-cocked, Director," Rule reminded him. "Now, how do you suggest we identify Whisper, and who her contact within the Unknown is?" he asked, regarding the director curiously. "Or even if either of them are the contact you're searching for?"

Son of a bitch and dammit to hell. He did not need this, Rule thought with an edge of carefully concealed anger. Investigating Gypsy's sideline wasn't his preferred course of action. Not when he'd prefer investigating that sensual, erotic side of Gypsy instead.

Jonas frowned, a severe, dark look that tended to make most Breeds extremely nervous. Rule had known him far too long, and knew far too much on him, to be nervous.

Wary in some instances, but never nervous.

"Commander Breaker, do I ask your advice on how to run the Bureau?" Jonas growled when the look had no effect on Rule.

"You don't have to ask," Rule quipped deliberately. "I believe I offer on a fairly regular basis. One of the reasons I'm considering that division directorship, remember? By the way, should I take it, Lawe, Diane and Thor will join me in the top-tier positions that have been outlined."

Jonas grunted at that as he tapped a single slowly extending claw tip against the desk. "Taking my best people, Rule? Now you're just trying to piss me off."

That was entirely possible, Rule admitted silently. If only he could piss the director off enough to make him drop this damned case.

He knew that wasn't happening, though.

"Distract you maybe." Rule shrugged as he admitted to the accusation but not his reasons why. "You're looking stressed, Jonas."

And Jonas had never looked stressed in all the years Rule had known him.

He watched as Jonas shook his head before wiping his hands over his face. "Just find the Unknown, Rule. They'll lead us to Gideon. Maybe then, Rachel, Amber and I can get some rest."

Gideon was the last link.

Anonymous files had been sent from Judd to the Bureau, after Liza had remembered parts of that ritual that hid her for so long.

The files had detailed the codes he remembered, outlined clearly the research notes he'd seen and advised Jonas that if Amber had been given the first injection and was still living, to make damned sure the injections continued on a schedule he'd listed as the same that the scientists overseeing Honor and Fawn had used.

There was no serum to continue, though. No one knew the formula and there were too many files of children, young adults and adults who had been a part of that research and had been a casualty of it.

So why was Amber still living?

Rule knew the questions, he knew where to find some sources for the answers, but what those sources knew, Jonas already had. They needed Gideon, and Rule was afraid Gideon just didn't want to be found.

Not even the one small favor the feral Bengal owed Rule would be enough to fix this problem.

"I'll get to work then." Rule rose from his chair.

He prayed he could find something, anything, to get Gypsy off that list.

"Rule." Jonas spoke his name carefully, hiding his wariness at the tone.

"Yeah?" Rule was a master of casual demeanor. He fucking worked at it.

"Orrin Martinez made another request to meet with you and Lawe. I'm advising you, as your friend, to make an appointment and get it over with."

As far as Rule was concerned, Orrin Martinez could go to hell. They had nothing to say to one another after the trouble the Martinez family had given them when they first arrived in New Mexico, especially Orrin's son, the chief of the Navajo Nation, Ray Martinez.

"Talk to Lawe." He shrugged. "As far as I'm concerned, I have no family here other than Isabelle and Chelsea. The male members of the Martinez family are just too far over the prick line to suit me."

Jonas's lips quirked. "Understandable, but not acceptable. Get it taken care of and get them off my back. Quickly."

With that, Jonas pulled up the computer once again, a signal that as far as he was concerned, the discussion was at an end.

It was, because Rule wasn't meeting with the old bastard or his family.

Leaving the office, Rule closed the door behind him before striding down the hall and heading to his brother's suite.

Lawe's mate, Diane, had found the information leading the Breeds to the capital of the Navajo Nation in their search for Honor Roberts and Fawn Corrigan. Perhaps she would have something on the Unknown as well.

Something that would get Jonas off Gypsy's back.

At least he knew there wasn't a chance of mating her. His animal instincts didn't even twitch when she was around. Hell, in the nine years he'd been checking up on her, watching after her, he'd become fond of her, he admitted. But even once she'd matured, those mating instincts hadn't appeared to even attempt to awaken.

Just his dick.

And in the past months, she affected that part of his body in a way that, for a few weeks, had made him wonder if he was going to have to run after all.

In all the years he'd watched her, checked up on her, ensured that she was safe and as happy as possible, she'd never known he was there. He'd brushed up against her, moved silently into her apartment as she slept, and more than once he'd allowed himself to tempt the hunger he'd realized he was feeling for her after she began maturing into a woman.

But he'd never gotten close to her in any way that would have allowed her to recognize him, or to come to know him until the past two months since the search for Gideon had led them to Window Rock.

So far, he had reined in his impulse to take her as a lover and ignored the restless sexual awareness plaguing him.

He should have taken advantage of the numerous offers for a one-night stand, given by both the human and Breed females. There were certain things a man learned about specific women quickly, though.

What he'd learned about Miss Gypsy Rum was the fact that she refused to bed any man or Breed known to have a promiscuous lifestyle or one who had already slept with a female she knew.

That had obviously narrowed the playing field for her.

But, he had to admit, it was refreshing to know a woman who actually stuck to her own rules, no matter the obvious flaw in them.

Rule was damned certain that she'd never had a lover, though.

But she was going to have one soon.

Women, their hearts, their luscious bodies, every aspect of them and every part of them that made them the amazingly complex creatures he so enjoyed, never failed to please him.

Perhaps that was why she drew him.

He knew the intelligence and the complexities behind the façade she presented. That mask of a shallow young woman was just that—a mask.

He suspected that was why she had made the list of possible Unknown contacts. And now, he was going to have to find a way to get her off that list.

To convince Jonas that she was just what she seemed to be. Even if he did know better.

The hurt she carried behind her bright smile and sensual, flirty demeanor haunted her waking moments as well as her nightmares.

He saw the woman who craved something she had no idea how to reach out for. A woman who imprisoned all her wild hunger behind a bottle of beer, a flirty smile and every party or good-time bar that could offer a spark of excitement instead of erotic heat.

And what she never displayed, was the deception and games that came with being a spy.

Not to mention the ability to sleep with whoever was needed to gain the information she sought.

No, the spark she needed had nothing to do with being a spy for anyone, let alone some group that no one could even confirm existed.

Rule had decided weeks before that he had her spark, and he intended to watch her burn once he set fire to her hunger. He'd just needed a reprieve from the investigations taking so much of his time first.

And the assurance that the desire hardening the flesh between his thighs wasn't Mating Heat.

The wild, animalistic genetics that often felt like a caged lion inside him were completely unimpressed with her. That shadow creature inside him was too damned busy searching for the Coyotes it so loved to fight, because that was one of the rare times Rule allowed it to come out and play.

Restless, driven to rid the world of the creatures that still gave their loyalty to the Genetics Council, his animal senses rarely even took notice of Gypsy unless he had the time to become aroused.

And that made for a very happy Rule Breaker.

And potentially, a very fucked Gypsy.

✦ CHAPTER 2 ✦

ONE WEEK LATER

Gypsy slipped into the underground entrance of the Navajo Covert Law Enforcement Offices and made her way tiredly through the steel-lined corridor leading to the elevator to the upper floors.

She checked her watch. Five minutes to spare.

She'd made it, but it hadn't been easy. And it sure as hell hadn't been a sure thing that she would make it back before nightfall to begin with.

Stepping into the elevator, she punched the button, leaning against the side of the metal cubicle as she smothered a yawn and waited for that little *ping* that indicated the ride was coming to an end. Which meant her week was coming to an end soon as well, and hopefully, at least one good night's sleep.

Straightening from the wall as the doors slid open, Gypsy stilled, her eyes narrowing at the sight of the man she'd come to see.

Dressed in dun-colored tactical pants and a matching T-shirt, he could have been hot as hell, if he didn't work at being an asshole so often. Light brown hair, brown eyes and a well-tanned complexion made him a real hit with all the other ladies he knew, though.

She must be weird, because she simply hadn't ever been interested.

"Hell, I usually have to track you down when I return," she drawled, standing straight and moving from the elevator as he glared at her.

What the hell had she done anyway?

"How long have you been back?" Cullen Maverick, commander of the agency, demanded, his tone dark, the snap in it irritating.

Damn, he must have already taken his prick pills for the day.

"How long does it take to get from the underground garage to here?" Mockery was usually the best and most effective weapon against his grumpiness. "Try chilling out a sec, Maverick."

"Then you've not been back long enough to realize there's a damned Breed APB out on your ass, right?"

She did freeze this time. She didn't just pause.

Coming to a hard stop, she pivoted and just stared at Cullen, certain she must have misunderstood what he said.

"There's a what?" she asked carefully, praying she wasn't giving away that panicked where-can-I-hide feeling beginning to shoot through her.

"You heard me," he snapped. "An unofficial Breed APB put out on you by Commander Rule Breaker. What the fuck is going on?"

"Unofficial?" She snorted at that one. Well, that happened just about every other day after she pissed one of them off. Or unless the director's baby wanted more "moo-cake." "When it becomes official, let me know."

Turning on her heel, she began tracking to his office, knowing damned good and well he wasn't going to take possession of what she had anywhere else.

Cullen wasn't fond of the security cameras picking up every move he made or the information exchanged between him and his men. Or his contacts, such as Gypsy.

Besides, her cover of irritating Cullen just for the hell of it had already been established and followed for years. Unless she was actually seen handing something over, then she'd be screwed. And so would he be. For a minute anyway.

His office door was locked, as usual.

Paranoid prick, she thought, respecting the hell out of him for being as suspicious as he was.

The *snick* of the lock being deactivated followed his hand moving into his pants pocket. Wrapping her hand around the knob again, she stepped inside the office and waited for the door to close behind him.

Once the room was secure, she removed the small case holding the nano-nit she'd collected from the spa in Broken Butte, New Mexico. She'd put it in place more than a month ago, in the manager's office where the majority of the information would go through.

Full audio and video.

The tiny bit of robo-electronics was incredible.

"Here you go." Smothering a yawn, she handed the small plastic case over to him. "Mission accomplished and all that."

He took the case—ultra thin, an inch square perhaps—and flipped it to his desk, still glaring at her.

Uh-oh.

Gypsy stared at the case, then back to Cullen as her lips thinned in irritation.

"I'm not in the mood for this shit," she informed him warily. "I don't know what your problem is . . ."

"If you're sleeping with that Breed, then kindly inform me now," he snapped, his arms going over his broad chest, his brown eyes snapping with ire. "Because he's making my life highly uncomfortable, Gypsy. Highly." The last word was a low, furious sound directed between his clenched teeth.

She almost flinched.

"What the hell has he done?" Her eyes went wide, disbelief and confusion smacking her brain as the depth of Cullen's anger finally registered. "For God's sake, Cullen, since when am I responsible for what some crazed Breed does?"

"Are you sleeping with him?" he bit out again. "So help me, Gypsy, if this is because of a damned lover's spat—"

"I'm not sleeping with him!" she informed him, outraged. "God, I've barely spoken to him."

Hell, she couldn't sleep with anyone. It was killing her.

What Breaker did was catch her gaze across a room, he wasn't picky which one, and she swore he was mentally fucking her at those times.

Taking her.

Pushing into her.

He made all her little feminine parts just perk right up and start prepping for the invasion.

Damned feminine parts.

"Then what the fuck is his problem?" Turning, he stalked to his chair, throwing himself into it as he continued to glare at her. "The man has been in every bar, nightclub and dive, legal and otherwise, and actually managed to crash too many fucking parties looking for your ass for the past week. Get him off the radar, Gypsy."

Get him off the radar?

She stared at him, wide eyed. "What does he want? God, Cullen, we've barely spoken. He flirts a little. His buddy, that damned Vanderale heir they've let run amok, pays more attention to me than Breaker does."

"I don't fucking care what he wants," he informed her furiously. "Get your ass out there tonight, Gypsy, and by God give it to him, or find a way to make him stop wanting it. Either way, get him off the fucking radar before someone decides to find out why one little party girl is so MIA that even the Breeds can't find her."

She stifled a groan.

The Commander was hot as hell. He did things to her libido that should be outlawed. That didn't mean she had time for this. No matter how eager certain *other* parties were for her to establish a closer, though nonsexual, relationship with him.

This was just uncalled for, though. She was tired. She wanted to sleep.

"Cullen . . ."

"Don't Cullen me." As he jackknifed in his seat, his glare took on a whole new meaning as pure fury glittered in his eyes and deepened his voice. "Get it done. Tonight. Or kiss this little side job of yours good-bye. You'll definitely be relegated to the damned phones, on midnight shift, for the next year if it's not taken care of. Now."

Fuck.

She really wanted to sleep tonight.

But she really, really liked her little side job too, dammit.

"Fine, tonight," she muttered, wondering what the hell had happened to her little world while she was gone. "But I don't see how any of this is my damned fault. I didn't do anything."

"You're not five," he pointed out sarcastically.

"Then stop reminding me of what it felt like to be blamed when I didn't do it," she informed him pointedly. "I was hoping to sleep tonight."

"Sleep after you get that damned Breed off your ass."

"I didn't invite him to get on it, Cullen," she protested, heading to the door.

"You did something," he grumbled. "Whatever you did, fix it. Reject him, kiss him, fuck him, I don't give a shit and don't want to know about it. But make him go away."

She slammed the door on the last order.

Dammit, she really wanted to sleep.

◆　　◆　　◆

Sometimes, it just didn't pay a man or a Breed to make a decision, Rule decided as he lounged against the bar at yet another honky-tonk on the list of known clubs Gypsy often found herself at.

Knowing he'd finally caught up with her hadn't helped his mood, or his irritation. She'd eluded him for a week and he was growing tired of waiting for her to get her ass back to town.

Rule was beginning to think he was going to have to actually chase her down if he was ever going to see her again.

A week between sightings was too damned long a wait, especially once he'd made up his mind to have her.

After going without the sight of her the past week, he was as antsy as an addict needing a fix and wondering if he should worry about that reaction.

And that just pissed him off.

Maybe he just had an addictive personality, he thought as he watched her and several of her friends stroll purposely onto the dance floor.

She was preparing to dance, and God bless her heart but she could turn grown men into slavering animals hungry to fuck whenever she danced.

The smell of their lust never failed to cause him to glower at any male unlucky enough to catch his gaze.

Maybe he was just too damned used to finding her whenever he wanted to.

Hell, he'd watched her practically grow up.

He couldn't count the times he'd slipped to Window Rock in the past nine years to check on the broken, traumatized child who had fought so valiantly against those Coyotes so long ago.

And he had to say, she'd grown into a hell of a woman.

She was wary and secretive, and the effects of the night her brother died were often apparent in her too-serious gaze.

But she'd turned into a hell of a beauty.

And he was a sucker for a woman in black leather too.

Miss Gypsy Rum McQuade had adopted a penchant for black leather just after her eighteenth birthday.

And she'd been driving him crazy just as long too.

Watching the dainty form, leather boots over her knees, short black leather skirt clinging to her hips and luscious ass, a black leather vest that flashed her bronzed belly and the upper curves of her full breasts, he couldn't help but grin.

He might have been drooling a little, and damn he hoped Dane Vanderale hadn't caught him.

But hell, that woman was built to tempt, seduce and deliver, all in one package.

Rule decided he was the Breed to collect on it too.

He was damned sure tired of all that lush, pretty body going unclaimed by him.

Jaw clenching, his cock throbbing, he watched as she moved.

Lifting her arms and moving her hips, her legs shifting gracefully in four-inch heels, her expression becoming exotic, erotic. Sexy enough to make a Breed have to force himself not to pant.

Long, long straight hair, so dark it was almost black and framing a dusky face so delicate he couldn't stop the hard-on straining the black mission pants he wore. Graceful and witchy, sensual and burning with a hidden fire, she made him want to burn with her, burn in her.

Fluid and graceful, hips and shoulders swaying, jade green eyes gleamed teasingly, long thick lashes at half-mast. Those eyes glittered with wicked promise—and cool distance.

A distance she'd used against him more than once in the past two months since Jonas had brought his investigation to Window Rock.

Tonight, she was just flat avoiding him, and her explanation for her disappearance was causing more than a few raised brows since she'd arrived less than an hour ago.

According to her, she had been at a spa in Broken Butte, New Mexico.

The local sheriff who had mated Jonas's sister, and a deputy, the sheriff's cousin who had mated another Breed, had checked into the story and reported back to Rule, mere minutes ago, that Gypsy had never been to that spa in Broken Butte. They knew, because it was no more than a front for the Bureau of Breed Affairs and every customer that came through its doors was completely vetted.

But who said she came in as a customer?

Rule refrained from shaking his head in frustrated disgust.

Gypsy was going to have to be more careful if she intended to keep doing these little odd jobs for one of her bosses, Cullen Maverick.

She was going to end up getting her ass burned at this rate. And if her ass got blistered, then his would be fried.

That thought and any other fled his brain, though, as her eyes met his and locked for heated seconds, and he swore the hunger that raged inside her began to burn him hotter.

Amid a floor filled with seductive, graceful women, sexual invitation gleaming in *their* eyes—eyes without the distance, without the reserve that shimmered in the very air around her, she stood apart with inexplicable awareness.

She gave herself to the music and that was all she was giving herself to, her gaze seemed to warn.

She didn't give herself to the men who attempted to draw her to them. She didn't give herself to the women who would have rubbed against her in sensual abandon. Nor did she give herself to the drunkenness or the drugs that flowed so freely.

She might be as secretive as hell, but purity flowed from her, even as he felt the dark, rich desire trapped within her—like a living flame.

She burned inside.

Rule swore he could see the flame burning there in the center of her eyes. Not the same flame easily glimpsed in a Breed's or animal's eyes in a certain light. This was a flame barely contained, burning from the center of the soul, trapped, aching to be released.

A woman aching to be touched.

"See what I see?" Dane Vanderale, the legitimate hybrid son to the first Leo and Rule's biggest headache, drawled through the comm link, the South African accent mocking. "She's avoiding you, Breaker."

"I see her," Rule stated into the mic that curled from the communications link set in his ear. "Find out where she's been yet?"

"She says the spa, but your sources say she wasn't there," Dane reminded him.

"Dammit, Dane, that's not what I want to hear," Rule growled.

Dane chuckled, the low, knowing sound grating on Rule's nerves.

"Best watch the hormones, old friend. What's that first rule? Run, don't walk, stumble or hesitate. Run hell for leather at first sign of Mating Heat? What else would you call such infatuation for one woman? If I didn't know better, I'd think she was your drug."

The accented drawl of amusement had Rule's teeth gritting in irritation.

"I think I'd know by now," he grunted.

He'd been close enough to her in the past years that her scent was as familiar to him as his own. And it had never changed since it had shifted from girl to woman the year she turned eighteen.

"So that's why you just keep watching the hell out of each other, huh?" Dane chuckled. "Tell me there, fraidy cat, when are you going to get up the nerve to tell the pretty girl hello tonight instead of stalking her like some perv as you have the past weeks?"

He'd told her hello several times in the past weeks. She'd pretended to ignore him as often as possible, though he was well aware she knew exactly where he was every second that he was in her vicinity.

She was damned wary around him, watching him carefully, almost suspiciously, and making his dick harder for the very fact that she was keeping herself so damned aloof.

Letting Dane rile him would be foolish at this point, though. The other man lived to piss off other Breeds.

Rule often thought he might even have a death wish.

"Let's not be a smart-ass tonight, Junior," Rule growled, using the insulting nickname Dane's father, the Leo, used whenever he became pissed with his son. "Now, answer the fucking question before I have to send your pelt to Daddy with my apologies for finally growing sick of your ignorance."

Dane growled, the sound far too close to the sound of the animal rather than the hybrid Rule knew him to be.

"Ah, and what a day that would be," Dane quipped. "The Leo would likely pat your back and adopt you should you be so brave as to attempt such a thing. Or give you the burial you're obviously searching for. Once I've finished with you, that is."

Crossing his arms over his chest, Rule directed a glare in the hybrid's direction. "Just answer the question, asshole."

"Where's she been?" Dane repeated sarcastically. "You neglected to mention that she was part escape artist and part invisible woman when you gave me the job of tracking her down. It's damned hard telling where she's been, from what I've managed to find out. Even her lovely little sister has no idea where she goes, according to Loki. Though she has mentioned a concern that you're going to show up at her sister's apartment looking for her soon. I bet the lovely Gypsy's expecting the big bad wolf. Think she'll be surprised when she gets the fraidy cat instead?"

"I'm gonna kick your ass, prick," Rule warned him.

"Yeah, yeah, take a number, nutcase." Dane actually laughed at the threat. "Be nice or I'll sic the big bad witch on your ass. Any woman living in an apartment next to a house with gumdrops painted on it has to be a real badass."

"She's no wicked witch, Junior," Rule drawled. "And she can feed me sweets anytime, right?"

There was one sweet he fantasized about on a regular basis, actually.

"Careful there, fraidy cat, she might be too much woman for a little kitty like you. You should let a real feline do this little job." The pure amused indulgence in the hybrid's voice had Rule shooting a thoughtful glance through the crowd to where Dane stood by the bar.

"Dane, are you drunk?" Rule questioned him.

The hybrid Breed lifted his glass with a mocking grin, dark sunglasses lying low on his nose so he could glance over the rims.

"Not yet," Dane sighed. "But the temptation is there."

Dane was unusually irritating, even for him.

"And what's with the damned shades? It's a bar, not high noon in the middle of the desert," Rule scoffed, wondering what the hell had gotten into the Breed.

Dane gave a short little nod in salute before turning back to the sight on the dance floor.

Pinching the bridge of his nose, Rule was tempted to close his eyes. But the band was breaking into another song. Something about what a guy had to do for the singer "if he wanted to be her cowboy." It was an old song, but one Gypsy seemed pleased to hear.

A second later his eyes widened, his cock grew impossibly harder and he swore he was going to have trouble breathing.

Son of a bitch, it was enough to make his balls tighten in pure appreciation as those lovely legs bent just enough, her head tipping back, her hips shifting, rolling, as delicate hands caressed the air from her breasts to her hips.

"God have mercy. But I love to watch her make grown men crazy," Dane breathed out in amazed appreciation instead as the tempting little leather-clad flame on the dance floor began working her entire body to the music. Hips, thighs, shoulders and breasts drew his gaze as she approached a table where four Breed Enforcers sat, just as entranced as Rule and Dane were becoming.

Gritting his teeth, he switched to the enforcer channel on his comm device.

"The first one of you morons to touch that woman will face me," he snapped into the line as Dane's short, surprised laugh barked across the link.

"Better run hell for leather, mate," Dane injected just below the laughter level.

Rule didn't answer the hybrid any more than the enforcers answered the order. Their eyes were locked on that image of pure, entrancing fire as she moved toward the table they were sitting at.

They weren't listening.

"Good luck, my friend," Dane advised him, his tone and accent thickening further as the beauty tossed her head, all that thick, thick silken hair brushing around her body as she moved closer to the table in response to the singer's demands that her "cowboy" take her for a ride.

The hard length of his shaft throbbed like an open wound, too sensitive and too hungry to be contained.

Despite the aching sensitivity of the engorged flesh between his thighs, his tongue showed no signs of the hormone filling the glands. All he tasted

was the beer he'd drunk just before catching sight of her and the peppermint and chocolate hard candy he'd finished before his gaze swept the dance
floor.

Narrowing his eyes, he prowled through the crowd and headed for the
table where those lucky-assed enforcers were enjoying a show no Breed or
human male could possibly contain his lusts through.

He didn't trust those damned Breeds leaning toward her not to touch.
Despite the order.

He stepped to the table between two of the younger enforcers; the
scent of their lust slapped at his senses, offensive, and pulling a dangerous
growl from his chest. And he didn't attempt to hide the savage warning that
the restless animal inside him ensured the sound contained.

The Breeds moved.

As one, they cleared the table, the sight of the female not nearly enough
to wipe away the more than two decades of training they carried inside
them.

That was more like it.

He ignored Dane's low laughter as he took the chair at the side of the
table and stared back at the surprised little minx with an obvious, silent
dare.

If she wanted to tease Breeds, then why not see how she fared teasing
a full-grown, well-trained, more than experienced Lion Breed commander
rather than a few young enforcers who still carried the scent of the labs they
were rescued from.

Lifting his hand imperiously as the waitress passed by, he caught her
nod from the corner of his eyes. The waitresses at this bar loved the excellent tips they received, not just from the enforcers, but from the Bureau of
Breed Affairs as well for reporting any indications or rumors of Council
soldiers lurking in the establishment.

He wasn't there for the waitress or the information, though. Evidently,
he was there to give one fiery little woman a Breed to torture.

Gypsy moved closer, hips swaying, her arms lifting above her head as
she moved directly to him. She positioned her legs to each side of one of
his, thighs spread just that little bit, her knees bent, hips moving with a slow
suggestiveness just above his knee that had lust flaming through his senses.

He swore he could feel the heat of her pussy radiating from between her thighs straight through his mission pants. Hot enough to sear a man's senses, wet enough to drown them.

And she was indeed wet.

The scent of her sweet juices had his mouth watering, his need to taste her racing through his system.

The tempting little morsel gave her head a toss, a smug little smile tilting the corners of her lips as the song came to an end and the music eased into a slower tune.

"Watch my drink, hybrid," he ordered Dane across the link as he moved before the lithe little vision could leave the floor.

Hooking his arm around her waist, he stared down at her obvious surprise.

Surprise? What the hell had she expected?

"Are you all tease?" he asked her. "Or is there a woman lurking beneath the promise in those pretty green eyes?"

Her brow lifted, laughter gleaming in her witchy gaze.

"It's all tease. And furthermore, purr boy," she drawled—and quicker than a Breed could blink she was out of his arms with a disapproving little frown—"you should know better than to manhandle me. You request a dance from me, you don't demand. And you sure as hell don't grab me like a toy."

And with that little proclamation, she moved away from him with all the haughty grace of an ice princess offended to her last perfect toenail. And completely unaware that in that single movement designed to break free of him, he'd recognized the slightest, well-trained, experienced shift of her hip, shoulder and one delicate foot.

Dane was, of course, rolling with laughter.

Rule couldn't help but grin as he kept the knowledge to himself. "I believe that might have been a dare."

Two months of circling each other with wary arousal and she'd thrown out a dare she should have known he couldn't resist.

"You're not a Coyote, Breaker," Dane reminded him, his tone surprisingly pensive. "Remember?"

To that, Rule could only grin. "Sorry there, Dane, just because Coyotes borrowed the phrase didn't mean Lions didn't start it. It's never dare a Breed, not never dare a Coyote."

Then, aware of the eyes watching him, the human's amusement, and the intriguing scent he was certain other Breeds were tempted by, Rule followed the scent of arousal that one little Gypsy Rum McQuade left in her wake.

◆　　◆　　◆

Oh God, was she insane?

Gypsy tried to breathe as she strolled across the dance floor to the bar, ordered her favorite beer, then leaned back against the counter and sipped at it. She was all too aware of the fact that Rule had yet to take his eyes off her.

Of course, it never mattered where he found her, he watched her, those neon blue eyes trying to sink into her soul as though he were determined to learn every secret she possessed.

And each time he did it, he made her hot. From that first look two months before across the distance of a crowded bar to the second that he'd strolled to the table of younger Breeds she'd danced for as she felt his eyes on her, searing her. Like a rush of sensation washing over her flesh, the knowledge that he wasn't taking his eyes off her had her thighs clenching, a damp warmth tingling against the suddenly sensitive, swollen bud nestled amid the slick folds between her thighs.

Dammit, she was creaming.

Again.

Oh hell.

She was creaming her panties for a damned Breed who made her completely crazy every time she came in contact with him. One who wasn't just making her body crazy, but was now putting out those unofficial APBs on her whenever he had a mind to.

That was just uncalled for.

No Breed should be able to do this to her.

No man, period, should be able to do it.

No other Breed had ever accomplished it.

This Breed should not be able to do it.

What had been mere interest as she avoided him over the past weeks at the clubs and bars where she made her weekly rounds was now turning into full-fledged sexual want. And sexual want was a mighty big no-no in her life.

That did not ensure that she put as much distance as possible between herself and the Lion Breed as he moved in beside her, though. He turned his big body to watch her profile as she stared out over the dance floor, that strange warmth she always felt from him reaching out to her.

"Courageous little thing, aren't you?" His gaze invited her to laugh, to share the amusement that threatened to warm parts of her that had been cold far longer than he could ever guess.

"Courage?" she questioned him with a hint of disbelief after taking another sip of the beer. God, what was she letting him do to her? She knew better than this. "That's not courage, it's disinterest, Rule. I told you before, I don't like the trouble that follows Breeds like a crazy ex-girlfriend."

But this Breed made her long to break her exile from the sensual, hungry nature that had risen inside her as she had matured.

"There are times I believe I would prefer the crazy ex-girlfriend," he assured her wryly, his lips quirking with a hint of bitterness as she felt the rasp of a single callused finger caressing across her bare shoulder. "As for trouble following us, it's not as though we ask for it." His declaration pulled her gaze back to him.

His eyes gleaming between thick, black lashes, he watched her, his gaze rich and warm, making her want to press herself against him, to still the ache for his touch that tingled across her flesh.

"No, you don't," she agreed with a sigh as the caress disappeared. "That doesn't mean I don't have a choice in dealing with the issues that come with you. Because I choose not to become part of that battle."

Just as she chose the life she led. And that life did not include joining Rule in some fly-by-night affair that would be over as quickly as it began.

"Interesting that you believe you have a choice in who you ache for," he stated, his voice rasping, his gaze intent now. "I'll have to remember to believe that one."

Sapphire eyes gazed down at her, filled with amusement and mystery. The look in them invited her to play, to put aside whatever hurt her, whatever she feared, and just play with him for a minute.

But Gypsy knew better than most the dangers of playing with Breeds.

It was a lesson she'd learned one blood-filled night that she would never forget.

"Such pretty eyes should never appear so somber and unhappy," he observed then, bending his head to her ear to be overheard above the music. "They should be filled with passion and a love of living."

Gypsy flinched, jerking back from him as she realized how close he'd come to her without her being aware of it.

She was getting too used to him invading her space every chance he had. Her body was damned sure getting too used to Rule doing so.

That was going to have to stop. It was going to have to stop right now.

"Is there a reason, Commander Breaker, that you have taken such an interest in me over the past months?" she asked suspiciously, narrowing her eyes on him. "Because it's starting to irritate me and I'm certain you have better things to do."

He smiled.

Completely male, completely assured, that look was pure, calculated trouble. "Actually, I'm just killing time and trying to keep you in one place before I go off duty here in about ten minutes." He tapped his ear and the tiny earpiece he wore. A communications device, she knew. "Besides, Control seems to think you must be guilty of some heinous act or two. I believe I might have even heard a few accusations such as breaking hearts and stealing kisses?"

Gypsy smiled with real amusement, laughter threatening to fill her voice as she stared back at him. "Does that line work for you often?" she laughed. "I would have thought a man of your experience could do much better."

He chuckled at her response. "Very good, Gypsy, very good. But give me a little credit. You blew my mind on that dance floor. I'm still recovering. Give me a minute and I promise you I will astound you with the many ways I can stake a proprietary claim without ever touching you once."

Her brow arched. "You would need a mind first." She wrinkled her nose mockingly. "I think I'll take my proprietary claim and head home. Now that you've found me, maybe you can rest too for a minute." Setting the remainder of her beer and several bills for payment on the bar, she gave him a little wave. "And I'll see if I can't remember to find a bar with a few less complications, not to mention a few less Breeds the next time I go out."

Proprietary claim?

Gypsy could feel a shudder racing through her at the very thought of Rule claiming her. That was a move her life simply couldn't accommodate, no matter how tempting it sounded.

She'd already had no less than a dozen calls since returning home that night. The calls had come from friends, family and even acquaintances, informing her that the Breed Commander Rule Breaker was questioning where she'd disappeared to.

As if it were any of their business.

She made a mental note to talk to Cullen and see what he could do to get the Breeds off her ass. After all, she had been doing a job for him while she was gone. She was certain he wouldn't want the Breeds aware of just what kind of job she was doing for him either.

Not that he'd seemed inclined to want to help her earlier. Once he cooled off, though, he might be in a more helpful frame of mind.

Leaving the loud, smoky confines of the bar for the clear, crisp Arizona night, Gypsy drew in a lungful of clean desert air.

She was growing tired of the bars and the often lecherous, always drunken attention she gained there. More and more often she put off her arrival at the various clubs and bars until late into the night.

Pulling her hair back and retrieving an elastic band from the snug pocket of her leather vest, Gypsy confined her hair to keep it out of her face. With the Jeep's top down, the long strands could become too tangled to comb before going to bed if she wasn't careful.

"Hey there, Gypsy Rum." Mutt, a Coyote Breed rarely known to smile when others were around, strangely enough often smiled at her.

He was cute as shit too.

For a Coyote Breed.

There were few of that species that Gypsy could tolerate being around, but Mutt was one of them. With his shy, hesitant smile so at odds with his kickass confidence and dry wit, he had a way of making her laugh even when she didn't want to.

He came into her parents' sweets and gift store often, along with two others, to buy the hard candies her sister, Kandy, made to sell.

He was especially fond of the butterscotch, she remembered, while Loki, one of his partners, enjoyed the cinnamon and Commander Breaker always went for the chocolate and peppermint.

"Hey, Mutt." Pausing, Gypsy smiled back at the Breed moving quickly from the pickup he'd slid from as she left the bar. "What's up?"

"You're leaving early." Tilting his head, he posed the question in a statement as the late evening wind ruffled his overly long dark blond hair. "You're usually still here after I leave."

"Things to do." Gypsy retrieved the ring holding her key fob from the pocket of her vest and casually activated the small Desert Sport II, a redesign of the ages-old Jeep that had always done so well in the deserts.

The motor rumbled with a powerful growl that reminded her far too much of the sound that had vibrated from Rule Breaker as she walked away from him. The Jeep's top retracted with smooth efficiency, tucking beneath the backseat and floorboard neatly in a matter of seconds as Mutt watched with raised brows.

"Man, I do love your ride, girl," Mutt murmured, tucking his thumbs into the pockets of his jeans and standing rather uncomfortably in front of her, his head slightly tilted as he watched her. "One of these days, I swear I'm gonna own one."

"One of these days?" she grinned. "I hear Breeds make a hell of a lot of money, Mutt. Go buy one."

His lips quirked wryly. "There's no way to make them secure without taking out the retracting hard top and completely changing the interior to make them resistant to laser and ammo fire. If I did that, it just wouldn't be the same. And if I didn't do it, then all I could do is watch it sit in a garage somewhere."

Her amusement dimmed in the face of his obvious disappointment.

His gray eyes flicked to the vehicle again, his jaw bunching as Gypsy narrowed her gaze at the small, almost hidden tip of the wand attached to his comm set curving toward his cheek.

He was attempting to delay her and wasn't exactly certain how to do so without rousing her well-known suspicious nature, it seemed.

Too late. Consider it roused.

Turning without so much as a good-bye, Gypsy strode across the wide paved road that separated the parking sections. She was in the process of gripping the door to slide into the driver's seat when her waist was shackled from behind and she was pulled back into a hard, muscular chest.

Again.

Heated warmth surrounded her, reminding her how chilled she often felt, how lonely she always was. And how very dangerous this man could be to her precarious senses.

"Now see, I was trying real hard to play nice." Laughter shadowed the deep drawl of his voice. "Rejection depresses me, you know. Makes me do dumb things just to get attention."

She rolled her eyes. "That's so lame, Breaker."

He chuckled behind her. "It could be so true."

"Doubt it. But what I don't doubt? Someone really needs to teach you how not to manhandle private property," she informed him, trying really hard to be angry. Unfortunately, arousal was converging on her like alternate forces of nature intent on destroying her resistance to him.

"So who has ownership?" he asked, his breath against her ear and sending a pulse of energy straight to the sensitive flesh between her thighs. "I'll take it up with him and ensure that those rights are transferred immediately."

She just bet he would too, then ride right back out of town the second his boss crooked his little finger.

She didn't think so.

"I'm going to file a complaint with the Bureau of Breed Affairs if you don't take your damned hands off me," she warned him, thrown off guard by his complete dominance and the shocking weakness attempting to spread through her system. Talk about conflicting responses. "Is that what you really want?"

She felt his lips brush her ear, a heated breath sending a surge of response racing through her. He felt too good. Too warm. And far too much trouble.

"All complaints are routed to me first." Amusement laced his voice, but there was nothing amusing about the iron-hard length of his shaft pressing against her lower back. "Shall I tell you just how quickly I'd delete that particular e-mail?" He inhaled her scent slowly. "How long do you think you'd delay sending it? Long enough to bring yourself to climax while imagining me between your thighs, filling you, driving you to release?"

Heat flushed her body, raced through her system and left Gypsy fighting for a semblance of common sense. Because he was right. So right. The second she slipped into her bed she would be reaching for one of the intimate toys she kept on hand to take care of the ache growing out of control and flooding her body.

Good Lord, Breeds and their effect on women should be outlawed.

"No one could accuse you of being humble," she snorted, pulling away from him even as she acknowledged that he was letting her pull away from him. "Or polite."

He wasn't releasing her because she was forcing him to, or because he had any constraints against making her retain that place in his arms. He was releasing her only because it was what he wanted to do.

She turned to him slowly.

"Before you make the mistake of spouting all that womanly ire I feel building inside you and demanding I keep my dirty Breed paws to myself—"

She had to laugh at the irritation that flashed in his deep blue eyes.

"Strange women you run with there, Breaker," she snickered. "It's not the paws that offend me. It's the arrogance and the attitude. I don't like being handled, by anyone. Don't do it, and we'll just keep getting along fine. How does that sound?" She had to laugh at him then, because he really did have the power not just to burn her alive with lust, but to also make her laugh. He charmed her, and she hadn't been charmed in a damned long time. "Do you often listen to the womanly ire, then?"

"I believe Breeds listen often when they can't smell the sweet scent of all that female honey spilling like hot syrup on a summer day," he retorted, his tone echoing with a sense of impatience. "I've yet to understand why women believe lies are so very important when they're most often more eager for a man's touch than they let on. The moment you obey them, disappointment has a tendency to mar the delicacy of their scent while they then become angry that you obeyed them. And that only makes for a horny, irritated, not to mention confused Breed."

"Because a man's ego, or a Breed's, doesn't need to be fed?" she asked, her eyes widening for effect at his obvious confusion. "Maybe we want you to work for what we have to give you? We do tend to believe we're worth a little effort, you know."

It seemed Breed males, just like their counterparts, the human males, could be so incredibly obtuse when it came to women.

"Breeds can smell their lies," he pointed out. "What's the point in lying when one will be so easily caught in the lie?"

Yep, obtuse.

But it wasn't the first such conversation they'd had over the past eight or nine weeks. Though it was the first time he'd approached her as blatantly as he had in the bar, and before she'd managed to get into her vehicle.

"Perhaps most women haven't watched those little documentaries the Breeds put out close enough." She had studied them for months. "And there could be the fact that even in those documentaries, there's very little layman's language. There's also the fact that you had to have used the most incredibly gorgeous, dangerous-looking, deep-voiced male Breeds living to narrate them. I suspect those Breeds were used in an attempt to distract us just as you meant to. The same can be said for the females used in those videos. The only intent in them was to fool the suspicious and to draw the unwary even deeper beneath your spell. Besides, women absolutely love ice cream, cake and chocolate too. Doesn't mean it's good for us, or that we eat it without first considering the calories it contains."

She'd already known this Breed didn't like games, nor did he believe in the chase. That was really too bad, because she was very experienced in playing games.

She was considered an expert at them, sometimes.

He only grinned at the accusation, those laser-bright blue eyes holding her gaze, encouraging her to sink beneath the waves of hunger she could feel beating at her resistance. "And did those videos draw you deeper as you denied yourself your favorite sweets?"

Leaning against the side of the vehicle, Gypsy crossed her arms over her breasts as she smiled back at him, shaking her head at the fact that men could be so hardheaded. She was very well aware of the fact that her position only plumped the curves of her breasts higher over the vest-style top she wore, drawing his attention. Momentarily anyway. She liked that about him; he didn't leer, despite the fact that she could almost feel his need to touch her.

"Sorry, Commander, they didn't fool me. And my chocolate and ice cream doesn't wake me up in the mornings, bitch at me for not cleaning, cooking and waiting on it hand and foot or leave dirty clothes lying around my house, so yes, I enjoyed it immensely."

His lips tilted into a half grin as he watched her closely while tucking his thumbs into the band of his pants, as though trying to find something to do with them besides touch her.

He stood, his feet braced slightly apart, muscular body not exactly relaxed, but neither was he poised for danger. Dressed in the black mission uniform most Breeds wore whenever in public, he presented a dangerous male allure.

Thick black hair fell back along his nape and framed the savagery in the hewn features of his face.

High cheekbones, firm, well-molded lips, and thick, thick inky black lashes surrounding brilliant sapphire eyes, while his shoulders were wide enough that a woman could convince herself of her safety while in his arms.

Or just in his presence, in the shadows of one of the most notorious bars in three states. She could stand there with him, enjoy the banter and not have to worry about some drunken wannabe Romeo groping her.

He was the epitome of everything Breeds were being portrayed as. Strong, intent, protective and honorable. And for the most part, they were.

But Gypsy knew just how dangerous some of them could be.

A flash of memory surged through her.

Lengthened canines gleaming in the dark as she screamed out in horror, saliva dripping from them as maniacal savagery reflected in the yellow-gold depths of the creature's eyes.

No matter how she fought, they tore at her clothes, shredding them, removing them, intent on raping her.

As he jerked her thighs apart—

She flinched, dragging herself back from the memory as a familiar band of panic tightened at her chest just before the sat phone in her vest pocket vibrated furiously.

"Gypsy, are you okay?" Rule moved closer, the scent of her sudden fear subtle, vying with the scent of arousal and the remnants of amused fun as he caught the distinct sound of the phone vibrating in one of the little pockets of her snug vest.

She'd been enjoying herself, only to have something yank her quickly from her joy as though to remind her of some pain.

A bleak pain so horrific that he could smell the agony of it even from outside the cavern where she'd huddled nine years ago, Rule remembered.

"It's time I leave."

He watched, denying the urge to pull her back to him as she slid inside the vehicle and pushed it into gear. The sporty little black Jeep tore out of its parking space and raced from the lot with a surge of power.

His eyes narrowed.

He was certain that motor was far more powerful than it should be.

Just as his attraction to the woman was.

Narrowing his eyes on the fading taillights of her vehicle, he checked the glands beneath his tongue carefully once more.

Breathing in, he pushed back his arousal, feeling the loss of stiffness in the eager shaft beneath his mission uniform and giving an imperceptible nod as the once-hard flesh lay dormant once again.

The beast that had been irritating the crap out of him, courtesy of his genetics, was quiet rather than roaring out in rage that a possible mate was escaping.

Hell, he halfway felt as though the animal senses inside him couldn't have cared less where she went or what she did as long as she didn't represent physical danger.

That meant no Mating Heat.

He grinned.

That meant Miss Gypsy Rum McQuade definitely wasn't his mate, no matter Dane's suggestion that his hunger for her indicated it.

Becoming addicted to her was a definite threat. But he could handle an addiction. He could walk away from it. Just as he had walked away from several of them while being tested in the labs for any weakness.

And that made her fair game, because he wanted nothing more than to fuck them both into exhaustion.

· CHAPTER 3 ·

Pulling into the parking lot behind the store an hour later, Gypsy watched in surprise as her sister's short-wheelbase four-by-four black pickup pulled in beside her.

Sliding from the Jeep, she set the roof into operation again, waiting as Kandy slid from her truck, closed the door and locked the vehicle before meeting her at the front of the Jeep.

"You're out late." Gypsy lifted her brows suggestively as she watched her younger sister.

Kandy was even more delicate than Gypsy. At five four, she sometimes looked far too tiny to even be a McQuade.

"Look who's talking," Kandy laughed back a bit nervously, her turquoise eyes gleaming back at Gypsy as they moved toward the downstairs apartment her sister had moved into the year before.

"Not so late for me," Gypsy murmured as Kandy unlocked the door, then followed her sister into the cool interior.

Flipping on the lights, Kandy instantly dispelled the shadows that filled the roomy, inviting openness of the apartment.

As in Gypsy's upstairs apartment, the door opened into a wide entryway that flowed into the open kitchen, dining area and living room. The rooms were divided by a long counter, inset with a chef's dream of a stove and oven.

Fall colors and dark wood gave the apartment an inviting warmth that

Gypsy's didn't have, while the scent of various baked sweets still filled the interior. Her sister could make a cake that would melt in the mouth and send the senses into orgasmic bliss.

Yet Gypsy knew, despite her parents' dreams, it wasn't a life Kandy really wanted for herself.

Unfortunately, Gypsy didn't think her sister knew what she did want instead.

"Did you check in with your guard dogs tonight?" Kandy set her purse on a table just inside the door as she slid her keys into it and glanced back at Gypsy. "Commander Breaker and his sidekick were convinced you'd been kidnapped, had run off to Fiji with a lover or were lying dead in the desert somewhere when they couldn't find you."

Gypsy rolled her eyes as she strode to the bar and sat down on one of the high stools as Kandy moved to the fridge.

"They finally caught up with me at the Crooked Toe," she drawled. "What is with those two anyway?"

Kandy paused as she set a covered pie dish on the counter and stared back at her sister in surprised amusement. "You haven't figured it out yet?"

The knowingness of her tone had Gypsy grimacing at her sister's knowledge that Rule Breaker's intent was no more than to get her into his bed.

"Don't start on me, Kandy," Gypsy ordered her, pointing an accusing finger at her with a fierce glare. "We're not going there tonight."

"He wants your body," Kandy announced, her lashes lowering as she gave her sister a quick wink. "Really bad."

"He can want on." She rolled her eyes before folding her arms on the counter and watching as her sister dished up apple pie, set it in the warmer, then moved to make coffee.

Kandy didn't ask if she wanted it, but then, it was rare for Gypsy to visit with her like this too.

Watching her sister as she moved about the kitchen, Gypsy felt the guilt and grief that filled her whenever she spent much time with the other girl.

Kandy had been ten when Mark had died. She had never known the brother Gypsy had known. The smart, incredibly funny, and always intensely protective young man who had given his sister her freedom while standing by carefully to ensure no one dared to hurt her as she tried out her teenage wings.

Her sister had seen the danger of slipping out, the parties, and the truth that monsters really did exist in the world. And it changed her life almost as much as it had changed the lives of Gypsy, their parents, his best friend, Jason, and Mark's former fiancée, Thea Lacey.

All of their lives had been scarred because of Gypsy's carelessness.

They ate the pie and Gypsy drank her coffee as the tension slowly began to build between them, just as it always did.

"Time for me to go to bed," Gypsy announced as she slid back her saucer and cup and rose from the stool before Kandy's nervous tension ended up affecting her further. "Catch you in the morning."

Throwing her sister a quick smile, she turned to head for the door.

"You didn't ask me why I was out so late tonight, Gypsy." Kandy's observation had her pausing and turning back to her.

Blue-green eyes watched her, the delicate, almost elfin features far too serious and, Gypsy realized, maturing when she hadn't been looking.

Just because she hadn't questioned Kandy's whereabouts didn't mean she wasn't well aware of where her sister had been. Like Mark, Gypsy took her sister's safety seriously. Unlike Mark, she didn't let Kandy know she did; that way, if anyone, especially the Council's Breeds, was looking for a weakness and found Kandy, they'd be convinced that the younger girl couldn't force Gypsy into giving her life for her.

Even though she knew she would do for Kandy just as Mark had done for her.

Die for her.

"You're nineteen, Kandy," she finally answered, swallowing against the sudden tightness in her throat. "I guess I thought you'd tell me if you wanted me to know."

A flash of hurt gleamed in the younger girl's eyes before she turned away.

"That's how it works, then?" Kandy picked up the dishcloth on the counter beside her, more to have something to hold on to than to actually clean the counter, Gypsy thought.

"I guess." She had no idea what was going on now. Her sister rarely, hell, had actually never questioned her about anything other than how her day was going.

"Then if I want to know anything about you, I should just wait for you to think to tell me because it's really none of my business, right?" Kandy questioned her softly, though Gypsy could see a gleam of determination in Kandy's eyes that didn't make sense.

"I don't want to fight with you tonight, Kandy," Gypsy breathed out roughly, reaching back to release the elastic band holding her hair back. "I'm really tired, and I just want to—"

"Go home and stare into the dark until dawn like you did while you were at home?" Kandy questioned suddenly, the quickness of the question catching her off guard, reminding her of why she stayed out so late most nights.

Gypsy flinched.

"Exactly. Good night." She moved to the door.

"Do you know what, Gypsy?" Kandy's harsh question stopped her as she opened the door and started through it.

"I'm sure I don't want to know," Gypsy sighed, keeping her back to her sister, aching at the bitterness churning inside her now.

"I didn't just lose my brother that night in the desert, I lost my entire family," Kandy whispered, the words, the grief in her sister's voice driving a brutal, sharp-edged stake straight into Gypsy's soul. "I became an orphan, and none of you ever realized it. Or maybe you just fucking didn't care."

Shock held her for long seconds, stealing her breath before she swung around to face her sister. But she wasn't there. Disappearing into her bedroom on the other side of the room, her door closing quietly, Kandy had evidently said all she had to say.

Gypsy shook her head.

Kandy was wrong.

Their parents had held on to the younger child desperately after Mark's death, terrified of losing their last, remaining favorite child.

They hadn't objected as Gypsy drew further and further away emotionally. Sometimes they had watched her helplessly, but they had loved Kandy.

Giving her head a hard shake, Gypsy left the apartment, closing the door behind her and listening carefully for the locks to engage. When they did, she forced herself to move to the stairs that led to her own apartment, and the darkness that couldn't be dispelled no matter how many lights she turned on.

She knew where her sister went on the rare occasions she stayed out late. Kandy liked to play poker and over the years, several of Mark's friends had taught her how to play it with deadly skill. The small amusement had begun when Kandy turned twelve and Mark's best friend, Jason, had arrived at the house to speak to her parents about the image consulting business that had been floundering sharply since Mark's death.

Kandy had been playing poker with a dummy hand at the small card table where Mark had taught them both to play. From there, as she'd grown older, he'd sometimes taken her with him to his card games when her parents were busy. Her parents had never, not even once, asked Gypsy to watch her little sister.

Not that she blamed them after she'd failed her older brother.

Jason and his friends got together monthly now and had been known to play for entire weekends.

And they always invited Kandy.

Stepping into her apartment, she made a mental note to call Jason— maybe he would know what the hell was going on with her sister.

Because Gypsy couldn't allow herself to figure it out on her own. If she did, she would have to admit that Kandy might not be an orphan, but in all the ways that mattered, she had definitely become an only child.

And the guilt of that would only open her to the nightmares she'd fought to put behind her so long ago.

◆   ◆   ◆

The next two days were relatively free of Rule and his sidekick, as Dane Vanderale was being dubbed. Rumor was that Jonas Wyatt had flown with his fiancée and child to D.C. to attend a Senate hearing that had been called regarding the reorganization of the Bureau of Breed Affairs that was being speculated on.

According to the press, despite the fact that there was no official announcement or details regarding the rumor, the Bureau of Breed Affairs and the Breed Ruling Cabinet were already in the process of expanding the offices when the Senate Oversight Committee on Breed Affairs had caught wind of it and called the immediate, private hearing.

It gave Gypsy the chance she needed to get a few jobs finished that she'd left hanging because of the distraction he represented. But she admitted, at least to herself, that some spark that had come into life when he began "harassing" her was no longer there.

Pulling the Jeep into the small parking area of her apartment that night after completing the final chore, she stared into the brilliance of the desert moon.

For the briefest moment terror raced through her, struck at her senses and reminded her of the danger she faced each time she entered the night-life and moved among the Breeds and their enemies.

Especially the enemies. The animals. The monsters that murdered, that raped . . .

A horror that had almost destroyed her once before.

A hard shake of her head pushed it back, her heart rate lowering once again as she activated the control that had the tough, flexible shell of the Jeep top rolling into place and locking securely.

This time, she pulled the remote fob from her jeans, and as she stepped from the Jeep and closed the door behind her, she automatically locked it before moving quickly for the comfort of the secure apartment.

She had a few hours to rest before her alarm reminded her that she was due at the Covert Law Enforcement Agency, where she manned the phones several nights a week in case any of the agents in the field called in for immediate help.

Once she returned home, she turned into just another party girl, just another woman on the hunt for her next dance, her next drink or her next potential lover.

Before she became the opposite of who she was, and what she always wanted to be.

As that thought drifted through her mind, the short knock on her front door had a frown creasing her brows. Stepping from the kitchen to the short wide entryway, she pressed the door camera, restraining a sigh at the sight of the man standing patiently on the other side.

"Come on in, Jase." Deactivating the locks, she watched as the man her brother had called his best friend stepped into the apartment.

Jase wasn't as tall as Mark had been, and he wasn't as handsome, but he was cute in his own way with short brown hair, deep brown eyes and a stocky rather than lean body. Dressed in dark slacks, black dress boots and a white shirt open at the collar, he'd obviously discarded his tie after leaving the office.

If it hadn't been for Jase, Gypsy didn't know how her parents would have survived after Mark's death. He'd taken over Mark's job at the image consulting firm, did all the things Mark had done to help her parents and Mark's fiancée, Thea.

He and Thea had married several years before, when Thea had been promoted to assistant DA in Window Rock.

"Hey, sweetheart." His smile wasn't as open and filled with love as Mark's had always been, but it was familiar even if she'd never stopped seeing a shadow of an accusation buried in the dark depths.

"Hey, Jase," she greeted him, allowing the brief hug he always insisted on. He was one of the few people who had refused to allow her to just disappear inside herself after Mark's death. "I was wondering when you would get around to a visit."

He shot her a chastising look as she moved away from him. "If you would come in to work occasionally instead of waiting for assignments, then you wouldn't have to wonder when you would see me."

She leaned against the counter as he took a seat on one of the stools on the opposite side.

"I've been busy." She shrugged. "I do have other jobs, you know."

He snorted at that, frowning. "How many times have I tried to get you to take full time at the office, Gypsy?"

McQuade Image Consulting was growing slowly, she knew, thanks to the way her parents had thrown themselves into the business after their eldest child's death and Jason's steady determination.

"I like the variety." She liked not seeing the pain in her parents' eyes whenever Mark's name came up.

Crossing his arms and bracing them on the counter as she busied herself straightening what didn't need straightening, he watched her closely for long seconds.

"Your mother called you earlier," he reminded her gently. "You didn't return her call."

No, she hadn't.

Lifting her gaze, she stared back at Jason quietly, coolly.

She didn't discuss her parents with anyone, even Jason.

"I need you to come in to the office in the morning," he said, concern filling his dark brown eyes. "We have a potential contract coming in and I'm going to need you and possibly Kandy both on this if I can get it to pan out." His expression hardened. "And don't even think about refusing, Gypsy, because your father has busted his ass to pull this job in and I won't have the fact that we're short a hand causing us to lose it."

Her father had taken on the business that had first been Mark's dream and steadily pushed it until it was a money-making enterprise.

"I'll be there," she promised, though her job as image consultant was one she tried to ignore whenever possible.

"Good." He nodded before his jaw tensed and he glanced at the bank of windows, carefully covered by heavy drapes. When he moved his gaze back to her, it was concerned once again. "I got your message earlier. You talked to Kandy the other night?"

"She was upset with me for some reason," she admitted, though she rarely did more than ask Jase what her sister's problem was whenever Kandy seemed out of sorts. Which wasn't often.

"I think she's upset with the world lately," he sighed heavily. "That damned Coyote, Loki, sniffing around her isn't helping matters either. Hell, I'm convinced he's making it worse."

The anger that filled his voice as he mentioned Loki didn't surprise Gypsy. Jason hated Coyotes. Hated them to the point that he was well known for it. His resentment toward Breeds in general wasn't hidden either.

"Loki's okay, Jase," she warned him. "You can't blame all Coyotes any more than you can blame all men for one serial killer, murderer, or—"

"Rapist?" he snapped.

Gypsy flinched.

"God, Gypsy, I'm sorry." Regret thickened his voice as he pushed his fingers restlessly through his hair before staring back at her in self-disgust. "I'm so sorry."

"It's okay, Jase." Moving to the refrigerator and pulling out a bottle of wine, she poured herself a glass before lifting it in his direction questioningly.

"Might as well," he nodded. "Then I'll head out of here."

She set the wine on the counter in front of him before sipping at her own and pushing her emotions, her equilibrium back into place. No, Jase hadn't meant to hurt her, she knew, but it had hurt all the same.

"So tell me," she suggested, leaning against the counter once again. "Taking Loki out of the equation, exactly what is Kandy's problem?"

Jase snorted again. "Can you ever take the Breed out of the problem if one is near? If you want my opinion, Loki *is* her problem. But she has no intentions of getting rid of him, so I guess we're just stuck until he leaves and she gets her heart broken." He shook his head wearily. "God, Gypsy, none of us have healed, have we? Even nine years later. Does Kandy really think this Breed is going to exorcise those ghosts for her?"

He finished his wine when Gypsy didn't comment, only ducking her head to stare at the floor, the tip of her boot, anywhere but at him. She didn't want to talk about Breeds. That wasn't Kandy's problem. She didn't know what was wrong with her sister, but she knew Loki wasn't the "wrong" in Kandy's life.

"Thea still has nightmares," he said when the silence became uncomfortable. "She still cries out for him in her sleep."

Her brother's fiancée had been attacked by a Coyote and nearly kidnapped as well the night Mark died. Thea had lost far more than her fiancée that night, though. Gypsy doubted the other woman would ever be completely over it.

"The attack she suffered that night nearly killed her, Jase," she reminded him. "It's the reason why she went into law rather than getting a business degree."

He shook his head slowly. "She always loved law. She was taking business because she wanted to be Mark's partner."

Jason stared off into space as Gypsy watched him sadly. He had loved Thea even before Mark had proposed to her, but Gypsy knew Mark had always been the other woman's first love. Likely, her only love.

"I'll see if I can get a minute to talk to Kandy tomorrow," he said, turning his gaze back to her and giving her a warm, tired grin. "I hear you're just driving all the men crazy as usual. Especially some Lion Breed commander that you're not giving the time of day to." Approval lit his brown eyes.

Gypsy shrugged. "The Breeds are okay, Jase, I just don't want their problems." It was her standard excuse.

"Thank God," he sighed. "Now, if I could just get Kandy to take the same stand, then I wouldn't have to worry about the two of you near as often, Peanut."

She forced herself to smile back at him even though she nearly flinched at the pet name. She hated it. It made her sick to her stomach every time she heard it. Yet she could never seem to tell him . . .

Don't cry, be brave, Peanut . . .

No, she wouldn't remember.

She busied herself putting away the wine, cleaning the glasses, chatting with Jason about Thea's long hours and anything and everything that would put distance between her and her memories.

Long minutes later, Jase said his good-byes and left. Hearing his car pull from the drive, Gypsy moved to the window and lifted the curtain cautiously to check for Kandy's truck.

It still wasn't there.

Where the hell was her sister and what was she up to?

It was time, Gypsy decided, that she figured out the answer to that question. And she had a feeling she'd better do it quickly.

CHAPTER 4

Two nights later, Gypsy was still trying to figure out where her sister was going after work every night. This had been going on longer than the Breeds had been in town, so she couldn't attribute it to Loki. Besides, she'd seen Loki at the last bar she'd been in, and he'd been confused as hell when she asked if Kandy was with him.

"Gypsy Rum!" An inebriated college boy, barely twenty-one, his alcohol-glazed eyes squinting, called out the greeting as Gypsy stepped into one of the busiest band bars on the Navajo Reservation border.

"Sober up, Slim," she ordered the kid, knowing the consequences if his father caught wind of tonight's overjovial state. "Daddy will be after your ass in a few hours if you're not home."

"Fuck him," Slim drawled, slurring the insult. "He needs a beer."

And no truer words had ever been said, she thought, throwing the boy a wave as she contained her laughter and moved for the bar while watching the crowd carefully for the sight of her sister among the throng.

Slap Happy's was filled every weekend with drunks, wannabe punks, biker dudes and biker babes, wicked Breeds and rogue Breeds, soldiers, warriors, male and female and every sort of desperado in between.

Tonight, she was betting it had maxed out the limit of allowable bodies, if the time it took her to get from the door to the bar was any indication.

Cops and criminals were known to share space here, as well as rogue Coyotes and Bureau of Breed Affairs enforcers along with any arm candy or wannabe sweet that could be had.

It was also one of the best rumor mills and gossip socials outside the private weekend or illegal desert parties that often sprang up on the reservation itself.

Unfortunately, patrolling Breeds and rogue Coyotes looking for trouble had managed to make the desert parties all but impossible to have. The private weekend parties had been scarce as well, due to the isolation of many of the ranches and small estates where they were held.

There were actually several scheduled in the coming weeks since news that the Bureau of Breed Affairs and the Navajo Nation were negotiating the possibility of locating a central Breed office in Window Rock. One that would focus on the enforcement of Breed Law, for both Breeds and humans, in the western states.

Until then, Gypsy was forced to resign herself to the larger, rougher bars instead to find the sister still two years away from being able to legally enter.

Loose lips and secrets discussed in the so-called anonymity of a crowd was another reason she was there tonight, though. According to one of the enforcers at the bar where Gypsy regularly met friends on Friday nights, Kandy had been seen here the night before with several of her friends. And that did not sound like her sister.

The band was taking a break for the moment, the holographic substitute band pelting out music instead to please the crowd on the dance floor.

She let a smile play at her lips as she wedged herself between two recognizable hard bodies at the bar and leaned over the teak counter.

"Kenny C," she called out to the bartender on the other end of the bar. "You're as handsome as ever, you baldheaded lothario."

Kenny laughed back at her. "Be there in a sec, honey."

Satisfied she had complimented her favorite bartender to his satisfaction, she wiggled between the two men, pressing at each of them until they shifted marginally, then waited.

"You are trouble waiting to happen, Gypsy Rum," Rule warned her as Kenny handed her the beer and smacked her an air kiss with a smile.

"So everyone keeps telling me." Turning her head, she shot the Breed a look from the corner of her eye, taking in all those sexy dark looks and sensual-as-hell features.

Her heart kicked up a few beats, just as it always did whenever he was around, while she became slick and wet, her thighs clenching as her moist interest for him threatened to cause her no small amount of embarrassment.

After all, Breeds could smell a woman's sexual interest.

Thankfully, if he sensed it, he never commented on it.

"One of these days, I might stop warning and start spanking." Too-long, too-lush lashes lowered just enough to make her breath quicken just that little bit as she turned to face the cavernous room and lifted the beer to her lips.

He followed the journey, his gaze lingering several seconds as she took a drink of the alcohol, clenching her teeth at the little bitter bite that hit her taste buds.

Rule and his sidekick, Dane, enjoyed the busy talk-filled bars just as much as she pretended to, it seemed.

"Careful there, sweetheart," Dane drawled, his South African accent sexy as hell but nowhere near as interesting as Rule's dark, growly tone. "You know what they say about teasing lions, right?"

She gave her eyes a playful little roll before sliding Rule another sideways glance.

"And I have a habit of shooting men who touch when they're not invited," she reminded them both. "Besides, I think Commander Breaker is intelligent enough to understand the word 'no.'"

Rule lifted the short glass of dark amber liquid to his lips and took a leisurely drink, his gaze holding hers as he obviously tried to hide his grin from her.

Evidently, she tended to amuse him, because he did that a lot while she was around.

"So tell me, luscious." Dane surprised her with the little pet name and sudden flirtatious air. "What exactly does one have to do to earn an invitation to touch?"

No way!

He did not just ask that question! And he did not just give her that suggestive little wink! After weeks of obeying her no-touch, no-sex rules, this heir to some imagined South African throne was breaking the rules?

This could get interesting.

A little dangerous, but interesting considering his family was one of the Breeds' main financial supporters.

"Overlook Junior there," Rule drawled, his voice lazy and mocking despite that little hint of a rasp beneath his smooth tone. "His keeper was called home and there's no one left to smack him around when he gets out of line."

Now wasn't this little sideshow quite the surprise and not exactly what she was used to from them? Not that a little flirting from them wasn't normal. It was. But this was just a shade beyond flirting from Dane.

Lifting the beer to her lips once again, more to kill time and watch the dance floor than out of actual thirst, Gypsy took another long, leisurely sip.

On one side Dane's emerald green eyes watched her with amused attraction. On the other side, Rule's dark blue eyes had her breasts suddenly tingling, her nipples tightening. And between her thighs her clit was so hard and swollen she knew she'd be masturbating the second she walked into her bedroom when she returned home.

"You're scaring her off, Breed," Dane accused Rule then, his voice smooth and mocking. "You should run along and finish chasing shadows." With a little flip of his fingers he dismissed Rule lazily. "I'll see that this luscious little morsel is well taken care of."

She nearly spewed her beer at the outrageous proclamation even as her senses skipped a beat, along with her heart, at his reference to Rule chasing shadows.

"You're joking, right?" she laughed incredulously when she managed to swallow the mouthful of beer.

Straightening from her slouched position against the bar, eyes wide, she stared between the two friends.

"He always acts out when Rhys isn't here to watch after him," Rule drawled, the lazy amusement in his tone at odds with the sudden spark in his vivid blue eyes.

Was that anger?

Not quite, she decided, but whatever it was had her finely honed instincts instantly wary.

What game were these two playing?

"It's starting to sound to me as though both of you need a keeper," she suggested, amused by them, despite her wariness and sudden curiosity about Rule's supposed search. "Is Rhys due back soon?"

Rhys or Ryan Desalvo, Dane's friend and sometime bodyguard, was always deflecting attention from the other man. She often wondered if Dane's habit of watching everyone was the reason why Rhys did it. So his friend could dissect and probe the psyches of those around him.

"Not real soon." Dane shifted a little closer, his large body crowding her, forcing her to slide to the side, her eyes narrowing up at him.

Despite his rough, blond good looks, emerald eyes and lazy humor, she could always sense his detachment, his overly intent curiosity whenever his attention settled on her.

As it was, now.

"Should I have a few of my enforcers toss his amused ass out the door?" Rule's lips were at her ear, his voice lazy and wicked, causing an indescribable warmth to slowly infuse her body.

Turning her heat to meet his gaze, she realized only then how close she had moved to him. Too close. Standing between his spread thighs, though he hadn't taken advantage of the position.

He wasn't touching her, though he surrounded her almost protectively.

His gaze held her.

Warmth and quiet amusement gleaming there, along with hunger.

A wicked, sensual, confident hunger that had her heart racing faster than before as her breath began to feel tight.

He made her want—

He made her want things she couldn't have, hunger for things she knew he could never sate.

Never even attempt to fulfill.

She wanted him to touch her. She wanted it even though she knew it would only make the need clawing at her worse.

Dane was saying something, his voice faintly mocking. She ignored him, as did Rule. His gaze was locked with hers, his lips so close to hers, tempting her, drawing her—

◆   ◆   ◆

The scent of her need—it actually outmatched the suspicion and that white-hot flare of curiosity that tinged the air.

Absently Rule ran his tongue over his teeth, just to be certain the glands beneath were still dormant. The scent of her need had his erection throbbing imperatively, his balls so tight with the need to spill his seed that it was nearing agony.

Jade green eyes were wide, filled with so many shadows and barely perceptible fears that he wanted nothing more in that moment than to see pleasure filling them. Hell, that was all he wanted every time he looked into the pretty green spheres and sensed the lust pulling them closer.

Her lips parted, that plump little lower lip feeling the damp caress of her tongue as it ran over it.

He could hear the thump-thump of her heart as it raced between her lush breasts, the curves defined and perfect beneath the snug little red tank top she wore.

That tiny bit of cloth paired with those butt-snug jeans and moccasin boots that laced up the sides of her shapely legs had him all but panting for her.

She made him hotter than he'd been in—hell, harder, hotter than he'd ever been. And now, as she stared up at him, her lips parted, that hunger blazing up at him, he was a second from taking that kiss he'd been long-ing for.

"Gypsy—"

The faint, barely perceptible buzz of a sat phone vibrating in one of her pockets—again—in a distinctive rhythm had Gypsy suddenly drawing up short.

Rule was going to hurt the caller, he decided.

Those intoxicating eyes widened, and a heartbeat later she moved from between his thighs, hurriedly stepping away from him.

Pulling the phone from her pocket, she quickly checked the number before her jaw tightened and that hint of fear became anger.

"I have to leave." Shaking her head, her scent suddenly tinged with an emotion he couldn't quite define, she hurriedly slapped a few bills on the bar.

There was a shadow overtaking her, a hint of fear and one of worry.

"Gypsy, wait—" *Fuck.*

Before he could stop her she turned, moving quickly to the door before disappearing into the night.

His eyes narrowed at her exit; the scent of her heat and hunger, marred by her fear, still lingered in his senses.

Along with it was the knowledge that until the small phone in her pocket had gone off, she had nearly been his.

Turning slowly back to Dane, he met the other Breed's narrowed, suspicious gaze.

Lifting the short liquor glass to his lips, the hybrid glanced to the exit she had taken before turning back to him with a shrug.

"Well," he drawled. "It would seem she may have a leash after all. Proprietary claim, I believe it was called."

Rule's glass slapped to the bar as his jaw clenched furiously. Turning, he followed the exit she had taken, determined to find out exactly who her leash might be. And when he did, as he told her before, he'd be taking fucking ownership.

Catching up with her, even on a good night, was a pain in the ass, and if he didn't keep his eye right on her, then she was gone just as quickly.

And he was damned sick of her disappearing acts.

Stepping outside and catching sight of her taillights as the little Jeep sped from the parkway, he turned to Dane questioningly as the other man stepped behind him.

"Loki tagged the Jeep at her last location, but there was a complication," Dane informed him somberly before he could ask.

"What kind of complication?" He strode quickly to the Dragoon, aware of Dane following quickly behind.

Dane was sliding into the passenger side as Rule closed the driver's-side door and activated the motor with a quick flick of a finger against the ignition pad.

"No sooner than he'd tagged it and finished programming the signal, the device malfunctioned. Returning to where she parked, he found the Jeep gone and the device dropped carelessly to the gravel."

Rule accelerated quickly as he pulled from the parking lot.

"Dropped? As in someone dropped it, or as in the mechanism that holds it to the vehicle failed?" he asked.

"The mechanism was still working, and at no time did Loki see her exit the bar by the front exit. Mutt was watching the back exit, and she didn't leave from there either. Though there were several windows on the other side where she parked, and one was open enough to have allowed her to slip away."

Gypsy was escaping rather than leaving?

Damn her, the evidence was racking up that she was possibly the contact Jonas was searching for, and it was starting to piss him off. Mostly because he couldn't deflect attention from her *and* cover her movements.

"Jonas wants that Jeep tagged, Dane," Rule reminded him, his voice short, wondering how the hell he was going to keep Jonas from tagging it. Pretty soon, one of Jonas's men would figure out someone was warning her of those devices.

Dane chuckled. "Perhaps it's time little brother learns he can't always have what he wants. Because it seems other interested parties are just as determined that it not be tagged."

Rule wisely refrained from commenting.

As the Dragoon pulled from the parking area, the comm link to the vehicle's communications beeped in summons. Flicking the control on the steering wheel, Rule answered it with a brief "Go."

"Commander, I have the vehicle in sight," Mongrel, one of Dog's Coyotes, reported with icy efficiency. "She picked up a tail just after pulling onto the main road. It's riding black on a parallel course and staying close."

Riding black. Moving with all lights extinguished to avoid detection and most likely using one of the side roads that ran along the highway to keep sight of her.

"Can you identify?" Rule questioned.

"Not without being seen."

Rule grimaced, wishing he'd driven one of the faster, more maneuverable desert vehicles rather than the Dragoon.

"Keep the shadow in sight if possible, but remain eyes on target until I arrive."

If Gypsy had picked up a tail, then he sure as hell didn't want to give whoever was following her a chance to get to her before he could. Just in case it wasn't friendly.

◆   ◆   ◆

Pulling the Jeep into the parking spot beside the stairs, Gypsy breathed out wearily before slapping the steering wheel in frustration when she saw her sister's truck wasn't back yet.

Damn Kandy.

She'd promised she was on her way home when Gypsy had spoken to her on the phone. That was the reason she had left so quickly rather than waiting to see just how terrified she would become if Rule actually tried to kiss her.

Not that she would have let him kiss her in the bar, she assured herself. She couldn't do that. Her reputation of refusing any man she met in a bar was golden. All it would take was one moment of weakness to undo years of work.

And Rule was quickly becoming her weakness.

He and Dane were steadily becoming known as "regulars" in the unofficial nightlife that existed around the reservation's Arizona–New Mexico border with the Navajo Nation. It wasn't as though they were strangers now.

If they weren't at whatever bar she pulled into when she pulled in, then they arrived within minutes of her taking the first sip of her drink. They had a few drinks, watching the younger Breeds and enforcers that Rule obviously seemed to feel so responsible for, and then they would leave and check out the next rowdy gathering.

And all the while, Rule watched her, those thick lashes slightly narrowed, those neon blue eyes gleaming with interest.

And arousal.

And God, he made her hot.

When the rhythmic ring tone identifying Kandy's number had vibrated in her pocket, it had terrified her. Because at that moment she had wanted nothing more than to—

"Are the sweets inside as nice as they are outside?"

A squeak of surprise and Gypsy was whirling around, almost reaching for the knife she kept tucked in the holster inside her boot.

Just almost, because she recognized his voice, knew who he was even before she turned. It just took a minute for her body to catch up.

"You prick, you just scared a year off my life!" Slamming both hands into the steel hard muscles of his chest as she let that first flush of adrenaline tear through her, she accomplished little else than bruising her palms. "What the hell are you doing here, Breaker? Trying to give me a freakin' heart attack?"

"Someone was following you."

There was no amusement in his eyes as there had been all week. No playful teasing in his voice.

He was flat serious.

She felt herself pale as she stared into his eyes and knew he wasn't joking.

"Who was following me?" Why would anyone be following her? What the hell was going on that anyone would take an interest in her all of a sudden?

"If I'd known who was following you, sweet pea, I would be following him instead of rushing here to make sure you were okay."

His voice sent her heart racing in something more than fear this time.

"I'm fine." Was her voice really trembling?

It was really trembling.

That look in his eyes was pure serious. And it wasn't just pure serious danger either. It was serious lust and intent. And she had a feeling she was not going to escape with a bit of flirting tonight.

"I can see that." He nodded slowly.

The black of his mission uniform blended into the night. With his black hair and bronzed flesh, his blue eyes almost glowed in the dark. And they were hot.

"Yeah." Shoving her hands into the back pockets of her jeans, she hurriedly jerked them out as those eyes lowered, sliding across the tops of her breasts as they pushed out against the snug tank top she wore. "Um, I'm fine. You can leave. If you want. I mean, yeah, you can leave." She felt like smacking her own head as the synapses between lips and brain seemed to misfire alarmingly.

What the hell was she supposed to do with her hands?

She crossed her arms over her breasts and that didn't work. Finally, she just shoved her hands into the back pockets of her jeans uncomfortably.

"You got here fast. How did you pass me and I didn't see you?" She cleared her throat, so nervous she swore she could feel her vocal cords trembling with it.

She would have noticed a Dragoon passing her in a heartbeat, and she knew she hadn't seen it.

"Of course I got here fast. I had to make sure my favorite girl was safe." His lips quirked just that little bit, his gaze lightening only marginally. "There's no one else to bust my ass on a regular basis."

"Because everyone else is trying too hard to get that tight ass naked," she retorted.

Oh shit, she didn't say that.

But she did.

His eyes narrowed on her. "But you're not, of course?"

"Oh no. Not me. I'm just everyone's best bud, haven't you heard?" And that wasn't bitterness in her voice now, was it?

But she knew better. The restlessness, the knowledge that the choices she had made over the years kept her life so sanitized it was painful, had the restlessness inside her growing until she felt she couldn't contain it any longer.

"I hadn't heard." He took a step closer.

Was she supposed to retreat?

Retreat? Um, yeah. She stepped back. "Well, I'm fine. You see I'm fine." Holding her hands back from her body, she went back another step. "You can go now. Where did you park anyway?" He wasn't parked out back. "Wherever you parked, be careful now. See you later."

But he wasn't moving to leave. Instead, he was moving with her, a step toward her for every step she took back.

"Are you scared of me, Gypsy?" His voice was lower, a little raspier, rougher. And she liked the sound of it far too much.

She moved back another step as he moved closer. Close enough that she could feel the warmth of his body.

A gasp slipped past her lips before she could stop it as her retreat was suddenly halted by the privacy fencing that hid her sister's front door from view of the parking lot and their parents' home.

"Rule—" She couldn't make herself say "No." Instead, her hands lifted to press against his chest, only to find them securely caught in his broad hands.

A second later he had them secured firmly over her head and pressed against the fence behind her.

Dominance.

Power.

Arrogant sexuality and pure confidence.

The combination was maddening and highly arousing. So arousing she was creaming her panties furiously.

"This isn't a good—" She knew what he was going to do. And she knew if she let him do it—

He didn't ask permission, he didn't give her a warning. Halfway through her own warning on the advisability of what she knew was coming, his lips covered hers, his tongue taking full advantage of her surprised gasp.

Too experienced, warm, with a hint of pure male determination, his lips covered hers and immediately set fire to her senses.

Chocolate and peppermint.

He tasted like chocolate and peppermint candy. Like pure sex and she wanted to lick him up one slow lick at a time.

His free hand cupped the side of her face as his thumb pressed at the tip of her chin, parting her lips further as his settled deeper into the kiss.

His lips plundered hers erotically. They licked over the plumped curves and at her curious tongue as his kiss assured her that he knew exactly what he was doing. And he knew exactly how to make it so damned good that she had no choice but to enjoy it.

And she was definitely enjoying it.

Her whole body was enjoying it.

His free hand moved from her chin to the back of her head, fingers tangling in her hair as he pulled her head back.

Releasing her wrists, his hand moved to her hip, gripped, then slid to her lower back before moving to the curve of her rear.

She was beyond fighting his kiss.

She was beyond fighting anything he wanted to give her right now.

Actually, she was more than ready to take more.

Gripping his shoulders and holding tight to him, Gypsy dug her nails into the black material of his uniform as he tugged at her hair again. The caress sent a radiant heat through her scalp and flooded her senses.

A groan, or a growl, rumbled in his throat as she arched to him.

A hard, heavy thigh slipped between her legs, the iron-hard muscle pressing firmly into the mound of her sex. The flesh there was so sensitive now that the contact burned through her jeans and the material of his uniform. Her clit was swollen, throbbing, the feel of her moisture easing from her vagina another caress against overly sensitive flesh.

Releasing her hair, his palm caressing down her back, to her side, then moving in a determined stroke to the ripe curve of her breast. There, his thumb found the tight, hard tip of her breast through the thin material of her tank top. The rasp of his callused fingertip sent hot arcs of sensation surging from the tight tip straight to the clenched, tension-filled area of her womb.

Pure, unbelievable pleasure began surrounding her, rushing through her veins, racing through her body.

Her hips tilted into the hard caress of his heavy thigh. Her clit rasped against the silk of her panties and denim of her jeans as his hard, muscular thigh flexed and rubbed against her.

For so many years she had wondered what it felt like, this pleasure she had denied herself for so long.

This Breed hadn't bothered to sweep past any objections she might have.

He hadn't given her a chance to object, period.

He hadn't asked for permission.

He hadn't even warned her.

He'd immediately flooded her entire body with such a rush of volatile pleasure that she couldn't deny herself more.

And more.

Her tongue met his over and over again, rubbing against it, licking it, loving the taste of chocolate and peppermint she found there.

His palm cupped her breast, tested the weight, and he made that growly sound again as he released his hold. His hand slid to her hips, pressing beneath the hem of her shirt, and a second later he found bare skin.

If pleasure had been a rush of pure, adrenaline-laced heat flooding her veins before, the second his callused fingertips and palm brushed over her midriff, it became rocket fuel rushing through her system.

His fingertips rasped her sensitive flesh with destructive waves of sensation that fed pure sensual intensity straight to the suddenly hungry depths of her pussy. Her clit didn't just throb now, it ached, hurting for his touch. Her nipples weren't just tight, but so swollen, so blazingly sensitive that the scrape of her bra over the tight peaks was nearly too much to bear.

Too much to bear, and yet it wasn't enough sensation.

Heat seared her nerve endings as a chill raced over her flesh, raising goose bumps along her arms as she shuddered within his hold.

His touch moved over her midriff to below her waist, halting there for a second before his lips tore from hers and Gypsy realized she was panting, desperate for air, yet just as desperate for his kiss again. A shaky moan left her lips and her lashes fluttered open as his kiss slid over her jaw to the sensitive line of her neck.

She arched against him helplessly, a mewling little whimper leaving her lips as his fingers tightened in her hair again, tugging at it. His teeth scraped against her neck, causing her to arch to her toes as a wave of exquisite pleasure exploded beneath his caressing lips and at her scalp at the same time.

She felt as though her nerve endings were racing to get as close to his lips and his tugging hand as possible. Her breasts were so swollen above his other palm that it was all she could do not to beg him to touch her.

All this was happening right here, in plain sight of anyone who might drive down the street behind the store.

It wasn't exactly the outskirts of town. She lived only two blocks from Main Street, for God's sake.

"Do we do this here?" he growled at her neck. "Or do we do this in the comfort of your bed?"

Her bed?

The implications of what they were doing exploded in her head.

"No."

Who was more surprised when she tore away from him and managed to duck beneath his arm to escape to the bottom of the steps, her or Rule?

As she stared back at him, the glow of his eyes, like neon flames, seemed to lick over her body in promise.

It was a promise that sent a bolt of fear tearing through her.

When his gaze met hers, there was a warning in them as well. One that stroked over her body and seared her senses like a brand and assured her that he wouldn't let her run for long.

"You don't run away from pleasure that extreme, little girl," he assured her, a confident smile curling at the corner of his lips.

"Watch me." She wasn't waiting around for him to actually touch her again and prove his words.

Jerking her house key from her back pocket, she fumbled for a moment before she turned and ran up the stairs. She heard him pounding up the steps behind her. A second later the key slid in, the door opened, and she jumped into the apartment, slamming the door behind her and sliding the deadbolt home just as she heard him reach the narrow deck outside.

A chuckle whispered through the door. "Who are you scared of, Gypsy? Me, or yourself?"

Him, she assured herself. It was definitely him scaring the shit out of her, not her response to him, not the knowledge that she was throwing her life away to have sex with a Breed if she continued this course.

"You are insane," she accused him, her voice rough. "Stop trying to seduce me, Rule. It's not going to happen."

The low male laughter sent a shudder of need clenching at her pussy.

"Tell yourself that while you're whispering my name and spilling all your sweet cream along whatever toy you use to get yourself off tonight, Gypsy." There was the slightest edge of knowing irritation as he growled the words.

Gypsy closed her eyes tight, knowing she would be doing just that and hating him for it.

God, she so didn't want to want him like this. Like he was the best thing since breathing and she needed him just as much as she did the air she took in. But even now, she ached to feel his lips on hers again and she could have sworn the taste of peppermint was lingering in her senses.

As she inhaled hoarsely, her fingers drifted over the tops of her breasts, her breath catching at the pleasure—

"I can make it feel better, baby," he crooned through the door. "All night, while you're screaming because the pleasure is so damned good, each orgasm so hot and exciting that all you want to do is reach out for the next one before the last one is finished pulsing through that hot little pussy."

"Go away!" Jumping away from the door, Gypsy turned to face the panel, heat surging through her as she had to force herself not to open the door for him.

"Sweet dreams, lovely Gypsy," he repeated, the amusement in his voice lazy and arrogant. "I'll see you soon."

See her soon?

"Not if I see you first," she muttered.

"I heard that. My sense of smell isn't my only talent."

Of course he had an excellent sense of smell. Of course he knew just how desperately she wanted him. That was her damned luck.

She was hot, the sensitive flesh between her thighs so swollen and needy it ached, her clit filled with such heat it was nearly unbearable.

He had to be able to smell it, because fate certainly wouldn't allow her to deny it.

Her face flamed with embarrassment. "I'm calling the sheriff."

He didn't answer.

What was the pervert doing now?

"Did you hear me? I'm calling the sheriff."

Listening closely, hearing nothing but the racing of her heart thundering in her ears, eyes wide, she tried to determine whether he was still out there.

The faintest sound of a Desert Dragoon starting up, its powerful motor echoing from the front of the building, had Gypsy racing into the living room to peek between the heavy curtains hanging there.

Gazing down at the lighted street, she watched as the black all-terrain vehicle eased from its parking spot and then, with a burst of speed, raced down the street.

"Playing with fire, Whisper? And here I thought you understood the rules? Tell me, did you even search his suite as you were supposed to?"

She laid her head against the window at the sound of the low, grating voice behind her.

She should have expected this.

◆ CHAPTER 5 ◆

"What are you doing here?" Turning, Gypsy faced the member of the Unknown who had accepted her as a contact only months after the death of her brother.

The same warrior who had given her the terms of her participation.

She must always remain a virgin.

Was he trying to make her insane now? Was every man she knew trying to drive her freaking crazy this month?

"Checking on you." Crossing his arms over his broad chest, the tall figure leaned against the frame of her bedroom door.

She didn't even try to see what he looked like, she knew better. The war paint that marked his face was done in such a way as to make it impossible to distinguish his features, no matter how close she came or how hard she attempted to find a distinguishing angle.

She spread her hands out from her body and gazed back at him mockingly. "All in one piece."

Literally. Even her virginity was still intact.

Which was all he was probably worried about.

"I had no doubt. But now, I wonder," he assured her, the confidence in his voice grating on her already heightened nerves.

"Then why check on me?" Moving from the window, she strode across the living room to the kitchen, glancing back as she passed the counter that divided the rooms. "Want a drink? I'm having one."

"No, thank you." His answer didn't surprise her.

Pulling the refrigerator door open, she snagged a long-necked bottle of her favorite beer and twisted the cap off in disgust before taking a long drink.

"You're twenty-four years old, aren't you, Whisper?" He spoke as she swallowed the bitter brew.

"What does it matter?" Turning to face him, she leaned back against the fridge, seeing the gleam of hazel eyes. The last time she saw him, they looked blue.

"You've remained a virgin for nine years in order to work with us. You've had no lovers, you have few friends and you began separating herself from your family even before Mark's funeral. Tell me, how long do you think you can remain isolated among the people who so love you? Or this Breed who seems intent on having you?"

She lifted her brow in a deliberate attempt to convey unconcern. "I walked away."

"You ran away," he retorted knowingly. "There's a difference."

There was a difference, and she knew it.

She simply didn't want to discuss it.

"When I can't run from him any longer, I'll let you know," she promised, tipping the bottle to her lips again.

"And what would happen to you if you stopped running?" Compassion filled his voice. "If you suddenly found you needed more than a drink to sleep on the bad nights?"

He nodded to the beer she was lowering.

"You think I drink to sleep?" she asked, amused. "Tell me, have you ever slipped into my apartment and caught me asleep?"

She knew he hadn't.

His head tilted to the side as he watched her, dissected her.

"Never," he finally admitted. "But I haven't tried to."

"Then try," she suggested. "But don't stay long if you do catch my eyes closed, because it never lasts."

She and sleep were not close personal acquaintances. But she and the nightmares that followed her were.

"That Breed won't be easy to turn away," he told her. "And getting the information we need will be impossible if you ignore him."

"Getting the information you need will be impossible if I sleep with him, remember?" she said, mocking him. "If I sleep with him, then you'll no longer answer my calls."

"I have voice mail. Leave a message. I'll always listen."

Gypsy narrowed her gaze on him as he slowly straightened from his position against the door frame.

"Are you rescinding the terms of my participation?" she asked slowly.

"That's not possible," he sighed heavily. "But should you break the terms of your participation, it doesn't mean I'll completely desert you. I'll just refuse to work with you further."

"Have you ever considered how ignorant that would be?" she asked him as she shook her head, disbelief reflecting in her voice now. "The information I pull in for you in a week's time amazes even me. I never use a computer, I never endanger myself or my friends, but you still get more information than you know what to do with. Would you really cut me off like that?"

"Of course."

Disbelief coursed through her. "For God's sake, why?"

"The same reason we should have cut your brother off when he and Thea Lacey became lovers. He became careless," he stated, his voice harsh now. "I won't take that risk with you."

"Mark wasn't the one who became careless," she sneered. "And we both know it."

"Gypsy." It was one of the few times he used her name.

"Don't Gypsy me." Anger surged through her.

Finishing the beer, she tossed the bottle in the trash before turning on the warrior furiously. "I was careless. And I refuse to discuss it. Now tell me why you're here, or leave so I can shower."

Silence stretched between them. A lengthy, tension-filled silence that warned her that the warrior was seriously considering continuing the confrontation.

God, don't let him continue the confrontation, she thought painfully. She didn't think she could bear it.

Finally, he shook his head, breathing out heavily.

"The information we suspected the Breeds have on the Unknown has been confirmed. We have a leak among our contacts, and we need to know who that leak is. We need you to find out who that leak is."

A leak?

"How many contacts do you have, exactly?" she asked then, tamping down her anger from moments before as she stared back at him suspiciously.

"The number wouldn't help you," he told her, the arrogance that was so much a part of him reminding her far too much of Commander Breaker.

"Okay then, a list of known contacts?" she asked instead.

"Such a thing doesn't exist."

When she would have argued that statement, his hand lifted in a gesture of silence before he continued. "There are six of us, and each of us has our own contacts that we're forbidden to identify. Even we have rules we have to abide by, Whisper."

How shocking.

"Forbidden to identify," she murmured, disgust curling at her lips. "Why doesn't that surprise me? That would just make it far too easy, wouldn't it?"

"I thought you'd see it that way," he agreed as though perfectly serious. "You enjoy doing everything else the hard way, I thought you'd appreciate that one too."

Clenching her teeth as her lips thinned, she propped her hands on her hips and faced him, knowing he would clearly read the mocking suspicion in her face.

"So how am I supposed to figure out who this contact is?" she snapped. "Am I supposed to sleep with Rule and forever give up my own dreams to do so?"

"Your dreams?" he argued with a muffled chuckle. "Working with us was never your dream, Whisper. It's your albatross. Your self-punishment and nothing else. You gave up your dreams for your grief, and you and I both know it."

God, she hated him.

"Go to hell."

It wasn't the first time they'd had this argument, nor was it the first time she'd cursed him.

"Been there," he stated with an edge of boredom. "As for how you do it? However you must, but we have to know what information they have, and exactly where they managed to unearth it. Nothing else matters. To survive, we have to remain hidden. Remain a fairy tale to our people. Somehow, someone's contact has managed to acquire enough information to identify at least one of us. If one of us falls, eventually we'll all fall."

Blinking back at him in shock, she gave her head a little shake.

"How do you know one of the Unknown has been identified?" she questioned him, suspicion and disbelief suspended for the moment. "You don't let anyone know who you are."

"I don't," he agreed. "What one of the others has done, I can't say for certain. All I know for a fact is that my contact within Jonas Wyatt's force assures me that one of us has been identified. He was unable to learn who, or how."

"You have a Breed contact?" That did surprise her. "He's in a better position than I am—"

"Jonas is also aware that the Unknown has a contact on his force," he snapped, anger edging into his tone now. "Whoever betrayed us knows far too much about us. Enough to assure me that the warrior that handles him has taken this person into their confidence. And that can't be tolerated or allowed to continue. And I can't trust the others to ensure that the identity of the warrior is not revealed. That leaves you with the task of identifying them. Because other than you and the Breed within Wyatt's unit, I have no other contacts that my fellow warriors aren't aware of."

So what happened to an Unknown when they were fired? Gypsy had a feeling the position didn't come with an out clause.

"You're certain Jonas can identify one of you?" she whispered.

"I was told that Jonas was overheard making the statement that the Unknown were no more a fairy tale than the Breeds themselves were and that he now had the information he needed to question one of them."

Yeah, that sounded like Jonas Wyatt knew exactly who he was looking for.

She knew Jonas too well to ever doubt he knew exactly what he was talking about. She'd heard far too many tales about Wyatt, and listened to far too many Breeds discuss him when they thought no one could overhear. He didn't make generalized statements. If he had what he needed to question someone, then he knew who the hell that someone was.

Her own experience with Wyatt nine years before, and again after he and his family arrived in Window Rock, confirmed her supposition. She'd even managed to secure two invitations over the past two weeks to lunch with Rachel and Amber, as well as Isabelle Martinez and Ashley, one of the Coyote females with whom she'd become friends.

She knew Jonas was determined, single-minded, and nothing mattered to him but his family and the Breeds. Their survival was his only reason for living.

Rather like the Unknown.

The Breeds were considered part of the People, their genetics a direct tie to past chiefs, medicine men, the sisters, and children who had been taken from the tribes during the years the Council was building its so-called army.

Her brother had revered these warriors. He'd dreamed of eventually becoming one himself if a position among the six ever opened up.

"Getting that kind of information will be extremely hard. Hell, it could be impossible," she muttered, making a quick mental list of the Breeds who might know what Jonas was doing. Though she doubted more than one, possibly two, would be privy to the information he had.

Rule Breaker would definitely be one of those Breeds, as would his brother, Lawe.

Jonas had several bodyguards; no doubt they knew quite a bit, but Rachel Broen was his lover. She would know everything Jonas Wyatt knew, and Gypsy knew Rachel.

A sickening feeling of self-disgust overtook her.

She couldn't reveal anything Rachel told her, even if the other woman did tell her something important. She knew what the Breeds were searching for and why, just not their actual identities. She had no information to give Jonas that would help him; her contact never told her anything, he merely took what she collected. And she believed him when she'd asked him if he could help Amber and he'd denied the ability. His voice had resonated with regret when he told her he couldn't.

"Watching your mind work is fascinating," the warrior said then, his voice reflecting amusement and disbelief. "At some point, my friend, you're going to have to realize how much your talents are being wasted as my contact. You could do far more with yourself."

Gypsy shook her head.

"Rule's suite was completely clean when I went through it last week," she stated, brushing aside his comment. "He keeps his e-pad on him, at least whenever I've seen him. It's never turned on when he has it, and he never pulls it free to use it."

She knew that because one of the programs the warrior had added to her secure satellite phone had been designed to hack into the device the Breed commander carried and download the information contained on it. But it would only work if the e-pad was turned on.

"You had to have overlooked something," he told her then. "When Breaker returned to his room, there was a definite indication of data being accessed or routed into his room from the hotel's cameras. He couldn't do that if he didn't have a computer there. The e-pads aren't capable of running a program like that. They can only read what's routed to them from a program existing on another device. And he wasn't carrying it in with him when he returned."

Her jaw clenched in frustration then. Getting into Rule's suite was easy, but getting caught would be easy as well.

Very easy.

The only person she knew close enough to Jonas Wyatt who might have the information, or a clue to it, was his lover, and the two women who had only recently become Breed lovers. One of whom was Liza Johnson.

She and Liza had visited once or twice since her Breed lover, Stygian Black, had brought her to the hotel for protection. Though the attack on her previously had caused more stringent protective measures to be taken, it might be possible to meet with her now.

Isabelle Martinez, the other Breed lover, was actually a relation. They were second cousins and close friends, though Isabelle hadn't been very social since the attack that was made on her as well.

Being a Breed lover wasn't exactly a safe position to have.

"Find out what you can, Whisper," the warrior sighed heavily as she watched him thoughtfully. "And quickly, if you don't mind. If Wyatt's contact has his warrior's confidence, then they could reveal all our identities. And I don't believe I'd enjoy being hauled into Breed headquarters and interrogated by the bogeyman of the Breeds."

She couldn't blame him for that one.

"As quickly as possible," she promised. "It may take a few days to make contact with my own sources, though."

"I'll look forward to your report." He nodded.

"Just don't hold your breath," she sighed.

He chuckled. "Never." He started to turn away before pausing and turning back to her. "I heard you've been trying to find out where Kandy disappears when she can't be found."

She had nearly asked him to help her when she began looking but had rejected it. She was certain Kandy wasn't in any trouble, but she could sense something wrong.

"Do you know where she's at?" Gypsy clenched her fingers on the edge of the counter as she prayed she'd been right.

"Mark's grave," he answered. "Maybe you should join her, Gypsy. Perhaps it's time to see the past from a new perspective."

Gypsy didn't move as he turned and disappeared into her bedroom, knowing that joining her sister at that lonely, desolate place was something she couldn't do.

Not now.

Perhaps not ever.

Something inside her tightened to the point that pain lanced her heart, drawing a ragged sob from her chest.

She didn't cry.

She never cried.

She'd shed all her tears the night Mark had fallen to the ground, staring back at her with such bleak sorrow.

His face flashed before her as her fists jerked up, pressing into her closed eyes as she fought against the image she couldn't seem to get out of her head.

Her stomach churned with memories she kept buried until these flashing moments of weakness, of agonizing realization. She couldn't breathe, and her throat felt so tight that swallowing nearly had her retching.

Why? Why had he told her that?

She would have preferred to just not know where Kandy was disappearing to and why she was staying out so late.

God, why was her sister doing that?

Why was she going to that place?

Gypsy hated that piece of ground.

She refused to go near it now, wouldn't even drive past it whenever her destination called for it. She always took an alternate route.

She couldn't bear the thought of looking over to that beautiful rise to see the black onyx stone that marked it.

"Why?" Before she could suppress the shattered scream inside her, it escaped her lips as her hand gripped a glass vase on the shelf next to her, which she threw with enough force to launch it across the room. "Damn you, why?"

Enraged, knowing she couldn't bear the walls closing in on her, she turned and made her way from her apartment and into the darkness.

Where secrets hid.

◆   ◆   ◆

The haunting, hollow cry of the young woman hiding in the apartment across from the sheltered copse of trees and the shadows where he hid had Dane grimacing with regret.

She was one of his greatest failures, he thought regretfully. Her brother was his greatest. How in God's name had he not been able to anticipate the betrayal that killed Mark McQuade, and in nine years of searching, why hadn't he found the bastard who had betrayed the young man and allowed that child to carry the blame?

It haunted him, knowing that whoever had turned McQuade's identity over to the Genetics Council wasn't the Coyote Breed who had died for it, though he had been no less guilty. The man who had destroyed that child's life had gotten away clean, at least for now.

Dane stared at the apartment, aching for the loss he hadn't been able to stop as a shadow shifted at the side of the building, then disappeared.

Remaining silent, Dane caught sight of the warrior again seconds later, moving toward him. He watched as his contact paused and removed the thin painted mask he wore before folding it and shoving it into his pocket.

His lips quirked at the thought of that mask. It had been fooling humans and Breeds alike for decades. It was a creation of the first Leo's, and one whose workings Dane had been unable to figure out to this day.

Removing a cigar from his pocket and bringing it to his lips, he then handed one to the Breed standing against the tree beside him.

Lighting the cigar, Dane then handed the lighter to the Coyote as well, waited as he lit his own, then accepted it back and pocketed it.

"The two of you are going to piss me off." The warrior moved over to them, glaring at them irately.

Pulling another cigar free of his pocket, Dane handed it to the newcomer before watching him use his own lighter to ignite it.

"How's she doing?" Dane nodded to the apartment as the warrior exhaled, irritation inherent in the sound.

"That has to be the most stubborn damn woman I've ever laid my eyes on," he bit out, grinding his teeth over the words. "She's been at this nine years now and has no intention of letting up. I thought you said that bastard who was all over her ass tonight was her mate?"

Dane couldn't help but smile. "He's her mate, I assure you." He did nothing to hide the heavy South African accent he carried.

"Yeah, that's why she's up there trying to figure out how to learn who's betrayed the Unknown when she's staring at the bastard who did the betraying."

Dane stared at the warrior, knowing far more about him than he was sure the man would find comfortable.

"All for the greater good, my friend," Dog drawled with a curious lack of accent. "We can't have a traitor in the ranks."

"Using her like this doesn't sit well with me," the warrior informed them, not for the first time. "And what the hell kind of mating was that anyway? Why is she up there by herself screaming like her soul is being cut out, if he's her mate? And ignoring the question's not going to make it go away, Dane."

No, this—warrior—was more stubborn than most. He wouldn't stop looking for an answer if he thought Dane was deliberately not answering him.

"I'm not certain yet why the mating didn't occur," he answered, his gaze returning to the apartment thoughtfully. "I am entirely certain, though, that she's his mate."

"How?" It was Dog who asked that question, confusion apparent in his voice. "How can you be so sure?"

How could he be so certain? Dane almost grinned, but he was far too aware of the other two watching him. He couldn't claim to have smelled it, because Dog was a Breed as well; he would instantly question why he hadn't smelled it.

That left the truth, which was far stranger than fiction.

Lifting his hand to rub at the back of his neck, he stared at both men a bit uncomfortably. This wasn't going to be an easy explanation and it was one he rarely made.

"I sense it," he finally muttered.

"Excuse me? You what?" Dog asked with his ever-present mockery, albeit thicker than normal.

"It's complicated," he gritted out, not enjoying the sensation of having others watch him as he so often watched them.

"You don't say," Dog commented wryly. "Why not explain it to us anyway?"

Shooting him a glare, Dane bit down on the tip of his cigar before clenching it between his thumb and forefinger and lowering it slowly.

"I told you, I just sense it," he repeated, forcing back his discomfort.

He'd be damned if he'd let that grinning jackass of a Coyote know that he felt a bit at odds trying to explain the little talent he had.

"Do tell," the warrior suggested, a bit more firmly than Dog had.

"Telling's the hard part," he admitted with a twist of his lips. "It's a knowledge that's there once I see them together. Rather like a gut feeling."

"Gut feeling, huh?" Dog was definitely laughing at him; thankfully, it was silent laughter.

Dane couldn't help but let his lips twitch, because with this Breed, he would definitely have the last laugh.

"And sometimes, all I have to do is hear a certain name on a Breed's lips to know who his mate is. Want to start naming names, *boet*?" The South African slang for "friend" slipped before he could stop it. A problem he was having more often of late.

Dog's eyes instantly narrowed as suspicion lit them, the gray darkening, flickering with a hint of anger.

"Stop letting him rile you, Dog," the warrior grunted in disgust from Dane's other side. "He tried that one on me last year. You have to know him well enough not to let him mess with your mind."

Oh, he could do far more than mess with Dog's mind. There was a reason he had sought out the Coyote and formed a friendship with him when he had. If this Breed didn't have friends soon, not just acquaintances or other Breeds who didn't care to fight with him, then he was going to be in a spot of trouble.

"You're going to end up in a world of hurt if you make the mistake of messing with what you assume is my mind," Dog warned him quietly.

"There would first have to be a mind within that thick skull of yours to mess with," Dane suggested mockingly before turning back to the warrior. "Rescind the virginity clause and give her a choice. I never understood why you put her under such constraints to begin with when you've done it with no one else."

Surprise reflected on the other man's face before instant denial filled his gaze.

"The hell I will." The warrior suddenly tensed, his brows jerking together in a frown as the tinted contacts he wore picked up the faint hint of color that Dane was certain he'd want no one to glimpse.

"Virginity clause?" Dog was far too easily distracted tonight, Dane thought with silent sarcasm.

Did Breeds have trouble with ADHD that he was unaware of?

"If I rescind the clause, she'll become suspicious," the warrior said, ignoring Dog's query. "She's too well trained for that, Dane, and you made certain of it. She'll instantly know she's being set up, and don't think she hasn't been listening long and hard for proof of Mating Heat whenever she listens to the Breeds talking. If she catches a whiff that it could be true and Rule's her mate, then she just might turn tail and run for good long before he does."

"She'll not hear anything there." Dog's assurance had Dane staring back at him now.

"Breeds gossip worse than old women," he reminded the Coyote.

"Not here, not about Mating Heat." Dog shook his head firmly. "Jonas put the word out before the first Breed headed out here nine years ago, I hear. He reinforced it when the search for Brandenmore's research pets led them out here again. And he made it clear, if word of Mating Heat is gossiped about, or the words 'mates' or 'mating' are mentioned, then he is going to start chopping off heads. Literally."

Dane shook his head before looking to the stars in search of help where his brother was concerned. That boy was a danger to himself sometimes, not to mention Mating Heat in general. The legend of the Mate Matcher was definitely sealing itself within stone. And Jonas with it if the other Breed wasn't extremely careful.

"Assuming she really is his mate," the warrior said then, "what happened tonight? Because he's damned sure not in bed with her."

To that, Dane could only shake his head, because he didn't have a clue. That didn't mean he wouldn't figure it out.

"Rule will run if he even suspects that's his mate," Dog stated then, causing that "something," that extra sense to shift inside him.

"His animal instincts won't let him run, from what I understand," the warrior argued, with a hint of a question in his voice.

Ahh, there was the key.

"It wouldn't matter if his instinct was a full-grown in-his-face Lion," Dog grunted. "That Breed even suspects his mate is in the area, might be in the area, or could be arriving at any time in the near future, and trust me, he's gone. He'll run."

"Why the hell would he do that?" The disbelief in the warrior's tone ran thick with amazement. "I thought male Breeds worshipped their mates or some shit."

"Or some shit," Dog grunted. "But Rule watched not just his mother's mate be dissected alive, but also his mother, because of the Mating Heat and the scientists' determination to view the effects of it on the living body. According to those gossiping Breeds you mentioned, he's that determined to protect his mate from even the chance of that happening to her. His belief is that the best way a Breed can protect his mate is to never mate her to begin with."

Dane sensed the surprise emanating from the warrior who believed that he knew all the secrets while hiding his own.

Children, he thought, restraining himself from shaking his head. Both of them.

They had no secrets at all where he was concerned, but letting them believe they did was a bit of fun now and then.

Even as amusement gathered inside him, so did a sense of knowledge where Rule Breaker was concerned.

The mating was there. Gypsy Rum McQuade was definitely his mate, but the animal, the animal senses rather, were far smarter than the Breed, evidently.

Dane turned to the warrior. "What do you think she'll do?"

The warrior crossed his arms over his chest, gazing back at him thoughtfully.

This man knew Gypsy McQuade better than anyone, even her parents, he guessed.

"She'll seek out her friends first," he finally answered. "Liza, Isabelle, and Jonas's mate, Rachel. Perhaps even the Coyote females. She knows them quite well and parties with them often. When there are no answers to be found there, only then will she go to Breaker."

"He would be the most direct route," Dane pointed out. "Why not go to him first?"

"Because he spooked her." The warrior suddenly grinned. "And he's the first man who's managed to do that. He has her so spooked, he just might have her running scared. And, boys"—pure anticipation filled the other man's voice now—"I've never seen Gypsy Rum McQuade run scared from any man or Breed. I'm damned sure looking forward to this one."

What the warrior wasn't thinking of, what he wasn't remembering, was that Gypsy had remained a virgin all these years to continue working with the Unknown for a reason.

She was trying to deserve to live.

She'd never forgiven herself for something that was never her fault to begin with.

Her brother's death.

She wouldn't give in easily, and if she did—if she did, he hoped Rule had the good sense to give her more to live for than she would believe she needed to die for. Just as he hoped that in Gypsy, Rule could find a mate he deemed worthy of fighting his fears for. Because in this world, in this time, being a Breed wasn't easy, nor was it much safer than it had been before.

Now, a Breed had so much more to lose.

Perhaps his father had been right last year when he'd suggested to Dane that it was time to place both woman and Breed in a position that neither could refuse nor run from. A position that would give that animal skulking inside Rule the best chance possible of claiming his mate before Rule realized what was about. And the best chance for the woman to be mated.

He almost smiled in satisfaction.

There were times when he and the old man were in perfect accord. Well, actually, often. They only really seemed to butt heads when the Leo began to suspect that Dane was out having fun when he'd told the Leo he was searching the world for his mate.

His father, despite his toddler twins who were giving him hell nowadays, was desperate to see his bachelor son settled and giving the Leo grandbabies to bounce on his knee.

Dane was just as determined to do otherwise.

He'd loved, deeply, sincerely. Mate or no mate, he'd loved one woman with a strength he'd not known he could possess. He'd loved her enough to give her to her mate and ensure that the dumb bastard deserved her.

Not that he ever had, but he was as close as any man would get, Dane had decided, aching a bit, as he always did, for her.

Still, he'd set this in motion nearly a year before, then just waited for his little brother, Jonas, to get a clue and finish the job for him.

Jonas was rather dependable in that area.

Thankfully, because Dane didn't think the title of Mate Matcher would sit as well on his shoulders as it did on his baby brother's.

"What now?" Dog asked, glancing at Dane curiously.

"Now"—Dane smiled around the cigar clenched in his teeth—"now, we dot our *i*'s and cross our *t*'s and see what happens."

The other two men glared at him in confusion.

Dane rocked back on his heels and grinned at them.

"It's time, gentlemen, to prepare a contract for our assistant director and ensure that he has no option to run."

· C H A P T E R   6 ·

The air of excitement that filled the offices of McQuade Image Consulting when Gypsy entered it several days later was nothing short of surprising. Normally, Hansel (God forgive her father's parents for that name) and Greta McQuade were with clients rather than in the offices across the street from the Gingerbread House, the sweets and gift store Greta's parents had turned over to their granddaughters.

They'd been busy building the small personal marketing business their first child had begun with them when he was no more than twenty. After Mark's death, they had thrown themselves into it and ensured that their lives were as busy as possible.

With Jason overseeing the offices and potential clients, her parents had concentrated on building the images, personal and business, needed to build their reputations.

Her father was still trim at fifty with very little graying in his hair. He was standing in the small conference room, a smile wreathing his face, his brown eyes sparkling in excitement.

Her mother was sitting at the long, dark walnut table, her chair turned to the side to face him, her green eyes filled with anticipation as her head turned and they both stared at Gypsy expectantly.

Despite her green eyes, Greta McQuade's features were pure Navajo, compliments of her maternal Navajo grandfather and paternal Navajo grandmother.

She was still slender, her five foot six frame delicate and well toned for her age. She looked ten years younger and sometimes acted twenty years younger.

Jason sat at the head of the table, grinning as he watched Gypsy, his gaze approving as they both noticed the fact that she had arrived on time for the meeting he'd called and dressed in soft light blue capris, sleeveless shell and white strappy flat sandals rather than jeans and a snug cami as she usually dressed.

Gypsy closed the door slowly, eyeing the three of them suspiciously as they continued to watch her as though she should be erupting with the same joy.

She didn't do joy so well.

She was inclined to suspicion and watching for whatever was about to disrupt her little world when they looked at her like that.

"Did we win the lottery or something?" she asked warily.

"Or something." Her father clapped his hands together in a gesture of building excitement, obviously ready to burst with whatever excitement filled him.

"Come in and sit down, Gypsy," Jason invited, his smile revealing his own excitement at the news they were obviously holding back.

"Do you want to tell her, Jase?" Greta asked, anticipation gleaming in her eyes as she gripped the armrests on her chair and glanced at her daughter. "I can't believe we actually did it."

Jason chuckled lightly, shaking his head. "I think this is Hans's news. He's the one who busted his ass to pull it off."

Her father shot Jason a look of gratitude before his hands gripped the edge of the high-backed chair in front of him.

"We just got that account we bid on last year for image development and social integration with the Bureau of Breed Affairs," he announced, sending a sharp edge of warning to explode in her stomach as she froze at the news. "They've contracted for a year's time, for their new division director and two business and civil liaisons at the new Window Rock offices of the new Bureau of Breed Affairs and Enforcement. The contracts are individual, for the positions and the Breeds filling them, rather than the

Bureau itself. If it works out, though, when they fill the remaining positions for this division next year, we'll have at least one of those as well."

Now there was a mouthful, and her father actually pulled it off without so much as a hesitation or a moment of stuttering.

Gypsy stared back at Hans McQuade, certain she couldn't have heard him correctly. "Image development and social integration," she repeated, trying not to swallow with the same fatalistic impression that anyone walking to the gallows would have used. "Really? I thought the bid was for corporate rather than personal development when you were discussing it last year?"

Corporate was easy. Corporate was what her parents did best.

Since when had they begun doing personal image development and social integration? Corporate mostly consisted of some well-placed ads and newsworthy stories as well as introductions to other business owners.

The Breeds were handling that end pretty well in the eastern portion of the United States. In the western states such as Colorado, the Wolf Breeds weren't quite as socially adept, though, and the Breed community as a whole had lost footing to the Purist militia groups rising up and attacking Breeds or working with the Genetics Council to capture and continue experimentation on them.

"The Bureau wants to step more into individual integration and image building than the Breeds Society normally focuses on. They believe that here in the West, that will be the best route to take," her father stated with an air of pride. "I'd actually proposed this first, but the Ruling Cabinet wasn't so certain of it, so they were considering a more general theme of increasing public support and awareness of the Breeds. I was certain if they went with the idea, we'd never have a chance at the contract with the bigger agencies vying for it. But Jonas Wyatt, along with Vanderale and Lawrence Industries, two of their main supporters, convinced the cabinet that my idea was perfect for the region and, as I'd taken the chance and carried the expenses myself to work it out and propose it to the cabinet, to allow me to have first shot at the personnel for the new Window Rock offices. As a sort of test project, they want to see what we can do."

Leaning forward, Jason drew her attention then.

"We'll move on to a more national project if this one is the success your father promised the Breeds it will be," Jason informed her, his expression filled with the same excitement her parents had. "This is going to be big for us, Gypsy. McQuade Image Consulting will finally be the company your parents dreamed of."

The company her brother had dreamed of, Gypsy corrected him silently. McQuade Image Consulting had been Mark's dream, not her parents'.

Or his best friend's.

Her gaze narrowed, her natural inclination to suspicion rising like a tidal wave and capsizing any hint of objectivity.

Unlike her parents and Jason, she knew a bit more about the Breed psyche and the fact that they never did anything on a more personal scale that wasn't somehow personally benefiting whichever Breed was maneuvering it.

Usually Jonas Wyatt.

"He's choosing one of his commanders to head the new offices initially, and there will of course be other positions. So far, five lead positions to start with," her mother continued, and Gypsy could feel that sudden clench of her stomach and the racing of her heart. "Several liaison positions in the Navajo Law Enforcement offices will be created as well. We'll work with his choice to head up the new Bureau offices and then move on to the liaison positions before we begin working with the others. We'll draw up a suggested schedule of events and placements to ensure that the commander and two liaisons have the most advantageous chances of creating and building the foundations for the right social and economic ties to begin repairing the rifts created by the purist societies. It's a wonderful opportunity for all of us."

Jason and her parents had enough connections, favors owed, and power backing by her mother's parents to ensure that the Breeds were indeed invited to the best parties and social events.

Gypsy turned back to Jason as he relaxed back in his chair at the head of the table. "I thought you didn't like working with Breeds, Jason," she reminded him, wondering why he appeared so excited as well.

Surprise spread across his face. "Gypsy, I don't have to be in love with the Breed society to do my job."

"Gypsy, that was rather unkind," her mother berated her then, an edge of disappointment filling her voice. "Jason has shown no discrimination to the Breeds, though all of us would do very well to be wary of them. We can still be excited over the fact that they're finally going to profit us."

Yeah. Let's get excited over that, she thought sarcastically, *while you hate them with every fiber of your being.*

Her father was less prone to blame all Breeds than her mother and Jason, but he rarely went against her mother either.

"I'm sorry, Mom, I was just a little surprised," she apologized, unwilling to upset her mother. "Was Mr. Wyatt forthcoming enough to inform you of the names of these Breeds he's chosen for the positions?" she asked then, panic beginning to well in her chest.

"We've actually met the two liaison appointees." Her father jumped in at that point. "I believe they're engaged to friends of yours? Isabelle Martinez and Liza Johnson. Malachi Morgan has accepted the position of Bureau liaison to the Navajo Law Enforcement Agency, while Stygian Black has agreed to accept the position of liaison to the Navajo Covert Law Enforcement Division. The commander there, Cullen Maverick, seems very pleased with the choice as well."

She nodded slowly. "You said there were three positions," she reminded them.

Her mother's smile dimmed partially as her father got that harried, worried look he always seemed to have whenever she was around.

"Mr. Wyatt wants to meet us to personally introduce the commander you'll be working with." Greta McQuade was watching her daughter anxiously now, though she was trying to maintain her excitement. "He even stated he'd run a full background check on the company as well as on you, and he's extremely confident of your ability to do exactly what's needed to ensure that the commander he's chosen as division director receives the best reception and chances of building a strong community network. We'll manage the two selected for the liaison positions, though we'll begin with Malachi Morgan and his fiancée, Isabelle Martinez. And Isabelle is such a wonderful girl. Not that it will hurt that she's the president's niece and one of our tribal chief's granddaughters, not to mention your second cousin."

Oh no, that wouldn't hurt at all, Gypsy agreed as she could feel the ax getting ready to fall.

Right across the back of her neck.

Her forced smile was completely lost on her parents and Jason. They were simply too damned happy with this contract to see that their daughter was less than enthused.

She wasn't normally a paranoid person, she really wasn't. But she didn't believe in coincidence either. And the very fact that this was happening only days after Rule, a rumored potential candidate for the position of division director, had warned her of his intention to check her bed out wasn't lost on her.

Her parents' business was small, their reputation sterling, but their list of clients wasn't exactly long. Even in Window Rock there were stronger image consulting firms than the McQuades'. Yet Jonas Wyatt had chosen her parents?

This was such a setup that it practically stank of being maneuvered. Then there was the fact that her parents hadn't mentioned the Breed commander's name. Probably because they had come into the store the day before to hear her raging about Commander Rule Breaker and his complete arrogance to Jason and Kandy.

They knew this was not going to be a smooth, seamless business relationship where she was concerned.

"So, when exactly are we supposed to be meeting with Mr. Wyatt and his commander?" she asked carefully.

"We're meeting this evening at the hotel, in Mr. Wyatt's suite. He'll be there, along with his wife, Rachel." Her mother frowned then. "I hadn't heard of their ceremony being performed as other Breeds have. Why do you think they didn't have one?"

Her mother was the queen of distracting questions, and she could see the desperation in her mother's gaze to distract her quickly.

"Their daughter's been too ill. They haven't married yet, though they rarely correct the assumption that a Breed ceremony was performed privately." Gypsy supplied the answer absently even as she quickly began processing information. "What time this evening? And isn't this a little short notice, especially considering the fact that I have no idea who I'm working with?"

"A bit, perhaps." It was Jason who spoke up as Greta watched Gypsy closely. "But as Director Wyatt has been quite concerned with information on the new offices opening on the reservation without an assigned division director and key staff, it's perfectly understandable. And his concern is very well placed. As are his plans to announce the new office and its DD at a welcoming ball that the president and chiefs of the Six Tribes are throwing in honor of the Breeds."

The look her parents shared, one of such pride and excitement, had her nearly rolling her eyes in disgust.

"What party?" No one had mentioned a party to her, and that was something she needed plenty of advance notice for. Notice that she knew she just was not going to get.

Her mother turned back to her, practically glowing again despite Gypsy's lack of excitement and her knowledge that she had just been distracted by her mother again. "We've been invited, as a family, to a welcoming ball being thrown in honor of the Breeds and the agreement between the Nation and the Breed Ruling Cabinet to locate the offices on reservation land. Mr. Wyatt wants to introduce you, as well as his selection as division director, to the press the day after the ball. It's an incredible opportunity for us as well as the Breeds. This could be what we've needed to pull in the larger contracts that other firms have gotten because of their greater visibility."

Gypsy nodded slowly, so certain of exactly what was going on that she had to grit her teeth to keep from informing her parents. This was no more than a heavy-handed attempt by Commander Breaker to ensure that she couldn't continue to ignore him as she had since the night he'd ambushed her outside her apartment.

There wasn't an image consulting business in the world that could do more for the Breeds' image than the Breeds themselves managed, one way or the other, to do for themselves.

They didn't need McQuade Image Consulting, they needed damned magicians to hide the machinations of the new division director, Rule Breaker. And while they were at it, it sure as hell wouldn't hurt to put a leash on the reigning director of the Bureau of Breed Affairs, Jonas Wyatt.

Wyatt was known as a man who kept his business promises, though; hopefully that meant he wouldn't destroy her parents' dreams when his commander didn't get the bed bunny he was hoping for.

And wouldn't her contact within the Unknown be jumping for joy at the prospect of her working so closely with the very enforcer they suspected was investigating them? The one they feared had found evidence to identify one of them?

"This is just what we needed." Her father was all but walking on air.

"This contract will definitely up the office's prestige." Jason was all but crowing like a cocky little bantam rooster, she thought in disgust.

"So, when is this little party?" she asked them, barely able to muster a false smile, let alone any excitement at all.

"Well, the party is a little short notice." Her mother was really nervous now, though. "It's in a week, but I'm certain we can accommodate the date."

She was going to scream.

"That is so past very short notice, Mother, that it's ludicrous. The only gowns we have at the moment are the ones commissioned for the Lanceister Ball. There's not enough time to commission for that ball and attend this one as well. And we've already committed to the Lanceisters; we can't back out," she reminded her mother, pushing her fingers deep, deep into the pockets of her capris to hide her fists. "Perhaps Director Wyatt should just look into a later announcement to the press. One that isn't so—"

"We've already discussed it with the Lanceisters and Mr. Wyatt, Gypsy," Jason informed her firmly, pointedly ignoring the sharp look she directed his way. Since when the hell was he king of the mountain around here? "The party was arranged a bit quickly, but the caliber of the guests demands a more formal atmosphere and dress. Never fear, there's time to arrange more dresses for this fall. You and your mother could even make a trip to L.A., perhaps, and do a bit of shopping there. Or New York."

She wanted to curl her lip into an insulting little sneer as Jason watched her with an unfamiliar gleam of triumph. What the hell was his agenda with this little party anyway? Getting her and her mother on a shopping trip? Did he really think it was going to work like it did in the movies? They'd come home all mushy-mushy and her parents would have forgotten the part she played in Mark's death?

She didn't think so.

But, as he said, getting new gowns wasn't an issue. It was the idea of such short notice for such a very important event. Press notices needed to be arranged, a list of guests needed vetting and discussions were needed with the reporters affiliated with McQuade Image Consulting to discuss the articles that would best portray the Breeds as benefiting the area socially and financially.

The fact that Wyatt was acting as though this were something that could just be thrown together worried her even more than the dress situation did.

She let Jason and her parents ramble on about opportunities, clients and contracts, unwilling to burst their bubble. Hopefully, Jonas Wyatt wasn't playing some cruel hoax at Commander Breaker's behest and could manage to do his magic as normal until her parents could pull in their own magic. If this was some game, or joke, then she just might sue.

Or threaten to anyway.

Even she had heard about the hungry volcano Jonas was rumored to introduce his enemies to on occasion.

It was enough to make her want to kick Wyatt *and* his commander.

"A car will be picking us up for the ball," her mother informed her as Gypsy came to her feet, preparing to leave the office. "You can have the next week off to get ready. Be sure to call the boutique this afternoon and see if Connie can get you in before the meeting this evening."

Connie.

Gypsy almost sighed.

That was a very subtle hint that her mother thought her hair needed trimming and her nails might need some work. Greta McQuade was very particular about appearance when it came to McQuade Image Solutions. She slid an unobtrusive look to her nails.

Okay, she might need a manicure.

"And the meeting with Director Wyatt and his commander is this evening, don't forget." Her mother was sounding more worried now than she had moments before. "I'll call Connie and see if she can't get both of us in within the next few hours myself."

Connie loved her mother.

The beautician had nearly gone bankrupt several years before, and it had been Greta McQuade who had used a few favors, worked a little magic, and within six months, Connie's salon couldn't keep up with the influx of appointments being requested. Gypsy had no doubt in her mind that Connie would schedule them within the next two hours.

"Just let me know," Gypsy replied in resignation.

She couldn't refuse the job, couldn't let her parents down like that. And from the small, satisfied smile on Jason's face, he knew it.

"Gypsy." Her father's quiet voice had her turning to him, his somber features warning her of what was to come now. And it was a discussion she simply couldn't face.

"Can we talk later, Dad?" She was not in the mood for another lecture.

"No, we can't." His firm tone had her tensing as she watched him warily, aware of Jason's frown as he sat forward slowly at the sound of Hans's sharp tone.

"I want to know what you're doing," he told her, his former excitement suddenly gone as he went from business owner to father in less than a heartbeat.

She gave him a deliberately confused look. "Doing?" Lifting her hands in a gesture of uncertainty, she gave her head a little shake. "I'm not doing anything. Mom said she was going to contact Connie. I need to go home, shower and figure out what I'm going to wear to this meeting and get ready for it."

The disapproval in his gaze had shame burning a hole in her stomach lining. Because most of that was a lie as well as a carefully worded reminder that a fight would only spoil this meeting for all of them.

"You were at one of the border bars last night. Director Wyatt mentioned it while we were talking this morning," he reminded her. "How does it look when our finest image consultant, our daughter, is a regular at one of the most disreputable bars in the state? Have you forgotten we fired one of your cousins for just such a thing?"

She rolled her eyes. "Come on, Milly was a tramp. She was screwing her way through the bars as well as drinking her way through them. Neither of which I'm doing. Stop worrying."

"That bar is dangerous, Gypsy." Her mother had slid her hands from the table to hide them. To hide her clenched fingers, Gypsy knew. It was her mother's way of coping and staying calm.

"That bar is fine—"

"That's what your brother said about that same damned bar a week before you were attacked and he was killed. He thought he could mix with that crowd and survive. He didn't survive it, and I'll be damned if I want to bury another of my children," her father burst out, causing her to freeze instantly.

She couldn't speak. For a moment, she couldn't breathe. For a moment, one bleak, horrifying moment, the memories almost overwhelmed her, almost broke her once again.

She made herself meet her mother's gaze and flinched, barely able to hold back a pain-filled cry at the accusation in that look.

In her father's, there was immeasurable pain.

She couldn't speak. She tried to. She tried to excuse herself, to apologize, but all she could do was see her father's face as it was when he arrived in the desert that night.

Bleak. As tearstained as her mother's. Standing next to the medic transport where her brother's body had been placed. They had both looked at her, then stopped and looked back at Mark before her mother had collapsed and her father had tried to deal with her loss as well as his own.

Gypsy had stood there, alone, until Jonas Wyatt and Lawe Justice had come to either side of her, their warmth holding back the icy desert night.

"I told you," she whispered as she felt Jonas staring down at the top of her head. *"Who could want me . . ."*

Turning, she rushed from the office, ignoring her mother's protest, her father's demand that she come back to the office.

From the corner of her eye she glimpsed Jason rising quickly from the table and her younger sister at the front counter, head down, her expression saddened.

Of course Kandy had heard the last of that conversation.

The door hadn't been closed.

Rushing past her, Gypsy jerked the door open and strode into the brilliant heat and sunshine that enveloped Window Rock before moving quickly to where she'd parked her Jeep across the street in front of the store.

She wasn't going to discuss her brother, or listen to another of her parents' attempts to excuse what had happened. They tried, she gave them credit. They tried so hard to pretend that it wasn't her fault that their son, their only son, had been killed because of their elder daughter. And for the most part, she let them. But more and more often her father was berating her for her evening activities, concern and suspicion filling his gaze each time he did so.

He didn't know what she was doing. She knew he and her mother suspected she was drinking too much, perhaps worried she was into more than just a few beers. After all, what more could they expect? Her determination to go to a party at fifteen had been the reason her brother was murdered by Coyote Breeds. The reason all their lives had been torn apart.

She couldn't reassure them. She couldn't tell them what she was doing. But she wouldn't have, even if she could. Let them think she was far less than what she was; it would only protect them if the unthinkable happened and the Breeds or the Unknown's enemies ever suspected her.

And protecting them was all that mattered.

Which was why she intended to have a nice little conversation with Commander Rule Breaker concerning his part in the contract her parents believed they were being offered.

He needed to understand, now, before it went any further. There wasn't a chance in hell that she was going to become his lover. Losing her virginity meant losing her last link to her brother, and she didn't think she could bear the guilt of it if she did so.

She'd lived so many years alone, without allowing anyone close enough to her to be harmed that she had no idea how to let anyone in anymore.

Even Khileen, once her best friend, rarely attempted to continue their friendship anymore. The Coyote Breed females Ashley and Emma had come closest to her, and nearly losing Ashley had given her more nightmares than she wanted to consider.

She didn't need anyone—

She couldn't finish the thought.

She escaped instead and assured herself she was strong enough to do this. She could resist Commander Breaker and any desire he filled her with.

Yet the taste of chocolate and peppermint lingered in her senses and left her craving more of the Breed's kiss.

Craving it enough that she began to worry . . .

CHAPTER 7

She found Rule several hours later, after missing the appointment with Connie and her mother, spending precious time hunting him down rather than preparing for that damned meeting.

He was on duty, she'd been told by several sources, no doubt in town someplace overseeing the enforcers under his command.

She found his Dragoon parked behind a small stand of cottonwood trees outside town where the new division headquarters were rumored to be located.

Not that he was alone.

Dane Vanderale was of course with him, as were Dog, Loki, Mutt and another Coyote she'd only seen a few times who answered to Mongrel.

Pulling the Jeep to a hard stop mere feet from the arrogant commander who of course refused to so much as step back an inch, she watched his eyes, intent, somber as he met her gaze through the windshield.

The others showed varying degrees of surprise, with the exception of Dane, who just laughed.

Slamming out of the vehicle, she stalked around the front of it to confront the Breed determined to drive her insane.

"You are behind this." She shoved her finger imperiously at his broad chest. "And don't even bother denying it. I know you're behind it."

She was almost shaking with anger and she was damned if she could even explain why the match had been struck to her temper. She just knew it was his damned fault. She just knew she needed someplace to expend that anger before it destroyed her.

◆　◆　◆

"Dog, Dane, find someplace to be," Rule ordered quietly as he saw the Jeep bearing down on them and glimpsed the set expression of the young woman at the wheel.

"Sure, Breaker," Dane drawled. "Tell me, should we worry about your safety or her virtue?"

"Go," he growled as the Jeep slammed to a stop within feet of him and she exited it like a whirlwind of fury.

Of pain.

Words wouldn't have struck at him nearly as deep as the agony rolling off her in waves and the sense that the tears trapped inside her were slowly drowning her.

He was only barely aware of the others moving for their vehicles as a slender finger poked toward him and jade green eyes darkened as she fought to find an outlet for the clawing, agonizing pain tearing at her.

"So what vile deed am I behind, Gypsy?" He frowned down at her, sensing that the gentleness that softened his heart to her would be instantly rejected.

No, she needed a fight. She needed to lash out and she needed to be held. But she would be damned before she would ask anyone to hold her.

"That crazy offer Jonas gave my parents." She was shaking with the anger, the pain. "Image consulting?" she sneered. "For what? You're masters of building your own image. Breeds were created for it. Master manipulators and scheming, calculating . . ."

He acted before she could say something that would only hurt her more once the pain tearing at her eased.

Reaching out quickly, gripping the hair at the back of her neck and pulling her head back, he covered her lips with his as a growl burst from his chest.

She was killing him with the hurt raging at her tender soul. She was breaking his heart with the scent of her loneliness, her utter desolate hunger and the unmistakable desire to just be held.

His Gypsy would never accept being just held, though.

But she did take his kiss.

Her arms latched around his neck. With a shattered groan her head tilted to the side as his lips slanted across hers. His tongue sank inside the hot silken depths of her mouth as she met it immediately with her own. Rubbed against it. Licked at him and tasted him as he tasted her.

Pain was replaced by pleasure and hunger in the space of a heartbeat. Her pleasure. His greedy demand. And God knew he was starved for her. So fucking hungry for her kiss, for the taste of her that it was killing him.

The skimpy little cami tank she wore and too-short cutoff jeans were little protection against his touch, against his intent.

His tongue played with hers, challenging her with little flicks against it. Nipping her lips if she tried to draw back, he picked her up easily, turned her and stepped to the opened back passenger door of the Dragoon.

Laying her back across the wide bench seat, he jerked the hem of her shirt to the full, lace-covered mounds of her breasts as he moved over her.

A flick of his fingers released the little front catch, spilling the lush curves to his waiting hand. Bracing a knee between her thighs to hold himself over her, as pleasure tore past their control.

He'd be damned if he could bear the pain she'd arrived with. Replacing it with hunger, with need, even if he knew her ire would be sorely raised later, was much preferable.

Much more enjoyable.

Moving his lips from hers, his kisses sliding to her neck, teeth raking against her flesh, a growl escaped him. A sweet feminine presence he hadn't known he'd opened himself to was suddenly within his senses. Her pleasure became a part of him.

Hell, this hadn't happened before. Her needs echoed through his mind as the impression of his lips against her nipples, his teeth nipping, pulling at them, his tongue stroking them sent a wave of heat ripping through his mind.

Lust clawed at him. His lips moved to her breasts. He was more than happy to fulfill that little need of hers. But as his lips covered a stiff, pointed little nipple and sucked it into his mouth, he became immersed in the needs clashing through her.

How had he ever enjoyed sex without this? Without the impression of his lover's pleasure rocking his senses and amplifying his own sensations? It was so damned hot he was ready to come in his fucking pants.

His cock was stiffer than it had ever been, the engorged head pulsing, throbbing desperately. He gripped her nipple with his teeth, tugged at it and felt the echo of sensation lashing with brutal ecstasy at her delicate body.

Her hips lifted again, the heat of her pussy, the delicate scent of it driving spikes of hunger through his senses rubbed at his denim-covered cock.

She needed. Needed his hunger, needed his touch.

Sliding his hand down her stomach, her rising anticipation struck at his mind.

A fierce groan, part growl, erupted from him as he sucked her nipple into his mouth again while jerking the snaps of her cutoffs free and pushing his fingers beneath the material.

Heat poured from her. Her juices were saturating her panties, then saturating his fingers as he slid them into the swollen folds.

Slick, thick, moisture prepared her for him.

The scent of her tempted him, the heated sweet juices making his mouth water for the taste of her.

Drawing back, he stared back down at her, seeing her closed eyes, the mask of complete, absorbed hunger on her face.

"Look at me," he rasped, the hunger tearing at him, straining his tenuous control.

Dark lashes lifted, green eyes stared back at him, dazed from her pleasure as he pulled his fingers from her pussy and brought them to his lips.

✦   ✦   ✦

Gypsy jerked beneath Rule as he brought his fingers to his lips, the hard flesh glistening with the rich layer of her juices a second before he began sucking the taste of her from them.

Then his hips lowered to hers, the hard wedge of his cock driving into the vee of her thighs again as he pulled his fingers from his mouth and lowered his head.

"I could fuck you here." The primal, graveled tone of his voice had her pussy clenching, more of her juices spilling from her vagina at the very thought of this powerful, erotic male doing just that. "I could strip that excuse for clothes from you and have you screaming with your orgasm within seconds."

She gripped his waist, her head tilting back, her hips rocking against his as he ground his cock against her.

"Is this what you want, Gypsy? Here? Now? Should I take all that sweet innocence in the backseat of a fucking war machine?"

"Shut up," she cried out desperately, her fingers suddenly curling into fists at the reminder that she was still innocent. Still a virgin. At the memory of why she'd never allowed herself to take a lover.

"Is this what you want?" he repeated, a hard hand gripping her ass and jerking her into the press of his erection between her thighs. "Tell me now. I'm two seconds from jerking those shorts from your body and giving you exactly what we're both dying for."

She shook her head desperately. Why wouldn't he just do it? Why did he have to talk about it?

"Here and now?" His lips lowered to her, the hint of her feminine taste against her tongue as he took her lips in a brief, hard kiss. "Right here," he repeated. "My dick sinking inside your sweet, tight pussy? I'll ride you until we're both dying from the pleasure if that's what you want."

She whimpered, the cry a ragged sound that shocked her, that reminded her how long it had been since she had truly cried. It reminded her how long she had needed to cry, to shed the agony destroying her.

"Just do it," she cried out, her eyes opening, glaring up at him until the sight of his expression, his eyes, finally registered.

Lust tightened his features, filled the blue of his eyes, but there was more there than just the sexual hunger burning inside him. Something she swore she could *feel*. It wasn't hunger. It wasn't need, sympathy, compassion or pity. Something that felt like understanding. Like warmth surrounding her ragged emotions, a soothing touch in the depths of her soul as her chest tightened and her breathing hitched dangerously.

"Let me go." She would not cry. She couldn't cry.

He eased back slowly, but before he released her he resnapped the shorts, fixed her bra and gently pulled her tank back in place before allowing her to sit up.

She jumped from the Dragoon, her back turned to him as she stood beneath the searing sunlight and drew in several ragged breaths.

"I know what you did," she finally whispered.

"What did I do that's so heinous?" A rasp of remembered pleasure and hunger echoed in his tone.

"The offer from Jonas to my parents. You were behind it."

She couldn't even turn to see the expression on his face as she forced the accusation past her lips.

"Did I now?" he asked, the dark, seductive tone sending sensation racing across her flesh as the need for his touch came dangerously close to addiction. "Why would I do that, Gypsy?"

"For this." She turned on him, her hand swinging out to gesture to the back of the Dragoon. "Do you really think that's going to get you into my bed?"

Grave, intense, his gaze met hers, held it. And she felt it again. That soothing warmth sinking inside her chest and loosening the shields between her and a loss of control she couldn't countenance.

"Gypsy." He sighed her name with an edge of chastisement. "I could have just taken you in that backseat and you would have loved every second of it. Screamed for me. Begged to come for me. I touch you and we both go up in flames. Do you really think I'd stoop to the trouble of playing games to get what I want you to give me willingly? If that were true, you would still be lying beneath me, your nails raking down my back as I fucked us both half crazy."

She flushed. She couldn't help it. Hunger, embarrassment, that warmth she hated feeling tugging at her emotions, urging her into his arms, against his chest, where he would shelter her as the agony buried inside her, tore free.

"Stop!" she cried out desperately, her fingers sinking into the hair at the side of her head in desperation for one crazy second as she swore he was inside her. "God, you're already making me crazy." She glared at him accusingly. "You don't have to fuck me into it. I'm already there."

"I think I need that extra, added little push into insanity," he told her far too seriously. "Shall we try it and see if it works?"

Her lips parted as she felt the disbelief suddenly covering her expression. She couldn't believe him. She couldn't control him.

His lips quirked with a hint of amusement as he watched her intently, his eyes appearing even bluer, more electric than before.

"The next time you need a hot little necking session, don't expect to get away so easily," he warned her. "The next time, you're going to be on your knees with my dick working between your lips in exchange for all my restraint. You can stay a virgin as long as you think you have to, but if you want to play, then you can share the pleasure. Because I fully intend to have my tongue buried in all that sweet cream filling your pussy."

That cream spilled copiously between her thighs, her vagina tightened with a hard clench of need and she swore her clit nearly exploded in climax.

His eyes darkened. "Get in that Jeep and get the fuck away from me, Gypsy," he suddenly growled, his tone darker now, warning. "You have about ten seconds before I rip those shorts off your body and sit you firmly on my face. When I've eaten you until your taste has me crazy to fuck, then I'm going to do just that. Fuck you. Right here, in the middle of the fucking desert . . ."

She ran.

Heart pounding, adrenaline coursing through her because she wanted it with a power that sent terror racing through her. It was all she could do not to strip for him, not to go to her knees and beg him to take her mouth.

◆　　◆　　◆

Dust flew as Gypsy reversed the Jeep before turning the wheel and speeding away from him even faster than she'd come speeding to him.

Propping his hands on his hips, he watched the vehicle as it disappeared around the curve of the highway seconds later, then blew out a hard, miserable breath.

Son of a bitch, his dick was stiffer than a poker, his balls so tight they felt knotted.

"Remind me to stay the hell away from the two of you when you get started." It was Dog who growled the words out.

Rule swung around to watch as the Coyote moved from the small rise of stones across from the Dragoon.

"I told you to leave," he growled, frowning back at the Coyote.

"You should have clarified," Dog breathed out roughly. "Damn, Breaker, you get any hotter with that woman and I'm going to think you're mating her or something."

Rule chuckled at the thought. "Not even the first sign of Mating Heat," he crowed.

Satisfaction wasn't filling him, though, and he sure as hell wasn't going to delve into that sudden tightening of his chest and the flash of something that felt decidedly regretful. Definitely angry.

Dog shook his head, his look thoughtful as he stared toward the direction Gypsy had disappeared before giving Rule another long, steady look. He shook his head, leaning against the side of the Dragoon. "So, are we going to discuss this little machination you have going on here or are you just going to keep winging it all on your own?"

Rule had to grin at the question. It didn't surprise him that Dog was suspicious. The Coyote had come out of the test tube suspicious, Jonas often accused. But Rule shook his head all the same.

"Don't know what you're talking about, Dog," he claimed. "Since when does a Breed have to be up to something just because he's determined to seduce a pretty lady?"

It was more, something whispered inside him. *So much more.*

He knew it was more.

He knew seducing was just the beginning . . .

He shook the thought away. It wasn't a mating, it couldn't be anything more than seduction where a Breed was concerned if it wasn't a mating.

Dog nodded slowly before straightening. "If you decide you need help, just let me know," he said, his disbelief clear. "Just don't wait until it's too late to be helped. It would suck watching your ass burn, Breaker."

He walked away then, heading back to the rise of stones and the Dragoon no doubt awaiting him there as Rule narrowed his eyes on him. What the hell did Dog think he knew?

There wasn't a chance in hell the Coyote could know the little traps Rule was laying in the area where several individuals were concerned. Just as he couldn't possibly know Rule was well aware of his and Dane's friend in the area.

Rule knew. It benefited him at the moment to keep his mouth shut, but he knew.

He just prayed Jonas never found out. Because if he did, then they were all screwed.

CHAPTER 8

Despite her attempt to run, Gypsy found herself unable to skip the meeting with Jonas and her parents that evening. She felt raw inside, ready to break apart at the slightest provocation, but she couldn't let her family down again, no matter how hard it was going to be to face Rule after she'd left him in the desert.

Gypsy had met Jonas Wyatt on several occasions in the past two months that he and his teams of Breeds had been in Window Rock searching for a rogue Bengal. The reservation and the Navajo capital itself seemed to be a haven for lost Breeds, hunting Breeds—and rogue Breeds.

It seemed that the rumors were true as well, that the reservation was now about to become home to an investigative branch of the Bureau of Breed Affairs.

Rather fitting, as a large number of them had been created from the stolen sperm and kidnapped girls of the Navajo that the Council had taken.

Dressed in a neat black pencil skirt and sleeveless white silk blouse, she moved from the Jeep before retrieving the black leather briefcase she'd brought with her. Sliding the strap over her shoulder, she pushed the door closed and locked the vehicle, then turned back to her parents.

"Where's Jason?" she asked. She was depending on his ability to distract her parents and ensure that this meeting went as planned.

"He had a meeting in Santa Fe that he couldn't cancel," her father informed her rather stiltedly. "You didn't wait around earlier to find out that he couldn't be here for this one."

Of course that was the reason why, she thought silently as she inhaled slowly, her gaze slipping to her mother. Because she hadn't waited around for the full brunt of the guilt trip, it was her fault she didn't know everything.

Greta glanced at the bag Gypsy carried for a second before turning her gaze to her disapprovingly. "This is just a friendly visit, Gypsy. Not an official meeting."

"I worked up a few ideas while waiting on Connie." She shrugged, thinking of the horrendously boring hours in Connie's salon, stuck in the VIP room alone while waiting for the chemicals on her hair to do their job. She'd missed her appointment, but Connie had worked her in anyway. Gypsy had wished she would have just told her to go to hell so she could escape the torturous hours alone. Connie and her assistants had done their job excellently, though. Her deep, dark brown hair now had the faintest streaks of sun-lightened browns and tawny blond peeking out.

"That wasn't necessary, dear," her mother murmured, as though Gypsy were some wet-behind-the-ears new consultant. "I'm sure Mr. Wyatt will let us know when he's ready for ideas. He's not a man who likes to be pushed, you know."

"Understood." She nodded, despite her confusion.

Since when did her mother protest being prepared? Since when did her mother profess to be an expert on how Jonas conducted business?

Because Gypsy knew damned good and well the Breed highly respected initiative. They'd had several discussions on that subject and several others the few times she'd visited Rachel.

Dressed in a sleeveless beige top and a soft, casual cream chiffon skirt, her mother looked relaxed and comfortable, so Gypsy let her keep her illusions. Her father wore his customary jeans with a white button-up, just as he would have if he were joining friends for dinner at the local café.

Neither of them wore any of their more business-related clothing, which was surprising considering their nervousness over this contract.

"Gypsy." Her mother stopped her as they neared the lobby entrance of the hotel.

Turning back to her, Gypsy saw the genuine concern building in the dusky features.

"Yes, Mother?" Damn, her mother was nervous. Gypsy didn't work directly with her parents very often, and only took the smaller contracts when her help was needed, but still, she would have thought she'd have seen this side of Greta McQuade before now.

"Please, be polite," her mother asked warningly, her green eyes shadowed, a bit harder than normal.

Be polite?

"Mother, when am I ever impolite to a client?" she asked, confused by this new worry her mother seemed to have gotten into her head.

"Anytime anyone, anywhere gives you the impression that you have to do something," her mother stated in disapproval. "Don't embarrass us, Gypsy."

Was her personal life now tied to the clients she helped her parents with?

"Greta, now isn't the time," her father murmured, casting Gypsy a faintly regretful look.

Don't embarrass them? Had they not wanted her help on this contract?

Her lips parted to ask what the hell they were talking about.

"Mr. and Mrs. McQuade. Gypsy, sweetie, it's about time you came back to see us." It wasn't a Breed who stepped from the lobby to greet them, but Thor Thorsson, a rumored ex-mercenary turned Bureau Enforcer who worked with Rule's brother's fiancée, Diane Broen. Diane also happened to be Jonas Wyatt's fiancée's sister.

But to her, he was just Thor, the big, strapping Viking look-alike who had taken one look at her two months before, grinned and said, "Hey, just what I've been looking for, a little elf to torment. Can I adopt you?" Then he'd pulled the braid at the back of her hair.

She'd informed him icily that she did not need anyone to take her brother's place.

Forlorn, his pale blue eyes had turned somber, "I wasn't asking if you needed a brother. I was trying to tell you I needed a baby sister."

Long, thick white-blond hair was brushed back from his face, his imposing features creased into a smile as his eyes met hers now while giving her a subtle little wink. A second later he bent, his arms going around her in a brief, firm hug before he drew back.

Sometimes, she was really afraid Thor knew far more about her than she was comfortable with him knowing.

"Hello, Thor." Gypsy smiled up at him, genuinely glad to see him. "I see you're recovering nicely from your accident."

The story that he'd been injured in an accident in the desert was bullshit. He'd taken a knife in the shoulder that had been meant for his heart two months before.

"I'm recovering fine," he promised with a wide smile. "So much so that Wyatt decided to put me back to work. I'm here to escort you up to his suite."

Her brows lifted. "Strenuous activity," she agreed, automatically handing over her bag to the too-handsome escort.

"That's what I tried to tell him, but he wasn't listening," Thor agreed before turning to her parents, blocking the entrance and waiting patiently.

"We do have an appointment," her mother informed him frostily.

"Mother, he needs your bag," Gypsy murmured, catching her mother's surprised look. "Security. We can't go in until you give it to him."

Confusion flickered in her mother's gaze. "I'm not comfortable with that." Greta frowned.

"You can leave the bag in your vehicle, ma'am," Thor suggested politely. "But I can't take you up until you do so, or until it's in our possession. You'll have it back before you leave, though."

Greta glanced at Gypsy worriedly.

Gypsy shrugged, confused by her mother's hesitancy. "Your choice."

Slowly, her mother turned the bag over to Thor.

"Thank you, ma'am." Nodding to her mother, he gave the bags to the female Breed who stepped out behind him.

"Hi, Gypsy." Emma Truing, the slightest smile edging her lips, accepted the bags from the enforcer.

"How's Ashley doing?" Gypsy asked as she noticed Emma's haggard expression had eased some from the past six weeks.

Emma's sister, Ashley, had been shot in the chest by one of the locals intent on kidnapping the niece of the nation's chief.

"She's recovering well," Emma promised, despite the shadow of re- membered fear in her eyes. "She mentioned the other night that she's missed talking to you."

"Tell her to hurry and get better," she told the too-somber Breed. "Things are getting boring without her around."

And that was no less than the truth. The private parties where only a select list of Breeds were invited were definitely suffering, not to men- tion the bars to which Ashley dragged Emma and some of the other Breed females.

"I'll be sure to tell her," Emma promised before turning and moving back into the lobby.

"If you and your parents will follow me," Thor said, "I'll show you up to Jonas's suite." His gaze met Gypsy's again. "Rachel's looking forward to seeing you. She and Diane were talking about that chocolate mousse cake you brought in with you last time. I gather they really liked it."

"I'll have to remember to make another chocolate date with them," Gypsy laughed as Thor chuckled, then turned and led the way into the hotel. "Amber especially loved my contribution to that little lunch."

"Where's the girl going with my bag?" her mother asked worriedly as they neared the bank of elevators.

"We'll get them back before we leave," Gypsy promised. "It's just a precaution."

"A precaution against what?" Her mother was clearly unsettled by the fact that her purse wasn't on her.

"Against weapons, I guess." Gypsy shrugged as they moved toward the elevator.

"Jonas has plenty of enemies, Mrs. McQuade," Thor stated as he led them into a waiting elevator. "No offense is meant. That's standard operat- ing procedure no matter the visitor."

Gypsy could see that her mother was still bothered by it, though, her troubled gaze meeting her husband's for a second as they stepped into the waiting elevator cubicle.

Catching her mother's eye, Gypsy glanced to the discreet metal signs in the cubicle. *Illegal audio/video devices punishable by Breed Law. All bags, cases and devices must be scanned for illegal electronics before meetings commence. Thank you for your patience.*

Discomfort flickered in her mother's gaze. Gypsy knew her mother's resentment of Breeds in general after Mark's death was behind her discomfort; still, it bothered her.

The ride up was a quick one. In less than a minute the elevator came to a smooth stop at the eighth floor and slid soundlessly open.

"This way." Thor stepped back to allow them to precede him from the elevator.

It was evident her parents hadn't been to the hotel since the Breeds had taken up residence. The entire building had been more or less taken over by the Bureau of Breed Affairs, and security was incredibly tight.

Moving down the hall, Thor turned up another long hallway, and halfway along the corridor four Breeds stood at attention, watching Thor and Gypsy's parents suspiciously. Heavily armed, brooding and looking far too dangerous in those black mission uniforms, not to mention far too good looking, they didn't take their eyes off the small group.

"The McQuades to meet with Director Wyatt," Thor told the guard at the door as Gypsy peeked around Thor's broad shoulder and shot the Breed at the door a suggestive wink.

His eyes crinkled just slightly.

For Flint, that was a fully formed sexy-as-hell grin. Or at least, that was as close as he came.

"Hello, Gypsy." Flint nodded as they moved past. "We've missed you."

"Evening, cutie." She greeted him just under her breath, knowing the Breed heard every word. "You're looking especially hot tonight."

He snorted at the compliment, while Gypsy caught the surprise on her parents' faces as they moved into the director's suite.

Roomy and opulently appointed, the presidential suite was decorated with classic desert hues, the furniture comfortable, the upholstery incredibly soft.

It wasn't Jonas and his wife who met them in the suite, though, but rather Lawe Justice, Rule's brother, and his fiancée, Diane.

They introduced themselves to her parents before greeting Gypsy with a smile and informing them that Jonas was running just a few minutes late.

As they waited, Diane sidled up to Gypsy. "Did you bring cake?" she asked in a hushed tone, drawing Greta McQuade's attention.

"I didn't know I needed to." Gypsy grimaced regretfully. "It was really short notice and Kandy didn't have any mousse cake. Next time, tell your boss to give me a little advance notice." Gypsy grinned back.

"You suck, McQuade," Diane accused her with a heavy sigh. "That cake was the bomb."

"I'll be sure to let my sister know," Gypsy promised, making a mental note to put Kandy in the kitchen whipping up chocolate mousse cake.

Lifting her finger in a sign to give her a minute, Diane turned away, obviously listening to whatever was being said in the earbud she wore.

"Excuse me a minute." She turned back to them with a quick smile. "I'll be right back. Lawe will get you a drink, and Jonas and Rachel will be out momentarily."

Diane disappeared.

Moving to the sofa, Gypsy took a seat, crossed one leg over the opposite knee and sat back to wait as she glanced at her parents while they took a seat on the matching love seat on the nearest side to her.

"You know them." Her mother seemed faintly confused by the fact that Gypsy was on such familiar terms with the Breeds they'd seen so far.

She shrugged dismissively. "I see them around a lot. We talk. I knew Ashley and Emma before Jonas and Rachel showed up. They asked for one of the chocolate mousse cakes the first week that Rachel was here and invited me to share it with them."

Actually, they'd begged her to make one and bring it to the hotel for Rachel's toddler, Amber, who had been having trouble eating. They had sworn the chocolate would tempt her.

And it had.

The little girl had been a giggling, chocolate mess when Director Wyatt had walked into the suite. And the sight of her, lifting her chocolate hands to him and squealing, "Da, moo-ie cake," had sent such a wash of emotion over his face that Gypsy's heart had clenched in her chest.

Now, two months later, Wyatt had her cooling her heels while he waited to tell her and her parents that the joke was all on them, she was afraid.

Asshole.

She wondered if Lawe and Diane would let her kick him then?

She was sure Diane would.

"You hadn't mentioned that you knew so many Breeds," her mother murmured.

"Yeah?" She glanced over at her mother again before surveying the scenery from the wide floor-to-ceiling windows on the other wall. "I didn't think it was important."

"How did you get to know so many of them? The bars?" her mother asked, her lips tightening in disapproval of where she had met them. "But it doesn't explain how you came to be invited here and now know Director Wyatt and his family so well. I can't imagine that's easily done."

Had her mother forgotten who had saved her the night Mark had died? Or were her memories just of her seeing her son's body on that stretcher, that ring of red at his neck?

A chill raced through her, cutting through the serenity she'd managed to project in the past hours.

Gypsy turned back to her parents and arched her brows. "I don't know, Mother, they like me, I guess," she said faintly. "That or they like Kandy's chocolate mousse cake."

It was probably the cake, now, but nine years ago, it had been Jonas who had sworn she would always have a safe place to live if her parents no longer wanted her.

Her mother frowned; her father just watched her with that faintly accusing look she found so disheartening. It was one of the few looks she couldn't read, and that made her nervous.

"You should have mentioned you knew them," her mother said accusingly.

She shrugged. "It didn't seem a big deal." More importantly, her parents never wanted to hear about the Breeds who came into the store, or those she'd become friends with. Actually, she didn't remember her mother ever caring who her friends were.

She turned back to the scenery, wondering if Jonas intended to come out and face her anytime soon.

As the thought went through her mind, the door on the other side of the room opened again and Diane returned, followed by Jonas and Rachel.

The director looked particularly sophisticated and handsome. His black hair had grown out a bit; his eerie swirling silver eyes seemed to see everything, know everything.

His smile was friendly and polite as he was introduced to her parents, then lit up with genuine fondness as Gypsy rose to her feet and accepted a quick hug from him.

"It's good to see you again, Gypsy," he said sincerely. "You need to visit more often."

That was Jonas. He was a kind man, but that kindness did not get in the way of whatever machinations he was involved in. It made it hard to hate him, easy to love him, impossible to trust him.

"I try, Jonas," she assured him. "But that three jobs thing, ya know?" She smiled up at him, comfortable with the affection but waiting for the shoe to drop.

"I told you when we first arrived, there's a job waiting for you with the Bureau." He gave her a firm, knowing look. "At any time you could have walked into a PR position in D.C. or in the liaison office in Window Rock we established several years ago. All you had to do was give me the word."

"And I told you," she reminded him firmly, "I'd kill you the first time you tried to run my office and then Rachel would hate me."

"All according to the circumstances, Gypsy." Rachel laughed as she moved forward for a quick hug as well. "It's wonderful to see you."

Gypsy returned the embrace, observing the practice she had seen with others when around women whose husbands or fiancés were Breeds. She let Rachel embrace her, aware that the other woman's hands never touched skin, but rather her back this time. The weather had been cool the last time they'd met and Gypsy had worn a jacket. Rachel had gripped her forearms then, leaning close but not really touching.

"Tell me, how's that little moo-baby doing?" After Amber had called the mousse cake "moo-cake," Gypsy had taken to calling her the little moo-baby.

"She was asking for moo-cake the other day." Rachel tried to smile, but Gypsy could see the pain and fear in her eyes.

"You should have called me," Gypsy chided her gently. "You know I would have had Kandy make one the instant I knew."

"Gypsy's mousse cakes are actually much better than Kandy's." Her mother spoke behind her then. "You should have her bake one of her own."

Gypsy shot Rachel a little wink, hoping she'd think her mother's bragging was just motherly loyalty.

"She didn't mention that when she was here before," Jonas said, moving behind his lover and placing his hand at her lower back as his gaze met Gypsy's. "I'll have to see if I can't get her to do that for us soon."

And he wasn't joking.

Great. Of course, Jonas would know it wasn't just motherly pride.

"I'm a very busy woman, Director," she reminded him with a cool smile. "And I understand I'm about to become even more busy with one of your commanders?"

Jonas chuckled. "I can see the suspicion in those pretty eyes, Ms. McQuade. Did you think the offer a ruse of some sort?"

"Perhaps not a ruse—"

"Good." He nodded. "Because the decision was taken out of my hands by Seth Lawrence and Dane Vanderale, two of the Breeds' most opinionated benefactors. They've been pushing for more individual press where the new investigative division and the division director running it was concerned; they just had yet to pin down their choice of DD and convince him to agree to the job. I'm happy to say, that was achieved day before yesterday."

She knew there was no hiding her surprise and she didn't even try to do so. She saved her energy for those times when hiding her emotions, truths or lies, was far more important.

"I see," she murmured.

"Jonas said you would instantly suspect him of some calculation." Rachel's amusement was thick as she glanced at her lover. "I warned him it was all his own fault."

At least his lover knew him well, Gypsy thought, amused.

"The rumors are vicious, Director," she agreed, allowing her smile to lose the cool edge as she glanced back up at him. "And several of your Breeds can be quite—charming."

She opted for politeness rather than rude or insulting at that moment.

"Don't think so highly of me quite yet," he warned her, his own smile warming his eyes. "My commander finally got around to informing me less than an hour ago that the two of you might not be on the best footing."

She felt it then.

That tightness in her stomach, the rush of adrenaline preparing to rocket through her system.

She had missed even more sleep than normal in the past few days because of that damned Breed.

Her eyes narrowed.

"Gypsy, I promise you, we only just learned of the fact that Commander Breaker may have"—Rachel cleared her throat delicately—"offended you in some way."

Oh brother.

Damn him. Damn him.

What had he done, kissed and told at the first chance?

She wished she had her bag. She needed something to strangle, and she assumed Jonas would prefer she strangle the strap of her purse rather than his commander.

"I didn't offend her, I kissed her."

Whirling around, all too aware of the fact that her parents were far too interested in this little meeting now, Gypsy lifted her arms, crossed them over her breasts, then threw her weight to one hip as she faced the Lion Breed.

"Definitely a criminal offense," she heard her father murmur behind her, his voice assuring her it was all he could do not to laugh at the predicament she found herself in.

At least he wasn't acting as though *she* had committed some criminal act by kissing a Breed.

Her mother was silent, though Gypsy swore she could feel that "mother" look of curiosity and disapproval boring into her.

The arrogance in Rule's face as he closed the door behind him and stepped into the room had her teeth gritting furiously.

"Commander, may I introduce Gypsy's parents, Hansel and Greta McQuade." Jonas moved ahead of her and drew her parents forward. "Owners of McQuade Image Consulting, who are being tasked with ensuring that your entrance into society and the division directorship happens seamlessly."

"Mr., Mrs. McQuade." Shaking her parents' hands, he then stepped back, his hands going behind his back, his legs spread, planted firmly beneath his height as he stared down at them with a grin. "That's quite a task you've taken on there. I hope I don't disappoint you."

Hansel McQuade could barely restrain his smile, and Gypsy watched in disgust as Rule turned on the charm. Of course, her father responded immediately. For all her appearances of warm graciousness, her mother's gaze told another story though.

"Greta and I will have the pleasure of working with your liaisons, actually. Gypsy has been given your account, but you can trust she's well qualified and knows exactly what she's doing."

"As I heard." Satisfaction began to gleam in his eyes. "And I must say, I'm quite happy with the choice of consultant tasked with handling me."

It was all she could do to contain her flush as his gaze met her, reminding her far too clearly just who had been handling whom no more than a few short hours before.

"Commander Breaker." Her mother stepped slightly forward then, shooting Gypsy a firm, warning look. "I'm certain whatever—offenses Gypsy may have felt will not affect her professionalism. I'm confident you're in excellent hands."

Wicked humor sparked in those electric blue eyes as they met her gaze. An immediate flush of heat began scalding her senses as that adrenaline just waiting to race through her now shot through her like rocket fuel.

Immediately her breasts felt swollen, her nipples far too sensitive. Her clit was throbbing, dampness rushing from her vagina as the sensitive inner flesh began to ache for his touch again. The memory of lying beneath him in the backseat of the Dragoon, his hips cradled between her thighs, their clothing a hated barrier between his cock and the needy depths of her vagina, raced through her mind.

"I agree with you, Ms. McQuade," Rule assured her mother. "I'm certain I'm in very capable hands."

Heat flushed her face then as anger began to fuel arousal and arousal began to burn like wildfire through her senses.

In capable hands, was he?

She was going to strangle him.

Neuter him.

She'd make him wish he'd never touched her to begin with, let alone continue to contemplate it each time she managed to escape him.

Her fingers curled into fists as she kept her arms crossed beneath her breasts, ignoring the look he flicked to the now too-sensitive curves.

And he was well aware of her arousal too.

She could see it in his eyes, see it in the sensual flames beginning to ignite there.

Suddenly, she could feel his touch just as she had felt it earlier. His fingers moving beneath her shorts, rasping against her flesh and sending pleasure racing through her body.

It was all she could do to hold back a shiver of response.

A chill of dread.

"Let's take our seats, then." Jonas broke into the erotic tension beginning to whip between them as he directed them back to the seating area.

She wasn't the least bit surprised that Commander Breaker took a seat on the other end of the short sofa she claimed. Her parents sat on the love seat next to her with Jonas, and Rachel took a similar sofa across from her.

"Shall I begin?" Jonas suggested, his gaze turning to Gypsy. "I happened to have been nosy." He grinned. "I went over the notes in the file you brought with you. Excellent, by the way, and many are similar to the list of concerns and suggestions that Dane and Seth were kind enough to text to me. We'll go over them, then adjourn until the ball next week. We'll make an announcement to the press the next morning, and hopefully we'll be able to get together to discuss our game plan within a few days of that. Agreed?"

Agreed?

Well, everyone else agreed.

"May I have my notes back, Jonas?" she asked sweetly, not at all happy that he had gone through them, but it had been no more than she had expected.

The grin that edged at his lips was still warm and affectionate as he stared back at her.

"I would . . ." He winced, then glanced at Rachel.

Rachel bit the side of her lip before staring back at Gypsy with amused discomfort. "I'm sure you'll want to see it to be certain, but I swear." She lifted her hand with a light laugh. "Amber managed to get hold of the papers and massacred them. I could have sworn she was jabbering 'moo-cake.'"

Gypsy felt her heart melt.

There was no way the toddler could have known she had eaten the last slice of Kandy's chocolate mousse cake that she'd slipped from the store before leaving for Connie's.

"We're going to have to get that kid a moo-cake," she decided. "Are you busy tomorrow?"

Rachel's smile was one of pleased surprise. "I have time tomorrow."

"Then Amber has to have moo-cake tomorrow. Tell her Auntie Gypsy will be around sometime tomorrow afternoon with goodies," she declared.

That baby would have moo-cake if Gypsy had to make it herself.

At least Jonas had notes of a sort, Gypsy thought as the conversation turned back to the contract the Breeds were offering McQuade Image Consulting.

By time the meeting was over, she was satisfied that the offer was legitimate, but more concerned than ever in regard to her own duties. Because the longer she sat there, the more she ached, and the more she craved that hint of chocolate and peppermint Rule's kiss held.

And she hated needing him. Hated it more than she could say because it threatened everything she was, everything she had believed about herself.

He was far too dangerous, and she was far too weak.

And she had no idea whatsoever how to combat either.

◆ ◆ ◆

"Did you replace the device?" Lawe entered the suite behind his mate and faced Jonas as Rule stood with his back to the room, staring out of the huge windows after Gypsy and her parents had left.

Tension filled Rule's shoulders as his anger seemed to shimmer in the air around him.

There had been a listening device in Greta McQuade's purse. It was very cleverly sewn into the lining and programmed to only record. Recording devices held a very different electronic signal than an audio device programmed to transmit.

Thankfully, Jonas scanned for any and all signatures. Then he scanned for anomalies if he found no signatures. If there was a scanner for it, then Jonas scanned for it. Still, it was more luck than anything that it had been found.

"It was returned." Jonas nodded as he moved behind the bar and poured himself a drink.

Lawe shook his head as the director lifted the decanter of whiskey in his direction.

"I actually expected Gypsy to have the device rather than her mother." Lawe shook his head in surprise. "Greta McQuade is no spy. Especially for the Unknown."

"And Gypsy is no traitor to her friends," Jonas sighed. "Especially those who saved her life. Her mother, though, was nervous as hell, according to Thor, when she was asked to turn over her purse."

Rule growled, turning to face him. "She knew what was in that damned bag. Just as she knew it would backlash on Gypsy."

The hard, chiseled lines and angles of his features appeared more savage than normal, his anger tightening them and causing his blue eyes to brighten marginally. In times of fury, his eyes practically glowed.

Lawe turned to Jonas. "Are you rescinding the contract?"

Surprisingly, Jonas shook his head thoughtfully. "Seth was inclined to, but Dane seemed hesitant. He wants to wait and see what happens from here."

"They're image consultants," Lawe retorted. "They could destroy Rule's chances of successfully settling into the enforcement bureau if they're of a mind to do so."

"Gypsy wouldn't allow it," Rule snapped, his jaw tightening as he glared back at his brother.

"What makes you think she wouldn't allow it?" Lawe moved to the back of the couch that faced him, his hands gripping it, fingers digging in as he stared at his brother in disbelief. "For God's sake, Rule, we already know she's involved with the Unknown up to her pretty little neck and doing everything she can to hide it, despite her knowledge that we have to find Judd and Gideon to help Amber. What's that if not a betrayal?" Lawe glanced at Jonas as well as he made the statement.

"Trust," Rule snarled. "She's worked with them for nine years. They protect the nation and its people. She knows that. If they told her they couldn't help Amber, then she would believe them until she's shown otherwise."

"I actually agree with him for a change." Diane, not exactly the gentlest of women when it came to traitors, moved next to Lawe, laying her hand against his arm comfortingly as Lawe watched his brother in disbelief. "Gypsy's a wild card, but she's damned loyal to friends, Lawe. Even I know that. Besides, she wouldn't allow her parents to destroy their own reputations in such a way. I think she should be told about the device, though."

All eyes turned to her. Jonas hadn't lost that grave, thoughtful look in his eyes, nor had Rule lost his temper. Yet.

"Why?" Rule questioned, his tone harsh. "What good would it do to cause her to question her loyalty to her parents? Especially if we can find a way to neutralize the threat Mrs. McQuade could represent."

Lawe stared down at the seat of the couch to hide his shock. Rule was concerned about the woman rather than Jonas's security, or any threat the McQuades could pose to the Breeds in general? Who had kidnapped his brother and left this lunatic standing before him instead?

"Rule, I highly advise against hiding this from Gypsy," Diane stated. "If she learns of it the wrong way, it could destroy the foundations of her life. She hasn't had a lot to hold on to since her brother's death."

Lawe stared at his mate and his brother now. They were discussing this as though Gypsy McQuade shouldn't be brought up on charges of breaking half a dozen statutes of Breed Law? She was a spy for an unknown sect of warriors that no one could identify.

Since when did that garner trust?

"Exactly. So why tear down her belief in all she has left?" Rule snarled.

Diane was shaking her head.

"Rule." Rachel moved into the living area from the bedroom, clearly aware of the discussion. "Her parents aren't the foundation of Gypsy's life. They haven't been since she was fifteen and stood alone in that desert while her parents stood apart from her. You forget, it was Jonas who gave her the acceptance she needed to survive when her parents were unable, or perhaps even unwilling, to do so. Gypsy's foundation is the code she lives by. It's her job, her friends and her determination to further her brother's work that ensure that she pulls herself out of her bed each morning. By withholding this information from her, you're taking away her ability to protect her parents and to learn more than we can as to why her mother attempted such a thing."

◆   ◆   ◆

Rule stared back at the group in disbelief before shaking his head in amazement, anger churning in his gut at the very thought of the pain that information would cause Gypsy. "Those are her parents. If she learns that they were attempting to betray the Breeds, then you'll strip them from her and that will destroy her."

"Keeping her in the dark is what will destroy her, Rule," Rachel assured him as she moved to Jonas, allowing his arm to wrap around her and pull her close to his side. "Yes, she loves her family, very much. But even I, a mere human, could sense the wall between them. A wall she placed there, I'm afraid. One that has ensured her parents have never really had a chance to get to know her. They had no idea she socializes with any of us. Her knowledge of individual Breeds shocked them. Our respect and liking for her simply amazed them, and even caused a bit of resentment perhaps. They have no idea of the woman their daughter has become in the past nine years, yet they could see that we do. That's why I say she has to know about that recording device. She has to know so she can feel she had the chance to protect them. If something happens to one of them. If one of them makes a mistake or God forbid does something so horrible that they're brought before Breed Law, then our knowledge of that device will be revealed. If that happens and her friends didn't give her a chance to save her family, then she'll see it as her failure to protect them, just as she believes she's guilty of her brother's death. And we'll all be just as guilty in her eyes, as she will believe she herself is."

Rule could feel his senses, hell, the fucking animal he was inside, pacing within the confines of his flesh and ready to roar out in rage.

He'd be damned if he'd allow her to take that guilt onto her already burdened shoulders. If she took much more upon herself, then he feared she might well collapse beneath the grief.

"Something happened since I saw her last," he stated, remembering the pain he had felt throbbing just beneath her serene exterior. "Something that's hurt her."

"Her parents," Jonas stated softly. "I would imagine, knowing human nature as I do, that in their resentment they feel they lost their daughter that night as well; they likely remind her often of the son. Her pain was edged with an incredible amount of guilt today. Just as her mother's disapproval even before they walked into the suite could be detected by every Breed they passed."

And the misty, barely-there image of her brother as he stood sadly behind her had touched Jonas's heart.

The brother, whose dedication and loyalty to Breeds and the Unknown alike could never be questioned, had turned to Jonas, staring at him demandingly before reaching out as though to touch his sister's hair.

A vision none could see but him.

A vision that convinced him of her innocence as nothing else could.

♦   ♦   ♦

Rule barely stopped the growl that would have vibrated in his chest.

Damn, his senses were far too agitated since coming to Window Rock.

Turning to Jonas, he met those eerie eyes for long moments. He might not trust Jonas when it came to his promise not to pair him up with his mate, should Jonas ever find her, but he did trust the other man's opinion.

With his free hand, the director rubbed at the back of his neck as the tension tightening through his body caused the rest of them to watch him expectantly.

He had the last word. Whatever decision he made, Seth Lawrence of Lawrence Industries, and Dane Vanderale, heir to the Vanderale dynasty, would accept without argument.

"Jonas, you said yourself she's riding a very thin line," Rachel said softly, obviously reminding him of an earlier conversation.

He gave his head a hard shake.

"Yes, I did," he finally admitted as his gaze connected with Rule's, then Lawe's. Finally, he nodded slowly, turning back to Rule. "I agree with Rachel and Diane, Rule. She needs to know about this. The debt we owe her brother can never be repaid, and turning against the sister at this point would only betray his sacrifices as well. But I understand your concerns. How do you want to proceed?"

"Me?" Rule snapped, restraining himself from hitting something as he forced himself to keep his arms crossed over his chest. "My suggestion was to not tell her at all."

"And now the—forget it." Lifting the whiskey to his lips, Jonas finished his drink before setting the glass on the bar. "She'll be here tomorrow with Amber's cake, I believe. I'll discuss it with her before she leaves."

"I'll take care of it myself," Rule snarled.

Like hell.

Where did that come from?

Rule almost blinked in surprise.

The words had jumped out of his mouth before he'd even realized what he was actually saying.

But Jonas didn't seem to realize how out of character his commander was behaving. Perhaps it was just him, Rule thought, watching the others closely for any sign that they noticed anything different about him.

They didn't appear to be.

Perhaps it *was* just him.

The irritation, the feeling that the animal inside him was somehow caged and pacing in fury, must be really whacking his mind.

"Rule, watch yourself with this," Jonas warned him. "This could be a ruse by the Unknown to use her parents to throw our suspicions off Gypsy, or an attempt to deflect our interest by pulling her parents into a potentially threatening situation. I want to know why Greta McQuade had that device in her purse and who put it there. And why she agreed to help them. We don't have unlimited time here. Gypsy can find out why it happened, or I will." His voice hardened. "Which do you believe she would prefer?"

Rule's eyes narrowed. "Don't give me ultimatums, Jonas," he growled. "You know that won't work with me."

"I'm not ordering you," Jonas stated firmly. "I'm telling you. I won't take any further risks with my daughter. Gypsy's a friend, not just yours, but mine and Rachel's, and even Amber's as well, and because of that, you have until after the ball next week to find out what the hell is going on. Then I'll find out myself."

Turning, Jonas moved from the room and entered the private rooms he shared with his mate. Even Rule caught the scent of Amber's pain and felt his chest tightening at the decisions Jonas was being forced to make to save her life. Decisions he knew kept the other Breed awake at night staring into the darkness as he searched for an answer.

"Rule." Lawe sighed wearily, and Rule could feel his brother's intent to try to dissuade him from the trust he felt for a woman he should have never trusted to begin with.

"Don't even bother, Lawe," Rule growled, determination hardening his jaw, tightening his body. "Everything inside me is screaming her innocence. I won't turn on her without cause."

With that, he left the suite, stalking down the hall and heading for his rooms. And, he hoped, a chance to figure out exactly what the hell was going on with the woman he hadn't mated, yet the only woman he'd been unable to turn away from in his entire life.

· CHAPTER 9 ·

He was waiting on her that night.

Leaning against the bar, watching the doorway with a smug, self-satisfied smile—and didn't he just look like the cat that ate the canary.

The man was positively sex served up with a side of luscious male muscles and sinful wicked looks. Something she preferred to admire from afar, if only her damned body and her Unknown boss would get with the program there.

Dane Vanderale stood with his back to her, and whatever he said to Rule had the Breed flashing him an irate look before his gaze turned back to her.

Was she supposed to be swooning? she wondered. Tearing her clothes off and spreading herself before him in thankfulness that he had persuaded the director of the Bureau of Breed Affairs to allow her parents to have that contract?

She didn't think so.

The very fact that she was even there that evening had more to do with a call from friends asking her to show up than either her contact or Rule.

Kandy had left the shop before Gypsy could ask her to make the mousse cake for Amber. Gypsy had found herself in the Gingerbread House kitchen whipping up chocolate mousse as she watched the clock, certain she would be up most of the night with it.

Thankfully, Kandy had shown up as Gypsy set the mousse into the fridge to chill, and with an irate glare at the mess in the kitchen, her sister had urged her to go "do whatever it is you do every weekend and get the hell out of my kitchen."

And Gypsy had done just that without argument.

She could bake, and she could bake well, but Gypsy was not all about the cleanup.

From the corner of her eye she watched as Rule narrowed his eyes on her where she lingered just inside the entrance. Her gaze moved over the crowd as though she weren't debating stepping up to the bar and shooting him. She sure as hell wasn't going to go panting after him like some bitch in heat.

The sight of a slender hand lifting into the air, waving enthusiastically, had her gaze turning to the owner, and a smile tugged at her lips. Hell, it had been too damned long since she had seen the Coyote Breed Ashley Truing and her sister, Emma, out having fun.

Two months before, Ashley had taken a bullet to her chest that the doctors had been certain she wouldn't recover from. She was recovering, just as Emma had promised before the meeting with Jonas, but others had mentioned over the past weeks that Ashley was different in some way. That there was a part of Ashley that may not have returned when she'd died on the operating table after being shot.

Breed genetics ensured that Ashley had healed quickly, though. In less than six weeks the Breed female had been strong enough that she was moving around easily and training to regain the strength she had lost.

Moving across the bar, Gypsy ignored the feel of Rule's eyes following her and the amusement she glimpsed curling on his lips as she made her way to the girls' table.

They weren't alone. The blonde with them, older by only a few years, was leaning back in a chair, watching the occupants of the bar broodingly as she nursed a bottle of beer that had been barely sipped from.

Sharone had been raised with Ashley and Emma, created first in the Russian labs, and often acted like the protective sibling she could very well be.

"Are the three of you having fun?" she grinned, her voice rising until she could be heard over the energetic tunes the band was pouring out to the crowd.

"Four," Emma informed her, leaning close as Gypsy took a seat next to her. "We finally talked Jonas into letting Cassie come out and play with us."

Gypsy looked around. "Where is she?"

Emma's lips twisted in perplexed amusement. "She's out there dancing with some guy. See all the Breeds congregated?" She pointed to what was indeed a mass congregation of Breeds next to the dance floor. "I bet her partner is pissing his pants."

Oh hell.

Poor Cassie. She was surrounded by glowering Breed Enforcers whose unrelenting stares were trained on the hapless cowboy Cassie was dancing with.

Gypsy could see them now. The young man was positively miserable, and Cassie was glaring at the Breeds.

What hell her life must surely be. Always followed, never left alone, never able to truly have friends.

"She never makes it for long," Emma revealed with a heavy sigh. "She talked Jonas into letting her go out while they were in Virginia last year. The Breeds he sent with her terrified anyone who even considered asking her to dance. She sat and got puke-faced drunk instead."

"Yeah, then the Breeds who took her out got their asses kicked for letting her get drunk," Ashley revealed with a slight smile. "I told her, she should have got hold of me before that bastard put a hole in my chest. Me and Em would have showed her a good time. We would have had to leave Sharone at home, though." Ashley nodded to the blonde on the other side of Gypsy.

"I bet that would have just upset the hell out of you." Gypsy laughed over at the disgusted look the other Breed female cast Ashley.

Sharone rarely got into trouble and was known to keep an eagle eye out for the other two girls. It often took both Sharone and Emma together to keep Ashley out of trouble, though.

"Why aren't the three of you out there dancing too?" Gypsy nodded toward the dance floor.

"With all those Breed Enforcers in attendance?" Emma looked at her as though scandalized. "I really don't want my alpha jerking me home and shortening my leash to the point that I strangle. None of us do."

"Just for dancing?" Gypsy tugged at her ear in confusion as she frowned out at the dance floor and the smooth, sinuous flow of bodies that moved in beat to the music.

"Our alpha is convinced we're pure and sweet with no sex drive and damned sure we know none of the moves we use while teasing those cowboys. If he even heard of us dancing as we do, he'd never let us out to play again." Emma even looked properly horrified.

"Is your alpha here?" she asked, looking around suspiciously. She usually heard when there were any alphas in the area.

"No, not the alpha, just every Breed who would ever tell on us." Emma grimaced. "Wherever Cassie goes, Jonas's best enforcers go. That means our alpha would be told because one of those Breeds this month is one of the Citadel's team commanders. He would tattle on us in a heartbeat."

They had sacrificed their own fun to give Cassie what she wanted, even knowing the total lack of fun the other girl would have.

Looking up, she watched as Cassie Sinclair stalked back to the table, lifted a glass of amber liquid and tossed it back furiously before giving in to a rough, shocked bout of coughing.

"There, there," Ashley murmured as she smacked the other girl on the back a few times. "That's it. Fine whiskey just makes everything better. Would you like another shot, dear?"

That gleam in Emma's eyes was positively devilish as she indicated to the waitress that she wanted another.

It wasn't going to make it better, Gypsy thought as she watched Cassie sit back in her chair, her gaze slashing mutinously to the dozen Breeds who moved to the table.

"They even have two female enforcers to go into the bathroom with her." Ashley leaned across the table as she indicated that Gypsy should move closer. "Or we would have just slipped her out the bathroom window."

She glanced at Cassie, seeing the damp gleam in her eyes as the other girl quickly ducked her head to hide the tears she had to blink back.

Damn, to let her go, then to send a dozen bodyguards to make certain she was miserable, was just cruel.

"Why not just slip her out of the hotel?" Gypsy asked, her gaze flicking to the furious Cassie. "They can't follow if they don't know she's leaving."

"It's hard to slip away from six Breeds parked on your ass every minute of the day," Ashley answered with a twinge of sympathy. "Besides, there's not a bar in a hundred-mile radius that doesn't have at least one Breed who would report where she was."

Oh, they so didn't know the area, or the bars, as well as they thought they did.

"What about the underground bars?" Surely Ashley and Emma had been to a few of them. "The Breeds there would die and go to hell before they'd tell on her. If she was caught there, so would they be. If there were even any there, which is damned rare. They might watch out for her, but they'll damned sure not ride her ass like a herd of ponies after a prized female."

Ashley's eyes narrowed as the others, even Sharone, laughed in surprise at the description. "You're kidding me. They have those here?"

Gypsy had to laugh now. "At least a dozen that I know of. Come on, bars are still strictly banned except along the reservation's borders. Even then, they're not allowed within the city limits. Do you really think we always want to make that drive? Especially those who live much farther from here?"

She could see Ashley's mind working now, the gears beginning to move, at first with a hesitancy that indicated she might still be recovering, then with enough strength to put that gleam she had lost back into her eyes.

Ashley hadn't changed, perhaps, Gypsy thought. She was getting bored. And that was something Gypsy well understood, the boredom. But she had also managed to snag the attention of the other women as well.

"I want to go." Cassie breathed out in sudden excitement. "Just one night, I want to be someone other than the crazy Breed Cassandra Sinclair."

Cassie wanted to be anonymous. That was something else Gypsy could understand. But a discussion on how to accomplish it wasn't going to happen here.

Suddenly, Cassie's gaze jumped to hers, narrowed and appeared brighter, a sky blue, lighter than Rule's, but so deep and pure it was almost mesmerizing before her gaze slid to Gypsy's side.

Cassie frowned, grimaced, then shook her head.

Gypsy glanced beside her, saw nothing but Emma, who had lowered her head as though intensely interested in the top of the table.

"Is there a problem?" Gypsy asked as she turned back to Cassie, letting the other woman read her lips rather than hear her words over the loud pulse of the music.

"Probably." The other girl could barely be heard. "But not yet."

Oooh-kay.

Yeah, she'd heard the stories about Cassie, and whatever it was the other girl saw or heard, Gypsy simply didn't want to know.

"Well, girls." Lifting her beer, she finished the cold liquid quickly before placing the bottle on the table and giving them all an amused look. "My bodyguards aren't here, if I even had any. And Daddy hasn't worried about my dancing since I was fourteen because he was never aware of it to begin with."

"I wouldn't be so sure about the bodyguards." She read Cassie's lips, as she seemed to have muttered the words to herself.

Whatever.

She hadn't had a protector since Mark . . .

Rising to her feet, she tipped her fingers to the other girls, ignoring their glares, and moved to the dance floor.

She was there to dance, and in her teasing, playful movements and flirtations with several of the males on the dance floor, she gained bits and pieces of the information she would later give to her contact. The pass of information would be deliberate tonight, though.

Gypsy had let them know several nights before that she needed specific information concerning any odd questions any of the Breeds were asking lately. She'd allowed them to believe she was asking because of Rule's interest in her when one of them had asked worriedly if she was being targeted, possibly, because of her brother's death and information it was rumored he might have had at the time.

This game could become dangerous fast, though. Breeds had exceptional hearing, and she wasn't the only one who was well aware of that. But she knew at least one of them had learned something. *SLAP HAPPY'S. BEFORE MIDNIGHT. XOXO.* The message she'd found tucked beneath the wiper blades of her Jeep that evening held the distinctive *XOXO* that she'd asked them to use.

Tonight, something was definitely going on. Even amid the loose-knit crowd where there were few real couples on the floor, getting a chance to get close enough to any of the four men became impossible.

A subtle wink by one of the older cowboys her brother had once been friends with identified the messenger, but getting close enough to get the information became hazardous. Each time they danced close to each other, one of the Breed Enforcers on the dance floor became noticeably nosy.

What the hell was going on?

Moving into step with the contact, James Herndon, she let his arm wrap around her waist. He pulled her to him, swaying, twirling her once, twice. She landed against his chest laughing as his lips moved directly to her ear. "Later."

The word, a distinct warning that would have had her tensing if he hadn't swung her around again, laughed at her as she caught herself against his chest, then glanced over her shoulder.

His expression stilled. All laughter, all humor wiping away.

Releasing her, he stepped back quickly.

Another arm came around her, twirled her around until she was staring into Rule's brooding, narrowed gaze.

He didn't look happy, and he didn't look in the mood to be teased.

In that instant the music moved from the hard, pulsing throb she was used to, to a slow, sensuous ballad that crooned the singer's hunger, her aching loss and need.

"You don't want to do that," he growled when she moved to push away from him. "Not here. Not now."

The warning in his voice was firm, dominant, and pushed some feminine button she hadn't known she possessed that urged her to just relent. To obey him, just this once, just in case he had a way of enforcing it in some erotic manner she couldn't fight.

"I don't slow dance," she bit out from between her teeth, her body longing to relax and melt against him even as she fought to remain stiff and unyielding. "Slow dancing with you will imply a relationship that doesn't exist."

She didn't want that. It would change the dynamic of who she was and the information to be gained in the circles she moved in.

"A relationship that doesn't exist? Who are you lying to, Gypsy? Because I sure as hell know better and you do as well," he informed her warningly as he moved against her, cajoling her, seducing her into sharing the dance, to share the intimacy he was inviting.

"You're taking far too much for granted," she retorted furiously, yet she wasn't fighting him either.

She was breathless.

She could feel the blood heating, pounding through her veins, the sensual side of her nature weakening far too quickly.

She ached for him. The flesh between her thighs became hotter, wetter, her clit throbbing as her sex melted and creamed for him.

It was impossible to deny she wanted him when her body refused to cooperate and remain cool and unresponsive.

"I haven't yet," he said softly as she tilted her head back to stare up at him. "But I'm certain I will before the night's out, Gypsy Rum. I'm very certain of it."

Before she could argue the statement or tell him to go to hell, he brushed his lips against hers, his tongue flicking in a quick little lick against her lips before he pulled back no more than a breath of distance.

The pleasure was shocking.

It held her in his arms, staring up at him in confusion as impulses, hungers and needs began firing through her body with a heat she hadn't expected.

It surprised her.

Shocked her.

His lips had lifted just far enough from hers to tease her, to make her wonder if he would speak, and when he did, if his lips would stroke against her again.

His gaze was locked on hers, unblinking, the blue of his eyes deeper than Cassandra's, more mesmerizing, holding her, making her wonder at what she saw reflected back at her.

There was so much in his gaze. A hint of another color, perhaps, a world of hunger, of need, a deep, brilliant pool of male lust so vibrant it made her wonder if he was even aware he was revealing it.

"Why?" she whispered.

Why her? Why was he pushing this when it was more than obvious she was hesitant to begin anything with him?

"Why not?" It wasn't the question, but the tone of voice, the look in his eyes, that shocked her.

Steel-hard determination, pure male hunger and narrow-eyed possessiveness struck at her, wrapped around her and made her wonder if she was smothering from fear, or breathless from anticipation.

"Leave with me," he asked her then.

Eyes widening before she could stop the reaction, she parted her lips to refuse, though forming the word didn't come easily.

"Just to talk." His finger landed against her lips, holding back what she wanted to say but couldn't. "I want you, bad enough to wait if I have to. But if I have to wait, at least torture me for a few hours."

"And that would be enough for you?" she quipped mockingly despite the flush of arousal that was beginning to heat her body.

God, how long had it been since she had allowed herself to want a man? If she even thought she would be attracted to one, she ran in the opposite direction as fast as possible.

"It's more than I have otherwise." The seductive roughness of his voice stroked against her senses as she wondered why she wasn't trying to run as hard and as fast as possible from him.

Gypsy breathed in slowly, deeply.

"I promise, no means no," he said.

For a moment, she wondered if he could read her mind, if he knew things about her that even the Unknown didn't know.

Things no one should know.

Slowly, she nodded, her senses exploding in disbelief as she realized what she had done. Then he was stroking his hand along her arm, catching her hand in his and drawing her from the dance floor.

There were too many eyes watching, she told herself. She had to leave alone. She couldn't leave with him. If she did so, then the rules would change. She would no longer be everyone's "friend" and would then be seen as a possible fuck instead.

That could destroy her ability to do the job she had been doing for so many years now.

She had to stop this.

She had to make him let her go.

So why was she moving with him instead, allowing him to curl his fingers with hers, hold her hand possessively as they moved through the exit and into the parking lot?

His arm slid around her, his fingers curling over her hip as he drew her closer.

"Your car?" he asked, pausing just outside the door.

Gypsy swallowed tightly. "My car. My apartment."

He nodded, following her lead to the Jeep, silent, watching her as she slid behind the wheel before he moved to the passenger side.

She was surprised he didn't insist on driving. She was surprised when he simply slid into the seat, buckled his seat belt and stared back at her expectantly.

"I've lost my mind," she muttered, then activated the engine, lowering the roof and then sliding the vehicle into gear and pulling from the parking slot. "This is not the smartest thing I've ever done."

"Do you always do what's smart?" he asked.

"If possible. Always, if possible."

He smiled back at her rather than assuring her it wasn't possible this time.

She had lost her mind tonight, but she promised herself she would find it as soon as he left. The second she was alone again she would find it, lock it up tight and make sure he couldn't steal it from her ever again.

She was going to make him crazy.

Rule could feel it coming.

The need to touch her, to taste her and to have her was burning through his system, engorging his cock and tightening his balls to a near-painful degree.

Watching her dance on that damned dance floor, her body swaying and moving against those other men as she laughed and flirted with them, had caused more than one growl to escape his control.

All that had kept him from tearing those men apart was Dane's order that the enforcers at the bar converge on her and ensure that she wasn't the contact their suspected spies were passing information to.

Jonas wanted that link, just as he wanted to know the threat they could become where Claire Martinez was concerned.

Jonas was certain Gypsy was connected. He was certain she was either one of the links who gathered the information and reported it to an upper contact, or one of the last links in the chain of information.

Protecting her ass was becoming difficult. Hazardous maybe, because Jonas was just a little too complacent about the direction and lack of results in this investigation.

Added to that, her parents' attempt to smuggle that damned audio recorder into the meeting was only increasing the attention on Gypsy, as well as the suspicion.

And none of it mattered right now.

Tonight, he didn't fucking care what Jonas was doing, was up to, or how he would handle it.

Tonight, Gypsy was his, in whatever way he could claim her, and as often as he could make it happen.

Giving her the information about the recording device her mother had brought to the meeting would wait. Not long, but it would wait.

◆   ◆   ◆

Pulling the Jeep into the small parking lot of her apartment, Gypsy parked, activated the roof and waited until it was secured before turning the motor off.

She drew in a hard breath, even as the scent of her need intensified, along with her confusion.

She wanted him, yet she didn't know why she wanted him. Why she was burning for him.

Stepping from the vehicle, he moved to the driver's side, opened her door and waited until she slid from the seat, swallowing tightly.

"I have a car coming for me in two hours," he told her, his lips quirking into a grin as her gaze flashed up to him. "Rest assured, sweetheart, what I want will take far longer than two hours to even get close to finishing. You're completely safe for the night."

He made a mental note to send Dog the message to pick him up at the appropriate time. He had a feeling it wouldn't do to allow her to catch him in even the smallest white lie.

"I haven't figured out what made you decide you should even be here," she told him, though she turned and led the way to the stairs leading up to her apartment. "You've just totally destroyed any peace I have when I go out at night now. Every Tom, Dick and Breed will think he can go home with me now."

Oh, he didn't think so.

He'd make sure every Breed who considered it knew the hazards and informed Tom and Dick of the claim already made on her.

"I don't think it will be the problem you're imagining," he told her, though, as she unlocked her door, her fingers tightening on the knob in preparation of turning it.

His fingers closed over hers slowly, stopping her.

Gypsy stilled, her head down, breathing hard. The warmth of her spread from her back to his chest, his entire body aching to feel her in ways he knew she wasn't ready for.

"I want you," he told her. "Until I ache with the need for you. But I won't take from you, Gypsy. I want nothing that isn't freely given. Nothing that you don't want just as badly as I want it."

She paused for long seconds, obviously battling not what she knew he wanted, but what she wanted as well.

"I believe you." She finally nodded, but that hint of fear still lingered in her scent. "Sometimes, what a person wants isn't always best for them, though."

He released her fingers, allowing her to turn the doorknob and push the door open before he carefully, casually maneuvered himself inside the apartment ahead of her.

His senses registered everything in less than a heartbeat. The animal genetics that raged so strong inside him were closer to the surface tonight, even before he'd left the hotel.

The scent of her permeated the apartment, sliding over his senses like a sensual caress. There were more subtle, softer scents. Those of her family, perhaps friends. There was no scent of sex or male intimacy. No other man had placed his mark on her territory as he intended to place his tonight.

"The light switch is on your left," she told him, waiting, her irritation edging along her scent now.

His lips quirked as he reached out and flipped on the light before drawing her inside.

"Sorry, habit," he assured her. "Some habits are better not broken, no matter the situation."

She nodded, moving into the apartment and closing the door behind her, automatically stopping to lock the deadbolt as well as the heavy chain lock between the door and the frame.

"I've lived here since I was eighteen," she told him, though he swore he could feel something that she was leaving unsaid.

"Your sister still lives with your parents?" he asked, following her from the small foyer into the combination kitchen and living room.

"The apartment downstairs." She gave a little shrug of her shoulders. "She moved into it last year."

The apartment was large, open and roomy. Large windows dominated three walls, while the other held an open door that revealed her bedroom and a large, neat bed.

She turned on several low lamps before moving into the kitchen.

"I have some wine," she told him, hesitating at the combination bar and counter that separated the two rooms.

"That's fine." He nodded. Not that he cared much for wine, but he could feel her nervousness building as he watched her.

Tilting her neck as though to stretch the tightness from it, she moved into the kitchen area, reached beneath the cabinet and pulled free a surprisingly recognizable wine.

It was one of the sweeter wines, he saw. The same brand the Pride Leader's wife preferred when drinking a glass before going to bed.

She opened it, filled two wineglasses, then set aside the empty bottle. Handing one glass to him, she led the way into the living room.

Rule watched as she curled herself into the corner of the couch, watching him as he sat, not too close to her, but not too far away.

She was too nervous.

He could feel her, ready to jump and run at a moment's notice as that elusive scent of fear strengthened marginally.

Turning his head, he stared at her for long moments, suspicion biting at his control as he sipped at the wine, watching as she did as well, and seeing the fine tremor in her fingers.

Fuck, he couldn't do this to her.

"You never date. You never allow any man to dance too closely to you and never allow them to even consider that they could have a chance to leave with you. You've had no lovers, and you've had no relationships. Yet you're twenty-four years old and I know you're not a cold woman. The warmth of you flows over my senses, and the scent of your feminine need has me so hard I'll carry the brand of my zipper on my cock long after I shed my pants. So tell me, Gypsy," he asked her, watching her stiffen until she was so tense a good wind could have broken bones, "why is your life in deep freeze?"

"You don't know what you're talking about," she lied, and that lie filled her entire expression as well as her scent.

"I intend to share that bed in there with you," he stated. "And don't bother denying any chance that I'll make it there. We both know I will. Before I do so, I'd like to know any obstacle that would stand in the way of the pleasure I can give you."

"Aren't you just as cool as you can be?" When she lifted her head, those witchy eyes glared back at him as she gripped the wineglass with both hands now. "You just state your intent and think I'm going to just follow along with you? Just because you decree it?"

Reaching forward, he placed his own wineglass on the low coffee table before turning back to her and lifting his brows. "It's a thought. I could live with the idea of it."

"Well, bully for you, badass." Gripping the glass in one hand once again, she lifted it to her lips, finished it, then all but broke the glass when she placed it on the table as well, but with a much heavier hand. "I knew this was a mistake."

She moved from the couch with a suddenness that had absolutely no attempt at subtlety.

He'd played with her in the past weeks, letting her get away, letting her run.

He was tired of watching her run.

"Oh, I don't think so." He was at her side, the fingers of one hand shackling her wrist as she stared back at him in surprise.

"I'm tired of being bullied by you."

He had to laugh at that. At the very thought of it.

"Bullied by me? Or having the truth become an object you can't push away like you push away those cowboys when they try for more than just a dance? I'm not bullying you, Gypsy, but neither do I intend to watch you run any longer," he promised her.

◆　　◆　　◆

He wasn't going to watch her run any longer? What she was going to do was kick his ass out.

"From what? You?" Her lips curled in derision. "Really, Rule, do you think you're the only Breed who's come on to me? Trust me, you're not."

"I'm the only one you've ever left with." The smile that shaped those too-damned-sexy lips should have been a warning.

In the next second he'd managed to swing her around, pulling her against the heat of his chest and holding her securely against him.

Why wasn't she fighting him?

She knew a few moves of her own, and she'd used them more than once to escape holds that were more forceful than this one. Yet she couldn't make herself fight. She didn't want to fight.

And that was far too dangerous.

"What are you doing to me?"

Gypsy couldn't force any of this to make sense.

This wasn't her. She didn't tell her secrets, not any of them. If she trusted anyone with one of them, then she would be tempted to trust more. And she knew better than that. Yet she wanted to tell him her secrets. She *needed* to talk to him, needed him to listen, to understand the why of so many things.

"I think we've talked enough—"

"I watched my mother die." His head turned to her, his eyes so brilliant they burned.

"What?"

"In those labs," he told her, his voice rough. "I've never spoken of it to anyone, including the brother forced to watch with me. We had two young siblings to protect. If we showed emotion, they would have been killed instantly. But we were forced to hear her screams and the screams of the Breed she loved as they were dissected while still living. The memory of those screams, of hearing the death of the woman who fought every day of her life to find a way to get her children, no matter that they were forced upon her, out of those labs, torments my nightmares. So should you awaken to my screams, perhaps you will simply awaken me, share your warmth and your courage with me, as I would do for you should the nightmares come to you as well."

The offer shattered her.

She felt her lips tremble as she stared into his gaze, saw the torment, the loss, the pain he suffered in a way that only made him stronger in her eyes.

"I would hold you through those nightmares if you allowed it, Gypsy." His fingers cupped the side of her face as he stared down at her.

"If I could," he continued. "I would hold the nightmares at bay for you."

"If I could, I would throw you out of my apartment and out of my life," she whispered painfully, her fingers gripping his forearms, feeling the hard muscles beneath the tough flesh as she stared up at him. "I don't want you here. I don't want you messing with my head and ruining my plans and my life."

"And what plans have I ruined, little Gypsy?" he questioned her gently, his eyes disbelieving as he brushed a soft kiss over her lips. "Your plans to exist like the perfect frozen little princess? To deny yourself something so basic as this?" The backs of his fingers caressed down her cheek, her neck, sending tingles of pleasure racing through her.

"You're the reason Jonas offered my parents a chance at that contract, aren't you?" she accused him, the way she'd been maneuvered still chafing at her.

He grinned. A self-satisfied, smug smile. "I would hate to have to attend the parties and gatherings I'm certain you'd send me to alone, if you could."

Her frown turned to a glare. "Because of you I have to wear a dress I had designed just for another event this fall. A ball that's damned near impossible to be noticed at without a dress as intriguing as it is unique. Your last-minute invitation to that Breed ball just ruined those plans."

The dress wasn't really the objection she had to it, Gypsy admitted. Hell, she'd admitted it to herself hours ago.

"Why do I sense far more than your ire that a dress is being sacrificed?" he asked gently, and she hated him for that gentleness.

She hated him for making her want to reveal things he had no need to know and to force her to attend a party she'd had no intention of attending.

"I hate being manipulated," she bit out between clenched teeth, moving to pull from him, expecting him to let her go.

Instead, his hold only tightened as a flash of male, dominant sexuality sparked in his eyes.

"And I hate aching, hungering for a woman who wants me just as desperately yet finds herself too terrified of the past to take what she wants."

The accusation struck far too close to the truth.

"So, should I just sleep with you and thank you very nicely for fucking me once you're finished?" she demanded with mocking sweetness. "Did you think that damned contract would get you into my bed, Rule?"

His lips curled with just a hint of amusement. "A man can hope, but I have to admit, I wasn't betting on it."

"You're an arrogant ass," she accused him roughly.

And she was insane. Somewhere she had managed to lose what common sense she possessed.

"It's time you le—" She didn't have a chance to finish the rest of the demand. His lips came over hers with a powerful, dominant force that had a surprised moan slipping from between them. Her hands rose to his shoulders, nails digging into the material of his shirt as she was drawn to her tiptoes, suddenly so desperate to get closer that the need was exploding through her senses.

She could taste the chocolate and peppermint candies he was known to enjoy. The taste of the sweet was licked onto her tongue as he pressed past her lips and stroked over it. It filled her senses and gave her a whole new appreciation of the candy.

The stroke of his hands down her back caused her to arch closer, pleasure rasping over the sensitive flesh, then exploding across her lower back as they slipped beneath her blouse.

Had she ever wanted to be touched in this way? Had she ever wanted a man to stroke her flesh, to tear her from the safe confines of her world and into a heady, chaotic storm of pleasure? Had she ever craved having all her plans for vengeance destroyed for a single man's touch?

She hadn't, she knew. Heat rushed through her as his nails scraped down her back lightly, rasping over her flesh and causing her to press closer to him. To rub herself against him as she felt the iron-hard, thick wedge of his erection beneath his jeans.

The impression of that erect flesh was large, too large, perhaps.

And she swore she could feel the heat of the engorged flesh through his jeans and hers as he pressed closer to her.

A tugging heat at her scalp had her head tilting back for him, her lips parting further as he began taking long, deep kisses from her. Sipping at her lips, nipping at them, only to rub the ache away with his far too experienced tongue.

"I want to taste you just like that." His head lifted, his lips only brushing against hers as she forced her eyes to open, to stare up at him.

"What?" She couldn't believe he meant—

"I want my tongue between your thighs, lapping at the sweet, hot cream I can smell dripping from you. I want to catch it on my lips, taste you on my tongue, then lick between your inner lips until it's buried in the sweet heat hidden there."

She gasped; her vagina clenched with such hard, involuntary spasms that the juices gathering there were suddenly forced to flow from her and further dampen her panties.

"You like that," he growled. "Admit it, Gypsy. You want my lips there."

His hand was suddenly between her thighs, cupping her mound, his fingers pressing firmly into the material where the moisture fell from her. The pad of his hand ground against her clit, rubbing it in short, erotic strokes that had her breath catching.

It was so good. So hot. She'd never even fantasized about a man touching her like this, of drawing such pleasure from her body that she suddenly wondered at the small amount of control she had over it.

"Your body knows me, Gypsy," he warned her, his teeth nipping at her lips as he urged her to part them for him again. "It knows the pleasure I can give it, the heated caresses and the sweet release."

A muffled cry, barely smothered, escaped her lips as his lips moved from hers and began spreading a line of kisses over her jaw and down her neck.

Sizzling arcs of sensation rushed through her system, burned straight to her clit and echoed in her womb.

God, she didn't know how to keep him out of her bed. She wanted to beg him to join her there now. Beg him to do exactly what he had just told her he wanted to do. To bury his lips between her thighs and taste the pleasure he was giving her.

"Rule. Oh God—" The small buttons at the front of her nearly sheer blouse suddenly released. The sides fell away, revealing the silk and lace of the nude bra she wore, the full curves of her breasts rising above the cups.

"Have mercy," he groaned, one hand cupping a breast as his lips pressed to the rise over its mate. "You taste like pure pleasure."

His tongue stroked over the sensitive flesh, the slight, roughened rasp causing shards of increased need racing through her senses.

She wanted his lips on her nipples. Now.

She wanted his mouth devouring them.

His fingers gripped the lacy top of the material, drawing it slowly over the firm flesh, scraping the material against her agonizingly engorged nipples.

They pushed out from the tip of her breast, pebble hard and aching painfully.

Gypsy had to watch. She couldn't help it. It was so erotic, so wicked, watching as his incredibly thick, long lashes lifted from the brilliance of his gaze as he watched her watch him.

His lips parted. His tongue peeked out, that roughness that covered it rubbing against her nipple.

Fire exploded in the tip.

It tore through her body in a rush of such pleasure she was certain she couldn't survive it. Certain she couldn't remain standing if he didn't stop, and knowing she couldn't bear it if he stopped.

Then standing wasn't an issue.

Sweeping her from her feet and lifting her into his arms, Rule carried her the short distance to the couch, laid her on the wide cushions, then came down over her.

His lips covered a nipple immediately, drawing it into the heat of his mouth and suckling it with firm, hungry draws of his mouth. The sight of his cheeks hollowing, his expression suffused with pleasure, was something she didn't know if she could survive.

The pleasure lashed at her nipple, and then as his fingers surrounded the other and began tugging and caressing it, the increased sensations tore free any further objections she might have been working on.

What the hell was she doing?

Panting for air, her fingers sliding in the warm, coarse thickness of his black hair and tightening as his teeth suddenly surrounded the tip and bit sensually, Gypsy could feel the sexual woman inside herself pushing free.

Releasing the tender tip, his tongue licked at it, stoking the already burning sensations arcing through her body and leaving her quivering in erotic need.

This was why, she thought hazily. Why she hadn't wanted to tease and flirt with the often-too-grim Lion. This was why she'd stayed as far away from him as possible.

Because he could do this to her.

He could make her lose control.

His caresses trailed from her breast, over her stomach to her hips and the buttons of her jeans. He flicked them open with experienced fingers, sliding beneath the material, moving closer to the humid ache tormenting her there.

And how much more was it going to ache if he continued? She couldn't let him have her. She couldn't let this happen.

His fingers pushed beneath her panties as his lips lifted from her breast and moved to hers once again, covering them. His kisses sipped at her lips, stroked them, stole reason and objection as his fingers continued their journey and slid between the lush, saturated folds of her sex.

Sensation lashed at her body as the callused tips of his fingers rasped through the narrow slit, parting the swollen folds before caressing lower, rubbing against the clenched entrance to her vagina.

The feel of her juices spilling to his fingers, eagerly welcoming his touch and tempting him further, had her thighs tightening in an effort to ensure that pleasure remained.

Oh God, just for a minute. Let her feel that rush of indescribable sensation for just a little while longer.

"Shh, it's okay, Gypsy." Rule's voice was thick, filled with hunger as she realized the whimpers she could hear were falling from her own lips.

"It's okay, baby, I promise. I have you. You can let go of my wrist, sweetheart."

She had hold of his wrist?

She had to force her lashes open, feeling dazed and uncertain as her gaze fell to where her nails were digging into his wrist.

Then the heated rush of moisture that spilled from her at the sight of his broad hand filling her jeans caused her hips to jerk upward. The punch of sensation that attacked her womb stole her breath.

"I'm just petting you, Gypsy. That's all."

Her eyes lifted to his once again, shocked, a cry parting her lips as his fingers rubbed at the aching entrance of her body and the hard pad of his hand pressed against her clit.

"I don't do this." She could feel the fear trying to ease into the pleasure, trying to destroy her acceptance that her body would feel pleasure with such mind-numbing force, that it could ache or want or grow wet for such a touch despite her knowledge of what she would have to leave behind.

"Yet how pretty you are as I pleasure you." His gaze darkened, his lips pulling back from his teeth to reveal the sharp, overlong canines as her body spilled more of her slick response to his fingers.

His expression was tight with his own pleasure. Yet where he was deriving that pleasure from, Gypsy had no idea. And as his fingers slid through the thick layer of moisture covering her folds to the swollen bud of her clit, Gypsy's thoughts splintered as a strangled cry of pleasure tore from her lips.

"Your body was made for pleasure," he crooned, his lips lowering to hers once again, taking brief, hard kisses that kept her aching for more.

His hand moved again, her fingers tightening on his wrist as he stroked from her clit to the entrance of her vagina and back again. Stroking, rubbing at each, sending waves of need clashing through her senses as her hips arched, her body begging for more.

Each stroke of his fingers tightened the pleasure building in her womb, in the tight throb of her clit and the ache in her pussy. She could feel it, like a band tightening between those pleasure points, stretching tighter, the need for more growing with each second.

"Rule," she moaned, though whether in protest or plea she had no idea. "Please . . ."

She had no idea what she was begging for, what her body was burning for. This was so unlike her own touch or the toys she kept that it was laughable to even compare the two.

This was addictive, brutally ecstatic, and she wondered how she would ever be the same now that she had known it.

With each stroke of his fingers between her thighs, her hips lifted to him, begging for more, aching to be touched deeper, harder.

Pulling back from the narrow entrance to her vagina, his fingers circled her clit, the firm, rubbing caress sending a shower of pure pleasure arcing through her body. The swollen bud throbbed, the ache tightening as Gypsy felt a building wave of sensation threatening to burst through her.

She had never known this could be pleasure.

She had shied away from any man's touch, pushed would-be lovers behind her and become their friend instead. She had told herself she could do without the touch or the aggravation of a man in her life.

And now, her body was intent on making up for lost time. It was burning in a Breed's arms, her hips lifting to him, eager for more as he rubbed at the tiny bundle of nerve endings, stroked them, kept her hovering on a pinnacle that became sharper by the second.

"Look at me, Gypsy," he growled, the rough rumble of demand rasping from his chest as her eyes opened for him.

Dazed, unable to fight past the waves of sizzling sensation building beneath his stroking fingers, she opened her eyes, her gaze locking with his.

"It's okay," he whispered, his breathing rough, as harsh as her own. "Let it have you, baby. It's only pleasure, I promise. Nothing to be frightened of."

Nothing to be frightened of? Gypsy could feel the waves of control-destroying sensation tightening in every cell of her body. She no longer controlled her own body. She no longer controlled herself, and it was beginning to frighten her.

She had to control this.

She had to know what was coming before she stepped into it.

"No." The hard growl in his voice had her body jerking as another powerful wave of sensation lashed at her as his voice rasped over her senses. "Stay with me, Gypsy. No fear."

The stroking, rubbing, diabolical touch of his fingers increased.

Her thighs tightened, his image becoming hazy as she stared up at him, the lashing, heated waves of pleasure growing, becoming hotter, brighter.

Her hips arched to him, her breathing becoming harder, faster.

"Rule . . . please . . ." She was suddenly frightened of where it would take her, how it would change her.

She wanted to pull back, wanted to wait, feel her way through whatever was beginning to tear through her.

"Give to me, Gypsy, just this," he groaned, the strokes shifting again, tightening.

Her eyes widened.

"I have you, Gypsy," he promised again. "I'll hold you right here, I swear."

She lost her breath.

A strangled cry rasped from her throat as her hold on his wrist tightened, nails digging in as an explosion of white-hot ecstasy ruptured her mind.

Her hips were jerking beneath his stroking fingers, her juices spilling from her again, a wash of rapturous moisture weeping from her as her head tilted back and a cry of agonized pleasure tore her apart at the seams.

There was nothing she could do but stare up him, so dazed, so lost within the clash of sensations, pleasure and need that did just as she had feared it would.

Somehow, it changed her.

Dog was waiting for Rule outside, leaning against the side of the building beneath the staircase that led up to the apartment.

The scent of Gypsy's pleasure still lingered in his senses, that explosive mix of hunger and newly experienced orgasm as it washed over his senses, nearly stealing his ability to realize the second when that pleasure had turned to fear.

As the waves of sensations eased inside her, the stiffening of her body hadn't registered at first. It had taken several long moments for Rule to gather his control around him and ease back from her.

And now, nearly thirty minutes later, he wondered if perhaps he should have stayed after she ordered him to leave.

As Dog straightened from his position, his eyes narrowed, flicking to the apartment upstairs thoughtfully, before he shook his head and led the way to the Dragoon. Rule slid into the passenger seat, propping his arm on the window frame as he stared pensively into the darkness while the Coyote pulled back onto the street and headed out of town.

He ran his tongue over his teeth again, just to be certain. He had a hard-on raging in his jeans that pounded in lust, but no true signs of Mating Heat.

"Cigar?" Dog extended the pack of thin cigars to him, his tone only mildly curious.

Rule accepted the cigar, then the pack of old-fashioned matches the Coyote carried.

Inhaling the sweet burn of the tobacco, Rule let the specially blended essence seep into his senses as the Coyote lit his own.

The window beside him eased down marginally to allow the exhaled smoke to escape as the Dragoon made its way through the streets of Window Rock at a legal speed.

Inhaling another draw of the cigar, Rule forced his senses to calm, his body to ease, but the hard-on straining his zipper refused to soften or relax in any way.

Damn, it had been all he could do to pull back from her. The need to strip the clothes from her exquisite little body had been almost more than he could control. He wanted to bury his cock inside the slick, hot little channel that beckoned him so bad it was like a fever inside him.

God help them both if it was Mating Heat, because he wouldn't, he couldn't allow it.

"I don't smell the Heat, just your arousal. And perhaps her release?" There was an edge of amusement to the Coyote's tone at the last observation.

"That would be none of your business, Dog," Rule assured him before bringing the cigar to his lips once again and inhaling.

"A mating, or her release? You may have to clarify which you would want my opinion on," Dog informed him with his normal sarcastic humor.

Rule turned his head and simply stared at him, knowing the other Breed and his propensity to create chaos wherever possible. Especially within the lives of those he claimed as friends.

"Ah, the release part." He nodded, though the smile that tugged at his lips assured Rule that didn't mean he would keep his observations to himself. "Still, there's no scent of Mating Heat."

Rule restrained a sigh of relief.

"I've often wondered, though," Dog continued just when Rule was beginning to hope the Breed wasn't in a troublemaking frame of mind.

"What exactly have you wondered, Dog?" he asked, enjoying the bite of the cigar again and preparing himself to hold back his temper. It was hard telling what would pop out of that Breed's mouth.

"Why you're so damned skittish about Mating Heat? Most Breeds bitch about it, joke about it and secretly long for it. You, on the other hand, are more than serious about running in the opposite direction should you encounter it. Why?"

Why?

Rule knew why. Just as he knew he wasn't in the mood to discuss it.

"If you don't smell the scent of Mating Heat, then don't worry about it," he warned the other Breed.

"Should I worry about it if I sense Mating Heat?" Dog asked then, though the humor in his tone had scaled back immensely.

Should another Breed worry about it?

"Only if you want to die," Rule warned him.

A chuckle whispered through the vehicle as Dog turned it toward the hotel after pulling away from town.

"You know, several Breed scientists theorize that if a mating isn't complete, then should the Breed part of the equation remove themselves from the mate's vicinity, it's possible that another Breed could come in and complete the bond. Especially if the substitute Breed is a blood relation of the true mate."

Rule remained silent. He'd heard that; Jonas had explained it to him in great detail actually when they'd feared that Rule's brother, Lawe, would deny the heat between him and his mate, Diane Broen.

Lawe had always felt his mate shouldn't be another Breed, or a warrior of any kind. He'd always felt a mate weaker than himself was what he needed. One who would be content to be protected within the confines of Sanctuary while Lawe stepped into a less dangerous role of security enforcement.

Instead, Lawe's mate should have been a Breed. She was a warrioress who commanded her own team of men and did so with exceptional ability.

"It's just a thought," Dog said then.

Rule turned back to the Coyote slowly, his gaze narrowing. "What's just a thought? If there's no scent of Mating Heat, then there's nothing to worry about."

"True." The Breed nodded.

Besides, Lawe had already given Rule his opinion of trading mates when Rule first saw Gypsy, first feared that she would be his mate.

He had his mate, and one he was well satisfied with. A mate strong enough to fight by his side rather than being content to hide behind the walls of Sanctuary, the feline Breed compound.

"We are now at Condition Beta. I repeat, Condition Beta." The radio crackled with the security protocols as the call came through from base over the vehicle's speakers.

Rule reached out and activated the two-way link.

"Commander Breaker responding to Condition Beta," Rule snapped into the link as Dog hit the gas, the Dragoon hitting top speed in seconds and racing through the night to the hotel.

"Commander Breaker, Director Wyatt requests immediate Blue Protocols be enacted. I repeat, enact Blue Protocols immediately."

He pulled the communications earbud he carried at all times from the small holster on his belt and clipped it to his ear. Activating the link, he waited for the beep that indicated secure status before identifying himself and giving the day's authorization code. "We have Condition Blue. I repeat, Condition Blue. Enact all security protocols. Director Wyatt has authorization until I'm on site."

Liza Johnson and Claire Martinez, were in danger again. The two women were too important to the Breeds to chance losing. They were too important to Jonas Wyatt to even consider allowing them to be in danger.

Twelve years before, Liza Johnson and Claire Martinez had been Honor Roberts and Fawn Corrigan, two test studies of one of the most important research projects that Brandenmore Research, a very well-hidden part of the Genetics Council's labs, had ever attempted. A project that created the drug now threatening Amber's life.

◆　◆　◆

Spinning into the back lot of the hotel, Dog brought the Dragoon to a jerking stop before Rule threw open the door and raced out to the enforcer running toward him.

"We had two six-man teams rush Liza and Claire's security force just after leaving the hotel for transport to safe houses. Backup arrived in time to secure their safety, but these bastards were good, Commander. Too damned good," Flint McCain reported as he met them at the back entrance, his expression savage. "Liza's secure with Enforcer Black and Miss Martinez is currently secured in Director Wyatt's suite. Blue Protocols are in force, but complete lockdown is impossible at this point."

There were simply too many guests in the hotel who weren't Breeds.

"Have we identified the teams?" Rule barked out. "Scent markers, any identifying DNA left?"

"Nothing. They struck, made an attempt to gain access to the Dragoons, then before we could get backup into place, they were gone. They didn't breech the Dragoons, but if backup hadn't been there . . ." Flint broke off, the message clear as they rushed into the hotel. "They left nothing to identify them, and we suspect scent markers were blocked."

"Get a crime scene unit at the site and on those Dragoons," Rule barked out. "And get me someone up here with a deeper sense of smell. They had to have left something to identify them, and I want it found. Now."

There was no such thing as no evidence, or no proof of identity. There was simply the inability or unwillingness to detect it. "Director Wyatt is reporting that Miss Johnson may have remembered something." Flint lowered his voice as they entered the elevator and headed for the top floor. "He wants you with him now."

Rule's jaw clenched. If Liza was remembering something more, then hopefully Claire wouldn't be long behind her. That meant the danger would only increase.

It was time to suggest removing both women from the area and completely out of sight rather than securing them in town, before the Genetics Council or, worse yet, the two women's former protector and now their would-be executioner, Gideon, managed to get to them.

If either party caught up with them, their lives wouldn't be worth shit and the Bureau would have no chance in hell of saving them, or Amber.

And that, they definitely couldn't allow to happen.

◆   ◆   ◆

Gypsy moved into the darkness, her hands pushed into the pockets of her denim jacket to ward off the chill of the desert as she stepped away from her Jeep and entered the abandoned garage on the edge of town.

The call had come through before the vehicle that arrived to pick up

Rule had managed to pull from the parking lot. The voice on the other end of the line had requested a meeting at the garage immediately.

"I'm here," she stated, coming to a stop in the middle of the garage bay she'd entered and staring around curiously.

"You always come when we call, don't you, Gypsy?" the voice reflected quietly. "You've never denied us, nor have you ever betrayed us."

She shrugged, a bit uncomfortable with this sudden reflection rather than the arrogance she was used to. "I came to you and offered my help, you didn't ask me for it."

"No, we didn't," the voice agreed, causing her to stare intently at the shadow as it shifted just slightly. "You didn't have to give your life, though. Just as we never expected Mark to give his."

For a single, brutal moment she was fifteen again, watching in horror, in agony, as the razor-sharp edge of that knife sliced across her brother's throat.

"Gypsy?" The dark voice pulled her back as he spoke gently. "This isn't what he would have wanted. He would never have asked this of you."

What the hell was the point of this meeting? Was she somehow being fired from a volunteer position?

How had she managed to mess this up?

"Do you not need my help any longer?" There was a curious sense of regret at the thought, at the loss she felt coming. Who would she be if she wasn't Whisper? She was no one's daughter, no one's sister; she could be someone's lover, but the risk would destroy her. What would that leave her?

"Your help has always been invaluable," he finally breathed out roughly. "But I would never want you to compromise your dreams, or your own life, for that help. I want you to understand that. Your brother was my friend, Gypsy. A good friend. And I know his dreams for you had nothing to do with the risks you take for us."

Gypsy shrugged again, telling herself she had to be wrong. "Is there something you need that you think will compromise that?"

"It's possible," he stated as she restrained a sudden, relieved cry. "You left the bar with Breaker and took him to your apartment. You've never done that. Is there a bond between the two of you that I should know about?"

"Are you asking if he was in my bed?" she frowned. "No, I haven't had sex with him, nor have I forgotten the conditions of working with you."

"Should a bond with this Breed develop, know that should you need to pull back in your work with us, we'll understand. But at no time would I ever be able to overlook it if you revealed your past work with us. Do you understand me?"

"I understand." Her fingers curled into fists at the remembered need to do just that. To end the lie she lived with just one person she could trust.

"Just before Commander Breaker left your apartment earlier, Liza Johnson and Claire Martinez were attacked on their way back to the safe house they've been assigned. They're fine, but already we're receiving transmissions among the Breeds that indicate she and Claire may be moved to a more secure and secret location. If this happens, then we need to know that location."

Just like they needed to know the information the Breeds had on them? Something she still hadn't managed to find, nor had she even managed to learn whether it actually existed.

"Rule doesn't seem like a man who tells his secrets to anyone, let alone potential lovers," she stated, her fingers curling into fists in her jacket pocket as she felt the fine threads of the spiderweb she lived within slowly tightening on her.

"Whatever you hear, see or perceive will be of the utmost importance to us," he told her. "We need Liza and Claire safe, but the Breeds have enemies even within their own ranks. I don't trust them to ensure Liza and Claire's safety."

"Are you going to attempt to take them yourselves?" she asked. "Liza Johnson's Breed fiancé would object to that, I'm certain."

"No doubt." Regret shadowed the voice. "But time is becoming of the essence. Should we take that route, though, we'll be certain to let you know the matter has been accomplished."

Gypsy nodded, though her stomach was twisting with the knowledge that she could be pulled straight into the middle of a battle between the Unknown and the Breeds. That wasn't a position she wanted to be in and one where she was terribly afraid she would end up.

The next days were a whirlwind of activity as Gypsy's mother pulled her into the preparations for the upcoming Navajo "Welcome to the Breed Community" Ball.

The dress was ready, but hair, nails and accessories had to be taken care of. There were meetings with the reporters they worked with, and long hours of discussions over what would appear in the Nation's press releases as well as the articles that would go out nationally and internationally.

Nothing the Breeds did remained local, in any way.

It was a relief when the day of the ball actually arrived. A week and she hadn't seen Rule, hadn't even glimpsed him, though she'd been told many times how he watched the doors of the bars he and his enforcers moved in, as though looking for her.

And how no matter the woman who attempted to gain his interest, none of them succeeded. They were gently rebuffed or distracted by Dane or one of the other enforcers.

There was also the knowledge that she might well be addicted to his touch too. Because each night her skin actually seemed to ache, to chill, and she missed feeling his warmth against her. She ached for his kiss, and no matter how many of those damned chocolate and peppermint hard candies she ate, she couldn't erase the need for his kiss.

Or the need for so much more.

As she dressed for the ball, a band seemed to tighten around her chest, a feeling of such loss overwhelming her as she realized she wouldn't be able to stay out of his bed if he offered again. And she knew he would offer.

The need riding her was too great, and Gypsy knew she wasn't strong enough to hold out against another erotic onslaught from the Breed who was becoming far too important to her in too many ways.

"I'm sorry, Mark," she whispered as she stood in her bedroom, dressed, her hair perfectly arranged, knowing that once again she'd betrayed him. "I don't know how to stay away from him."

Would her brother have been angry?

She closed her eyes, remembering his smile, his laughter—

"It's not in you not to love, Gypsy. I raised you better than that." The memory of the conversation that had come on the heels of yet another forgotten birthday by her parents surprised her.

"I don't need their stupid old presents or their happy birthdays." She *shrugged, her arms crossed tight over her aching chest. "They don't matter to me. No one matters but you."* She *looked into his somber eyes. "You never forget my birthdays, do you, Mark?"*

His smile was incredibly gentle. "And I'll never forget one of them," he *promised. "How could I forget the day my favorite girl started screaming like someone was killing her when she heard my voice?"*

He'd told her that story so many times.

"But I shut up when you held me." She *finished it for him with a smile.*

The hug he gave her had eased the hurt, as had the cake and the surprise pizza party in town with several of her friends from school.

But her parents hadn't been there. Her sister hadn't been there. They'd been in California on another business trip. Mark had refused to go, but Gypsy hadn't been invited.

He wouldn't have blamed her, she thought. But he wouldn't have blamed her for his death either.

"What do I do?" she whispered into the silence of the bedroom. "What do I do with my life now, Mark?"

Because she knew, once she let Rule take her to his bed, Mark would really be gone in ways he hadn't been in the past nine years. And despite the aching regret, the pain, she knew it was inevitable.

Rule Breaker. The name said it all. Because he was making her break the rules she had lived by. Forcing her to realize she was more than just Mark's sister.

And that was something she had never wanted to do.

◆　　◆　　◆

Listening to the lost, pain-filled voice through the audio device Jonas had placed in her room, Rule lowered his head and rubbed at the bridge of his nose in frustration.

Dammit, he should be there with her. Holding her.

Behind him, Jonas was quiet as well, and Rule swore he could feel the emanations of the director's regret.

"We've had that fucking bug in her room for a week now, Jonas," he growled, still furious that it had been placed there without his knowledge. "If she were meeting with anyone there, we would know it."

The director was becoming more calculating, he thought. The device had been in place for two days before he'd gotten around to telling Rule about it. Not that Jonas told him everything, but this he would have expected to know about.

"I still remember that night," Jonas sighed behind him. "She didn't cry. I don't think she's ever cried, because each time she's in my presence I swear I can feel those tears ripping her apart."

No, she hadn't. And Rule felt it himself, just as he'd felt the pressure inside her increasing later.

"Then stop this fucking investigation," he snarled, pushing the desk chair back with heavy force as he came to his feet. "Leave her the fuck alone."

He faced the other Breed as he rounded on him, watching the silver mercury in Jonas's eyes swirl like storm clouds boiling on the horizon.

"I don't smell Mating Heat," Jonas stated casually.

"What, one of your schemes not working so well this time, Mate Matcher?" he accused furiously.

"My schemes always work, Rule, one way or the other. You should know that by now. The question here is, am I scheming?" Jonas pointed out without so much as a hint of arrogance. He was pure confidence instead. That was what pissed off his enforcers the most.

"You're always scheming," he growled, pacing to the bar for a drink, all too aware of the silent presence of his brother Lawe and Lawe's mate, Diane.

"That's enough, Jonas," Lawe spoke up.

Rule flicked his brother a look of false amusement as anger pounded at his temples. "Still trying to protect me, big brother?"

"No more than you still try to protect me, little brother," Lawe answered quietly.

Rule tossed back the drink before setting the glass carefully on the bar and staring back at Jonas with narrowed eyes.

The director stood in front of the windows again. He liked to dare the bastards if they got a chance to actually take a shot, he'd once claimed. That hadn't changed with his mating, only his security protocols had changed.

They'd heightened.

Dressed in black slacks, a white long-sleeved shirt, sleeves rolled to his elbows, his feet encased in specially made black dress shoes that would probably outkick any combat boot, he was the epitome of sophisticated style.

Hell, he'd come out of the labs he was created in with that same bearing, that same look in his eyes.

"Have it removed," Rule told him quietly. "Or I'll remove it for you."

A black brow arched imperiously. "Really?"

Rule didn't change his stance. He didn't tense; by God, he'd known what he was going to do the minute he'd heard the pain trembling in Gypsy's voice.

"I took the position of division director," he reminded Jonas. "We signed the agreement and the bylaws, and you don't have the power to continue anything that I decide has no merit."

Jonas's gaze flickered. "You'd sacrifice Amber for a woman who's not even your mate?"

"Goddammit, Jonas, she doesn't have what you want," Rule snarled, enraged.

It was the pain in her voice. That ragged self-loathing and bitter regret was killing him.

"She's the contact we're looking for and you know it." Still, the director's tone was quiet, without heat, without anger. As though he were simply pointing out a particular piece of information.

"Not anymore, she isn't. If she ever was," Rule growled.

He'd taken her out of it when he'd left her apartment the week before. He'd called her fucking contact and made his wishes clear. Gypsy was out, starting now. Hell, he should never have agreed to allow her in it to begin with.

Jonas nodded slowly. "Probably for the best." He surprised Rule with the comment. "She wasn't cut out for it."

"And what makes you think that?" This time, his arms went over his chest powerfully, aggression surging through him.

She was the best damned contact the Unknown had. The only one that no one had been able to identify.

"She refuses to use her friends," Jonas revealed with a shrug. "Both Rachel and I, as well as Ashley and Emma, have dropped several pieces of particularly useful information in an attempt to ascertain if she was indeed the contact. That information was never acted upon. Good spies understand the fact that friends are their best contacts."

Not Gypsy, Rule thought wearily as he dropped his arms. Her friends, the few she claimed, were sacred to her. After all, she hadn't had family since the night she had stood in the dark: cold, hurt, aching to be held only to have her parents turn to the child they had lost instead.

They'd never understood that they may have lost a son, but Gypsy had, at the very essence of her soul, lost her father.

"Let her go, Jonas," he repeated, though the demand lacked the anger of moments before. "You know her as well as I do. If she had what you needed, you would have had it long before now. Hell, you wouldn't have had to come here to get it. She would have contacted you."

Silver mercury. Jonas's eyes seemed to swirl, to storm within as he stared back at Rule.

"We'll see," he finally murmured. "We'll see."

◆   ◆   ◆

The limo Gypsy rode in to the Breed ball with her parents was one of the most opulent she had ever seen. The leather was so fine, each stitch detailed, the scent of it luxurious.

It was almost, just almost enough to make up for the fact that she'd had very little time to prepare for this ball. At least she had a gown, even if it was meant for another event.

Layers of soft, delicate blue and green chiffon brought to mind emeralds and a sun-kissed sea as they shifted across each other. Each layer of the material was sewn together to blend and shift the colors as she moved, bringing attention to not just the delicacy of her figure, but also the dress itself.

Strapless, the delicate, hand-embroidered chiffon and lace cupped her breasts perfectly within the V-shaped bodice and revealed a tantalizing amount of cleavage.

Layers upon layers of chiffon fell from beneath the bodice like a waterfall of exquisite material as the slit that ran the length of her leg to her thigh teased with hints of soft flesh and emerald-threaded silk stockings, while a sixteen-inch train followed behind her. The front hem was the perfect length to cover the tips of her pale green heels, yet not long enough to trip her should she forget and let the toe of her shoe trap it.

She wore her mother's emerald, sapphire and diamond necklace, the tiny jewels gleaming against her sun-kissed skin like tiny brilliant stars. Sapphire and diamond posts glittered at her earlobes, while the emerald tennis bracelet emphasized and drew attention to the sapphire and diamond ring she wore on her right hand.

The jewelry emphasized rather than overwhelmed the gown, while her lightly tanned skin glowed from the colors laid against it. Her green eyes appeared darker, the addition of shadowed, muted colors of her makeup about them giving her a sultry, mysterious look while the glossy light bronze lipstick drew the eye to the soft pout of her lips.

Her long dark hair was pulled back from her face, the sides held at the top of her head with a diamond-studded comb while tiny individual sapphire, emerald and diamond clips, barely larger than half the size of the head of an eraser, were secured in the waves.

Greta McQuade wore far different colors than her daughter. The bronze A-line chiffon and tulle gown had rich amber embroidered lace shoulders and bodice that covered her from her breasts to her still-trim hips. Bronze and amber chiffon fell to her matching bronze heels in the front while a short train trailed behind her. Amber teardrops dripped at her ears, while a matching amber gem fell to point just between the tops of her breasts and amber pins secured the shoulder-length waves of her hair into a neat twist atop her head.

Her father's black tuxedo was the perfect foil for both his wife and daughter, he'd proclaimed before leaving the house, still despairing over the fact that Gypsy hadn't invited a guest to accompany her.

She'd almost thought that perhaps Rule would invite her to attend with him. When she hadn't heard from him after asking him to leave that night, a week before, she'd felt strangely disappointed and more than a little hurt.

The limo drew up to the crowded hotel entrance, waiting as the chauffeur opened the door and several couples exited. She recognized the tall, darkly handsome Dash Sinclair and his wife, Elizabeth, Cassie's parents. Reaching in after helping his wife from the limo, Dash then drew his ethereally beautiful daughter from the car.

Cameras flashed with an explosion of light as the Sinclairs moved to the hotel entrance and journalists called out for pictures.

There was a brief pause as the small family allowed a few shots before moving inside the hotel. Behind them, the Wolf Breed alpha, Wolfe Gunnar, and his wife, Hope, exited the same limo. The couple paused several times for pictures; the tall, muscular Wolf Breed held his petite wife to his side, unsmiling but not unfriendly.

Mingling along the entrance, Breed Enforcers in their dress uniforms stood alongside many of the more popular faces from the Breed society.

Tanner Reynolds and his wife, Scheme. They were the PR team that had used their charm and natural ability to draw support to pressure several nations into paying handsomely for the fact that many of their government leaders were found to be participating further with the Genetics Council.

Pulling the car to a stop, their chauffeur moved quickly from the front of the car and within seconds was opening the door for her father.

Hansel McQuade reached in and helped his wife from the car, and Gypsy was incredibly pleased to see Jonas Wyatt stepping to them, shaking hands with her father as cameras flashed in a kaleidoscope of light.

Then a hand reached inside to help her exit onto the red carpet.

It wasn't her father.

She knew that hand.

Intimately.

Gripping it, Gypsy met Rule's burning gaze as she stepped from the limo, not even caring if a single flash caught the shift of color she'd designed her gown to have if such a thing happened.

Her heart was suddenly racing, her breathing tight and restricted as her flesh tingled at the nearness of his hard, heated flesh.

"Miss McQuade," he murmured as he drew her to his side. "I trust you've been well since I saw you last?"

"Quite well," she assured him, staring up at him from beneath her lashes as he drew her along the walk. "And you?"

His head lowered, his lips touching her ear. "Hard."

Gypsy, who never blushed, felt a flush of heat warming her face as pleasure tightened her womb and her pussy wept, aching for his touch again.

Light exploded around them at that moment, as it seemed every cameraman there wanted a shot of the tall, imposing Breed whispering into the ear of the unknown female on his arm.

Ignoring the questions hurled at them, Rule drew her to the hotel's entrance and into the lobby behind her parents. Three sets of wide double doors were thrown open to the main ballroom at the top of the wide curving staircase.

They didn't leave the journalists outside, though. Gypsy felt a glow of satisfaction at the sight of several cameramen taking notice of her parents with Jonas Wyatt and his fiancée, Rachel, as they stopped outside the ballroom to chat.

This was what her parents needed. As much as they loved the candy and gift shop they'd given their younger daughter to run, it was the image consulting business they dreamed of making a success.

"Isn't your sister attending?" Rule asked as he drew her to a stop several feet from the small group.

"She's arriving with a date," she told him quietly. "There's a Breed who's been hanging around the store who invited her several weeks ago. She hadn't even told us."

Kandy was keeping her relationship with the Breed quiet until she'd learned her parents were attending the same ball she had been invited to attend. Funny, but Greta hadn't displayed the same disapproval toward her younger daughter as she had Gypsy.

"They're still seeing each other?" he asked her curiously.

"Loki?" Her lips twitched at the name. "Considering Navajo history, I would have thought she would know better."

Thankfully, her sister wasn't so easy to fool. Just because her father had named her Kandy Sweet didn't mean she tried in any way whatsoever to live up to that name.

"Miss McQuade." Jonas surprised her when he turned to her. "If you'd join us, I'd like to introduce you to one of the Breeds' greatest assets, Cassa, and her husband, Cabal St. Laurents."

"I've followed many of your stories, Mrs. St. Laurents." Gypsy shook her hand, pleased by the firmness of her grip.

"Thank you." Cassa smiled back at her as she looped her arm over her husband's elbow. "It's nice to see Rule looking like the arm candy he should be rather than glowering at the other mates for enjoying the position."

The Bengal at her side muttered something as Gypsy held back the frown that would have pulled at her brows. She sure as hell didn't want one of those popping cameras to catch a frown on her face.

"Oh." Cassa's eyes widened. "Sorry, dear, the mate reference just slipped out." She smiled at Gypsy again, a friendly, warm smile. "Rather like referring to one as a date."

Gypsy's lips twitched. Even *she* knew better than that, but she allowed the reference to slide.

"I hear your parents have accepted the contract Jonas offered for their services," Cassa remarked then. "I've been telling him for a while now that image consulting begins at the individual level, but he never seemed overly fond of the idea."

"You have good ideas sometimes, Cassa," Jonas drawled mockingly. "It's just so very rare that they're compatible with Breed Law."

Now Breed Law, she definitely knew about—the laws that governed every legal or contractual, criminal or enterprise endeavor involving any Breed, or Breed affiliate, including but not limited to wives, children, siblings, parents, lovers or intended spouses, and how the government had to deal with them. More than a century of detailed horrific experiments backed up by recordings of some of the most vile acts humanity could commit had ensured that nearly every government that had been sued by the Breeds at the onset of their discovery had been willing to pay up rather than face the combined individual lawsuits that would have been brought against them in international court.

Cassa rolled her eyes at Jonas's remark as they stepped into the ballroom entrance and began moving down the wide staircase.

The alphas of each community stood at the bottom of the stairs along with the president of the Navajo Nation, Raymond Martinez.

Gypsy had never personally cared for Ray Martinez, though along with everyone else, she adored his father, Orrin, and brother, Terran.

Accepting the elbow Rule held out to her, she descended the stairs along with him, aware of the flashing bulbs and the knowledge that by offering his arm to her, Rule Breaker, considered one of the most eligible Breed bachelors, had ensured that her picture, as well as that of her parents and their reason for being there, was splashed across every society page known to man.

This was more than she could have hoped for where her parents were concerned. But she also acknowledged that it would begin making it much more difficult for her to collect the information the Unknown depended on her to collect. She was the neutral party, so certain individuals hadn't cared to brag about strikes being planned against the Breeds by the groups determined to destroy them. Just as she had been told of Breeds in hiding, trying to escape or to find a place to rest before traveling farther. Usually, the information she received was of Breeds traveling through the area looking for work that wouldn't require an ID. Many wanted to stay under the radar of humans and Breeds alike. Those Breeds, the Unknown were well equipped to help.

As they grew closer to the line of the alphas and their wives and the president and Mrs. Martinez, the president's chief of staff moved to him, whispering something in his ear.

Gypsy watched as he listened attentively before making his excuses and moving away.

"Is everything okay?" she asked Rule, knowing that the almost invisible little earbud communicator he wore would ensure that he knew every little detail of every little thing going on.

He nodded easily enough, but she could see the look on his face as Ray and Maria moved from the ballroom.

"Is Claire here tonight? Or Liza?" She hadn't seen either girl for weeks and realized she'd missed their steady, friendly presence as she met up with them a few nights a week.

"Jonas and Stygian didn't want to risk their safety for a party." He shook his head. "They're secure for now."

"Are they allowed visitors?" She needed to see them, to reassure the Unknown they were indeed fine and content with their security.

He glanced down at her. "The three of you are good friends, aren't you?" he said softly.

"I like to think we are," she replied. "I've missed them."

"I'll discuss it with Jonas later," he promised, and then the formal introductions to the alphas were made.

Callan Lyons and his wife, Merinus, seemed more relaxed and at ease than Wolfe and Hope Gunnar, while Dash, Elizabeth, and Cassie Sinclair gave the appearance of indulged amusement at the pomp and ceremony the Navajo Council had insisted on.

Well, not the Council, she'd heard. One of the president's aides had informed her the night before that it was Ray Martinez who insisted on pretending he had the same bearing and presence of any foreign dignitary. But then, Ray had always thought himself far better than others in the same social class as himself.

Shay Anderson, Raymond Martinez's presidential aide, and a close friend of Gypsy's, had stopped by the apartment before Gypsy had left for the evening, furious at some of the president's comments where the Breeds and tribal chiefs were concerned. Those comments nagged at Gypsy. Bothered her for some reason she couldn't put her finger on.

"So, have I made up for Jonas forcing you to wear your special dress?" he leaned closer as he asked the question, a hint of laughter in the rough voice.

Gypsy flushed at the reminder of her comments regarding the ball and how it interfered with her plans for the one she'd had her dress designed for. "I owe you an apology for that." She sighed as he took flutes of champagne from a passing waiter. "I didn't mean anything offensive. Rightfully so, whenever the Breeds are present, attention focuses on them. It's just that my parents have worked so hard to draw attention to their image consulting firm—"

"Enough, sweetheart." The grin that curled his lips was far too sexy. "According to Callan's sister, Dawn Lawrence, it was indeed a sacrifice you were making."

Her eyes widened in horror. "You told her what happened?"

She had actually met Dawn Lawrence several times when she'd traveled to Window Rock with her husband, Seth. Dawn was quiet and amazingly astute and possessed such a dry wit that she and Gypsy had gotten along wonderfully during the two hours the other woman had spent in the candy shop.

"Not hardly, she would have hit me with something," he snorted. "I merely proposed a hypothetical situation and she looked at me as though I were to be pitied while informing me of what a colossal ass a man would be to allow such a thing to happen."

Yeah, she could see Dawn telling him exactly that.

"I was angry with you," she informed him. "You can be amazingly arrogant, Mr. Breaker."

And so very wickedly sexy.

She hadn't been able to forget his touch, or the pleasure she'd found in it. That didn't mean she wasn't very well aware of the decision she would be making by becoming his lover.

She was twenty-four years old, and in the years since she'd caused her brother's death and made her bargain with the Unknown, she'd never desired a man more than she desired atoning for the life she'd helped those Coyotes to take.

Each time she'd considered taking a lover, guilt had swept over her. If the Unknown learned of it, she would be forced out of the small circle her brother had been a part of. She would no longer be able to continue his dream to help ensure the Breeds' survival.

And if she wasn't there, picking up the information it seemed others missed, then there was every chance it would result in a death somewhere, somehow, because she had once again cared more for herself than for those at risk.

If she ignored the need burning inside her any further, though, then it might well destroy her anyway. It was like a flame she couldn't extinguish. A hunger she couldn't ease. And she knew—to the depths of her soul, she knew—that she wouldn't be able to deny him tonight.

For the past week her need for him had taken on a life of its own. A craving she couldn't seem to shake for the taste of his kiss, the touch of his hands. At times, she could actually feel her womb tightening, tensing with the need to find release from his touch again. And no matter how often she'd tried to masturbate, suddenly the touch of her own fingers was completely ineffective.

Rule turned her on to the point that her body hadn't stopped burning since the second she had laid eyes on him two months before.

Finishing the champagne, Gypsy set her empty glass on a nearby tray, watching as Rule talked to his brother and Diane.

Diane stared back at her with a twinkle of amusement in her gaze as they waited.

"One of these days, I'm going to buy one of those nifty little hearing aids that amplify conversations around me," Gypsy remarked, her voice low, though she knew Rule would still hear every word. "I'm simply too nosy."

Diane gave a low, light laugh. "You learn how to wait patiently while they're together."

Gypsy's brow lifted dubiously. Wait patiently?

"Oh, I rather doubt I'd learn that fine art," she commented. "Unless I knew my curiosity would be appeased later, that is."

"There's always the chance," Diane assured her as her fiancé winked back at her, then turned back to Gypsy, her expression filled with warm amusement. "So, are you looking forward to actually pushing that particularly growling Lion into society? I think I'd be intimidated."

"Intimidated, no. Certain it will work?" Gypsy laughed. "I have a feeling he'll actually own the Navajo Nation once he's finished. Though, trust me, my parents are looking forward to it as well," Gypsy assured her. "Dad's been attempting to gain the notice of the Ruling Cabinet for years with his alternative methods of image and social marketing."

"It's something that certainly won't hurt. And I must say"—Diane stared around the brightly lit extravagance of the ballroom—"being spoiled in such a manner once in a while is rather nice."

"Then I'm sure you'll enjoy the social side of the process that Mom and Dad have planned," Gypsy assured her. "The plan Dad's putting together for you and your fiancé is one of his best. I think you'll approve."

Diane's brows lifted. "Shouldn't Lawe be the one to approve it?"

Gypsy tilted her head and regarded the other woman seriously. "In most cases, men leave social organization to either their secretaries, their lovers or their wives. I've never seen and rarely heard of a man who enjoyed making certain his own social schedule worked with the image he needed to present. In most cases, they're neither aware nor do they care which party they attend, as long it's a business opportunity. It's their wives who know to cultivate friends among business associates, and to ensure those that are cultivated are a general match to the lifestyle and interests they share as well."

Diane watched her closely then. "And for Rule, how will you cultivate his image with no wife or lover to help him choose the friends and business associates that match the life he leads outside the office? Or the life he wants to lead?"

"There's a process," Gypsy assured her before briefly explaining the observation and evaluation process before a detailed social agenda was proposed.

"Very interesting." Diane nodded before turning back to her fiancé, as he now stood at her side.

He and Rule had abandoned whatever they were discussing once she and Diane had begun discussing social agendas, interests and some males' unwillingness to pay close enough attention to the friends they were developing from among their social set. Those were the clients McQuade Image Consulting wanted.

The businessman who had built himself from his toes up and did so with exacting precision and instinctive force would be wasting his money unless he was looking to suddenly change his entire business model.

"It sounds like a wife," Lawe drawled, his blue eyes twinkling as he looked between her and Rule. "Have you actually worked with many men who needed such help?"

"Normally, the client has a wife or girlfriend with some knowledge of the business associates whose goals match his," she told him. "It's a rare opportunity to be able to work with men as successful in your fields as you are, who haven't yet begun acquiring the footholds you want socially. I believe you and Diane especially will enjoy the program my parents have come up with."

"And what about Rule?" Lawe nodded to his silent brother. "Matching him with like-minded family men won't be easy."

"Matching Rule with men who share his interests as well his vocation will be far easier than you think," she assured him.

"And women?" Diane asked, her brows lifting. "I know socially, an advantageous marriage is usually important."

Why did she suddenly ache? She shouldn't care if he would consider a marriage that would suit his position and the life he wanted to build.

"As I've seen, Breeds are generally pretty adept at choosing women who suit them and their lives exactly," she finally answered, hoping she had managed to hide the hurt that filled her. "I trust Rule can do the same."

"Finally, someone with at least a little confidence in my ability to choose something," Rule snorted as his arm went around her waist to draw her to his side. "Now, the band's starting to play. I want a dance. You can tell me if my dance moves are adequate or if they need some work too."

She doubted very seriously that anything about Rule Breaker needed any work. But she let him draw her to the dance floor and assured herself that the continued ache in her chest had nothing to do with the earlier conversation or the implications of it.

◆　◆　◆

"Well?" Diane demanded as the couple moved far enough away from them that there wasn't a chance Rule could hear their conversation.

Lawe liked that about her. She understood he wasn't just hers, that he was Rule's brother, Jonas's friend. That he was an enforcer as well as a role model to the newly freed Breeds. There was never any jealousy in her as he'd often scented from the wives of the human males he'd met over the years.

She encouraged his friendships, pushed him to have hobbies and often chided him for not resting enough.

And he was delaying answering her and he knew it.

"I'll be damned if it makes sense." He shook his head, careful to keep his voice low as he spoke.

"What doesn't make sense?" she asked, frowning back at Rule and Gypsy. "At first thought, there's not a chance they would suit each other. A good-time party girl? Who knew she was such an excellent social image developer?"

"She's not his mate," Lawe stated softly, sadly even.

Diane stilled, then turned back to him in shock. "Are you certain?"

Lawe continued to watch his brother and the woman resting in his arms as they swayed to the music.

"She carries his scent," he frowned, trying to make sense of it. "But it could be because they're lovers, nothing more. There are no similar scents of lust. With mates, there's a scent they share, whether its lust, love or some other emotion that develops into love. They don't share it."

Diane turned back and watched the couple as well. "If she's not in love with him, then she's falling."

Was she? There was definitely something there, but Lawe couldn't make sense of what it was.

He'd drawn their scents in countless times, and each time he'd done so he'd sworn he'd sensed Rule's senses drawing further away from him. As though the animal part of him were hiding.

But why do that? What would it serve Rule or his senses to weaken themselves in such a way? What could be so important that the animal felt the need to hide it?

A sudden suspicion slipped into his mind, causing his eyes to widen.

"What?" His lovely mate turned back to him, frowning as she stared up at him. "You've thought of something?"

He shook his head slowly. Son of a bitch, why hadn't he figured it out sooner? "I know my brother."

"Meaning?"

She knew him, his lovely mate, and she knew how it bothered him when he'd felt Rule drawing so far away from him when they'd first arrived in Window Rock, and then especially so when Rule had offered to trade mates with him, when there was no mating scent on him.

"She has a very subtle, barely there, unique scent that I can't place. Rule's senses are suddenly shuttered, as though the animal part of his genetics is hiding from me. Or perhaps from any Breed senses, period."

"I'm getting impatient, Lawe." She sighed and he had to grin. She was dying to know if Gypsy McQuade was Rule's mate.

"She's his mate, but he's not mating her," he explained, wanting to laugh at the chances that Rule's animal could actually act in a manner so separate from the man it inhabited.

"You're not making sense." She shook her head.

"Rule's determined he'll never risk a woman as Elder risked our mother," he explained, sobering at the thought of Morningstar Martinez's horrific death. "The thought of ever facing even the chance of losing someone so important as a mate has him stubbornly determined to ensure that if he ever senses her, he has the option of running as fast and as far from her as possible."

"I know all this, Lawe," she drawled. "Get to the punch line already."

"The punch line?" He wrapped his arms around her, drawing her to his chest as he danced her onto the dance floor, carefully staying clear of Rule as he spoke. "Rule's animal senses his mate. The animal is determined to possess her, to own her heart, but knows that should Rule consciously realize what she is to him, he's going to run."

"So basically, the animal, or his subconscious instincts, is hiding the fact that she's his mate?" she asked, disbelief coloring her voice.

"Exactly." It was simply all he could do not to laugh at the position his brother had managed to find himself in. "No one can convince Rule she's his mate, because the animal is holding the mating back until there's no way Rule can run from her. Only then, only when he has no other choice, will his animal instincts snap back into place and initiate the Mating Heat."

"Mind over matter," she breathed out, shocked far deeper than Lawe himself was.

"Pure stubborn will," Lawe amended, stroking his hand down his mate's back, feeling the heat, the warmth of her, and knowing that if he lost her, he'd follow her as soon as he sought vengeance for her.

There was no way he would be able to survive the never-ending hell of existing without her.

"So, how do you intend to make him realize he can't run from her, or deny her any longer?" Pure anticipation filled her voice.

"Bloodthirsty wench," he chuckled, bending his head to brush a kiss against the mating mark, which a wide collar-style necklace of gleaming silver hid. When his head rose, he knew that his own satisfaction filled his gaze. "For the moment, I'm just going to watch him bury himself in the hole he's making. Once he's realized what he's done, I want to sit back and enjoy the show."

He simply couldn't help it. Rule had pushed him, prodded him, enraged the Lion inside him and generally had Lawe ready to kill him as he fought to accept the woman he had mated. Dealing with his brother and his own instincts hadn't been easy, and Lawe had sworn that when he had the chance, he was going to make sure Rule suffered his own mating hell.

⋆ CHAPTER 13 ⋆

She fit him.

The odd thought drifted through his mind as he danced with Gypsy, the slow, gliding steps of the waltz suddenly making sense as they moved together.

She did this with the same grace and sensuality that she danced to that country tune in black leather, or the vintage rock in a white lace skirt and cowboy boots. With such inherent eroticism that his balls tightened with the need to spill his release and ease the granite hardness of his cock.

Tonight, he was determined to have her. His suite was ready, clean sheets graced the bed, candles were lit and ready for the moment he entered the room with her. A bottle of her favorite wine was chilling and he was hard enough to fuck her for hours without softening.

She had orgasmed in his arms, her juices spilling over his fingers as he held her to him in her apartment. He understood that going further would have been far too soon. He sensed she was only now learning that such pleasure could exist. That she could shake with the need for his touch, plead for her release.

He intended to show her far more tonight.

He'd gone to Jonas as soon as he'd asked Dawn why Gypsy was so damned upset over a dress. Her laughing chastisement that he had ruined a chance she felt her mother and even perhaps she had possessed to make a certain impression had been the explanation that suddenly made sense.

They were image and social building professionals. Having their pictures premiere in the right places would of course be important to aid the growth of her parents' business. To do that, a certain look would have to be achieved; somehow, by reputation, standing, wealth or a unique dress, they would have to be noticed. She had felt he had taken her chance to be noticed.

He'd ensured she was noticed tonight in ways she could never have been at any other party.

When the music moved from a waltz to a slow, sensual tune, he pulled her further into him, feeling her arms curl about his shoulders, her head resting against his chest. And God, he wanted her. He wanted her until he was burning with it.

A natural burn, he assured himself. Had there been anything more, she wouldn't have been able to hide it from his senses. Mating Heat wasn't burning within her; simple, pure desire made stronger for the fact that she had been hiding from her own sensual nature for so long was all that burned within her.

As Gypsy and Diane had chatted, Rule had given his brother her request that she see Claire and Liza. The two girls had mentioned a desire to see friends and had named Gypsy especially. Before they left the party, he hoped Jonas would approve the request.

Whether he did or not, Rule was determined he would have Gypsy.

Then, soon, he would have to put his foot down where her nightlife was concerned. It was too dangerous for a Breed lover to run the night without security, and at the moment all units were taken up with protecting Claire and Liza.

She would understand, he told himself. Being his lover would make her a target. Too many forces would assume she was his mate, and he couldn't explain that to her. The ban on explaining mating or Mating Heat to anyone but a mate was strictly enforced.

It was a thin line he would have to tread.

"I'm ready for a drink," she mumbled lazily from where she rested against him. "And didn't you say something about a buffet?"

"Hungry, are you?" He smiled into her hair before allowing her to draw away from him and leading her to the edge of the ballroom.

"Like you wouldn't believe," she informed him, her green eyes glancing back at him with sultry hunger.

Shadowed, exotic, her gaze was filled with need and the memory of his fingers stroking her to release.

"Your parents seem to be enjoying themselves." He nodded to where Wolfe and Hope were joining Callan and Merinus at the table where the McQuades were sitting.

The opportunity to discuss the electronic device her mother had attempted to bring into that meeting more than a week ago still eluded him. Seeing the pain, the betrayal she would experience, feeling it, would enrage him.

And God knew, Gypsy didn't need more pain where her family was concerned.

"My parents are probably in seventh heaven at the moment," she told him with a light laugh as they made their way to the connecting ballroom that had been set up with a dozen or more food and dessert tables.

They each filled their plates before collecting a glass of wine. Rule led her to one of the tables in the corner of the room where the low lighting was dimmer, the candles reflecting a small pool of intimacy.

The various items that filled their plates were finger foods. Shrimp, vegetables, tenderloin, lamb and chicken chunks served with a variety of cheeses, crackers and specialty breads.

In the low light that hid them from view, Rule selected a small chunk of lamb, held it in his fingers, then reached across the table to tuck it at her lips.

Surprised, her gaze darkening at the implications of the action, Gypsy stared back at him. Lips parting, she took the morsel of food before her head dipped, her lashes lowering as she ate.

Hell, his tempestuous little Gypsy had a bit of shyness.

Along with the lamb, she also hadn't chosen several other delicacies. Those he fed to her as well, watching as her face flushed and scenting the heat of her body rising.

She was relaxing with him, easing in his presence. Where before there had been wariness, a hint of fear and rejection, there was now shy acceptance.

How much more accepting could she become? he wondered. Not that he was about to test her boundaries here, at a ball where her parents and sister were in attendance. He would never allow even a chance of her becoming embarrassed by her family seeing the naked sensuality he could draw out of her.

Leaning close, he talked to her instead. He answered what questions he could about the Breed society, and laughed with her over some of the more outrageous tabloid stories. And for some reason, he wasn't certain why, he told her about the brother and sister he suspected had died when they were taken from the labs.

Grave regret filled her, a well of sadness that reached out to him and attempted to soothe him, that she wasn't even aware she possessed.

There was no way anyone could suspect this was the woman Jonas believed was a part of the Unknown. Anyone with that shadowy group was as merciless as the Breeds when it came to protecting the innocent, immature creations humankind believed they had created. There wasn't an ounce of mercilessness inside this woman.

Stubbornness, yes. But never could she kill without thought, in cold blood, just on the suspicion that someone was a threat to the group itself.

As the night deepened and the crowd in the buffet room thinned to only them, he reached across the table and stroked his fingers over her hand.

"Come upstairs with me," he said, anticipation surging through him as her gaze lifted quickly to his, the scent of her arousal thickening.

"That wouldn't be a very good idea." She stared back at him, her relaxed enjoyment of the night fading as uncertainty filled her.

"Are we going to play games, Gypsy?" he asked, his voice as gentle as he could keep it as his cock throbbed like a demon starving for the taste of her.

She looked down once again, though she didn't pull her hand from his grip.

"I would be a lousy lover for you, Rule." She finally smiled nervously, shaking her head as she lifted it, her eyes filled with her belief in that statement.

"I think I'm the only judge of who would or would not suit me in my bed, Gypsy," he refuted, his voice low. "Come on, try me on for size, then decide if I fit as you need me or not."

"And if the size is wrong?" Amusement flashed in her eyes. "Won't it be a little too late to decide I'd made the wrong decision?"

"I promise not to kiss and tell." His brows lifted suggestively. "And I sure as hell don't come and tell."

She flushed again. He couldn't wait to watch that intriguing heat spread from her face, along her neck and over her breasts as pleasure began to fill her.

She was breathing raggedly, her breasts rising and falling quickly beneath the bodice of her pretty gown as she tried to find a way to talk herself out of wanting him.

He could feel her doing it, coming up with all the reasons why she shouldn't lie in his arms and scream out her release.

Rising, he pulled her unhurriedly to her feet, ignoring the indecision on her face as he drew her to the exit, then the short distance to the elevators.

Her heart was racing so fast, so hard she was nearly shaking with it as excitement churned in the air around her.

Rule drew her into the elevator as the doors swished open, pulled her into his arms and, as they slid closed, lowered his lips to hers.

Her kiss was as sweet as his favorite hard candies, he thought, and just as hot. His tongue licked over her lips, parted them, then stroked inside for a deeper, intimate exploration.

Still, she stood hesitantly before him, her lips parting for him, her tongue touching his despite her wariness, her intent to pull back rising alongside the arousal burning inside her.

Gripping her wrists, he drew them to his shoulders, his hands stroking down her sides before reaching her hips and curling his fingers over them.

She kissed him with a hunger that drove spikes of pure raw need straight to his balls. As she stretched against him, reaching for him now, a moan whispered past her lips as her hips tilted and he pulled her into the thick ridge of his cock rising beneath his slacks.

Pulling his head back, his control threatening to slip, Rule stared down at her, his gaze narrowed on her sensually flushed features.

"I'll be lucky if I make it to my suite," he groaned. "You go to my head faster than liquor."

◆　　◆　　◆

She went to his head faster than liquor?

Gypsy could feel her blood racing through her body, pounding at her clit, in the sensitive tissue of her pussy, and wondered how a kiss would have a woman so ready, so hot and so eager to fuck for a man's touch.

She didn't want to wait. She wanted to take him here, now. She wanted his tongue against hers, pushing between her lips and making her even more delirious with pleasure as his hands pushed the material of her dress to her hips. She wanted him to drive that hard, heavy flesh rising between his thighs into the torturous ache between hers.

When his lips refused to kiss her hard enough, hot enough, her fingers speared into his hair, gripped the coarse strands and tried to hold him in place.

She needed so much more than he was giving her.

And it didn't make sense.

This was too dangerous.

He might not kiss and tell—or whatever version of it they were about to do—but that didn't mean the Unknown wouldn't know. They were masters at knowing, especially the one she had made contact with.

Yet pulling away, denying him, was impossible.

She couldn't taste him deep enough, couldn't feel the power of his kiss sinking far enough into her and couldn't make herself care about anything but needing more and more of him.

And that wasn't like her.

But then, she hadn't been herself since the night she had glanced across a bar and met his gaze so many weeks ago. As though she had been waiting for him all her life.

The *ping* of the elevator was only a distant sound, but the feel of Rule suddenly lifting her into his arms and striding from the cubicle was anything but distant. It was the most amazingly sensual act she had experienced to date.

"This is insane," she whispered, burying her lips against his neck to test the tough flesh with her teeth before licking over the place where her teeth had bitten.

And he wasn't protesting the feel of her sharp teeth at his neck either. If that rumbled little growl in his chest was anything to go by, he just might have enjoyed it.

She wondered if she could get him to bite her.

A shudder raced through her at the thought, the slide of moisture between her thighs further wetting her already saturated flesh.

"Good God, what were you just thinking?" he groaned as he set her on her feet next to the door of his suite. "Because your hot little pussy just went supernova on me."

He swiped the security card through the reader, pushed open the door and took a second to test the air before he strode into the room.

The door locked behind them, enclosing them in a world of flickering candlelight and sensual warmth that filled the living area and the bedroom as well. It was like walking into the most romantic dream she could have conjured up. The preparations he had made gave the room a sultry, erotic feel, and a dreamlike quality that he only added to as he carried her to the bedroom.

He didn't set her on her feet next to the bed. Instead, he laid her back on it, following her down as his hands began gathering the material of her dress and pushing it above her knees.

His lips were on her neck as he shed his jacket, tore at the tie and shirt until he had tossed them to the floor as well, then kicked his dress shoes to the floor. His lips began moving over the firm upper swells of her breasts, leaving a trail of fiery pleasure in the wake of his kisses.

He was moving so fast she couldn't keep up. She couldn't process the pleasure or the sensations, and the dizzying surges of them were making her feel overheated and rushed.

If he would just slow down . . .

Gypsy fought to pull in much-needed air as she panted beneath him, feeling him tense above her, his hands moving from where he'd been pushing her dress farther up her legs to clench in the blankets beneath her.

"You okay?" he suddenly growled, his lips at her neck, then her jaw, brushing against them at a much slower pace as she tried to pull her own senses back now.

"I'm okay." At least, she thought she was.

Hesitantly, she lifted her hands to the hard abdomen straining above hers, her fingers curling as she allowed herself to stroke the tight, bunched muscles.

His skin wasn't soft, it was tough and at first appeared completely free of any body hair. But it wasn't, at least not completely. Beneath her palms she could feel the ultra soft sensation of tiny, almost invisible hairs beneath her touch.

And she loved the feel of it.

She stroked to his chest, his hard shoulders, then down again to the clenched abs to where he'd only managed to free the button that held his slacks closed.

Lifting his head from where his lips had been caressing the shell of her ear, Rule eased further above her, his weight held with unconscious strength on his powerful arms.

"Your pace," he swore, though his voice was hard, tight. "I swear it, Gypsy. Anything, everything you want. All at your pace."

All at her pace?

Anything, everything she wanted?

Did she even know exactly what she did want from him past this pleasure, his touch, the warmth of him—

He watched her as she stroked his shoulders again, then lifted her hand to brush over his lips.

She hadn't seen him enjoying the small chocolate and peppermint hard candies tonight, but she had tasted the sweet essence of them in his kiss.

And she craved more of it.

She was going to do this.

Hunger and fear flashed through her, running side by side as a part of her mind watched in horror, unable to believe the wanton he was drawing out.

Her fingers found the zipper of his slacks and began to slide it free, loosening the material over the straining flesh of his cock.

She couldn't believe she was doing this. Couldn't believe she was actually throwing away her chance for redemption, for forgiveness—she was throwing it away for this Breed and a pleasure unlike anything she had known before.

"Gypsy, baby, do you know what you're doing?" he asked as her fingers moved from the zipper to the heavy length of iron-hard flesh that rose from between his thighs.

"I told you, I haven't done it before," she whispered, stroking her fingers along the throbbing, heavily veined shaft.

From the wide, silken knob to the pulsing crest, then to the tightly drawn sac beneath. Every inch of him was so hard, heated and insistent for her touch.

She couldn't encircle the heavy width with the fingers of one hand, so she contented herself with stroking him from base to tip, feeling the flesh clench and pound beneath her touch as she felt her entire body beginning to burn for his possession of her, for her possession of him.

She lifted her head and laid her lips against his chest, her tongue peeking out to taste. And she craved so much more.

Pulling back, her hands flattening against his chest as she pushed at him.

"I want to touch you." That wasn't her voice, so low and echoing with a pleasure that bordered pain.

"Gypsy, baby," he groaned, but he moved.

Rising from the bed, he quickly discarded his pants and his socks before completely surprising her. Kneeling on the mattress with one knee, Rule wrapped his arms around her and lifted her to him, lowering the zipper of her dress as he stared intently into her eyes.

What had happened to her touching him? To him lying back for her? And why wasn't she protesting?

He removed her dress slowly, satisfaction filling his expression as he pulled it from her, then tossed it carelessly over a nearby chair. Clad now in nothing but French-cut white lace panties and the black stockings with the iridescent emerald green thread sparkling within them, Gypsy felt the need burning inside her heating further.

His fingers hooked in the band of her panties, and a second later they were falling forgotten to the floor as Rule stared down at her, his face flushing, becoming heavy with erotic need as he knelt beside her.

Once again, the engorged length of his cock drew her touch, her hunger. There were things she had imagined doing to him, had never believed she would have the chance she now had. She didn't want to watch it slip past her and somehow lose the chance to ever do it again.

"I need to touch you," she whispered, rising until she was kneeling on the bed in front of him, her hand stroking down his chest. "Just for a little bit."

He caught her hair in the fingers of one broad hand, a tight, brooding grimace pulling at his lips as she moved to taste him.

Her tongue lapped at the hard muscle of his chest, her teeth scraping over it as she felt his body tense further. He moved one hand between them to grip the base of the heavy shaft tightly as the thick crest pulsed in demand.

Gypsy let her hand follow his, stroking down past his abs to the broad head of his cock. She gripped the thick flesh once again and stroked it, learning each pulse and throb, each heavy vein that pounded beneath the silken, tightly stretched shaft.

Her lips moved lower, following the path her fingers had taken to the heavily engorged crest as it rose beseechingly to her lips.

A small drop of pre-cum beaded at the slit, tempting her to taste him. When her tongue swiped over the droplet of moisture Rule groaned as though he were being tortured rather than simply tasted.

His entire attention was focused on her.

The lean hard contours of his body were tight with pleasure as Gypsy parted her lips, her tongue reaching out once more to lick over the knob, before curling beneath the flared edge as her lips descended over it.

His teeth snapped together, pleasure rocking his body with jarring force as Gypsy sucked the head of his cock into the snug heat of her mouth.

Her tongue lashed at the overly sensitive crest, tucked beneath it and rubbed heatedly at the flared edge. With one hand she stroked down the hard column of flesh, then back up, cupping and stroking his tightened scrotum with the other.

A muttered growl escaped his lips. Pleasure arced from his balls to the head of his dick. Her hot little mouth sucked at him, drawing him deep before pulling back, licking and caressing the sensitive head before suckling it erotically once again.

It was torture. It was the greatest pleasure he'd ever known.

He couldn't help spearing his fingers into the silken weight of her hair. Bunching the strands in his hands, he held her head in place, staring down at her as he fucked her mouth with slow, shallow strokes. Watched her lips redden and swell, her eyes glaze with arousal as the scent of her need washed over his senses.

"So sweet and hot," he groaned, the sight of her expression suffused with pleasure enough to send a furious pulse of sensation racing through his testicles.

She was exquisite.

Tightening her mouth on him, she sucked at the throbbing cock head harder, creating a damp, wet haven for the shuttling crest as he moved against her. He wouldn't last much longer and he knew it. He couldn't last much longer. He'd waited far too long to have her, teased himself with the thought of taking her for far too many nights.

Before she could tempt him further, though, he moved back. He pulled himself from the liquid heat of her mouth as her eyes flew open, surprise and need gleaming in the dark green depths.

"Lie down for me, my wild little Gypsy," he growled, lowering himself and forcing her to recline back on the bed.

Her lips were honeyed heat as he took them again, parting and welcoming as her tongue tangled with his, then arching closer for more as he pulled back to sip at her lips.

She was pure, feminine heat and erotic promise and Rule knew that even without Mating Heat, she would be damned hard to walk away from.

If he decided to walk away from her . . .

God help him if the Heat decided to ambush him, because it would kill him to tear himself from her now.

Gypsy gripped Rule's powerful shoulders as his lips moved down her neck; the force of pleasure lashing at her nerve endings had her crying out and arching closer. His teeth raked over her neck, his lips and tongue easing the little hurt as he made his way to her collarbone, then lower.

He kissed over the rise of her breasts to the aching points of her nipples. Covering one painfully hard tip, his tongue curled around it, licked it, loved it, as he suckled at it deeply. Lava-hot pleasure enveloped her senses as her hands tightened on his shoulders, her nails unconsciously kneading the tough flesh.

Electric heat zipped from the tortured tip of her breast to strike at her womb, clenching it furiously before racing to her clit and swelling the little bud tighter.

His hand was between her thighs, sliding up the inner curve of one before cupping the saturated heat between her legs. His fingers eased between the pouty lips to find the heavy juices spilling from her. His touch rasped over the clenched entrance of her sex. There, his fingers rubbed, stroked. They set up a firestorm of ecstatic pleasure, barely entering her, rubbing at the sensitive nerve endings just inside the entrance.

His lips moved from one nipple to the other, sucking at each, his tongue licking and stroking as she arched to him. Desperate need tightened inside her, clenching her muscles and whipping over her flesh.

"Rule, please . . ." she begged, arching, writhing beneath him as so many sensations seemed to converge on her at once.

Hunger and need, emotions she had fought back so long, were now rising inside her so fast, so hard, she couldn't force them back.

Emotions she hadn't realized she'd kept hidden so well from herself.

Rule lifted his head then, staring down at her as she forced her eyes open to stare into the wild hunger of his gaze. His lips curled into a devastatingly sensual smile.

"Ah, baby," he crooned. "I intend to please you. Very, very well."

Holding her gaze, he lowered his lips once again.

Gypsy couldn't hold back the gasp that escaped her as his lips moved between her breasts, his tongue stroking over skin she hadn't realized could be so sensitive.

Then he moved lower.

Stroking over her midriff, down her stomach, those slow, devastating kisses moved between her thighs. Broad palms pressed against the outer curve of her upper legs, spreading them wider and wedging his shoulders between them as his lips moved to the curls at the top of her mound.

His cheek brushed against the softness, his breath feathering the neat fluff as she arched involuntarily, her hips lifting for him, her thighs falling farther apart.

The touch of his tongue was such a shock of pleasure that Gypsy couldn't hold back her cry. Nothing should feel that good.

His tongue swiped through her juice-laden slit, stroked around her clit, flicked against it and sent brilliant waves of sensation tearing through her body. Only to ease back, to lick lower, to tease and torment the entrance to her vagina.

Pure arching pleasure flashed through her so hard and so fast that Gypsy found her torso lifting from the bed before falling back. Her heels dug into the mattress, hips lifting, a cry tearing from her as his tongue pressed inside, licking at flesh that responded with pulse after pulse of quicksilver pleasure and yet more of the thick essence of her need.

She couldn't seem to catch her breath.

Her body was burning with need, her clit so swollen, so desperate for release—

"Oh God, Rule, please." She arched again as his lips returned to her clit, his tongue licking in a tight, blazing circle around the little nub.

She was so close. She could feel ecstasy reaching out to her, teasing her, tempting her to fall into the flames only to refuse her at the last second.

Rule pulled back, delivered a fiery kiss to the tortured bundle of nerves before suckling it into his mouth and tormenting her with the nearness of release again.

She was crying out for him. She could hear her voice, broken and pleading.

Suckling at her firmly, his tongue rubbed against her clit, stroking, caressing and licking, tightening her womb, her pussy, her thighs.

Release ripped through her like a vicious storm, shaking her from her head to her toes, pouring through her senses with a downpour of rapture that rained through her entire body.

Gypsy could feel herself opening, a part of herself she hadn't known existed fracturing inside her soul. As though some inner wall were all but falling to rubble as the heat enveloping her seemed to pour from him, into her, then back again.

Collapsing back to the bed, she felt Rule move over her, his larger, harder body covering her. Forcing her lashes open, Gypsy watched as he gripped the thick base of his cock, nudging the crest against her entrance before his gaze lifted to hers.

"That's it, baby, watch me take you," he whispered as the thick crest parted the folds of her pussy and pressed against the snug entrance. "Sweet Gypsy. God help me, so much damned pleasure."

The groan sounded torn from him, ripped from his chest as Gypsy watched the head of his cock press deeper, only to pull back, glistening with her juices before pressing inside again and delving deeper.

Her head fell back against the bed, pressing into the pillow as pleasure erupted through her flesh at the heavy stretch and burn of her vagina. Rule eased back, only to return, rocking against her, inside her, stretching her and burning her with a pleasure that had her nails digging into his shoulders, her neck arching as a cry tore from her lips.

She felt his muscles bunch as he pulled back again, his body tensing a second before he powered inside her with a quick, hard thrust that sent a flare of pain arching through her vagina a second before the invading heat stilled, buried mere inches inside her, thick and throbbing.

"Gypsy?" His rough, animalistic tone had her lashes lifting, confusion filling her as she realized he was staring down at her as though shocked.

"Don't stop," she whispered, running her tongue over her dry lips as she shifted experimentally against him, a heavy mewl of pleasure escaping her lips at the throb of his cock against her inner flesh.

Then he moved again.

Rule pressed deeper inside her, that feeling of fullness intensifying, heating until she was lifting her hips higher, desperate to take all of him.

Each time he pulled back, easing the burning stretch and ecstasy of the pleasure building inside her, her breath would catch, protest rising inside her. Then he powered inside her again, deeper, fuller.

Her world shrank, narrowed, consisted of nothing but the pleasure crowding her senses, the sensations racing through her, building atop each other as his hips began to move faster, harder.

He thrust inside her with heavy strokes that kept her senses shocked and stunned with the alternate pulses of pleasure and pain, fire and fullness. Writhing beneath him, Gypsy cried out his name, the feel of his pelvis stroking the ultra sensitive bud of her clit as the flared head of his cock stretched her inner muscles, stroked and discovered nerve endings even Gypsy hadn't known she possessed, sent her senses flying.

Each measured, hard thrust tightened that coil of sensation building in her womb and echoing in her clit. Each stroke sent so many lashes of pleasure, striking arcs of heat and excitement rasping across her nerve endings that she feared she wouldn't survive it.

Pounding inside her, the jackhammer thrusts built the agonizing pleasure, pushing it higher, sensitizing her further and tightening her body until she swore she felt the sun erupt inside her pussy.

A storm of sensation exploded through her. It flared through her, blinding heat followed by flames of ecstasy licking over every nerve ending, stroking and caressing some internal trigger before setting it off and sending clashing rapture reverberating through her senses.

She was jerking in his arms, crying out his name. Her vagina tightened on his cock as she felt the heavy throb, a thickening of the already wide shaft and that first, heated pulse of his release jetting inside her.

A second later, her arms were empty, her body was empty, the burning rapture shut off mid-orgasm, leaving her confused and cold before she realized his body no longer covered hers. He was no longer finding his release inside her.

Hell, he wasn't even in the bed with her.

He was standing next to it, his breathing harsh, his blue eyes vivid and wild as he stared down at her, a snarl on his lips revealing the sharpened canines as his cock stood out from his body, thick and hard and glistening from their combined dampness.

"Rule?" she whispered, her chest suddenly tightening, a feeling of impending doom weighing on her soul and stealing her breath.

"I have to wash up." His voice sounded odd, too thick, too heavy. "I'll give you a ride home when I get out of the bathroom."

He turned and stalked to the bathroom, slamming the door behind him two seconds before she heard the sound of the shower.

The shower?

He was taking a shower?

She stared down at her body, seeing the smear of blood on her thighs, staining the sheet between her legs. She was slick from her need for him, her body still throbbing with remembered bliss.

He would take her home after he washed up?

Why? What had she done wrong?

◆ CHAPTER 14 ◆

God, what had he done!

His fist rammed into the shower, a ceramic tile cracking as Rule's teeth gritted furiously, the torment racking his brain to the point that he didn't even feel the pain to his knuckles.

Gypsy's expression was branded into his head. That pale shock, her eyes rounded and dark with pain and confusion, then the color brightening as he'd made that dumb-assed statement. Her eyes had filled with tears even before he'd managed to turn from her and rush to the bathroom.

He'd left her lying there when he wanted nothing more than to push inside her again, swear he was just fucking crazy and give them both that electric, fiery pleasure he had been immersed in before he'd felt—

It.

His dick was fucking iron hard, pounding with the abrupt halt he'd forced on his release, the sensitive flesh just beneath the flared head fucking aching. Aching like a sore tooth right there where the mating barb was supposed to be located.

He checked his tongue against his teeth. Fuck. Son of a bitch, there were no fucking swollen glands, no mating hormone, nothing but that god-be-damned spot pulsing so violently he could see the flesh throbbing where it shouldn't be.

Wrapping his fingers around his dick, he pressed the pad of his thumb against the hard throb, but all he felt was a tighter tension and slightly higher degree of sensitivity.

Was that normal, or was he was just so damned on guard for a mating that he was only now sensing it?

It couldn't be a mating, could it?

What the hell was happening to him?

A mating barb didn't extend from beneath the cock head without a mating. Without that wild taste in a Breed's mouth, the crazy need to fuck his mate insane, only to have the overpowering lust shoot through him again and again.

Rule felt no weakness, no hard dick twenty-four-seven. Just whenever he so much as thought of Gypsy.

But he knew what he had felt as that first pulse of his release shot from his balls. He knew what he was feeling now just beneath the pad of his thumb. Surely, he would have known if he had felt it before.

Wouldn't he?

His breathing was rough, hard as he stared down at the offending part of his body as he forced himself to release it, watching the flesh pulse like a heartbeat just beneath it.

It had to be something else, he told himself as cold water sluiced over his flesh and covered his cock, having little effect on the burning hunger ravaging his senses.

He was powerfully sexual, he knew that. He couldn't count a high sex drive as a possible mating sign. He had a high sex drive anyway. Most male Breeds did. They simply loved to fuck and did it whenever, wherever they could. They loved sex and they loved women, and petting them, rubbing against them, sensing their pleasure and satisfaction.

It was like a drug. A high.

And Gypsy's pleasure had been like no high he had ever known in his entire life. Hell, he had been so attuned to her pleasure that he swore he felt the echoes of her release beginning to strike so deep inside his senses that he wondered if it sank to his soul. Something else he'd only heard of happening with a mate.

But the mating signs weren't there.

He couldn't even call the strength of her echoing pleasure a mating sign without anything else to go with it. And the feeling of—something—a heat and sudden building tightness beneath the head of his cock just before he came had been so damned odd he'd jumped from her and rushed to the shower before he could risk the mating barb extending from his cock.

Once it was free, there was no going back.

How many times had he heard that?

Once the mating barb extended and locked inside his mate, there was simply no stopping the mating.

He shut the shower off, standing there, his flesh still hot, the need for Gypsy still pounding through his system like a fever he couldn't stop.

But not just the need to fuck her.

He wanted so much more from her than just the incredible pleasure that had raced through his senses.

Mating Heat was all about the sex. It wasn't about the rubbing, the touching, seeing the laughter in a lover's eyes or feeling her joy as it wrapped around him.

Mating Heat was weakening. It took over the senses and erased everything but the need for the mate. He'd sensed that ravaging force in his twin, Lawe, when he'd found his mate. His brother's lack of control, the inability to sense anything around him but Diane.

And he'd sensed it even before then, years before, confined in a cell, all too aware of the scent of his mother and the Coyote they called Elder in the labs. The scent of their need, of their building desperation had haunted that fucking lab. The scientists never forbade the Coyote soldiers from taking the female prisoners. But never before had one of them mated a breeder.

Morningstar had literally birthed a pack, four offspring, before her body had suddenly become infertile.

Or it had been, before Elder.

Before her Coyote rapist had mated her and caused her death.

That desperation to set her and her young free, to have her, no matter the cost, had been the cause of her death as well as her mate's.

Rule knew he couldn't let that happen to any woman he mated. If he mated, if he let himself weaken that far, then it would be far too easy to take Gypsy from him.

She wasn't a fighter.

She wasn't a Breed.

She was resourceful, smart. She'd spied for the Unknown for nine years without ever being identified until Jonas put his too-intelligent mind to work on finding one of their contacts.

But she wasn't trained to survive.

And she couldn't be his mate.

His dick slowly lost its desperate stiffness as he stared down at it, frowning in confusion, wondering what the fuck his body was doing.

What crazy shit was happening to him and how the hell was he supposed to fix it?

It couldn't have been the mating barb. He wouldn't be losing the hard-on if he were even close to the beginning stages of Mating Heat. It wasn't possible from what he'd heard.

So it couldn't be a mating, he thought desperately. It had to just be one of those damned anomalies Breeds came in contact with damned near every day of their lives.

They weren't human and they weren't animal, and their bodies weren't normal. That made some interesting reactions sometimes.

That had to be what had happened this time.

A smothered grunt of amused irritation left his lips as he began thinking hard. Jerking a towel from the towel rack, he fought to come up with a reasonable explanation for what was no doubt going to be a furious lover once he left the bathroom.

Had he really told her he'd drive her home after he washed up?

He ran the towel quickly over his hair, shook the remaining water out of it and drew in a quick, hard breath. There was no such thing as a reasonable explanation, but maybe a partial truth would work. She made him feel a pleasure that no other woman had ever made him feel, and it simply shocked the hell out of him.

That was the truth, and he thought maybe Gypsy could sense the truth sometimes. A certain expression, the way her eyes darkened when he held something back from her, or when he hadn't exactly told her the truth.

It was a suspicion he couldn't prove yet.

Snapping the towel into the bathtub, he exhaled roughly and opened the door, stepping back into the bedroom.

"Gypsy, baby, I'm sor—" He looked around the empty room.

Before he could stop it, an enraged snarl erupted from him, an animal's fury pounding through his veins with such suddenness that it was shocking.

The man he was became the secondary part of his senses. The animal jumped forward, suddenly free, suddenly enraged, though not at the woman. No, the animal was enraged at the man and clawing beneath his flesh as he tore free of the inner restraints.

Because of the man, his mate had run.

Before Rule could stop the impulse, his hand slashed out, claw marks raked across the wall, the shock of seeing that primal, impossible sight snapping inside him.

Claws?

His fingers, blood smeared, the tips of strong, lethally sharp claws extending from the tips—

Another snarl tore from him, nearly a roar as animal instincts clashed with human ones and nearly overwhelmed him once again.

"Back off, goddammit," he snarled furiously, reining in the animalistic impulses tearing through him.

He had to think.

Blood pounded hard and fast through his veins, chocolate and peppermint teased his taste buds, and that sure as hell didn't make sense because he hadn't had one of the sweets in days.

Drawing in a deep breath, her scent, her emotions, he clenched his teeth against another snarl that rose from the animal trapped inside him.

Gypsy was gone.

Her dress and her shoes were gone.

The little clutch purse she had carried was gone.

There was nothing left of her but the scent of such overwhelming pain—and God help him, shame.

He'd shamed her, humiliated her.

Pushing his fingers through his hair, the animal growled out at the silence of the room as self-disgust filled him with a suddenness that was shocking.

What the fuck had he done now and how the hell was he going to fix it? Because as God was his witness, he would have to fix it. Mate or no mate, barb or no barb, he had to get her back. He was beginning to suspect she was far more than any lover, and even without Mating Heat, a mating mark or mating hormone, he wasn't going to be able to do without her.

He hadn't marked her, but he knew that somehow, some way, she had marked him. The thought of that wasn't as distasteful now as the thought of it had been, even hours ago. As though in the midst of their pleasure, in acknowledging that he'd never known so much with another woman, he'd dropped his guard enough to realize she was much more to him than he'd allowed himself to believe.

He wasn't going to let her go.

He'd hurt her, he knew that. He could scent how much he had hurt her. But she would have to forgive him. He would find a way to make her forgive him.

And if he didn't?

Some part of him mocked his confidence.

He wouldn't entertain the thought that she wouldn't forgive him. He couldn't. If he did, then the animal pacing and enraged inside him just might break the leash restraining it and do something that would well and truly shock the man who controlled it with such force.

And Rule didn't know if his pride could take too many more shocks.

◆　◆　◆

Huddling in the corner of the elevator, her head down, Gypsy was all too aware of the three Breeds who stood silently on the other side of the car.

They had been striding down another hall as she ran for the elevator, holding her dress to her breasts because she'd been unable to zip it all the way. Her mother had zipped it earlier, and Gypsy had been unable to finish pulling the tab up in Rule's room.

She'd had to wait on the elevator in the hall, too aware of the Breeds striding toward her, silent, suspicious as they most often were. Struggling not to sob in agony, she'd stood with her head down, burning with humiliation as they moved silently to stand in front of her while she pressed her back into the wall.

She didn't want them to see that her dress wasn't zipped, but when the elevator doors had slid open, they had stepped back and she knew they'd wait until hell froze over if she didn't step in first.

Keeping her head down, she had done just that, moving to the corner of the car before turning and staring at the floor.

No one had spoken.

She didn't even know if she knew the Breeds. She couldn't bear to look them in the face. If she knew one of them, she wouldn't be able to hold back the humiliation and the pain. It would have poured from her eyes in such grief that she wouldn't have been able to stand it.

"We're on our way down, sir," she heard one of them answer, the link she supposed. "We'll meet with you at the west elevators if you don't mind."

Everyone referred to Rule as Commander, so it wasn't him. Not that Rule would care, she thought. No way in hell would he really care whether he drove her home or not.

What had she done?

How had she managed to mess it up?

Was there some unwritten rule she was unaware of when it came to orgasming? Had she done something so unforgivable as to cause him to jump from her before he even finished his release and rush to the shower?

She lifted her fingers to her lips to still the threat of trembling. She was not going to cry over him here, in front of other Breeds who would no doubt tell him. Breeds who would laugh with him over the stupid little human who couldn't hold her emotions back.

That must have been what it was.

As her release had whipped through her, she remembered fighting to hold back the words she knew he wouldn't want to hear. Had he somehow sensed how deeply she was coming to love him without her saying the words?

Shame burned inside her, blazed through her cheeks and burned a path straight to her soul. And she knew the Breeds in the elevator could smell it.

Who else would know once the elevator came to a stop in the lobby?

God, she hoped the journalists were gone. She couldn't bear to be seen like this.

The elevator slid to a stop, the subtle *ping* announcing the end of the ride sounding as the doors slid open.

She moved quickly from it, striding across the lobby with what she hoped wasn't obvious hurry. If she was lucky, very very lucky, then no one would even notice her.

◆ ◆ ◆

There was no missing the smell of pain that agonizing, Lawe thought as he and Diane watched the elevator doors slide open. They had stepped to the bank of elevators less than a minute after the enforcer had contacted him with the strangely worded request that he meet him there.

He and Diane watched as Gypsy McQuade stepped from the doors the second they slid open, her shoulders shaking as she held her dress to her breasts and moved quickly for the lobby exit.

"Sir." The Wolf Breed, Dagger, stepped forward, a hard frown on his face. "Commander Breaker didn't notify security of his mate, and it seems she's in some distress."

There was a heavy tone of irate disapproval in the Breed's voice. One Lawe couldn't blame him for.

"It seems Commander Breaker neglected to inform me as well," Lawe muttered as Gypsy rushed past the doorman and moved to the side of the entrance, and the shadows she was no doubt attempting to hide within as he turned to Diane. "I was wrong. The mating scent is like a damned red flag now."

"Of pain," Dagger growled.

"Damn him," Diane whispered beside him.

Lawe could only shake his head, reaching back to rub at his neck and send a small prayer heavenward. Rule was determined to destroy himself and his little mate, it seemed.

"Go," Diane urged him. "You have all that freaky Breed sense going on, you'll know what to do and say far better than I will."

"You could come with me," he urged her gently.

"Go," she waved him away. "I'll just want to convince her to go with me and kick his ass. That's not what she needs. Don't worry, I'll wait right here for you."

Bending his head, he brushed a quick kiss to her lips before following Gypsy, waving the doorman back as he moved for his phone where it lay on the small counter just outside the doors. No doubt, his first instinct was to contact Jonas Wyatt. Lawe really didn't think Rule needed Jonas poking his nose into this right now.

Gypsy stood to the side of the entrance, just out of sight of those inside, huddled in the shadows.

Pausing, Lawe breathed out heavily before stepping to her, watching as she quickly shifted to hide the fact that her dress was still partially unzipped. Shrugging his jacket from his shoulders, he gently laid it across hers, pulling the edges together in the front.

She looked up then, her pretty dark green eyes bright with unshed tears.

"Tell me," he said softly, his voice filled with an understanding he feared would never be enough for whatever Rule had done to this young woman. "What stupidity has my brother acted on this time?" Barely brushing the soft flesh beneath her jaw, he urged her to glance up at him as he smiled back at her gently. "I believe the scientists may have dropped him on his head one time too many when he was a babe."

She didn't smile back at him. "No stupidity," she whispered instead. "He's just a man."

"A Breed," he corrected her, thinking it an oversight.

She shook her head slowly, her eyes dazed with confusion and such aching hurt that it tightened his chest.

"No," she denied, her voice thickening as she swallowed. "He's just a man."

Whatever Rule had done, he had cut so deep into her woman's soul that Lawe actually feared now that repairing it might be impossible. He hadn't just hurt her feelings, he thought, shocked; Rule had sliced her open.

And that simply wasn't like his brother.

Of the two of them, Rule had been the one more prone to cuddle and spoil his lovers. He laughed with them, teased them more than Lawe ever had. He had never, at any time, done anything more than hurt their feelings when he moved on.

"What has he done, Gypsy?" he asked her again, urging her to confide in him. "Perhaps, whatever it was, he didn't mean to hurt you as deeply as he obviously has."

"Hurt me?" She jerked her head up, staring back at him with patently false surprise. "There's no hurt, Enforcer, I promise. He even offered to drive me home. I simply preferred to find my own way. That's all."

The blatant lie almost had his lips curling in another smile, one that would assure her he had seen through it. But the white-hot agony pouring from her deserved far more than even a facsimile of humor.

As he stared down at her somberly, her lips suddenly began to tremble before she lifted her fingers and forced them to stillness.

"I want to go home," she whispered, and she felt so lost, so very alone that his heart absolutely broke for her, and he was reminded vividly of that night, nine years before, when she had whispered those same words.

"Carl," he called to the doorman.

"Yes, Enforcer Justice?" Carl maintained his distance, though he too watched Gypsy worriedly.

"Would you call down and have my driver pull my car around, please?" he asked the doorman.

"Yes, sir." Carl moved quickly to do as he was asked, calling down to the Breed parking level where one of the enforcers on duty would be waiting in case they were needed.

Then he turned back to Gypsy and ached to find a way to comfort her. Unfortunately, there was little he or even Diane could do. The scent of mating wasn't as strong as he'd scented on others, but it was there. Another male's touch could be extremely painful during Mating Heat. He couldn't even pat her delicate shoulder. Diane couldn't give her one of those girl hugs that she was forever giving her friends.

Gypsy was forced to stand alone, without comfort. And for that, Lawe thought, his brother deserved to have his ass kicked.

◆   ◆   ◆

She had been a virgin and Rule had known it. He had been her first, her only lover, and didn't she feel stupid as hell?

Used.

She felt used and cast off.

Unwanted.

The humiliation of it left her feeling so raw, so damned helpless that she didn't know how to handle it.

He had just jumped off her and all but demanded she leave.

He would take her home after he washed up?

As though she had left him feeling dirty.

Her stomach roiled at the thought, pitching with such agony that she wondered if she was going to throw up. Piercing, white-hot humiliation and such pain she didn't know how to bear it. Her knees felt weak from it, her stomach tightening with the bitter waves of it. She just wanted to escape. Escape and find some way to hide from it.

◆　　◆　　◆

Lawe flinched.

God, the emotions his brother's little mate was feeling. This tiny, delicate woman who had been meant to share his brother's life had such agony rolling from her that he could only stare at her in confusion.

How had Rule managed to hurt her?

Whatever he had done, he had hurt his tender little mate in ways she should never have known after the mating had begun.

His car pulled to the curb then, the Breed driving it stepping from the car and moving to them, his gaze curious as he too scented Rule's mark on her.

The Breed opened the back door for her.

"Come on, Gypsy." Careful to keep his jacket between his touch and her arm, he helped her into the backseat of the car, then bent and waited until she finally turned to look at him miserably. "If you need a friend, Diane and I, both of us, are your friends, I promise you. Call us if you need someone to talk to. Sometimes, Breeds, by their very nature, can be incredibly stupid. Perhaps, whatever he did, isn't something he realized had hurt you."

She simply nodded before turning away from him, her fingers linking and unlinking as she stared down at them.

Lawe shook his head, straightened, then closed the door gently on her.

"Take her home," he ordered the enforcer before his gaze hardened warningly. "And if you so much as breathe a word of her scent, even to Rule, then you'll answer to me. Do you understand?"

The enforcer snorted mockingly. "Hey, Breaker wants to cut his own nose off, then that's his business, right?"

"Exactly," Lawe agreed. "Keep believing that. I'll have a team follow behind you and set up security for her. I don't want her running around unprotected until Breaker gets his head out of his ass."

"Or you pull it out for him?" The enforcer grinned before turning and hurriedly moving to the driver's side, sliding inside, and a second later, the car pulled away from the curb.

Lawe shook his head before returning to the lobby and his mate where she waited. He couldn't help but stop in front of her, and as her gaze lifted to his, he cupped her face, his lips lowering gently to hers for a brief kiss.

"Have I told you lately how blessed I am in you?" he asked her, adoration rising inside him as tears filled her eyes.

His hardened mercenary had to blink back her emotion and the tears that would have escaped at his declaration.

"And I love you, mate," she whispered. "With all my soul."

And his brother would throw his own mate away? Cast her away and live without her? Wrapping his arm around his bloodthirsty little warrior, Lawe drew her into the elevator and led her to their suite.

Perhaps he should have gone to Rule's room and kicked his ass, but he decided to wait. Once Lawe was in his room and the quiet was close around him, he would do what he had been doing since he'd realized Rule was closing himself off from the twin bond they had shared for so long.

At first, it had just pissed him off that his twin would desert him. But once he'd realized why Rule was doing it, it had made more sense. Hell, he didn't want Rule sensing the pleasure Diane gave him any more than Rule wanted to sense it.

The link was still there when they needed it, so he didn't worry as much about it. Especially when he was able to slip back into that link without Rule's awareness of it, just to make certain his brother was doing okay.

For a week or so, he'd worried. Then one night Lawe sensed Rule's instincts pacing, growling. Realizing his brother slept, Lawe had shifted through the impressions his brother's animal senses had been telegraphing, almost as though asking for advice.

Lawe had seen the woman, felt the animal's need for her, his brother's denial of her, and he'd grinned.

Animal sense to animal sense, Lawe had sent back the impression of Rule accepting it, no matter his denial of it. But had his brother's animal, his subconscious, somehow known Rule would have actually run?

Breeds were far more than just human with a few added features. They were both human and animal, and not always in equal measure. The face of the human might greet each day, but many times, Lawe knew, even for him, it was the animal that was aware as they slept, waiting for trouble, watching the human's back.

Sometimes, in those Breeds with the stronger genetics, it was almost as though the human and the animal simply shared the same body. He'd often sensed that in Rule. Despite his brother's control, his denials to the contrary, it was often the animal senses that guided him.

What if the man had suddenly sensed what the animal was trying to hide from him?

He grinned at that.

God, to have been a fly on the wall. Gypsy probably thought his brother was fucking crazy. Or would, once she'd gotten over the pain.

And maybe, he thought, he could have helped, should have done more. But Rule had gotten himself into this mess and he was going to get himself out of it. If he was too stubborn to accept that his animal would never have accepted a mate who was too weak to be the woman he needed, then he'd just have to suffer until he realized the truth.

Or until Lawe decided he'd suffered enough and felt sorry for him.

He'd wait till morning, Lawe decided. Then he'd decide if his brother deserved the help.

"Going somewhere, Breaker?"

Rule paused outside the hotel lobby, his gaze narrowing as a whiff of cigar smoke reached his nose and Dane Vanderale stepped from the shadows of the hotel.

Mockery filled the hybrid's expression, but his eyes were cold, hard. Like frozen emeralds.

"I'm busy, Junior," Rule sneered, almost hoping the bastard would give him the fight he was itching for since he'd stepped from the bathroom and realized Gypsy had run.

Dane leaned against the side of the hotel, holding the thin, aromatic little cigar loosely between his fingers.

"I'm almost tempted to give you what you're looking for, cub. You're a dumb little fucker, aren't you? I didn't expect that of you." His gaze never wavered.

Rule gave a harsh snort of laughter. "Dumb little fucker, am I?" he asked the other Breed mockingly. "You're really itching for a fight tonight, aren't you? Too bad, I'm not in the mood to give you what you're after."

"No more than you were able to give your pretty little mate what she was after," Dane tsked as Rule suddenly froze in disbelief.

"And you called me a dumb little fucker?" he growled, feeling, *feeling,* something wild and animalistic rising too close to the surface of his skin as fury began to boil in his blood. "She's not . . ."

What the fuck?

The words he would have bitten out in fury were locked inside him, a snarl emerging instead as though a part of him refused to allow him to utter the words.

It wasn't a part of him. Animal instincts—the animal that resided just beneath the skin was suddenly enraged. With him.

Dane laughed.

A low, savagely cruel sound that had the hair at Rule's nape prickling in warning.

"Do you know, Rule, I've sensed your mark on that girl since she was no more than fifteen years old. As I stood at her brother's casket, mere feet from her, the scent of the animal that paces inside you marked her, even then."

"What kind of fucking game are you playing, Vanderale?" Rule was in the other Breed's face before he'd realized he was moving.

Eye to eye, he glared at the man who could easily break the back of the entire Breed community if he had a mind to, and wanted nothing more than to plant his fist in his face.

"Game?" Dane drawled as though the only threat he was in danger of was boredom. "No game, Breaker. Even if you were too stupid to realize the animal that paced inside you was keeping you out of that cave the night Jonas and your brother's teams rescued her, that didn't mean others were near so stupid. Even your brother caught your scent that night and turned to find you nowhere near. But that animal inside you was. It was there, watching over its future mate."

That night.

The night Gypsy's brother had died and she had nearly been raped. Jonas and Lawe had been in that cavern with her. Each time Rule had attempted to join them, to be certain nothing more was needed, something had stopped him. Held him back.

He'd excused it, telling himself the girl was too traumatized for more males to be crowding around her. Yet he'd paced outside that fucking cavern—

He'd smelled her terror. The horror of what she'd seen, of what had happened or nearly happened to her. He had sensed the agony that had screamed from her, and he'd snarled at the knowledge that nothing could ease it.

"Ahh, you remember now, don't you, whelp," Dane sneered.

"I haven't mated her," he bit out.

"Because that animal inside you has held back, knowing you're too buck fuck stupid for such a brave, courageous young woman." Dane smiled as though finding pleasure in that thought. "Go ahead, cub, run." He flicked his fingers to the road. "Go play elsewhere. Because I'd almost bet if you leave, then I just might have a chance of completing that bond with her myself. I could use a pretty little mate like her—"

As though suddenly a spectator to his own actions, Rule felt like a man watching in vicarious pleasure as the animal inside him erupted in a fury unlike anything he'd ever known. Before the Breed, one of the strongest Rule knew, could anticipate his action, Dane found himself flat on his ass, the razor-sharp claw-tipped fingers Rule hadn't known he possessed before tonight pressing into vulnerable flesh, tasting Dane's blood.

Rule could see the blood staining the claws. He could smell it, though he was reasonably certain the hardened tips pressing into the hybrid Breed's throat weren't causing fatal damage.

Not that Vanderale acted as though he gave a damn. He was still smiling in cold, brutal mockery, despite the smell of his blood in the air.

"Rule." It was the sound of his brother's voice, once the alpha who ruled the small pack Rule had been born into before the labs were overthrown, penetrating his senses.

They weren't in those labs anymore.

And Lawe wasn't his alpha.

In this matter, no fucking man, or Breed, commanded him.

The animal snarled.

The enraged, primal sound that tore from his throat, directed at Dane, would shock him later. For now, he could only let the animal reign.

Dane actually flinched at the sound.

That reaction, as small and involuntary as it was, was all he needed.

Bounding back, Rule fought the savagery mounting inside him until slowly he felt the claws retract once again, just as the lobby doors swooshed open and Jonas, along with six hard-eyed enforcers, stepped into the predawn night.

"Do we have a problem?" Jonas made no move to give a show of strength. He didn't cross his arms over his broad chest, prop his hands on his hips or glare.

He voiced the question evenly while the silver in his eyes swirled like thunderclouds preparing to burst.

"Ah, little brother." Dane was back on his feet, relighting that damned cigar. "Did you come to rescue me?"

Dane was seriously amused now. And that was dangerous. Even the animal inside Rule stepped back a safe distance until it could ascertain the hybrid's next move.

Jonas grunted at the question. "Actually, Dane, I think whatever sliced your throat should have gone for your tongue." He turned to Rule then. "What the *fuck* is your problem?"

"Goddamned nosy-assed Breeds," Rule growled, refusing to back down. "Get the fuck out of my business."

"He ran his little mate off," Dane drawled, though he kept a wary eye on Rule now. "In tears. I scented them even as she rushed from the lobby earlier. Newly mated, hurting and frightened. Shamed." He turned to Lawe. "Sorry, Justice, but that jacket of yours that you placed over her shoulders did nothing to dilute the scent of the Breed that marked her."

"There's no fucking mark," Rule snarled.

Dane gave a mocking little sneer, but it was Lawe's reaction that held Rule. His brother frowned back at him as though disappointed.

"I didn't mark her." Rule shook his head. "I would know if I bit her, dammit."

"You did something," Lawe assured him then, and Rule knew if there was one thing his brother wouldn't do, he would never lie to him. "It was weak, Rule, but the mating scent was there. And the Breed who drove her home reported that the scent only grew stronger after she left. Whatever you did, she's in Mating Heat."

She would be in pain.

He hadn't fully satisfied her. Not enough to still the fires that would begin burning in her.

He rubbed his tongue against his teeth to still that faint irritation—

And he froze.

The glands weren't swollen, they weren't really sensitive, yet it was there. A faint taste of sweet heat he couldn't quite identify. An unfamiliar sensitivity.

He shook his head sharply.

What the fuck was going on?

"He doesn't believe he marked his little mate when she was no more than a child," Dane drawled then, directing the comment to Jonas.

Rule watched as Jonas's gaze flicked to Dane before he shook his head warily, warning the hybrid from saying more. The truth was in the director's eyes, though, as they met Rule's once again.

"I didn't touch her," Rule snapped as he turned on Dane again. "What the fuck kind of monster do you take me for? To suggest I'd touch a child in such a way?"

Surprise flickered in the icy green eyes. "I don't believe you mated her. I said you marked her. You found a way to have your scent placed on her, and it stuck. Just as nature intended it to."

"The hell—"

"You gave the female enforcer present there your shirt to put on her as we pulled those Coyotes off her body. You collected her blanket and handed it to the enforcer who brought it in to her," Jonas broke in. "He's not lying, Rule. Even I sensed your claim on her that night."

Rule shook his head in confusion. "I only saw her for a moment."

They all turned to him then.

"When?" It was Lawe who asked the question roughly. "You were never in the cavern other than those first moments."

"The hell I wasn't," Rule snarled back. "I was there long enough that the scent of her pain was like an insult to my senses. It was my weapon that fired, along with Jonas's, and killed Grody. I saw what they were going to do to her. Do you think I stayed out of the cavern? That I'm not intelligent enough to know how to direct cleanup and keep my eye on what the hell is going on as well?"

He'd shot before he'd even processed what was going on.

That huge fucking Coyote had been between a child's thighs as she screamed for her brother. Those jagged, wrenching screams of rage and pain had been more than the animal inside him could allow. Two others held her down while two more waited behind their leader to have their turn with her.

Rule barely remembered those moments. Seeing the horror of it, the scent of her pain and fear, the agonizing scent of her self-blame and terror that had wrapped around her like a living blanket, had enraged him.

He'd taken out two of the Coyotes before the other shots had been fired.

"Hell, I didn't even realize—" Jonas shook his head, staring at Rule as though seeing him for the first time. "When I first realized she'd been claimed, even I was unaware it was you for a while."

"I didn't fucking claim her," he snapped. "She was a child."

What did they take him for anyway?

Rule scratched at the irritating little itch beneath his tongue by rubbing it against his teeth again.

Fuck this.

He'd had enough.

He turned, stalking off into the parking lot and heading for the secured parking area where he'd left the Dragoon he'd driven in the night before.

"Where the fuck are you going?" It was Lawe, moving in beside him, who dared to ask that question.

Rule paused long enough to snarl out, "To get my fucking mate."

His mate?

To ensure that the cackling South African bastard with a death wish didn't make the mistake of touching what wasn't his to touch. Because Dane's death could cause Jonas more problems than he caused the director breathing.

"It may be too late, Rule." His brother caught at his shoulder, forcing him to a stop despite the animal snarling inside him. "Listen to me, dammit, I don't know what you did to her, what you said to her, but the woman who left here tonight was not the woman who went up with you. Whatever happened, she was . . ." Lawe breathed out roughly. "It was like you broke something."

Rule's jaw tightened. "She's still the same woman. I didn't break anything, dammit. She's pissed."

"She's not pissed," Lawe denied in confusion. "You changed her, Rule. You took something from her, and I don't know if you can fix it."

Jerking from his brother's grip, he threw a disgruntled snarl his way before turning and moving more quickly than before for the Dragoon. Lawe was wrong, he had to be wrong. Gypsy would forgive him, she wouldn't have a choice.

She was his mate.

The Unknown had trained her once they'd realized they couldn't control her. As Gypsy stepped to the window that looked out on her parents' home, she had only a second to wonder at the instinct they'd used to prepare her for any eventuality. Because Breeds were slipping around her apartment like shadowed wraiths.

Quickly pulling the satellite phone she'd safely stored in a hidden pocket of her dress, she dialed her contact's number.

"Whisper?" he answered before the first ring had completed.

"Extraction needed from primary residence," she requested softly. "Importance classified as immediate."

"Negative. Extraction denied."

Denied?

She couldn't have heard correctly.

"Breeds are surrounding the primary residence," she fought to speak, her throat tightening in near fear. "Extraction imperative."

"Extraction denied, Whisper," he answered again, this time, more gently. "You slept with Breaker. You're marked as his mate."

She was barely aware of her head shaking slowly, denial ripping through her senses at the knowledge that no extraction would be forthcoming.

"What? . . ."

"You were told no lovers for a reason. Take a human lover and his prejudice could prejudice you. A Breed lover, and the chances of becoming mated and giving that lover complete loyalty was far too high. This is the last time this number will be answered."

"You promised," she retorted, her voice hoarse. "You said you would never desert me . . ."

"I said I would always listen to my voice mail. You didn't just take a lover, Whisper. You made certain I can't interfere. Not for a Breed mate," he informed her, his voice soft, though without mercy. "The Breeds coming for you were sent by your lover. Our protection is no longer required."

The line disconnected.

Gypsy didn't pause to think.

In a matter of seconds the dress was lying on her bed in a heap of rich material as she dug into the side of her mattress and pulled the black skin suit she used to slip through the night when she herself didn't want to be seen.

Pulling the tough material of the form-fitting pants and long-sleeved shirt on, she slipped the scent blocker from a hidden pocket, tucked it quickly under her tongue and hoped she had enough time for it to take effect.

She was praying they weren't expecting her to leave the apartment and weren't watching for her. If they were, as well trained as they were, then her chances of escaping would be limited. And she was betting they would be watching for her.

Was that why Rule had jumped from her?

Had he somehow sensed or scented something that gave her away? Had she somehow managed to leave her scent behind the night she had searched his rooms? Whatever she had done, if she had done anything, there was no doubt no chances would be taken in their effort to take her now, if she was indeed his mate.

She'd heard whispers of mating, though not since Jonas Wyatt and his men had arrived in Window Rock.

Mating was forever, it was told. White-hot sexual need, blinding hunger, complete loyalty. Not a single Breed wife, lover or so-called mate had ever given the secrets of the Breeds to anyone willing to tell them.

Each one had fallen easily beneath her Breed's spell.

She sure as hell wasn't going to make it easy for them. She was going to get the hell out of there and get out fast. She had never depended upon her contact or the Unknown to ensure her safety. Mark had taught her better than that. He had died awaiting help, awaiting extraction. She'd always sworn she would never make the same mistake.

Less than a minute later she was moving silently down the narrow, dusty steps set between the walls, a little hidden access her brother had shown her in the old store when she was barely a teenager. This was the reason why she had taken the second-floor apartment rather than the first. There was no access to the staircase from the first floor. And no way to know that it led to a small tunnel that exited on the same small street where the only other person who might help her lived.

Cullen lived in a small house at the end of the street, his sheltered backyard less than ten feet from the exit.

Her contact had told her once that if she was ever in trouble with no way to contact him or, for whatever reason, unwilling to contact him, Cullen would help her. Besides, Cullen was her boss, and she knew he liked her. Surely he wouldn't turn his back on her too?

But was it really only what she deserved?

The distant thought had her breathing hitching on a sob.

She'd never paid for leading her brother into a trap, not really. Not as she had expected to. Was this her penance instead? To realize that despite years of trying to ensure loyalties, she'd failed at the most elemental level and was just as alone as she had been the night she stood in the dark watching her parents turn from her?

If it was her punishment, she'd accept it. She couldn't fight what couldn't be changed.

But God, surely there was someone she could depend on.

She knew Cullen, and she trusted him.

At this moment, she had no other place to turn. The Unknown considered her compromised, Rule had thrown her away. He wasn't sending Breeds to protect her. To secure her perhaps, but not to protect her. Somehow, she must have betrayed herself, that was all it could have been. There was no reason for Breeds to be surrounding her apartment other than to arrest her for some reason.

She'd read nothing in Breed Law about any statutes against running from the asshole Breed who didn't know how to be a lover.

Climbing silently from the ravine above the storm drain the tunnel led into, she checked the area quickly before making her way into the tree line that surrounded Cullen's adobe house.

The small house was inconspicuous. It was a bachelor's home, but Gypsy knew things about that house that she doubted anyone else knew. Things her brother had told her about ways into it, out of it and a maze of hidden caves beneath it. She had no doubt in her mind that Cullen was well aware of them as well.

It wasn't the only house in town with hidden access, or hidden tunnels. It wasn't the only house with a history, and her brother had, for some reason, made certain she'd known about all of the ones he'd been aware of.

Moving slowly to the back of the house, she kept her eyes moving constantly, watching the shadows she hovered within, certain no one would be watching for her there, but unwilling to take any chances.

Sweat gathered along her body beneath the wicking fabric of the outfit she wore. The unusual summer heat soaked her skin and her hairline far quicker than usual. The fabric felt itchy against her flesh, the arousal Rule had left burning in her body tormenting her now. The fact that she couldn't just ignore it was pissing her off too.

She wanted to hate him.

Tears threatened to spill from her eyes as she paused next to one of the large trees at the edge of the house. Forcing herself to catch her breath for a second, she watched the area carefully, desperately searching for some sign of Cullen.

Or any Breeds that could have followed her.

Nothing moved but a light breeze. Nothing could be heard but the sparse traffic several streets over and the crickets that chirped playfully among the leaves of the trees.

Reaching to her hip, she slid the sat phone from her belt and activated it silently to call Cullen before barging in on him.

"No need to call. I'm right here."

The low, cross male voice had her ducking quickly and moving to the other side of the tree as her weapon cleared its holster.

"It's Cullen, Gypsy," he sighed.

Stepping from behind the tree, she faced him warily, her emotions uneven, fear, anger and desperation filling her.

"I'm being hunted," she whispered. "And denied extraction by someone

I've been helping. I was once told you would help . . ." But not if the Unknown themselves denied her.

Her voice was too rough, the tears she held back too close to falling. She'd been betrayed by the lover she'd given up retribution for, and by the small sect of warriors she'd dedicated her life to for nine years.

What was there left to lose?

"Come on." He strode past her to the back door. "I knew you'd end up here when I received the report of those Breeds positioning themselves around the store. I'll put some coffee on and you can tell me what the hell's going on."

Tugging at the neckline of her black shirt before rubbing at her shoulder and the irritation of the material, she followed him silently until they were safely locked on the other side of the door. The room they stepped into was shadowed and cool.

He didn't turn any lights on, but it was far easier to see him now. He moved through the kitchen they'd entered before stopping at the coffeepot and flipping it on. The sound of hot water flowed into the filter as the scent of coffee reached her senses.

"Did you take one of the scent blockers?" he asked, his back still to her.

"Yes," she answered, staring around the kitchen curiously. "I came through the tunnels, but the entrance to them should be safe."

For the most part, Cullen's home was devoid of personalization. The normal appliances were there, but little decoration with the exception of a small crystal fairy and a six-inch dagger with a mother-of-pearl hilt sitting on the small breakfast counter between the kitchen and darkened living area.

"It's your apartment." He shrugged. "Your scent permeates it anyway. Your escape should have been undetectable if anyone entered it."

Turning back to him, she frowned at the comment. "If? Why would they have been there if not to come after me? They were surrounding the place like SWAT or something."

He grunted at that. "They were there in a surveillance capacity alone. Trust me, if they were there to take you, you wouldn't have seen them before they were in the apartment. The threat wasn't from the Breeds sent to watch out for you, it's the Breed who should be arriving at your place the moment he's realized you've run from him. The security team was sent to protect you until he managed to get his head out of his ass."

Her heart jumped in her chest. "What do you mean by that?"

Choosing two cups from the cupboard, he poured their coffee before picking them up and turning back to her to nod at the breakfast counter. "Have a seat. We have to talk."

She suddenly felt like a teenager being called down by the principal. She'd not even experienced that in school.

"Why are Breeds surrounding my house, Cullen?" she asked as she slid into one of the high stools and pushed back the hair that had fallen over her shoulder.

She hadn't even had time to braid it before running. It still hung down her back in a riot of carefully arranged curls as the front and sides fell from where it was secured at the crown of her head.

"This is a fucking mess," Cullen sighed roughly as he lifted his cup, pausing at his lips as amusement flickered in his gaze. "Amusing, but a fucking mess."

Her eyes narrowed at the casual arrogance in his voice.

"And what has you so damned amused?" Leaning forward, her forearms braced on the counter as her gaze narrowed on him, Gypsy promised herself she wouldn't tell him what a complete asshole he was being.

"You have me amused." Once he made that cryptic comment, the cup touched his lips and he sipped from the heated liquid.

He didn't appear in any hurry to tell her exactly what had him so damned amused at her expense, though.

As he returned the cup to the counter, still watching her silently, Gypsy sat back on her stool, her head tilting to the side.

Crossing her arms over her breasts, she watched him angrily, waiting, and it wasn't patiently.

He merely stared back at her with a hint of a smile on his face.

"What kind of game are you playing with me?" she asked him, suspicion beginning to grow within her. "And why?"

She'd known him for years, had worked for him at the Navajo Covert Law Enforcement office for the last few years. He had been a friend of her brother's, though he hadn't arrived in Window Rock until after Mark's death. He'd quickly become a friend of her parents', and of hers and Kandy's. She had always known he was arrogant, but this cool, merciless amusement she hadn't seen in him before.

"No game, Gypsy," he promised, flashing her a quick smile as he lifted the coffee cup to his lips once again and sipped. Lowering it, he sat back as well. "My only intent is to do whatever I can to help you. I knew Mark was an informant for an unidentified group that aided the Breeds, and I greatly admired him for it. Just as I've always suspected you were as well."

Well, didn't he just know a whole lot of nothing.

At least, according to him.

"You aren't part of that group, then?" She had wondered, she had hoped he was part of it, just for her own safety.

"Don't ask questions." His voice hardened, as did his gaze. "You're only going to waste our time, and we don't have long before that Breed you ran from finds you."

"I took the scent blocker." Her head was shaking before she could stop it.

"There are instances when the scent blocker doesn't work," he informed her, his voice still as hard as stone, his gaze icy. "I rather doubt it's working now. Any Breed who gets within a quarter mile of this place will know a Breed mate is in the vicinity once he catches the scent of Mating Heat I'm sure is rolling off you at the moment. At the most, we may have an hour before he arrives, simply because it should take that long before a team passes by here. If we're lucky."

If they were lucky.

The irritation along her flesh was growing worse, amplifying the longer she sat there. The arousal Rule had left burning within her not only was still there, but it too was worse than it had been before she left her apartment.

And she'd read of those symptoms in the past, in the tabloids and gossip rags that carried the outrageous stories of "Breed Mating Heat."

"What's going on? Mating Heat is supposed to be a rumor, nothing more." Could that really be what was going on inside her? She could feel a difference in her body that didn't make sense, in the arousal and physical need for him. But it wasn't supposed to be real . . .

She might not have a lot of experience in arousal or sex, but even she knew she shouldn't be growing painfully aroused without a reason. And she'd left her reason in the shower after he'd jumped from her as though she sickened him.

"Are there other instances when the blocker doesn't work? I searched his suite a few weeks ago; could he have somehow learned I was in his rooms?" she probed when he didn't answer her. There wasn't a chance Rule had learned she worked with the Unknown, but he could have somehow learned she was in his rooms.

"I doubt he has a clue." That gleam of curious amusement. "If he had, then he would certainly not have taken you to his bed. Instead, he would have charged you for crimes against Breed Law." A quick glance at his watch. "I would guess you have perhaps forty-five minutes now."

He wasn't helping her.

"Then if we're short on time, perhaps you should tell me, if I'm his perfect special mate," she sneered, "why am I here instead? Why would he be searching for me at all when he was the one who rejected me?" Her breath hitched involuntarily as the pain ambushed her, thickening her voice, pushing tears closer to the surface. "How did I mess up, Cullen?"

Surprise registered on his face as sympathy filled his gaze now. "You're always so certain you're the one who's messed up," he said gently. "You've done nothing wrong, Gypsy. Maybe you finally realized there was more to life than vengeance when you slept with your Breed."

If she had, then she'd found out quickly just how wrong she was, hadn't she?

She rubbed at her arms nervously, the sensitivity increasing as she felt wariness rising inside her. And perhaps even a hint of fear.

"How do you know—?" She broke off when his expression immediately darkened.

"That you're his mate?" he broke in. "I know because you suddenly have two teams of Breed Enforcers that Jonas Wyatt can ill afford to put on surveillance for one unimportant party girl, and trust me, little girl, Commander Breaker won't be far behind. And I know because several Breeds I'm in contact with notified me immediately upon catching the scent of it as you rushed by them when you left the hotel."

"Why?" she cried out, the pain-filled anger that burned inside her setting fire to her emotions, her denial. "Why the hell would he come after me? He didn't want me, Cullen."

"You're his mate." He leaned forward intently. "He may be shocked, surprised. As I understand it, most male Breeds don't handle the initial mating phase any better than their human mates, but it won't have taken that territorial, possessive-as-fucking-hell animal inside him long to convince him that there's not a chance he's going to really let you go."

His mate. This couldn't be possible. The stories were warped, many hinting at depravity, at sexual acts that Gypsy just couldn't believe.

The stories in the tabloids had supposedly been proven to have no basis. They still abounded. With each engagement or marriage between a Breed and their partner, the stories would flare up again for a day or so before dwindling away.

She couldn't believe it was true. It was so farfetched, surely it was impossible.

"Stop shaking your head," he ordered brusquely. "Didn't think there could be a grain of truth to the rumors in the tabloids?"

"Impossible." Jumping from the bar stool, she faced him furiously now, fighting to deny what he was suggesting. "Trust me, if mating existed, then I wouldn't be sitting here with you, Cullen, I'd still be in the bed with him."

There was no denying it had happened. He knew she had slept with Rule. Evidently he had a very reliable Breed contact after all, just, hopefully, a delusional one.

Gypsy watched him warily now. "If you have a Breed contact, then why weren't you asked to search those rooms?"

Cullen grimaced. "Evidently whoever they are, they don't trust me enough to contact me regarding it. I was to be your backup. Nothing more. And my contact within Jonas's organization is a very clever ploy I suspect to enable him to gain his own contact within the law enforcement community."

"Why you?" She watched him carefully, wondering now how far she could truly trust him.

"I'm commander of the Covert Law Enforcement Division, Gypsy. Who else would have the information they need when it comes to any secret activities in the area?"

And she knew that, she really did.

Lifting her hand to her forehead, she could feel the perspiration gathering there as her senses continued to riot while arousal tightened her sex and spilled the silky release of her juices.

"Gypsy, whoever you spy for, it can be very dangerous. As I understand it, Jonas already suspects your involvement, though Rule has fought him over it," he told her grimly. "Don't allow either of them to become certain. It could be more dangerous than you realize." The cold, hard edge to his voice had her watching him closely.

"Yeah, I'm just going to take out an ad for that one." She glared back at him.

He snorted at that. "Breeds have a way of convincing their mates to trust everything about them. To trust their ability to hold their secrets. But *you* trust *me*, Jonas has a way of figuring it all out and using everyone to his own ends. Whoever's behind the protection of the Breeds here in the nation, I wouldn't want to fuck with them. They have a way of becoming brutal."

They had cut out the tongue of the informant who had helped the Coyotes identify her brother. Her parents had received the letter that had been left tucked in the pocket of the dead man.

We, those not spoken of, have taken retribution for the death of your son, the pain that fills your daughter, and the loss your family now suffers. Know that Mark's work, his dedication and commitment to our people will never be forgotten, nor will his family. Sleep easy when darkness falls, and know that we are the ones who will now stand guard over those you love to ensure that evil never again takes from you those you love most.

But nothing could bring Mark back, nothing could erase her part in it and nothing could erase the fact that she'd betrayed her family again when she threw it all away for a Breed she sickened to the point that he had to jump from her and run to the shower.

"I swore I wouldn't tell anyone anything when I began working with them. Not that I know anything to tell anyone," she bit out furiously. "But, even if I did, I definitely wouldn't tell Rule Breaker."

She had no intentions of speaking to that bastard again, let alone giving him so much as a single one of her suspicions.

He glanced at his watch again and looked up at her. "He'll track you here, Gypsy. Soon. Breeds never let their mates remain unprotected."

"What do I do?" Her heart began racing in dread.

She couldn't face him again. Not this soon.

"Here's what I suggest you do." He leaned forward intently. "Slip back out of here and go back to your apartment. If he sees that slick little night suit you're wearing, or realizes you've taken a scent blocker, then you're fried, baby. He's going to know you're the spy he's searching for. Here." Reaching into the front pocket of his shirt, he pulled free a small pill, similar in shape to the scent blocker. "Within fifteen minutes this will reverse the blocker and leave your system clean. Take it now."

He laid it in front of her, watching her with sudden amusement once again. "Unless you're of a mind not to trust me."

She took the pill warily, placed it on her tongue and let it begin to dissolve. When it had properly broken down, she washed it down with the remainder of the coffee before taking a deep breath.

"You're throwing me to the wolves, aren't you?" She asked him then.

He wasn't going to help her escape Rule.

If Rule was even coming for her.

"The lions actually," he corrected her, a quirk of a smile edging at his lips as he watched her curiously. "I'm confident it's in your best interests, though."

"Oh, I'm sure you are." Setting the coffee cup back on the counter carefully, she stared back at him. The anger burning inside her was far stronger than it should have been. Far stronger than it would have been normally. Because normally, she would have felt she had a choice. In this instance, Cullen had reminded her that she might not have a choice. And that infuriated her.

Even more infuriating was the feeling that in some way, he was attempting to maneuver her exactly where Rule wanted her to be.

"What you've done for the group you've worked for has been commendable, Gypsy," he said then, his voice gentle, soft. "Let yourself live now. You deserve it."

Yeah. Right.

As she stared back at him, anger pulled her lips tight, suspicion edging at thoughts that weren't becoming overwhelmed with a sexual need nearing critical.

"Do I? Whether I do or not, it seems I'm not working with them any longer anyway." Despite the gentleness of his expression, there was no mercy in the somber intent of his gaze.

Oh yes, she definitely had her suspicions. She wouldn't reveal them, not now. Far better to hold on to them for the moment.

"Go home," he urged her. "And in a month, if you still want to run, I'll help you myself."

"A month? Why a month?" What did that length of time have to do with anything? What game was he playing with Jonas Wyatt and with her?

"You tell me, in a month." Rising to his feet, he watched her with that quiet gaze, that hint of calculation. "Rest, Gypsy. Consider it a bit of a vacation, despite the aggravation of your Breed. You've earned it."

Had she? Why didn't she feel as though she had earned it?

"Go home, Gypsy."

Go home?

She didn't think so.

There were far too many Breeds there. One too many, no doubt. And that one, she couldn't bear to see again.

But she did leave Cullen's house. She even let him watch her disappear into the storm drain and let him think she was moving through the tunnels and returning to her apartment.

But if that was where Rule intended to be, then Gypsy intended to be just as far away from there as possible.

Once inside the tunnel, she turned down another shadowed path. There, stuffed inside a crevice and resting on a narrow ledge, was a pack she checked and changed often. Several changes of clothing, a weapon, sat phone, cash and the keys to the powerful black motorcycle she kept stashed in case of emergency.

This was definitely an emergency, she decided.

Of the worst sort.

"What do you mean, she's not in the apartment?" Even the animal that had been pacing erratically inside him came to an immediate stop to stare at the Breed unlucky enough to have to give him that information.

"We've used heat sensors and infrared, Commander. The sister is in the lower apartment, sleeping. The upper apartment is empty." The Wolf, Cole Dagger, stood relaxed but on guard as his dark gaze remained steady despite the growl Rule was unable to contain.

"You're certain it's Kandy in the lower apartment, not Gypsy?" Rule had to be certain. He was holding on to his rage by the thinnest thread.

And his fear.

The fear that she had been taken.

That she could be taken.

That a scalpel could slice into her delicate flesh as she screamed until her voice broke, until her scent was a red haze of agony in the air around him. That because of him, despite his wariness, his constant vigilance against coming in contact with his mate. Despite all his precautions, he had failed her.

"Commander?" Dagger questioned him, his tone holding the faintest sound of wariness. Not fear, but definitely a sense of high alert.

"Rule, ease it back." Lawe stepped next to him, calling Rule's attention to the fact that he was glaring at the Wolf as he reached out to the added strength his brother offered no matter where he might be in the world.

At that moment, Lawe's hand landed on his shoulder despite the discomfort he knew Rule might feel at this point.

There was no discomfort, though. His entire body, every sense was alive with the agonizing knowledge that his mate could be in danger. There was no pain greater than that.

His gaze bored into the Wolf's. "Find her." His voice felt rough, jagged. "Find her before anyone else does."

He didn't bother to make a threat. The flicker of Dagger's dark gaze and the scent of concern, of immediate intent to do what was required, was all that mattered to him.

The Wolf nodded, turned and immediately loped into the night as Rule fought against the primal rage building inside him.

"We have men at the bars?" he asked his brother.

"Heading there now," Lawe assured him. "You need to pull back. If she sees you like this, Rule, you'll terrify her."

What she would see was the animal in his eyes, eyes that gleamed in shades of blue so brilliant they were nearly neon.

"She ran." The snarl was impossible to hold back.

Swinging his head around to meet his brother's darker gaze, Rule glared back at him, his hands clenching the weapons holstered on both thighs.

"Did she have a reason to run?" Lawe asked softly. "Think about that, Rule. What reason did you give her to run?"

"I didn't harm her." He knew what Lawe was thinking. That somehow he must have hurt the woman that the animal inside him had claimed. The woman the man had already fallen in love with.

"Physically," Lawe agreed. "I would never have imagined you had hurt her physically, Rule. But what happened otherwise?"

What happened otherwise.

What the hell *had* happened?

Explaining it was a bitch, but he knew hiding it wouldn't work, as Lawe would just keep probing until he figured it out.

"I pulled away as I felt the barb emerging." Releasing the hilt of the blade holstered at his thigh, he pushed his fingers through his hair restlessly, his senses continually testing the air around him for Gypsy's scent.

"You did what?" Lawe stepped back, staring at him in shock, as though the information was far too much to take in.

"What?" Rule growled, furious, humiliated with his own weakness. "I could feel it emerging. Fuck." He turned away from his brother as the other man blinked back at him, the disbelief growing. "What the fuck is your problem?" he snarled as he immediately rounded on Lawe once again.

"You pulled free of her before releasing?" Lawe cleared his throat as though suddenly uncomfortable with the conversation.

Rule shifted, suddenly even more unwilling to discuss this subject than ever before. "Maybe, just as it began." His teeth clenched at the admission.

"And umm, exactly at what stage was your mate in?" Lawe asked, wincing as he rubbed at one side of his face uncomfortably.

His mate had been locked in her release, holding to him, her delicate little nails digging into his shoulders as the fist-tight sheath surrounding his cock rippled around him with a fiery pleasure that had shocked him.

"Fuck, Rule! No damned wonder she ran out on you." Lawe's eyes widened, filling with shocked amusement as the memory surged into Rule's conscious thoughts and echoed into Lawe's.

That damned link.

Rule pulled back immediately, breaking that awareness they had of each other that enabled them to draw on the other's strength or knowledge.

"That's not even the worst of it," Rule muttered, unable to meet his brother's gaze now. "I told her I would take her home after I showered."

Why had he done something so insane?

"Shower?" Lawe sounded confused.

"Cold shower," Rule muttered.

"A cold shower?"

"Are you a fucking parrot all of a sudden?" he snapped out, his anger surging at Lawe's response.

"Parrot? No." Lawe shook his head, one hand bracing on the butt of his automatic laser weapon where it rested against his own thigh. "But Rule, I have to say, tonight I'm beginning to wonder if we're truly brothers."

Rule snorted at the comment. "I've been questioning it from the day we were told. Never made sense to me either."

Though for far different reasons than his brother's, he was sure.

"She's going to kick your ass," Lawe chuckled then, turning from him to stare around the darkness and the Breed shadows hidden within it as they awaited their orders.

Two-man teams had been sent to all the bars the Breeds knew of. Those that were public, private and underground. Still, two hours after she had stepped into her apartment, she hadn't been seen.

"She's welcome to kick my ass," Rule breathed out roughly, turning and staring into the darkness, desperate to see her walking through it. "As long as she's safe."

As long as the soldiers and Breeds still operating on orders from the Genetics Council didn't get their hands on her. As long as the scientists still living, intent on deciphering the secrets of the animals they had created, didn't cut into her.

"Stop, Rule. Let those memories be. No good can come of remembering them."

Swinging around, he released an animalistic snarl from his chest as he bared his teeth at the Breed who had stood by him, behind him or in front of him for as long as he could remember.

"She's alone. Any Breed in the vicinity will scent the Heat. They could take her." The thought of it had his teeth snapping together as he fought to bite off the growl of renewed rage.

"And losing control of yourself will do nothing but endanger her further," Lawe rebuked him firmly.

He hadn't lost control of himself since the labs. Since his mother's youngest cubs had been sent away and he'd been informed they were too weak to be allowed to live.

Rage burned inside him when he'd learned the little Cougar Breed female had been lost. It was one of the reasons he'd been so secretively protective of the main Pride's Cougar sister, Dawn Daniels, until her mating.

Now, fighting back that demonic fury was harder than it had ever been. The animal inside him was demanding freedom. Demanding that it be allowed to protect its mate no matter the consequences or the blood that flowed. It demanded that the man step back, and Rule couldn't allow himself to step back. He knew the rampage of fury the animal could create.

Still, his guts tightened as another growl tore from his chest, that inner fury he kept locked so deep inside himself rising closer to the fore as each second passed and Gypsy wasn't found.

· C H A P T E R 1 8 ·

There was too much energy.

It surged inside her. It laid waste to any concept of controlling the need to move, to undulate in sensual abandon. Her body was a mass of electrical stimulation with no place to discharge.

And it was driving her insane.

The underground club, Caine's, was a country-pop-rock free-for-all where dirty dancing was almost required and the things that happened in the corners of the rooms weren't dared to be mentioned in polite society. It was a club she rarely came to. But tonight, a Coyote group was headed there. A group that promised to hold the key to some much-needed information.

A year before she'd overheard a Coyote soldier discussing a lab in the western United States and hinted that it was still in operation, carefully hidden, fully funded and still experimenting on both Breeds and humans. The soldiers heading to the club now were rumored to be coming off duty rotation there before heading to another assignment.

This was the information her contact had been trying to get to her the week before when he'd been forced to abort the exchange of information. She could have had advance notice. She could have eliminated the mistake she'd made by going to Rule's bed, and already had plans in place and questions prepared that would draw out the information she needed.

Now, she was working without plans, without backup and without the careful control she'd always depended upon to ensure that the suspicious, scent-sensitive Coyotes never picked up on the fact that each question, each smile, each flirtatious comment was no more than a careful deception.

Until her much-sought-after Coyote team arrived, though, she was going to dance.

Her lashes lowered over her eyes as Ashley, Emma, and Sharone danced with her, Gypsy sipped at the beer she'd carried onto the dance floor with her and fought back tears. She'd been fighting back tears since she'd left that damned hotel the night before.

"Hey." She turned quickly to Ashley rather than allow a lone teardrop to fall. "Cassie couldn't come with you?"

Her gaze lacking the sparkling excitement it once held, Ashley still managed to give her a slight smile. "Jonas has her on lockdown for some reason," she called back over the music, the hint of Russian in her voice giving it a mocking undertone.

"Let's go rescue her," Gypsy suggested, ignoring the amused, mocking horror that flashed in the Coyote female's gaze while her sister stared back in pure fear.

"We don't fuck with Wyatt, Gypsy." Emma shook her head, shoulder-length dark hair flowing around her face as the Russian accent crept into her voice as well. "He's damned scary."

Gypsy snorted at the description. "He can't kill us."

"He can make us wish we were dead once he gets finished telling the alpha all our dirty little secrets," Ashley informed her, leaning close, her gaze intent. "We do not let the alpha know all our dirty little secrets."

They tiptoed around their alpha as anyone else would a rabid animal.

"I can't believe the three of you are scared of your alpha," she laughed back at them.

"Two," Sharone informed her. "Those two"—she pointed to Ashley and Emma—"are terrified of their alpha because they know damned good and well he would have nightmares for weeks if he knew what they were doing. And he would ensure they did it no more."

"Sharone's the good little Coyote soldier," Ashley smirked, a hint of her former self in the sudden sparkle of merriment in her gaze. "She never gets into trouble."

Sharone merely rolled her eyes, but Gypsy could see the concern in the other woman's gaze as it drifted around the room.

She might be a stick in the mud, as Ashley and Emma called her, but she was intuitive, cautious and rumored to be a stone-cold killer whose efficiency, lack of emotion and attention to detail was nearly unparalleled among the female Breeds.

Despite the hard, fast pace of the music, the driving tempo and the perspiration that poured from her body and dampened the black cami top she wore, Gypsy was still burning inside. She could feel the moisture collecting on her bare skin, running in small rivulets here and there. It was a caress that drove her crazy, that made her ache for Rule's touch.

That ache was becoming deeper, hotter. She moved with the music and found herself drifting, remembering his touch. His lips at her throat, her need to feel his teeth raking against her flesh.

As his lips had caressed her shoulder, she'd waited. Ached. Needed to feel his teeth there.

His touch was an addiction.

She was seeing that now.

What they called Mating Heat was a compulsive, overpowering drug. One taste. One kiss, and she'd become something, someone she wasn't.

She wasn't a lover. She'd known that since the day she'd been told she couldn't have one and still avenge her brother's murder.

Hips swaying, her body moving sensually as languid need burned ever hotter inside her, Gypsy railed at herself for her decision that night.

She'd given to him, given him everything only to learn that everything was either too much or not enough.

"We should go." Ashley's suggestion had her eyes opening as she lifted the beer to her lips and sipped at it lazily, her gaze raking over the club.

"Why?" The Coyotes weren't here yet. She still had information to get.

If the Unknown didn't want it, then she knew many, many groups still involved in routing out the hidden labs who would want it.

Hell, Jonas would want it.

She could just work for him.

The thought was almost amusing.

"Because it's nearly dawn?" Ashley drawled, her tone amused, her eyes flat and hard.

Gypsy let her gaze wander over the club again, her skin suddenly prickling with a latent warning of danger. She could feel it stroking against her flesh with an icy stroke.

"Bye-bye." She waved back at the three girls as they seemed to share a concerned look. "Catch you at the next party."

She wasn't going anywhere.

Sleeping with Rule wasn't nearly the compensation she would have imagined for giving up her entire life. What the hell had made her do something so irrational to begin with?

Mating Heat should be outlawed anyway. It made a woman's heart do things that her head knew was inadvisable. Things that hurt worse than facing the loneliness.

The music shifted, pounding harder, faster. Turning from the three girls, Gypsy opened her eyes once again and found herself confronted with a broad, male chest.

It wasn't Rule's chest.

Her gaze lifted.

Lifted.

Wow, now this dude was fucking tall.

And he was pissed.

Six feet six if he was an inch, super long black hair pulled back in a low ponytail and Celtic green eyes. Eyes so bright, so lacking in warmth or mercy that they were like a frozen sea.

"You are becoming a nuisance, Ms. McQuade." And his voice was like serrated gravel, rough and sharp with a deadly baritone.

"Oh God, we're dead." That was Sharone behind her.

"Will we get that lucky?" Emma sounded completely terrified.

"We're screwed. He'll tell the alpha . . ." Ashley was actually whispering in the sudden silence of the club.

"Stop already!" Gypsy turned on the three girls with a furious hiss before turning back to the guy with freaky-as-hell too-green eyes. "Who the hell are you anyway?"

"Their worst nightmare if you don't leave this establishment this moment," he stated firmly, frozen sea green eyes gleaming icily back at her.

"Go now," Ashley gripped her arm.

The pain.

It struck at her with a suddenness that had her jerking from the female

Coyote violently, causing all three of them to jump back as Gypsy swung away in a graceful pivot. She cleared not just the female Coyotes, but also tall, dark, and who-the-hell-ever.

They stared back at her, shocked, four gazes each going slowly to the military-perfect, well-trained stance she had taken.

And in that second, Gypsy realized that this man knew things about her that even Rule couldn't suspect yet.

The music was pounding again, loud and hard, the beat racing through her bloodstream and thankfully covering from others' gazes the perfect stealth maneuver that had swung her away from Ashley as well as the male attempting to reach out for her.

The Breed grinned, displaying strong, white, wickedly sharp canines at the side of his mouth.

"Breed," she muttered, eyes narrowing.

"You have no idea." Emma was shaking her head as Gypsy read her lips.

"Go!" Eerie green eyes shifted color and became more frozen as he made the demand.

She didn't have to hear the tone to know the order in it.

"No."

He stared back at her with an intensity that was almost frightening. She had to admit, that was one damned freaky look.

Still, she turned her back on him, flipped back her hair and made her way to the bar. She ignored the looks. She ignored Ashley's nervous calling of her name behind her.

Her friends might be scared of Mr. Freaky, but she wasn't.

Tonight, she would be damned if she was scared of anyone.

Not Mr. Freaky, and not some half-assed Breed mate who thought she should be waiting whenever he decided to get around to claiming what he'd thrown away to begin with.

"Ms. McQuade." The deep drawl directly behind her had Gypsy turning again as she reached the bar, anger flaring in her at the sight of the tall Breed towering over her.

"What the hell do you want? And who are you anyway?" she practically yelled at him as the music rose in volume, thundering through the crowd filling the club.

"If you aren't willing to leave for your own safety, perhaps you'll leave for Commander Breaker's." His head lowered to allow her to hear him over the music. "He should be pulling into the parking lot at any moment—"

She didn't wait around to hear anything more.

A curse sizzled from her lips, causing the Breed to draw himself stiffly erect as she turned and moved quickly for the entrance.

Dammit, he shouldn't have been able to find her so fast. She'd spent the day laying a false trail to other locations before choosing this bar to dance away the pain throbbing inside her soul. She'd been here less than an hour, not even enough time to drive the aching hurt from her chest let alone the restless anger burning inside her. All she'd wanted to do was dance it away for a while until the Coyote unit she'd heard about arrived. Then she could have immersed herself in the game of extracting the information she needed, listening and getting to know the Coyotes.

As she rushed from the exit, intent now on getting to her motorcycle and finding somewhere else to hide, it took a second to realize that a hard, muscled arm had manacled her waist before she was able to react.

There was no pain.

There was no panic.

That didn't mean she intended to allow him to take her wherever he was suddenly all but dragging her.

"Let me go!" Fury erupted inside her as the heat of him, the strength and pleasure from his touch began sinking inside her.

"The hell I will," Rule snarled, holding her securely despite her struggles and attempts to escape.

She could see the Desert Dragoon he was driving, still running, the driver's-side door thrown open as bright light pierced the darkness at the side of the building. There were Breeds standing around, hard-eyed, without mercy, without compassion and heavily armed as they watched the area closely.

"I'm going to kick your ass." The cry was torn from her as the sudden hunger to feel his lips against hers ached with near-debilitating hunger.

As though his sudden nearness, his touch, just the fact that he was there were enough to remind her of the pleasure he could give her with a strength that had her sex rippling, clenching with the need to be filled again.

"Fine, kick my ass. Do whatever you have to, sweetheart, because I'll be damned if I'll let you go now."

She was pushed into the Dragoon before she could brace herself against the frame to hold herself back. She tried to grab on to the steering wheel to give herself leverage, but somehow he managed to brush her hands aside.

She was in the passenger seat before she really understood exactly how he'd managed to get her into it.

Reaching for the door handle, Gypsy gave a furious growl that would have easily rivaled any Breed's as she felt Rule's broad hand curve around the nape of her neck to grip her securely. The other grasped her chin, turned her to him as he tilted her head back and stole the kiss she lied and swore she would never have given him willingly.

Chocolate and peppermint.

Just a hint of the candies he enjoyed teased her senses before the heated sweetness suddenly overwhelmed her. Hunger rose like a ravenous beast, no longer that irritating fire simmering inside her. It was now a full-fledged blaze, burning through her body, tightening her womb and parting her lips to accept his kiss.

Rather than fighting, she was demanding more with a suddenness she found herself helpless against.

Her hands were in his hair, clenching, pulling him to her as she felt the fiery lick of his tongue against hers.

Peppermint and chocolate.

Once more, it simply teased her senses. Tempted her as his tongue rubbed against hers, his lips moving sensually over hers.

She couldn't help herself, couldn't stop the need for more of him, more of that intriguing taste.

Her tongue rubbed against his, the unique taste of his kiss becoming more heated as tongues caressed and lips devoured each other in a hunger she was helpless to avoid or fight.

Why couldn't she fight him?

She'd had no defenses against him from the very beginning and it didn't make sense.

This need.

This hunger.

It speared inside her, ripped away any lies she would have told herself and refused to allow her to hide from the hunger that built daily inside her.

"No . . ." Her moan was weak, the protest filled with the confusion that had kept her off balance since that first night she'd seen him.

Laying his forehead against hers, he stared back at her, his blue eyes appearing lighter than before, pinpricks of black appearing to flicker in the pale blue background.

"You ran from me." Lips pulling back from his canines, one hand tightened in her hair, the other cupping her jaw to keep her head turned up to him. "You shouldn't have run, Gypsy."

"You shouldn't have treated me like a whore," she shot back, the anger that bloomed inside her over the past hours exploding with the same suddenness with which the arousal and hunger had exploded inside her.

"And you think that's how I treated you?" He frowned back at her, his gaze gleaming with anger.

Jerking from his hold, she was furiously aware that it was only because he allowed her to.

Her hand gripped the door handle and pulled, intent on escaping him with the same desperation he'd used to escape her body earlier.

Except the door didn't open.

Instead, the Dragoon was racing from its parking spot, the speed and power of the vehicle assuring her there would be no escape until he allowed it.

"The doors are secured until I release them. One of my enforcers will take your cycle to the hotel. You and I are going to talk," he growled, both hands on the wheel as he glared into the night behind the state-of-the-art windshield.

Digital holographs lit the glass. Speed, location, outside temperature, GPS tracking and satellite tracking were all subtly lit within the glass, giving him any information he might need on the area surrounding them as he turned onto the main road and headed into the night.

"And just what do you think we have to talk about?" Gypsy asked him then, her voice a mocking sneer as she crossed her arms over her breasts and turned back to him slowly. "Mr. Freaky who decided to ensure I was running out of the bar right into your arms? Or how about why you couldn't even stomach ejaculating while you were having sex with me?"

Or, they could discuss what made him think she was his damned mate.

Revealing her knowledge of that, though, would give away the fact that she had sources that she shouldn't have.

Sources a regular party girl wouldn't have.

"We could definitely discuss your perception of my actions." The roughened sound of the growl rumbling in his chest had a chill racing down her spine. "As for whoever the hell Mr. Freaky is . . ."

"Six and a half feet tall, frozen green eyes and black hair a woman would kill to have herself?"

No expression, not so much as a grimace crossed his face.

"Rhyzan Brannigan," he finally stated. "What the hell was he doing there?"

"You're asking me?" Incredulity filled her voice as she stared back at him in amazement. "Excuse me, Breaker, I think I was the one who asked who the hell he was to begin with. I can't even mind my own damned business anymore without a Breed insisting on horning in on it."

◆ ◆ ◆

The deceit.

Unlike other lies, Gypsy's deceit wasn't tinged with the scent of blood or rot, but he could smell the lie all the same. And like the rest of her, it simply intrigued him. She was the most complicated, stubborn, confusing woman he had ever known.

But at that moment, the deceit, the subject of it and her whereabouts after running from him added up to one thing only.

The Unknown's contact.

And there wasn't a doubt in his mind that Rhyzan Brannigan had finally managed to sniff her out. The new assistant director of the Bureau of Breed Affairs had said he would do so. Rule had just been certain he could keep it from happening.

"Why are you looking at me like that?" Narrowing her gaze on him, she stared back at him with all the ire of a woman scorned.

She wasn't just his merciless little spy, but scorned as well, at least as far as she was concerned.

"Rhyzan Brannigan is Jonas Wyatt's preferred choice of assistant director of the Bureau of Breed Affairs," he told her, giving a tidbit of information that no one else had known. "Jonas is preparing to inform the Breed Ruling Cabinet of his choice once he's finished here in Window Rock. He's also one of the Bureau's best investigators. The only reason he would have been at that bar would have been to identify a spy for an underground group of Navajo Warriors called the Unknown. They call her Whisper."

Her expression never changed.

"And that has exactly what to do with me?" Voiced low, offended, furious, her tone nearly had a smile quirking at his lips.

She was good.

Son of a fucking bitch, she was too damned good, and she was too damned guilty.

"Nothing," he assured her. "But that's likely why he was there. He'll be Jonas's second in command if he's accepted into the position by the Ruling Cabinet. Identifying Whisper was his last assignment before taking that position once approval is formalized."

"Whatever," she breathed out, anger still searing her tone just as deceit seared her scent. "You've still managed to sidestep the original issue with all the grace of a crippled bull in a china shop. Why not just tell me how I managed to sicken you to the point that you had to shower, and get it the hell over with."

As she turned to face forward, the scent of the deceit began to disappear beneath . . .

Pain.

God, he'd hurt her, and he would cut off his own arm before doing so deliberately.

No—she blamed herself for it? She actually believed she had somehow sickened him? Hell, Lawe should have just kicked his ass when he had the chance for allowing that to happen.

"You were not at fault for what happened in that bed, Gypsy," he stated, self-disgust filling him at the lash of humiliation that suddenly surrounded her.

What had he done?

His clumsy ignorance had sliced at her soul in ways he'd never have allowed if he hadn't refused to accept what the beast inside him had evidently known for years.

"Really? So it wasn't my body that you jumped from and rushed to the shower as though dirty? Right?" The low, mocking drawl accompanied by the shame, hurt and distrust that whipped in the air around her nearly caused him to flinch.

Self-control was all that held back that reaction as his hands tightened on the steering wheel. Clenching his teeth against the self-disgust he could feel rising inside him, Rule fought to remind himself that it could be fixed. Their kiss had been infused with the mating hormone; even now it filled the glands at the sides of his tongue, waiting to spill to her once again as their lips met.

She would have to forgive him. They were mates. Mates didn't separate, at least not for long, and that had happened only once. Besides, the separation had been between a Coyote and his mate, not a Lion and his mate.

"The reasons why are complicated," he forced himself to say despite his discomfort.

He deserved the discomfort, he told himself. What his mate felt was far worse.

"I hate that word." The studied disinterest in her tone had him flicking a look at her expression as his lips tightened.

This wasn't the place to discuss what had happened. It wasn't the place to remember what had happened. Those memories were steeped in such agony, in so many nightmares that sometimes he wondered if he would ever be free of them.

"I hate that word as well," he assured her, grimacing at the tight, hoarse sound of his voice. "Nonetheless, it's the truth. Hopefully, once we reach—"

A red alert shot on the windshield before he could say anything more. A heartbeat later, two more joined it as he thumbed the link to Control.

"Control, identify bogies four point six miles behind my mark," he requested.

"Unable to establish link to Control," the computer announced.

"Computer, activate satellite link," Rule commanded as he shifted the Dragoon into higher gear and thumbed the accelerator.

"Satellite link jammed," the computerized voice reported. "You have three vehicles approaching at a high rate of speed. All identifying transponders are deactivated or unable to respond. Activating covert protocols."

The lights went out. Dashboard lights, headlights and running lights went black while the windows darkened further to hide the glow of the faint illumination of the holographs on the windshield.

"Computer, activate Alpha. Navajo. California. Seven. Six. Niner."

The computer repeated the code.

"Affirmed." Rule acknowledged the request that he'd given the correct command. "Activate and begin a repeat pulse emergency signal."

"Activating."

He shifted the vehicle again, its speed increasing as Gypsy watched the display on the windshield, her expression intent.

"Do they have a lock on the Dragoon?" she asked as she watched the red pinpoints indicating the unidentified vehicles gaining on them.

"Computer, process any means of detection locked on our position," he commanded clearly.

"No electronic, satellite, cellular or radar locks detected," the computer reported as Gypsy glanced out the window to verify their position.

"Computer, display GPS and landmarks," Rule ordered rather than questioning Gypsy. "Answer all queries from McQuade, Gypsy Rum. Code Alpha. Foxtrot. India."

"All queries verified," the computer answered.

"McQuade, Gypsy Rum. Alpha. Foxtrot. India," Gypsy spoke clearly as she continued to watch the hologram. "Display all routes not currently provided."

◆ ◆ ◆

She needed to see the back roads. If there was no radar or GPS lock on them, then whoever was behind them, if they were looking for her and Rule, was counting on them to remain on the main road.

"All routes, mapped and unmapped, now displayed."

Her eyes narrowed on the maze of lines that suddenly streaked over the hologram.

"Computer, display only routes leading to the Navajo Suites Hotel. Each individual direction to be highlighted in differing colors."

"All routes leading to the Navajo Suites Hotel displayed and highlighted as requested."

Gypsy nodded at the new display.

Checking the red pinpoints still far enough behind them to ensure that they couldn't physically see the vehicle, Gypsy glanced back at the map.

"Just tell the computer what you need," Rule told her quietly as she used her finger to follow a particular route.

Giving the computer the various detour routes, many that were unmapped anywhere but on Breed mapping systems, she sat back and waited.

Within seconds, the computer was giving Rule the first turn from the interstate, just in time to keep the vehicles behind them from getting them in sight.

Whipping the wheel, Rule took the turn quickly.

"Half mile there's dirt," she advised him. "Dawn's coming, they'll see the dust trail unless you slow down."

She heard the frustrated growl in response, but he slowed considerably and commanded the computer. "Engage dust dispersion."

"Dust dispersion engaged," the computer answered.

Gypsy kept her eyes on the display as the first faint streaks of dawn began to emerge. The Dragoon was moving quickly, ensuring that the vehicles behind them couldn't catch sight of them before they hit the next county road.

The red alert points continued along the interstate, bypassing the turn they'd taken completely.

"Computer, keep bogies in sight and continue to contact Control . . ."

"No," Gypsy told him quietly. "They'll have your transponder number, possibly to the vehicle as well as your phone. They have to have or they wouldn't have known you were headed to the hotel rather than my apartment. If they're using traditional GPS, then your vehicle transponder will still appear to be on the interstate, though very soon, they'll realize it's not. Block your transponder and satellite number until we're closer to the hotel."

He was silent for long seconds before giving the computer the command and listening silently as it was confirmed.

Hell, he should be confronting her over the information she had. Jonas was going to blow a gasket, because the connecting routes she gave the computer to use weren't listed as connecting on the Bureau's GPS files. Which meant they weren't listed on anyone's files. That information, added to her knowledge of transponder and satellite signal tracking, was like a fucking nail in the coffin where hiding her was concerned now.

Fuck, this was a mess.

A mess he had no idea how to save his mate from.

CHAPTER 19

They arrived at the Navajo Suites without incident and pulled into the valet parking, where a Breed Enforcer stepped forward as Rule moved around the Dragoon to open her door. She stepped from the vehicle mutinously, glaring at him, full female fury gleaming in her eyes.

The moment the threat of danger had passed, she had sat back in her seat silently and completely refused to speak to him.

Just what the hell he needed. His mate angrier than ever at a time when he needed her cooperation the most. And he couldn't blame anyone but himself.

If he hadn't been too damned stupid to realize exactly what had been going on over the past few months . . .

If he hadn't been too damned stubborn to claim what was his when he'd first suspected who she was to him, and offered instead to trade his helpless, vulnerable mate for Lawe's warrior mate . . .

No wonder his brother doubted they were actually kin.

Hell, Rule was beginning to wonder why Lawe had even claimed him after that ridiculous offer. Because no woman could fit him more perfectly than his Gypsy.

And no doubt Lawe felt the same way about his own fiery mate.

"I would prefer to go home," she told him as his hand curved around her upper arm to escort her inside the lobby.

"I would prefer you hadn't left to begin with and had given me the time

I needed to explain what was going on," Rule bit out, furious with himself more so than her, but furious all the same.

"Yeah, I really wanted to wait until you managed to disinfect yourself before you gave me a ride home." She was clearly offended.

Tugging at the grip he had on her arm, she made the journey across the spacious floor just as difficult as possible without calling attention to the fact that she was there involuntarily.

"I'd stop attempting to piss me off while it's still possible for me to maintain control, sweetheart," he advised her. "Because, trust me, you have no idea the edge I'm riding right now."

For all her anger, for all the pain and hurt feelings that flowed through her, though, the smell of her heat still managed to intoxicate him. Arousal spiced with a hunger he couldn't quite decipher fully. Emotions he couldn't identify quite yet created an exhilarating scent that had his dick iron hard.

Talking would definitely have to come later.

First, God help him, first he needed to show his fiery little mate exactly who she belonged to. Exactly why she couldn't continue to fight him this way. If it didn't stop, then there wasn't a chance in hell he could protect this incredible gift he'd been given.

It was his place to protect her. And he was beginning to suspect she was going to need more protection than he had ever imagined.

She was his mate.

His mate.

She was his.

One woman.

A woman he was beginning to suspect could complete him in ways he had never imagined.

✦　✦　✦

Stop attempting to piss him off?

Who the hell did he think he was?

Glaring up at him, standing stiffly beside him as they stepped into the elevator, Gypsy was all too aware of the fact that no matter how hard she tried, she couldn't really fight him.

She could have escaped him a dozen times during that damned ride.

She knew exactly how to deactivate the door locks on those stupid Dragoons. Yet she had been unable to make herself do so.

Instead, she had sat silently, refusing to respond to his attempts to talk to her, to ease the anger still simmering inside her. To soothe the aching hurt that still lanced at her heart.

It wasn't just anger or hurt, though.

She ached for him.

Especially since that kiss had fired every freaking neural receptor in her system.

She ached for him with a power that shocked her and infuriated her. Because she should hate him.

She should hate what he was doing to her. What her body was doing to her and her complete inability to make it stop or to control it.

The arousal, her hunger for his touch, his possession, had her stifling a scream of outrage.

Because it wasn't fair.

Her jeans had to be damp. She knew her panties were soaked. Her nipples were so damned hard that each rasp of her bra against them only primed her higher for his touch.

Hell, his touch was all she could think about.

His touch.

His kiss.

His lips on her nipples, between her thighs.

Her thighs clenched at the thought. Her fantasies hadn't come close to the pleasure he had given her, even before he'd jumped from her as though she sickened him.

The pleasure had been incredible. It had whipped through her, searing her body with increasingly powerful sensations until that edge of release she'd touched had been a second of pure nirvana. A pleasure unlike anything she'd imagined in her life.

And she had a damned good imagination.

The elevator doors slid open on the floor where his suite was located. Tightening his grip on her upper arm once again, he all but dragged her to the doors, where he pressed his thumb to the biometric lock—a new installation, she noticed suspiciously—opened the doors, then pulled her inside.

God, had he somehow figured out she was in his suite—

That thought was abruptly cut off.

Before Gypsy could do more than draw a breath, he'd pushed her against the door, his lips covering hers as his hands curved around the back of her thighs and lifted her. Dragging her legs around his hips, he used his body to hold her against the door as he ground the hard wedge of his cock against the sensitive mound of her pussy.

The whimper that left her lips was embarrassing.

Hungry, desperate need. Like a friggin' cat in heat was what she sounded like.

Her hands slid into his hair, her lips parting beneath his as she accepted the hard thrust of his tongue against her own before the subtle taste of spicy sweetness had her attempting to lick at the invader demandingly, her lips closing on it to catch as much of it as possible.

Each taste seemed to push her higher. As though the teasing heat of his kiss were enough to stroke her senses to a fever pitch of arousal.

Her knees gripped his hard hips, another moan escaping her throat as the heated strength of the heavy shaft ground against her. The firm pressure stroked denim and silk over the swollen bud of her clit as her hips tilted to get closer to the caress.

Oh God, this was what she needed.

He was what she needed.

And she needed more.

Her nails bit into the fabric of his shirt. Clenching it, pulling at it, she fought to get closer to him. The feel of his flesh stroking against hers, the heat of his skin warming her.

She'd been so cold. Brutally cold. She'd burned on the inside, frozen on the outside as she fought every instinct demanding that she find him.

"You've destroyed me," she whispered as his lips slid from hers to take firm nips and stroking tastes of her jaw. The caresses had nerve endings screaming out in pleasure, the sexual tension ratcheting higher inside her as she still tried to fight the needs clawing at the flesh between her thighs.

Her pussy was so swollen, so sensitive that the heat of his cock could be felt even through the barrier of their clothing.

"The hell I have," he growled, nipping at the upper curve of her breast as he tore the edges of the skimpy top apart. Buttons flew across the floor, and a snarl dragged from the depths of his chest voiced his satisfaction as her breasts were revealed beneath the skimpy lace of her bra.

The bra didn't last long. She was certain the front closure would never work again as he jerked it apart as well, filling one hand with the swollen curve of her breast.

Sensation tore past misgivings and distrust to ensure that there was no chance she could deny him. Instead, the demands tearing at her senses had her crying out at the fear of rejection instead.

The rough pad of his thumb brushed over her nipple, the pleasure spearing straight to her womb before lashing at her clit.

"Please." The moan was a shocking plea.

Gypsy Rum McQuade didn't beg a man for anything.

But she evidently had no problem begging this Breed for his touch.

Overwhelming, overpowering,

The hunger was riding her harder, faster, and his touch wasn't keeping up. He was going too slow, pushing her too high, too fast, flooding her body with such pleasure that it bordered pain.

When his lips covered one hard, peaked nipple, drawing it into the heat of his mouth as he began to suckle firmly, Gypsy swore that a charge of pure, undiluted pleasure exploded in her womb.

Her pussy wept in need, her clit throbbing with it as she fought to get closer to the heat and hardness pressing against it. Yet no matter how she fought to get closer, she couldn't get close enough.

"Stop torturing me," she cried out, her fists clenching on his shoulder as she ground her head against the door.

"You've tortured me." The rough growl of his voice sent a shiver racing up her spine; unfortunately, it was a shiver of pleasure.

She bucked against him, her breath catching as he nipped at her nipple, an erotic little pain that had her gasping with the exquisite sensation. Gasping even as she tried to grit her teeth against the wild urge to give in to him, to submit to whatever he wanted.

She didn't beg, and she didn't submit. No matter how much she might want to, or how desperately she had begged moments before.

Her fingers slid into his hair, clenched, pulled hard.

Her nipple popped from his mouth with a slight sucking sound, his gaze moving to hers, narrowing.

There was a warning that she had no intention of heeding. A demand that she had no intention of obeying.

"Do not—"

"Let me go." She had to force the demand into her voice rather than begging as she had moments ago.

"Gypsy—"

"I'm no toy," she informed him, pushing at his chest. "You can't throw me away one moment, then demand that I submit to you in the next. I won't have it, Rule."

Maniacal arousal throbbed through every vein, burned every nerve ending in her body. Talons of need clenched at her lower stomach, tightening in her womb as the sensitivity of her clit became painful.

She needed.

She needed so much more than he was giving her . . .

His hand moved, too quickly to avoid him. It buried itself in her hair as he pulled her head back. His lips slammed over hers again. His tongue speared past her lips, peppermint and chocolate a taste that teased her senses, becoming more addictive as her tongue licked over his, her lips attempting to catch it, to catch more of the addictive taste.

She was only distantly aware of his hand releasing the band of her jeans. Then the feel of the zipper loosening at the side of her boots. His lips moved to her ear, nipping, taking stinging sips of her lips as he undressed her, controlling her with effortless ease.

"Freaky fucking mating drug," she moaned as his lips moved to her shoulder while he maneuvered her to drop the bra and remnants of her shirt to the floor.

His teeth raked against her shoulder, sending a rush of fiery sensation shooting through her senses.

The need to feel his teeth there, nipping harder, *biting* . . .

Whimpering at the pleasure, the needs rushing through her like a conflagration of flames, Gypsy could only follow his direction as he moved her legs, forcing them to the floor as he dragged her jeans over her hips.

As he lowered his head, his lips found the tight point of her nipple again, sucking it in, surrounding it with such heat, such pleasure that she could only cry out and surrender to the hunger building inside her. The pleasure from his hands stroking over her thighs, pushing the material from her until she could kick it from her legs.

She was naked, burning for him.

The stroke of his fingers along her inner thighs had her legs parting for him, her breath stilling in her chest, heart racing.

"Oh God, Rule, please," she tried to scream, but could only beg.

Parting the swollen folds, his thumb raked her clit as his finger pushed demandingly into the clenched, hungry depths of her pussy. It rasped over inner flesh so sensitive she felt her legs weaken, knees shaking at the ecstatic rush of sensation raging through her.

Slick, saturated, her juices wept like heated honey along his finger, easing the penetration as the desperate, milking clench of her muscles attempted to hold it inside her.

"Don't stop." The demand rose unbidden from her lips as she felt the smooth, slow withdrawal, the caress of his finger inside her, driving her higher. "Don't stop, Rule."

"Never again," he growled, his tone harsher, closer to the animal it was said lived within him. "Never again, Gypsy."

Before she could do more than cry out, he had her in his arms, lifting her and moving to the next room and the bed awaiting them. Laying her against the comforter, he turned, sat on the bed and hurriedly removed the boots laced on his feet.

Gypsy's fingers clenched the blanket beneath her, her lashes lifting, staring at the broad expanse of his naked back as he rose again. Turning, staring down at her, holding her gaze, he shed the black mission pants as his gaze seemed to shift, darken, then turn brighter.

What would she do if he jumped from her again? How could she bear the pain? "I won't let you go. Not this time, Gypsy." The words were a hard rasp as he came over her, spreading her thighs with his hard, well-muscled legs and bending to her until his lips could touch hers again.

Whatever raged inside him, whatever emotions tore at him, she glimpsed in the fiery blue of his eyes, the hard, intent expression on his face. She wanted explanations. She wanted to know what she had done, why he had pulled from her so quickly before, but the needs tearing at her stilled those questions for now.

Lifting her hands, she slid them up the perspiration-slick planes of his hard abdomen, the broad expanse of his chest until she was curling her fingers over the tight, flexing muscles of his shoulders.

"This doesn't change anything," she whispered, more because she was weakening and she could feel it.

Amid the ravaging hunger for this Breed, the addictive need for his kiss and the anger that swirled inside her was something more. Something she didn't want to look at too closely. Something she couldn't afford to look at too closely.

"It changes everything," he assured her.

Before she could find the will to argue, the broad head of his cock was pushing against the swollen folds of her pussy, parting them, then stretching the entrance to the clenched, hungry demand inside.

A small cry escaped her again, breathless, yearning as her flesh stretched for him, parting with such painful pleasure that her lashes fluttered closed on a weak catch of her breath.

She couldn't stand to watch him further, to see that hint of agony on his face, to sense that there was a cost he would pay in taking her.

◆　　◆　　◆

Helplessness had never been a feeling Rule had known since the moment the labs he and Lawe were confined in were destroyed. Escape had been planned for, it had been planned exactingly for years, and even then, he'd never known complete helplessness. He'd refused to feel it.

Now, he was helpless.

The mating hormone pounded through his senses, rushed through his body like a drug that set fire to all his senses. Taking her was imperative. Marking her was a hunger destroying him, because doing so meant marring the perfect, sweet flesh that he loved touching.

Gritting his teeth until his jaw knotted, he tightened his hands on her thighs, holding them wide as he knelt, poised at the entrance of the slick, fiery folds of flesh cupping the broad head of his cock.

Flames licked at the sensitive crest, raced to the tightly drawn sac below and had the heavy, broad shaft throbbing in desperation. The animal that prowled and paced inside his body had taken control and there wasn't a damned thing he could do about it.

Except enjoy it. Enjoy the most exquisite pleasure he'd ever experienced in his life.

She'd managed to hide from him for two days. Two miserable, agonizing days spent while the demons of the past tortured him with the visions of the fate she could be facing. Two days of a building hunger that knotted his balls and had the stiffness of his cock increasing until he swore the need to release would kill him.

There would be no running from this woman.

No escaping his mate.

Running his hands higher along her thigh as his hips rocked against her, he found the sweet, saturated folds with his thumbs. Parting them to reveal the swollen, distended little bud of her clit, he thrust harder against her, filling the entrance to her cunt with the throbbing crest of his cock.

God, he didn't know if he was going to be able to hold back long enough to bring her to release first.

A growl rumbled in his chest at the thought, a denial of such a thing occurring. Nothing mattered but her protection and her pleasure. If he could do nothing else, he would give his life to protect her and every second he could beg, borrow or steal to bring her pleasure.

Exerting the slightest bit of pressure at the sides of her throbbing little clit, he rocked against her further, pushing the stiff erection deeper inside her as her breathless little cry had his abdomen tightening in agonizing pleasure.

He'd never known pleasure like this. Never known that taking a woman could be so damned exhilarating. Even that first night, it hadn't been this damned good. And that only proved the rumors he'd heard of the pleasure to be found in a mate's arms.

"This is insane," she cried out, her head thrashing against the bed as her hips jerked against him, pushing him deeper as he watched the soft flesh hugging his cock part further for the heavy width of the shaft spearing inside her.

Fuck, it was so damned erotic.

The sight of her slick dew soaking her silken folds, lying in a thick layer against the most delectable flesh. As his erection parted the folds, it clung to him, glistening on the heavily veined shaft as it was forced from inside her, coating him, slicking her.

The excess of her moisture did nothing to ease the clenching tightness of her pussy, though. It flexed and milked the thick crest penetrating her before sucking at it, trying to draw him deeper. He could feel her stretching for him, hear her cries as she took each inch he worked inside her.

She was so tight. So tight and sweet and hot that it was all he could do to bear it. Like a heavy fist clenching and unclenching around the sensitized head and shaft as he fucked inside her.

"That's it, baby," he groaned as her hips jerked again, burying him deeper still. "Take me, just like that. So fucking tight and hot."

He lifted his gaze to her face, watching as her lashes drifted open. As her gaze met his, the short little nails tipping her fingers clenched on his lower arms and bit into his skin. An erotic demand, an assurance that she was as lost to the pleasure as he was becoming.

"Kick your ass later," she moaned, her hips shifting, pressing, working his cock deeper as he fought to keep from taking her like the animal he knew he was. Hard and fast, riding her until the explosion took them both.

"You do that." The snarl in his voice warned him—

Ah God, he had to hold on, just a moment. Just a minute. He could feel the tight hug and flex of her cunt on his shaft, working it, stroking it. She was close. So fucking close to coming for him.

Let him take her like the man he wanted to be—

"Rule—" It was that edge of panic in her voice that pulled him back, that reminded him of the unique way the animal had of showing itself.

"It's okay, baby," he promised, pressing deeper, the sharp sensitivity just beneath the head of his cock assuring him that release was rapidly approaching. "I swear. It's all okay."

An involuntary flex of his hips had the silken flesh gloving him tightening further, clench and release, stroking him like a silky, slick fist, so fucking tight that the pleasure ripped through his balls.

Her gaze was locked on his, the heated kiss of her juices against his cock head an added pleasure that tore at the fragile thread of his control. He wasn't going to make it much longer. He couldn't make it much longer.

Pulling back until only the head of his erection remained inside her, Rule thrust against her sharply, burying halfway, pulled back, then drove his cock hard, deep, to bury full length inside the slick, too-snug flex of the sweetest little cunt he'd ever been inside.

The pleasure . . .

The sweet, brutal ecstasy . . .

It was all the animal needed to break free.

◆   ◆   ◆

His eyes—the brilliant blue flared, darkened and brightened a second before it overtook even the whites of his eyes, the pupil becoming a perfectly round pit of coal black that reflected a sheen of blue from the color around it.

It was a lion's eyes. A blue-eyed lion that stared back at her, that watched her with savage intensity.

Panic threatened at the edges of her mind. It would have overwhelmed her if he hadn't pulled back, surged partway inside her, then eased back once more before a hard, driving thrust buried him to the hilt inside her.

She couldn't scream. There was no breath left to scream. As though that thrust were a trigger, the penetrating pleasure-pain exploded through her senses, raced through her bloodstream and blinded her with a wave of white-hot, blue-tinted ecstasy that completely overtook her world.

It wasn't pleasure. It wasn't ecstasy.

It was something so far above it that she could only convulse beneath him, thighs tightening on his hips, her breath suspended, and the knowledge, an innate distant knowledge that something so far outside belief as to be completely unbelievable had occurred.

Something that she feared had bonded him to her in ways she had never believed she could be tied to anyone. Let alone a man.

Or a Breed.

The feel of what the tabloids called a Breed barb becoming engorged beneath the head of his cock, locking him inside her as it pulsed and throbbed, stimulating that too-sensitive area just behind her clit, inside her vagina. Heated, caressing as Rule released inside her, the jetting heat of his semen adding an additional sensation that spurred her pleasure higher.

It was too much to bear.

Too much pleasure. Too many sensations.

Far too many emotions . . .

CHAPTER 20

The two days she'd spent running from Rule and his Breeds had been exhausting. So exhausting that fighting him once he found her would have been impossible. At least, that was the excuse she used that afternoon after coming awake, wrapped tight in his arms.

Not just his arms. One muscular leg was thrown over hers, anchoring her to the bed. Behind her, the stiff, thick length of his cock pressed against her lower back, reminding her why she was there.

He hadn't wanted her until by some stroke of ill luck, nature had decided to use some freaky hormone to bind her to him. Now, he decided he wanted her? Wanted her so much that he had her locked to him like a well-loved wife?

She so didn't think so.

"Let me go." She pushed at the arm lying over her, the anger of the past two days rising inside her even as the arousal began a hard, heated simmer between her thighs.

Dammit, she hadn't even had a shower yet. After he'd taken her, after that "something" had locked inside her and sent her spiraling into a complete rapturous meltdown, she hadn't even had the energy to keep her eyes open, let alone drag her ass out of the bed to shower.

Damn him.

"Dammit, let me the fuck go." She rammed her elbow into his side with enough force to bring him instantly awake.

"What?" the grouch grumbled, his arm tightening around her.

"Get your damned leg off me, Rule," she snapped, infuriated. "I have to get out of this bed now."

"Why?" He snuggled sleepily against her back, which only pissed her off further.

"I don't need a damned body cuff," she informed him furiously as she struggled against him. "Now let me the hell go so I can go to the bathroom."

A grumbling little growl vibrated in his throat, but thankfully, he released her, albeit slowly.

"Hurry," he mumbled, burying his head in her pillow as she glanced back at him.

Irritation surged inside her. He had just completely fucked up her entire life and all he wanted to do was sleep?

"Yeah, I'll get right on that, asshole," she muttered with a silent snort before heading quickly to the bathroom.

She could smell him all over her. That man-and-midnight-storm scent with a hint of peppermint and chocolate. Hell, she was starting to crave chocolate because of him.

She really needed to convince herself she hated him. That was what she needed to do. Maybe then that mating hormone stuff would just go away and leave her alone. Because right now, it was making its presence known by sensitizing her clit and the inner muscles of her sex in a way that was highly distracting.

She had things to do today. She didn't have time to lie around in bed with a crazy Breed.

He had to be crazed. What other explanation could there be for him jumping away from her as though she were diseased two nights before, then spending two days canvassing the Navajo Nation in his search for her.

Crazy-ass, that was what he was.

And those eyes.

As she flipped on the shower and adjusted the temperature, a shiver raced through her at the memory of his eyes. The whites hadn't existed. His entire eye had turned blue with the exception of the black, center pupil. Like a lion. Like a predator.

It was damned sexy . . . no, it wasn't sexy, it was damned freaky, she amended furiously.

Collecting the items needed for her shower, she stepped beneath the stinging spray, lowered her head and let the water beat down on her.

She wanted to cry now. She hadn't cried in nine years, and she wasn't going to start now because it sure as hell wouldn't help. It didn't solve anything. It would just make her head hurt. And the last thing she needed was another headache. The man lying in the bed in the other room was enough headache for any woman.

Washing her hair quickly before conditioning the long mass of dark brown strands, Gypsy tried to keep her mind off the ache her body was turning into, and on the rest of the day instead.

It was late afternoon.

She had a meeting scheduled with her parents at their home office regarding that stupid contract they were signing with the Bureau of Breed Affairs. Jonas had announced that the new office would be opening but had held back the news that an assistant director and several liaisons had already been appointed.

That announcement was supposed to come after the initial phase of introducing Rule, Malachi and Stygian to the business community in the tri-county area had been accomplished.

Her mother already had a schedule outlined that was guaranteed to strip Gypsy of the last of her patience where Rule was concerned.

Rinsing the suds from her body as she turned beneath the spray, she was somehow not surprised to come to a hard stop as her shoulder hit the immovable obstacle that stepped into the shower with her.

"Showering without me?" Rich, normal blue eyes stared down at her as steamy water sluiced over the hard-muscled, darkly tanned flesh of his body.

God, he was almost a work of art.

There wasn't an ounce of fat on his body. The power beneath the tough flesh was obvious, just as the intelligence that gleamed in his eyes couldn't be missed.

"I would love to." Her smile was tight and she knew it.

She didn't want a confrontation while she was naked, but that gleam in his eyes assured her that he didn't mind at all.

Rivulets of water curled around his neck, running in narrow streams down his body as her gaze tracked them. They curled over and around the heavy width of his erection before falling down his powerful legs.

Not that she bothered to follow the path along his legs. Her gaze stopped on the heavily veined shaft spearing out from his body. The heavy throb of blood beneath the flesh matched the pulse evident in the flared crest that pointed demandingly toward her.

His cock screamed intent. Throbbing beneath her gaze, clenching as she licked her lips nervously, it was a temptation she really needed to refuse.

She might play the seductress, but as Rule knew, until two nights before, she'd never been with a man. She hadn't gone parking, she hadn't almost had sex, she hadn't been a false virgin with the experience to please a man to any point.

But God help her, all she wanted to do was fill her mouth with the fierce throb of the stiffly engorged, flared crest of his cock. She wanted to lick it. Suck it. She wanted to feel it throbbing like that on her tongue just before he began fucking her mouth because he wanted her so bad he couldn't control the urge to do so.

She'd dreamed of that more than once since seeing him for the first time.

A moan whispered through the air around her as she felt his thumb and the side of his finger grip her nipple, tugging at it, tightening on the nubbin of flesh with a firm strength that sent shards of sensation racing straight to her pussy.

What the hell was she doing?

Licking her lips again, she obeyed the need that had her lowering herself to her knees, losing the pleasure attacking her nipple for a pleasure she couldn't deny herself.

Leaning forward, lips parting, she felt one hand lock in the hair at the back of her head, and her lashes fluttered with the sharp sensation of his fingers clenching the strands as he tugged at them.

Her tongue met the engorged crest first, curled around it, licking it as her lips followed, drawing him inside the hungry depths of her mouth.

Okay, she'd read books.

She'd seen it on some of the late-night, hard-core movies she'd watched over the years. She knew the basics. And Rule seemed to be appreciating those basics immensely.

"Ah fuck," he groaned above her as she gripped the base of the shaft firmly and began moving her mouth and tongue over the sensitive head.

"Gypsy, sweetheart. That's it. Fuck. That's it, baby, suck me deep just like that."

Just like that. As deep as she could take him as she worked her fingers over the hard shaft, feeling the blood pound in the thick veins beneath the iron-hard flesh.

The hunger assailing her wasn't as unfamiliar as she wanted to convince herself it was, though. Over the years, her body had reminded her often that she was a woman rather than just a tool for vengeance.

The ache in her pussy and swollen clit was amplified, but many nights she had spent in her lonely bed masturbating, to the point of tears because the release she needed wasn't there.

Yes, she too had been a false virgin, no matter how her anger wanted to pretend otherwise.

She wasn't a virgin of any sort now. She was no longer a tool of vengeance, and she would pay for allowing that to happen later. Right now, she was just a woman—a hungry, aching woman. One whose senses were completely filled with the Breed whose cock was shuttling between her lips. Her tongue licked and stroked hungrily over the hot flesh as the taste of him and her hunger for him raged out of control.

His hand was locked in the hair at the back of her head, clenching and pulling at the strands, sending arcs of explosive sensation racing through her, over her.

A heavy pulse flexed beneath the erection she held captive, a hint of salty male and midnight teasing her taste buds as pre-cum escaped the narrow slit at the tip of his cock. The taste brought a low moan from her lips, the need for more than a teasing hint of his pleasure rushing through her system.

Tightening her grip at the base of his shaft, she slid her free hand from his thigh to between his legs to find his tightly drawn testicles. As her fingers caressed him there, finding the spheres hidden beneath her touch, he groaned her name.

The sound of it was a hoarse, growling rasp that sent her senses spinning in pleasure. The sound of a man's pleasure shouldn't send sensation racing through her with the same strength that his touch would. Or with the same pleasure.

Yet it did.

Her womb clenched, her clit swelling impossibly further as her pussy slickened for him.

Sucking the thick flesh deeper, Gypsy held it deep within her mouth, her tongue working against the sensitive underside as she suckled the broad head, loving the taste and feel of him in her mouth.

The intimacy of it. The pleasure she swore she could feel emanating from him seemed to wrap around her, sink inside her and whip the conflagration of sensations rising through her senses higher than ever before.

◆　　◆　　◆

What the fuck was she doing to him?

Rule felt every muscle in his body tightening, burning, pleasure rushing through his flesh like a thousand tingling slashes against every nerve ending in his body. The feel of her mouth drawing on the sensitive head of his dick was destroying him. The pleasure was tearing through him, raking across his senses and giving a part of him that had been wild, uncontrolled and inconsolable completely to the woman kneeling before him.

As her tongue pressed firmly against the underside of his cock, he could feel the brutal pleasure gathering just beneath it. The flared head pulsed and swelled further even as it tightened with agonizing pleasure. He could feel the barb that would only distend once he was buried inside her, surrounded to the hilt by her lush heat, pulsing in time to the blood rushing through his veins.

Adrenaline called forth by the pleasure tearing through him filled his senses. That rush of power and strength was an incredible high during battle, but rushing through his system now, powered by Mating Heat, aflame with the scent of her hunger for him, it was like nothing he had ever known.

Even the powerful hallucinogenics, the incredible drugged highs and mind-numbing lows he'd experienced in the labs had nothing on the sensations ravaging his senses now.

There was no such thing as control. There was no holding back.

His fingers locked in her hair, his gaze locked on the ecstatic expression of her face, he knew that control, reason or holding back was nothing he wanted when it came to the lush eroticism of this woman.

His mate.

"Gypsy, now is the time to pull back." The animal was taking control.

Rule could feel his senses expanding, narrowing, centering on the woman and nothing more. On the hunger clawing at him, beating in his soul and demanding he take her.

Possess her.

Imprint upon her the fact that she belonged to him.

This was his mate.

She was the man's woman. The man's heart.

But she was the animal's mate, and here, at this time, the animal ruled. The creature that existed within his genetics, within the soul of the man, had been held back long enough.

As her lashes drifted open, her pretty green eyes dark and filled with hunger, gleaming with feminine defiance, Rule lost the battle.

◆ ◆ ◆

Gypsy could feel him. He was close. His testicles were drawn tight, his cock throbbing, the crest flared and pounding fiercely as the taste of salt and male arousal teased her senses.

She'd wondered what it would be like with him, loving him with her lips, with her tongue, feeling him thrusting past her lips until he found his pleasure with her.

She was certain it would happen within seconds.

"Gypsy, now is the time to pull back." The sound of his voice was so ragged then, so harsh and animalistic that she knew what she would see when she opened her eyes.

She told herself to keep her eyes closed. She didn't want to see what would meet her eyes.

But she had never listened to that inner voice as she should, so why should she start now?

Her lashes drifted open.

Brilliant, neon blue filled his gaze, his entire eye. In the center, the black iris had morphed, slitted just a bit to assure her that it wasn't the man staring back at her. The animal his genetics were drawn from watched her, and he was tired of waiting on the man to—

"No." The protest was instinctive as he pulled back, removing the treat she'd believed was within seconds of releasing into her mouth.

He snarled at her. A low, feral sound that had her eyes widening, a gasp tearing from her as she suddenly found herself staring at the shower wall. Behind her, one hard hand gripped her hip to hold her in place as the other planted itself between her shoulder blades, pushing her forward firmly.

"Damn you—" She froze the second she'd moved to struggle against him.

Suddenly he was covering her, sharp canines, dangerously strong, gripping the muscle at the bend of her neck as he growled a low, harsh warning.

She should have been terrified.

She should have been fighting.

Instead, she lost her breath, gasping with a surge of such incredible pleasure that her lashes fluttered in a gesture of instinctive submission to him.

She would hate herself later, she decided. Maybe tomorrow.

Maybe next week.

She wasn't going to do anything to dull or take away from the incredibly erotic sensations rushing through her body. Pleasure stormed her senses. It exploded at the sensitive flesh of her neck, spilled through the rest of her body, and when the hard crest of his cock pressed against the swollen folds of her pussy, her juices had her so slick, so ready for him that when he pressed against the entrance, the tip of his cock wedged inside easily.

Then came the real pleasure.

Gypsy's back arched, a cry tearing from her lips as the first heavy thrust buried only a few inches of his shaft inside her. Steamy water flowed around them, blocked only marginally by his broad back. It heated the cubicle further, steaming the glass door, filling the area with a moist heat that only further sensitized her flesh.

Pulling back, he gave her only a second to draw another breath before he was plunging inside her again, then again. Four heavy thrusts before he lodged fully inside her, stretching her, sending sharp spasms of incredible pleasure piercing each nerve ending inside her pussy.

Her fingers curled against the shower floor, the tile smooth, warm beneath her. Above her, Rule was harder, hotter. Buried inside her, his cock throbbing, pounding against her overstretched vagina and clouding her senses with a drugging pleasure.

She was crying his name, begging, and she had no idea what she was begging for until he began moving.

His fingers tightened at her hip as he planted his other hand on the shower floor in front of her. Gypsy braced her shoulder against the clenched muscles of his arm, turning her head and biting into the tough flesh as he began thrusting fiercely inside her.

Each penetration was a shock of agonizing pleasure. The rasp of the flared crest against her inner tissue stoked the need to climax to a painful level. She was crying out his name, her pussy clenching on each quick thrust, desperate to hold him inside her. The iron-hard width stretched her until each thrust exerted just enough pressure to her swollen clit to drive her insane there.

Her senses were being thrown out of control. Pleasure intensified to the point that she was certain she couldn't stand another second. Couldn't bear the need to orgasm for a heartbeat longer, only to be thrown higher. To burn hotter.

"Rule, please. Damn you, let me come," she cried out, feeling his tongue licking against the flesh clenched between his teeth as a rumbled growl vibrated against her back and at her ear.

His hips pounded against her rear, his cock shuttling hard and deep, caressing and stroking the oversensitized flesh of her pussy until she thought she would go mad with the sensations tearing through her.

"Please," she moaned against his bicep, feeling it flex beneath her lips. "Please, fuck me hard. Harder."

He growled, the pace increasing, the iron-hard flesh shafting inside her faster, harder, stroking and burning through flesh as the delicate tissue clenched and tightened around each thrust until she felt that inferno building inside her reaching a critical peak.

The hand gripping her hip slid between her thighs, finding the agonizingly swollen bud of her clit with the callused tips of his fingers.

That touch against live nerve endings screaming out for him shattered her. It began with a rapid-fire implosion that stole her breath. Ecstasy crashed in upon her senses, drawing her body tight as her teeth bit into the hard flesh of his bicep.

Lightning struck at her clit, speared into her pussy, then gathered in force to clench at her womb as it suddenly went from an internal influx of pure pleasure to a series of fiery explosions of such ecstatic fury that her sight blurred to a whitescape of brilliant, bursting light.

She was unaware how hard she bit into his bicep as she felt the internal detonations overtake her. She was only barely aware of his teeth penetrating the flesh at the bend of her neck and shoulder. Each sensation was just another white-hot burst of rapture shuddering through her body, jerking her in his grip as she felt the additional thickness of that added erection inside her, locking him inside her.

The feline Breed barb.

She could feel it locking into the area of her G-spot, rasping and caressing flesh so well hidden on a woman that it took a very experienced lover to find and caress it properly.

Nature had given the feline Breeds a little additional help there, just as it had in other areas. Several rapid-fire bursts of sensation struck at her sense as Rule locked inside her. They amplified the release ripping at her senses, sent her flying higher, until she was nothing but a creature of pure sensation. She wanted, needed, nothing but this pleasure.

This Breed possessing her.

She was lost and she knew it.

Gypsy could feel the imprint of that truth searing inside her soul. She was lost to him. There was no escaping him, because she knew, mating be damned, she would never be able to do without this pleasure again. And that terrified her. Because anything a woman couldn't do without was guaranteed to destroy her when it was taken from her.

◆　　◆　　◆

What the fuck had he done?

What the fuck was going on?

Son of a bitch.

Son of a bitch.

It was all he could do to hold his weight from her as he found they'd both collapsed to the floor of the shower. Warm water still flowed around them, though the heat that had filled it earlier was absent.

And he needed to get his ass off his mate and turn off the water before she became chilled.

The thought of that actually had him moving. Every instinct inside him warned him that protecting her, no matter how slight the danger or effect on her health, was of paramount importance.

What did she do to him?

This wasn't Mating Heat. Mating Heat was the inability to be apart. It was the need to fuck, to procreate, no matter the obstacles.

This wasn't Mating Heat. It was the animal's response to the man's automatic thoughts about a woman he was trying desperately not to love. And he'd already failed.

Forcing his muscles from the limpest stage they had likely ever known, Rule moved to his feet, quickly turned off the water, then knelt to help his mate from the shower tiles.

"Just go 'way," she mumbled as he lifted her into his arms before placing her on the wide built-in shower seat and grabbing a towel.

She slumped against the corner, eyes closed, her long hair hanging in sodden ringlets around her face and dripping water down her breasts and on her thighs. Her head rested against the corner of the shower, the green of her eyes gleaming between her lowered lashes.

"Get dressed or something." Her voice was still sleepy, lazy, no doubt the reason why she surprised him when her hand flashed out and jerked the towel from his grip.

This was a bad thing, he thought as she draped the material over her to cover her breasts and thighs. No one else, no matter who, no matter the circumstances, could have jerked that towel from him so easily. Never had he allowed his guard to drop to that point.

That didn't excuse the fact that she had moved much more quickly, and with a precision no civilian could possess, to ensure that she acquired the towel from him. And she didn't even notice the fact that she had moved so easily, and with a training he was certain she wouldn't want revealed.

"Why are you looking at me like that?" The smell of her distrust was offensive.

Rule grimaced. The animal was still far too close to the surface, the pleasure of moments before still lingering too strongly within his senses.

"Let's get you dried off, hotshot," he told her, kneeling in front of her and taking the towel from her, despite the struggle she gave him.

Starting with her hair, he blotted the excess water from it gently, aware long moments later that she was growing frustrated with his ministrations. The long, water-heavy ringlets were particularly pretty, though. The straight effect she sometimes achieved was nice as well, but he was fond of the waves and little curls. Drying it too quickly, too roughly could cause the strands to frizz. He knew she wouldn't like that. He'd never seen her hair frizzy or at any time less than silken and healthy looking.

"Rule, what the hell are you up to?" She was watching him with far more distrust than even moments before.

"I've just been drying your hair." Finishing the last of the long curls, he brushed them gently behind her shoulder as he evaded her attempts to grab the towel back.

"Fine, you dried it." She glared back at him. "Now give me the damned towel. I'll dry myself."

The scent of her distrust only grew and, even more disturbing, also a sense of fear as he'd continued attempting to dry her. Why would taking care of his luscious little mate cause her such distress?

Narrowing his eyes, Rule did as she asked, reached out and pulled another towel off the shelf on the outside wall to finish drying his own body.

Seconds later she found the strength in her legs, rose to her feet and quickly wrapped the towel around the slender curves he would have enjoyed watching a bit longer.

Tossing his own towel to the corner of the shower, he moved from the cubicle and headed to the bedroom. The scent of the continued distrust and that edge of fear had been joined by the hint of pain.

Dammit. She was tempting those crazy fucking animal genetics into surging free again. And that was something he'd prefer to ensure never happened again. Well, unless he was buried deep inside her again.

Pulling on a pair of jeans, he zipped them quickly, aware that his cock was still hard enough to ensure it wouldn't be long before he was indeed buried inside her again.

Until then, he'd wait patiently.

It wasn't long before she moved into the room, glancing at him nervously before moving to the dresser. There—his brow lifted as she found the drawer that held his shirts on the first try.

Lifting a dark gray T-shirt free from the top of the pile, she unfolded it, drew it over her head, then pushed her arms into the sleeves and let it fall over her body before dropping the towel.

Those animal genetics—

He normally cursed them; in this second, he was doing more than cursing them. The animal snapped inside him. A hint of a scent. The awareness of something not just right as his normally dependable senses failed him.

He'd come into this room weeks before, aware of the slightest scent that he should have recognized, only to have it elude him.

It wasn't eluding him now.

"Where did you get the scent blocker the night you searched my room, mate?" he asked her softly. "And who provided it?"

How had she given herself away?

Her gaze was locked with his, normal now, all evidence of the animal he shared his genetics with no longer present. But there was no way she could hide her response and she knew it. She was caught. She could feel it. She could see it in the flare of anger that lit his eyes and tightened his body.

"What are you talking about, Rule?" That didn't mean she had to go down easy.

He'd already destroyed the plans she'd made for her life so many years ago. Nine years she'd spent vowing to avenge her brother's murder and to make up for being the cause of it.

He chuckled.

It wasn't a comfortable sound, she observed, watching him nervously. And she really wished he'd snap the band of his jeans and put on a damned shirt. Socks. Maybe some shoes too. That would definitely make her feel more comfortable. Though not in any less trouble, she was betting.

"You know." Leaning against the dresser she'd just pulled a shirt from, he watched her curiously as he crossed his arms over his broad, naked chest. "Several weeks ago my room was gone through. A scent blocker was used, but what the intruder was unaware of is that the perspiration they left throughout the room wasn't safe from detection when the room belongs to the intruder's unmated mate."

Unmated mate? It was all she could do not to roll her eyes, but she was pretty fucking tired. His bathroom sex had pretty much sapped what little energy she'd gained while she slept earlier.

"You're reaching, Rule," she breathed out roughly, certain there was really no getting out of this, at least without really lying to him, and that, she found suddenly distasteful.

A spy who couldn't lie? Hell, wasn't that one a first?

His gaze focused on her like a laser, brightening, the blue iris enlarging just enough to send her heart racing.

"Then," he continued as though she hadn't spoken, "when we picked up those tails last night, you knew exactly how to pull up the GPS on the Dragoon and evade whoever was following us. How did you know that, Gypsy? No one outside the enforcers who use those vehicles knows about the new systems that went in just before we left for the op in Window Rock. That, or the transponders and satellite phone trackers we carry. Especially no human civilian."

She shrugged nonchalantly, rather enjoying the game he'd started. At least for the moment. She was certain that the time was coming, though, when he wasn't going to allow her to deny her knowledge of where she'd gained her information for long. And God help her, she could only pray he didn't get Jonas Wyatt involved with this.

"Someone must know about it," she informed him, as though the subject were no more than amusing. "Because I had to have heard about it somewhere. Though it's really not that dissimilar to the GPS and backup systems used by National Law Enforcement."

"And how would you know about their GPS and backup systems?" He latched onto that immediately. "Last I heard, National was just as proprietary about their technical information as the Breeds are."

"More so, actually." She smiled. "I guess it's all according to who you have as friends, Rule. I have a lot of friends. And remember, I do work part-time at the Navajo Covert Law Enforcement office."

He actually grinned. Ducking his head for a moment, he stared at a point that could have been his bare feet. He was shaking his head, though, and that smile was flashing a bit more of the healthy canines at the side of his teeth than she found comfortable.

His head lifted enough to stare up at her through the veil of those thick, inky lashes. The gleam of those blue eyes, barely glimpsed for the long lashes, was entirely too wickedly sexy. It made her stomach kind of jump.

"Yeah, you have a lot of friends, baby," he said softly, causing her heart to trip nervously. "And whoever the fuck trained you did a damned good job of it. Had any Breed other than Jonas questioned you, then I have no doubt you would have convinced them you were just the party girl you pretend to be. But no other Breed would have seen your response when you jerked that towel from my hand. And I know, only training can create the quickness you used in doing that. Just as only training could have taught you the move you used last night when Rhyzan made the mistake of touching you in that bar. And yes, one of the enforcers watching that little move described it perfectly as I was pulling in."

Gypsy widened her eyes innocently. "That is one freaky Breed, Rule. You should keep him out of the general public if you really want to convince the public you're harmless."

"Is that what we're trying to do?" he asked her.

"Isn't it?" She kept her appearance amused, archly mocking, and prayed she could pawn off the racing of her heart and her nervousness on the simmering arousal still vibrating through her body.

"You're not distracting me," he warned her then. "You're calm, giving all appearances of being slightly confused, a little nervous but game to play along. Damned good training, just as I said. But I'm probably the one person in the world you're never going to be able to fool whenever you attempt to lie to me. I know your scent more intimately than any other Breed ever will, and I'll catch that hint of deceit creeping out. You won't have to say a word. I'll know you're preparing to deceive me before the words ever leave your mouth."

Well, wasn't he just damned sure of himself?

Gypsy moved across the room then, watching him warily, as though she were indeed just as confused and nervous as he indicated she was playing at. They both knew he was right, but nothing could hurt her, or him, if she didn't admit to it.

"Look." She gave a nervous little laugh that wasn't entirely faked. "This has been really interesting, Rule, but I think I'd prefer you find another game to play."

He tracked her with his eyes alone, but when she reached the door, a dark rumble suddenly filled the room, causing her to stop and stare back at him in surprise.

"You haven't denied searching my room yet, mate," he reminded her.

Gypsy cocked her hip, mimicked his stance with her arms crossing over her breasts and glared back at him.

"You didn't ask if I had searched your room, *Rule*." She stressed his name rather than using the title of mate in the mocking tone she wanted to use. "I did just that the first time you threw me to the bed and had your way with me, as soon as you left the room afterward. And I didn't even need a scent blocker to do it nor did I have to break in, if you'll recall. I don't know what you think I was looking for, though. I wanted a drink of water, and wanted to know exactly where I could find the T-shirts when I needed one." She plucked at the front of the gray shirt mockingly. "Is there anything more you want to know?"

"I want to know why, even while revealing that you did indeed go through my room that night, the scent of your lie is still pouring from your body?"

"What lie?" Distress filled her voice now. "What are you accusing me of, Rule?"

She knew damned well what he was accusing her of, and the very fact that he was so damned confident, and pushing a little more with each sentence out of his mouth, had her consciously battling her rising nerves.

"Jonas is looking for someone, Gypsy. An informant for a secretive sect of warriors located within the Nation that's known to aid Breeds and humans attempting to escape and forever disappear from the Genetics Council. Finding that informant is imperative. It could be all that's standing between life or death for Amber."

She hated Breeds.

And she was beginning to hate this mating crap and didn't even understand what it was. What she did know was that it was all she could do to keep from giving him what he wanted. She wanted to tell him the truth so damned bad she could barely stand it.

"And do you think if I were this all-important informant that I would stand by silently and allow Amber to die?" That really bothered her. She would never stand for anyone who would watch that child suffer.

Uncrossing his arms, he straightened from his slouch position and stared back at her directly. "I believe you would question whoever you worked for, you would ask if they had what we needed and they would lie to you. You're human, baby, you would have no idea when an experienced liar is lying to you."

Her fists clenched as the anger she was trying to hold inside since he'd dared to infer she would allow anything to happen to Amber began to burn inside her.

"And you think I would just accept someone's word if I were this sought-after informant?" she charged him, feeling her expression tighten, the tension beginning to ratchet through her. "Is that what you think, Rule?"

"I think you would trust your contact," he breathed out wearily. "And your trust isn't easy to acquire. But if they told you they couldn't help Amber, then they're lying, sweetheart. They're hiding two individuals known to have been part of the experiment that created the drug that baby was injected with. Both of them had and most likely still have photographic memories, and both of them know exactly how to help her."

"Then why not search for them?" Turning, she jerked open the door and went through it a second ahead of him as he attempted to catch her.

And she knew why he'd attempted to keep her in the bedroom then. Sitting on the other side of the door were his brother, Lawe; Lawe's fiancée, Diane; and the Coyote female, Ashley.

Her gaze narrowed on them. They would have clearly heard the conversation in the other room.

"What are they doing here?" she asked succinctly, fighting to hold on to her temper as she turned to face Rule accusingly. "What are you pulling here, Rule?"

Ashley stepped forward, her expression concerned as she gripped the weapons strapped to both thighs with tense hands. "I asked Lawe and Diane to get me in to see you. You must not have heard the knock on the door. When you did not answer, I begged them to allow me into these rooms to await you."

"Why?" This was her friend, yet Gypsy had learned over the years that those you trusted the most were often the ones most determined to deceive you.

Propping her hands on her hips, Ashley stared back at her with cool gray eyes now. "I can smell your distrust, Gypsy . . ."

"I really wish everyone would stop talking about my fucking smell," she snapped, catching the amusement in Diane's gaze and the suspicion in Lawe's. "I'm getting really tired of hearing about it."

"Fine," Ashley harrumphed. "I cannot deny I overheard that conversation and your mate's accusation that you are the one working with the Unknown. I don't agree with him." She flashed Rule a hard look. "But I had to speak with you before you learned something from someone you may not believe is your friend." Distress darkened her eyes as a hint of uncertainty filled her expression. "Tell me, please, that you know that even if no other Breed believes this, I believe you are my friend and a friend to the Breed community. Please, Gypsy." She glanced at Rule apologetically before turning back to her.

"What are you talking about now?" This was going to drive her crazy. Swiping back long strands of hair that had fallen over her shoulder, she faced the Coyote female angrily, wondering if there was even a reason to be angry with her.

"Please, Gypsy." There was something so vulnerable, so desperate in Ashley's gaze that Gypsy couldn't lie about something so elemental.

"I believe you're my friend, Ashley," she answered, frowning, foreboding rising sharply inside her. "And you know I've always considered you my friend."

"Ashley." Rule stepped forward, his expression, his tone gentle as though he knew what was coming. "It's okay. I promise. I'll take care of this."

Ashley's lips thinned. "This is not the time for you to weaken yourself further with your mate, Commander," she informed him as Gypsy watched Rule's expression with narrowed eyes. "I believe, more so now than when I learned this information, that you are the wrong person to handle this matter."

The way he rubbed at the back of his neck and grimaced, his gaze moving to his brother beseechingly as Lawe gave him a look that seemed to suggest he was crazy for asking for help, would have been endearing if she hadn't been certain it would negatively impact her.

"I told you, Ashley—"

"And I told you, Commander." Ashley straightened to military stiffness as she glared back at him. "You are the wrong choice. Please allow me to take care of this; as her friend, I demand the right to do so now."

Rule grimaced. "I'll take care of it, Ashley."

"Overhearing a conversation you began convinces me otherwise," Ashley snorted. "As it does Cassie. She urged me to come here this evening and take care of the matter. She and I both agree, your attempt to protect her is worthy of you and your feelings for her. But keeping this from her has not protected her. And now, it will only harm your place in her heart. So you may take it up with Cassie if you do not like it."

The girl's Russian accent gave her voice, even when angry, an almost charming cadence.

"Let's just get this the hell over with," Gypsy suggested as Rule appeared ready to deny Ashley the opportunity to discuss whatever it was with her, once again. "I'm hungry and I'm pissed off and I really just want to kick Breaker's ass with a little privacy, if none of you care."

"And here I wanted to sell tickets," Lawe murmured.

"Well, doesn't it just suck to be you?" Who was more surprised, she wondered, when she turned on the amused Breed fiercely.

Definitely, his fiancée, or mate?—she was amused, but surprised. Lawe Justice was more than just surprised, though. His gaze narrowed, became more blue, more mocking than ever before and just slightly warmer perhaps as he glanced at his brother.

"Let's just get this the hell over with," Gypsy snapped before turning and leading the way back to the bedroom. "Come on, Ashley, whatever you have to spill, just go ahead and spill so I can figure out what just happened to my damned life."

It had gone to hell in a handbasket, that was exactly what was happening to it, and it was all Rule Breaker's fault.

Every damned second of it.

"Gypsy, I'm sorry." Ashley closed the bedroom door, facing her with a glimmer of sympathy in her eyes as Gypsy threw herself into the chair next to the bed, slouched against the back and watched her friend with something less than patience.

"Just say it, Ash," she sighed, knowing she wasn't going to like it. As she understood it, any time Cassie Sinclair was involved with anyone's life, things just happened anyway. But it seemed to her that that applied to any Breed, not just that particular one.

"The day you were here for the meeting with Jonas, along with your parents." Ashley didn't shift nervously or appear in any way uncertain. She stood straight, spoke quietly.

"Yes. I remember." Gypsy nodded, her fingers tightening where they rested against the arms of the chair. "What about it?"

"Do you remember how nervous your mother was about releasing her purse?"

Gypsy straightened in her chair, leaning forward as a premonition began to tingle at the back of her spine.

"She was nervous about meeting with Jonas," Gypsy said, remembering even at the time how odd her mother's behavior had been. "This was more than a week ago, Ashley; what does it have to do with anything?"

"We found an audio transmitter hiding in the stitched lining of her purse, Gypsy, and her scent wasn't one of nerves, it was one of deceit."

Gypsy felt herself freeze inside.

There went that scent thing again, she thought distantly. Breeds were always smelling things. She wondered if they ever grew tired of having everyone's emotions fill the air with such scents.

"You have to be wrong." She couldn't even look at the other woman as she whispered the words. Staring at the wall across the room, she remembered that meeting. How nervous her mother was, almost frightened as her purse was taken.

Even Gypsy had noticed her odd behavior and had been confused by it.

But this?

Her mother had tried to slip an audio device into the meeting with Jonas Wyatt? Why? Why would her mother or anyone else be interested in a simple business meeting? That didn't make sense.

"That is not all, Gypsy," Ashley told her. "Since that day, I, Emma and Sharone have been investigating the reason why your mother would do this. We learned that she was not unaware of the device, as we had hoped. Rather, she had agreed to have it hidden in her purse, and she and whoever she has aligned with plan to have another hidden even more discreetly at the next meeting."

That couldn't be true.

Gypsy couldn't take her eyes off the wall across from her, couldn't meet the eyes of the woman she called her friend. She could hear the sympathy in Ashley's voice, the kindness, and knew if she saw pity in her friend's eyes, then she simply wouldn't be able to bear it.

"How . . . ? How do you know this?" she asked simply, wondering why she wasn't vehemently denying her mother's guilt in this. Why wasn't she calling Ashley the liar she would have called her at any other time? Why wasn't she fighting the crime her mother had committed?

"I know because Breeds are much better at hiding listening devices than are image consultants," Ashley whispered, misery filling her eyes. "Emma, Sharone and I have the recording of your mother discussing this in her home with a male we could not identify. She intends to try again at the next meeting. She believes Breeds are responsible for her son's death. She believes she will get away with this now, certainly, if she's caught because of your association with Commander Breaker."

Gypsy was well aware of Breed Law, just as she was aware of the fact that Jonas Wyatt could have had both her parents arrested for crimes against Breed Law for attempting to bring that device into the meeting. The fact that he hadn't, and that Ashley was coming to her now, made her wonder just exactly what the director was planning, or what he would want from her at a later date.

"Is that all?" Gypsy asked then, hearing the exhaustion in her voice, the distance.

She had been in this place, inside her own mind, only one other time in her life. The night Mark had died. She had prayed to never find herself there again.

"No, it is not all," Ashley stated. "Please look at me, Gypsy. Do not hate me for this. I demanded that I be the one to tell you these things because of our friendship. I do not want to lose the unique bond I've found with you, my friend. But if I must, to ensure that you are told the truth with the respect I believe you deserve, then I will risk it."

Gypsy turned to her then, the distance still pulling her back from the situation, though Ashley's statement forced her to return to reality.

"The respect I deserve?" she asked, confused.

Ashley swallowed tightly, her gray eyes filled with somber regret, though thankfully no pity.

Ashley's sad little smile actually made her chest ache. "If there is any person in this nation that I know would never betray the Breeds, Gypsy, then I believe that person is you. Whatever the scent of deceit is that Rule detected, and that I have caught a hint of on occasion, I know it is not a desire to hurt or to in anyway see the Breeds harmed. That is not in your nature. You have helped me and Emma so many times during our visits here. You introduced us to friends, to those who have aided us countless times. You deserve to be given this information by a friend. By one who understands the pain you feel when you believe your honor has been betrayed by a loved one."

"Believe it was betrayed?" Gypsy whispered past the tight ache in her chest.

"I have come to know your mother a bit in the time I've been coming to Window Rock," Ashley reminded her. "Kandy's sweet shop is a favorite of many Breeds, and many of us have spoken and laughed with her. She is not a cruel or mean person. And I can't think she would mean the Breeds harm. But an explanation must be forthcoming. To see your mother suffer the public repercussions of her act would destroy Kandy's store as well as your parents' business. I believe that is not in the best interests of the Breeds, or in your best interests."

Breeds weren't often known for their understatements, but that one was a doozy.

Gypsy found herself nodding, making the action without a conscious decision to do so, still feeling cut off from what was happening around her.

"I'll take care of this, Ashley," she promised. "Thank you for being the one to tell me."

Could she have borne having Rule give her this information? It was bad enough being aware that he knew.

"Rule was angry that Jonas ordered that you be told," Ashley told her. "He wanted the information held back from you, just as I did as well, at first. I believed that whatever her reasons, your mother's actions could be overlooked, as no harm was done. And I believe Jonas would have heeded our request had we not learned that for some reason, your mother was determined to slip that device into the next meeting with Jonas and that she blames all of us, despite appearances, for a death that affected us all. One that saddened so many."

An audio transmitter? What could it do other than allow someone to hear what was being said?

A memory surfaced then. Slipping such a device that her Unknown contact had given her into a meeting with a suspected Pure Blood commander. She hadn't been told what it was for. The meeting had been a mere business luncheon with a small advertising company that had been in Window Rock for more than a decade.

Within hours after Gypsy had left, the computers in that office had gone down and the next morning Navajo Law Enforcement had swarmed over the building, arresting not just the owner but many of the employees as well.

According to the report that had filtered out after the arrests, those computers had autonomously sent out files to the Covert Law Enforcement Agency that implicated not just the owner but many of the employees in strikes against the Breeds as well as collaborating with soldiers working for the Genetics Council to betray Breeds suspected of hiding from their former creators in the Navajo Nation.

It had confirmed the information she'd uncovered that the Unknown's audio devices were much more than simply tools to listen in on various meetings. They were technological weapons and they were used with the utmost efficiency.

Had that device worked and Jonas Wyatt's computers been attacked, then she and her parents would have been immediately arrested for crimes against Breed Law.

What was going on? Who was using her mother and how the hell had they managed to convince her to do something so insane, no matter her beliefs?

"Gypsy, I am not sorry I chose to be the one to tell you—"

It was that stoic, forlorn expression that had Gypsy moving. Jumping from her chair, she moved quickly to the little Coyote Breed female and immediately embraced her, barely holding back a flinch at the pain the contact brought her.

To say Ashley was surprised was more an understatement than before, but Gypsy acknowledged that she surprised herself even more. She hadn't realized how close she had become to the Breed females until this moment. Until she had seen the regret and the fear in Ashley's eyes that she had destroyed her friendship with Gypsy.

"Stop," Gypsy ordered as she pulled back and released the other girl slowly. "This wasn't your fault, Ashley, and you're right, I couldn't have borne having anyone else tell me."

The knowledge that her parents had attempted to betray Jonas, Rachel and that precious baby, Amber, was ripping at her soul. Her stomach was cramping with it, building a pressure behind her eyes that she hadn't truly felt in years.

Tears.

She hadn't really cried since Mark's funeral. Would the tears come now? She hoped not. The agony she remembered feeling the last time she cried was an emotion she never wanted to feel again.

"Gypsy, perhaps she has a very logical reason." Ashley tried to comfort her, her delicate expression filled with pain.

"Perhaps, Ashley." She tried to agree as she moved slowly to where her clothing was still crumpled on the floor and picked it up. "I'll take care of it, though, I promise."

"If you need to talk, Emma and I are truly your friends. I hope you will remember that and not become too angry once you've had time to consider what I've told you."

She could only shake her head as she turned back to the girl. "Do you think I'll change my mind and hate you later?"

"I think maybe that is how I would feel if I had a mother, and she had not confided in me over such a decision," Ashley agreed.

"But mothers don't always confide in their daughters, Ashley," she told the girl bitterly, sadly. "Sometimes, things happen— Daughters make mistakes sometimes that their parents can't forgive."

"No, Gypsy—" The other girl moved to cross the room when the bedroom door opened.

Rule stood in the doorway, his expression heavy, torn. His blue eyes raged back at her, brilliant and concerned as Ashley turned to him quickly.

"Ashley, you should leave now," he told her gently as he stepped inside the room, his gaze moving to the Breed female with a hint of gentle demand. "Lawe and Diane are waiting for you to accompany them to dinner, I believe."

Ashley nodded, then turned back to Gypsy. "If you need me . . ."

Gypsy gave her a small facsimile of a smile, but she couldn't promise to talk later. She couldn't promise she would even see the girl later. All she wanted to do right now was run. She wanted the silence of the desert enfolding her, the solace she'd always found in the wild, barren land surrounding her to sink inside the ragged wounds that were being uncovered in her heart.

Laying her clothing on the bed, Gypsy faced the man who seemed determined to claim her now.

"Where's my motorcycle?" She was shocked at the ragged edge of her voice as she smoothed her hands over the material of the shirt covering her hips.

"If you need to go somewhere, then I'll take you." He stood relaxed, but his eyes watched her too closely, and she was very much afraid he saw far too much as he held her gaze.

"How long do you think that will work, Rule? How long do you think I'll stand for you taking my independence and choice away from me? I want my cycle in the front of this hotel in thirty minutes, and you *will* allow me to walk out of here alone. I need to see my parents."

"Not alone." His voice deepened, the growl that had seen her backing down earlier echoing in his chest again.

That growl didn't scare her any more than she would allow anything else to scare her.

"Don't make me run, Rule," she warned him instead. "I promise you, neither of us will enjoy the experience."

Fury gleamed instantly in his gaze. The whites disappeared beneath the full blue, the black pupil dilating, and she knew she was facing a Breed who was more animal than man.

"Run." He was suddenly in her face, daring her, challenge evident in the animalistic rasp of his voice. "Go ahead, mate, run. I'll enjoy the chase and when I catch you, I promise you I'll make damned sure you never consider such a fucking foolhardy action again. Do you understand me?"

She backed up before she meant to. It wasn't fear that filled her, but nerves.

Because this man, this Breed, would keep his word in ways she was sure she would never forget.

• C H A P T E R 2 2 •

Exhaustion had seeped into Gypsy over the hours she and Rule had engaged in a silent, nerve-racking standoff in his room. The meeting scheduled
with her parents was canceled. No surprise there, she thought painfully as
Rule and Jonas discussed the option just after Ashley left.

Finally, desperate to find a moment to breathe that didn't include his
too-intent stare, she'd retreated back to bed.

She needed to think, to consider how to work around what she couldn't
go through. Rule would employ whatever means it took to keep her from
leaving the room. That meant she would have to find a way to slip around
him and make her way to her parents' home.

God help her, what was in her mother's mind to take such a risk? What
had she done, Gypsy wondered, to make her mother chance her very life
like this?

Where had she messed up?

Gypsy knew she had to have done something, she had to have made a
mistake somewhere. What had she done to give anyone a chance to use
her mother in such a way? And no doubt it was her fault. Her mother would
do anything to protect her children after she lost her oldest child, and Gypsy
knew her mother had suspected for years that there was a reason her elder
daughter continued to attend the desert parties and clubs that had initially
given the Coyotes the chance they'd needed to draw Mark out and kill him.

Would she now be responsible for her mother's death? Were her actions risking the rest of her family despite all her precautions?

Could she bear to lose anyone else she loved to her own reckless decisions?

Huddled beneath the blankets, dry eyed, aching, she stared into the slowly darkening room, unaware of the moment her eyes finally closed and sleep claimed her. There was rarely peace to be found in her dreams, though.

Especially at night.

Gypsy had made a habit over the years of remaining awake until dawn began lightening the sky. She'd learned that if it wasn't dark, then the nightmares didn't come near as often.

The room was only just darkening as sleep took her this time, though, and that darkness began spreading through her, dragging her into memories she'd forced to the furthest depths of her mind.

Her parents had taken Kandy to New York with them that week. It was her sister's first visit and teenage shopping trip. They'd left Gypsy with her older brother, Mark. Ten years older, strong, always laughing, he spoiled her, but he watched out for her. Everyone knew if they messed with Mark McQuade's wild baby sister, then Mark would come calling.

That night she and Khileen Langer, the Wolf Breed Lobo Reever's stepdaughter, had planned to attend a desert party that many of Gypsy's school friends were attending. But it was also an adult party, and Mark always attended those with her, or she didn't go.

"Mark." She stepped into the living room, where he was working intently on his computer. "I'm going out with Khileen to a party in—"

His head jerked up, his green eyes feverish, making her wonder if he'd been drinking that night.

"No!" The harsh denial shocked her.

She'd overheard her parents talking about how much Mark had been drinking lately, and how worried they were for him. Staring up at him in shock, Gypsy felt the hurt that came from any sharp word that her precious brother gave her. Not that there had been many, which was why this one stopped her in her tracks.

"But you said—"

"I said no, Gypsy, get back to your room now! And stay there for a change

instead of aggravating the fuck out of me." Then he threw the whiskey glass he'd been drinking from at the wall to her side.

She felt herself pale.

Tears filled her eyes and for a moment, there was something in his gaze that might have been fear. And agonizing regret. As quickly as it had been there, though, it was gone.

"Go to your room, Gypsy," he rasped, his expression hardening in an instant. "We'll discuss these parties later."

Her lips trembled as she ran back to her room, slamming the door behind her before moving straight to her bedroom window.

Her temper was the bane of her existence. She'd gotten into more trouble over the years because of her inability to control her anger than because of anything else. She was even worse when her feelings had been hurt.

Mark had hurt her.

Pushing some money into the pocket of her jeans, she moved to the window, slid it open soundlessly, then shimmied over the sill. Khileen would be there in a few minutes. The other girl had called minutes before when she'd turned into town. With Gypsy's parents gone and her normally loving brother home, Gypsy had intended to beg prettily that he come with them to the party that they wanted to attend in the desert that night.

It was an agreement she and Mark had made after the first party he'd caught her sneaking out to. He would go with her whenever he could, watch over her and Khileen, make sure they didn't get hurt or didn't do anything stupid, and she agreed to never attend one without him.

That agreement had worked for a year now, until tonight.

Moving quickly, Gypsy made her way from the house across the street, then around the candy shop her parents had named the Gingerbread House.

The large two-story house and attached apartments had once been her parents' home, a gift from her mother's family when they married.

She was waiting in front of the store when Khileen made the turn onto the street in the little convertible her stepfather owned, music blaring.

Gypsy watched herself from within the dream. She could feel the tears she'd been holding back that night and the fear she'd felt that her brother had acted so oddly.

She watched as she jumped into the little car with her friend, apprehen-

sive that they were going to the party without Mark to watch over them. He always watched over them and made certain the older boys and young men who attended the parties didn't bother them.

The music was blaring, and they were laughing, though Gypsy had still felt that edge of fear riding her. They weren't aware of the motorcycles that shot from behind the rising stones until their lights were suddenly shining brightly in the rearview mirror, blinding Khileen.

Everything happened so fast then.

Two of the riders jumped from the cycles to the car as Khileen screamed and began jerking the wheel. One of them was slung to the road, but the other managed to jerk the wheel, causing the vehicle to nearly flip as it came to a shuddering stop at the side of the road.

Rough, cruel hands were gripping Gypsy's hair as the remaining rider began pulling her from the open top. Behind them, an older-model Dragoon came to a hard stop as Khileen cursed rougher than her stepfather's cowboys and the gears of the car made a harsh, screeching noise.

As Gypsy screamed and fought, she could still feel herself being forced from the car, her feet slipping over the top of the door as the little car shot back onto the road. It swerved dangerously, then in a burst of speed disappeared from sight.

Khileen had gotten away.

Thank God, her friend had managed to escape.

But Gypsy hadn't.

Screaming, terrified, she was thrown to the ground as a pair of heavy boots were planted in front of her. Hard hands gripped her hair, jerking her to her feet as agony lanced her head.

"Gypsy Rum McQuade." A harsh voice laughed down at her as a smile filled the cruel, scarred face. "Shall we see if you're as sweet and innocent as you look, baby?"

She stared up at him, seeing the curved canines, the cruelty in eyes that gleamed red in the light of the full moon and the vehicle running several feet from them.

"Let me go," she cried, struggling to break the grip he had on her.

And he laughed. "After looking for you for so long? I don't think so. I've waited far too long to invite you to my little party tonight."

She hadn't seen his other hand draw back, but the blow he delivered to the side of her face numbed her mind, her senses, with the torturous pain that suddenly exploded through it.

Darkness filled her vision as the lights suddenly went out, and Gypsy was left in a mindless black pit of agony of near unconsciousness.

They hadn't been merciful.

It had taken her hours to force herself back to awareness. When she returned to consciousness, she realized she had been taken deep into the desert. She was only dimly aware of being dragged from the vehicle, then tied to the bumper. Drifting in a world of dark pain.

Blinking, her gaze blurred at first, it had taken her precious seconds to focus her eyes on the man kneeling in the dirt about twenty feet away from her. He looked older somehow, and hurt. The bruises and blood on his face were horrifying to see.

"Mark?" Her voice had been weak, shaky. "Mark, I want to go home."

She was so sorry she had left the house. She shouldn't have. He'd have listened to her if she had just waited to talk to him again.

"I know, Gypsy." He stared back at her, his eyes so sad, so filled with pain.

"You fucked up, McQuade. Trusted the wrong person." The harsh voice of the Coyote who had knocked her out caused her to flinch in terror as her brother's gaze suddenly became so bleak, so pain ridden that Gypsy knew she would never forget the sight of it.

"Let her go, Grody," her brother demanded, though his voice wasn't strong like it usually was. It sounded very defeated.

Grody just laughed, a sound so evil that Gypsy couldn't help crying. And she hated those tears. Because when Mark saw them he grimaced, and she was certain he was disappointed in her. He always told her she was allowed to cry, that it was his job to be brave. That girls needed to cry. She could still think and plan, even with tears, he'd promised her. But her head hurt so bad, and she was so scared she couldn't think.

"I couldn't believe it was you, McQuade." Grody laughed again as he moved from behind her and walked slowly to where her brother was kneeling. "I was shocked as hell when our contact identified you. You just didn't seem like the geek type, ya know?"

Her brother wasn't really a geek, he just knew how to make a computer do whatever he wanted it to do. His broad, strong hands could fly over the keyboard and within seconds he would be crooning to it, caressing it with his voice in a way that made Gypsy laugh at him.

"Who identified me?" Mark asked then, and even Gypsy could read the defeat in his voice, in his expression.

Oh God, if Mark was giving up, then this was really bad. Mark couldn't give up.

She couldn't hear what Grody said when he leaned close and whispered the name in her brother's ear. But she watched his lips. She had paid very close attention to his lips, wanting to know who to kill later. The word was forming, as though in slow motion, and she knew, just as she always knew, what Grody was whispering to her brother. She knew, but somehow, for some reason, it was as though her gaze blanked, darkened, stealing the image. Except this time, it was shorter, the darkness more shadowed than absolute, almost giving her the secret she'd fought to remember for nine years. Then, Grody was straightening and chuckling at the tormented shock in Mark's expression, and the betrayal.

She knew who it was, why couldn't she see the name? She knew that the man who had betrayed her brother was his friend. She could tell from Mark's expression it was someone very close to him.

Mark nodded slowly, his gaze meeting Gypsy's as he stared back at her intently, a message in his green eyes that she fought to decipher.

"Any last words, kids?" Grody asked then, his amusement evil, his voice sending cold chills raking at her back.

"Mark?" Her voice trembled, terror shaking through her as she fought not to scream again, not to lose control, though she couldn't stop her tears.

"Don't cry, Gypsy," he told her as the Coyote, Grody, had laughed at him. "Don't cry, and be brave, Peanut. Do you hear me?"

Grody moved behind Mark then, gripping his long hair and suddenly jerking her brother's head back until his neck was stretched painfully. And a second later a knife pressed against the side of his neck, so sharp that the edge immediately had blood welling against it.

"No! Oh God, please. Please. No!" Gypsy screamed, begging, crying as she struggled against the ropes holding her to the front bumper of the vehicle. "Oh God, please. Please don't hurt him."

"Listen to her beg, Mark," Grody laughed as her brother's gaze met hers.

Be brave, Peanut . . . he mouthed. I love you.

He never told her to be brave. He always comforted her and told her she was allowed to cry. That little sisters didn't have to be brave, that was what brothers were for. And now, she had to be brave.

"Please. Please," she cried out, screaming, begging as she fought the ropes until her wrists burned and she could feel the dampness of her blood. "Please don't hurt him."

"Will she beg so pretty when I'm fucking her, McQuade?"

Her brother didn't have a chance to answer him. Immediately, Grody moved the knife, digging it in deep and slicing it over her precious brother's throat.

She was screaming. Screaming and fighting the hard hands that were on her, shaking her as someone yelled her name . . .

◆　◆　◆

"Wake the fuck up, goddammit. Gypsy, wake up now."

Rule could feel something exploding in his soul as he fought to wake her, staring into her wild, unseeing green eyes as they had jerked open, the way she had gasped as though trying to scream, though no sound had emerged.

The terror in her eyes had drawn his animal instincts to the fore in a surge of such fury it would shock him later. Until then, he was determined to force her awake. Shaking her, holding her to him as he yelled at her, terrified he was losing her to whatever demon had control of her.

Just as quickly as her eyes had opened, unseeing, that terror an agonizing mask that had rage surging through him, she was awake.

Blinking, perspiration and silent tears running down her face, she parted her lips as she gasped for air. Rule could feel her nails suddenly pricking his flesh and watched as she quickly realized what had happened.

Nightmares of the night her brother had been murdered. The night she had been abducted into the desert, where a Coyote had not just murdered her brother before her eyes, but had nearly raped her before the Breeds had arrived to make certain he never murdered another brother or tried to rape another sister.

"My fault," she whispered, her voice hoarse with tears as she stared up at him now, shuddering so hard he was surprised her teeth weren't shattering. "My fault."

♦   ♦   ♦

Gypsy could feel the tears that still ran from her eyes, the pain that pushed them free of her control as she was jerked from the nightmare.

She had never been awakened by anyone while the nightmare held her in its grip. At first, because her parents hadn't known about them. It was years before she had actually screamed through one of them. That happened only rarely. And never had they awakened her, then jerked her against them, their arms wrapping around her as Rule did now.

Her cheek was pressed to his bare chest, tears dampening the tough skin as one hand cupped the back of her head, while the other ran comfortingly up and down her back.

"I have you, baby," he was whispering roughly, rocking her just a little bit. "It's okay, Gypsy, I have you."

He had her?

Her breathing hitched as she fought to get a handle on herself, to stop the tears she hadn't shed before now.

She wanted to push him away from her. She was angry with him, she remembered that. But she couldn't make herself do it. No one had comforted her since Mark's death. Not because her parents hadn't wanted to, they had tried. Because she hadn't deserved to escape the pain and the remembered terror.

Because her selfishness had caused Mark's death, and she couldn't let herself forget that.

But she had forgotten it.

"Let me go." She couldn't let him weaken her further, but neither could she force any real demand into her voice. Because the terror was still there, lodged inside her soul and burning through her memories. A fear that drove spikes of agony tearing through her because she couldn't make it stop. She couldn't make the guilt and pain of that long-ago decision to disobey her brother go away.

"It's okay, baby," Rule whispered, his caresses soothing, gentle, though his voice was that harsh rasp he used whenever his eyes began changing, when the animal side of his genetics began showing itself.

"I'm okay." But she wasn't. It had been years since she'd had the nightmare. Of course, it had been years since she had allowed herself to sleep deeply too.

Pushing at his chest, she tried to put some distance between them, tried to get away from the warmth of his body. Because she was suddenly no longer fighting the remnants of that nightmare. Now, she was trying to tell herself she should be fighting the arousal rising inside her. Not that her senses were paying any attention to her. They were in a free fall to ecstasy with no intention of slowing down.

She had to get a handle on this need for him, especially in light of what she had learned the day before. She had to think, to figure out what her mother was up to and how to keep it from backlashing on the woman who had already lost one child too many.

Besides, she couldn't allow herself to depend on him, or to believe he'd never walk away again. He'd already walked away once.

And showered as though he'd dirtied himself with her.

Unfortunately, even remembering that wasn't enough to dim the hunger driving her.

"Would you please just let me go?" There was no way she was going to force her body not to ache for him if he didn't stop holding her as though she would break if he weren't careful.

"Let you go? When I can sense your need?" he asked, that growly sound in his voice deepening to a wicked, sexual sound.

"Sense my need, huh?" Her fingers curled against his chest, feeling beneath her touch the superfine, all-but-invisible hair that covered his body. "Is that another word for smelling it?"

"When I say I *scent it*, it seems to upset you," he murmured as his lips brushed against the bend of her neck and shoulder where he had bitten her the night before in the shower.

"How would you like it if I could smell every emotion or reaction you have?" she questioned him roughly, her breath catching as his tongue swiped over the little wound.

The pleasure that surged through her at the contact stole her breath. Like a thousand tiny, heated caresses over her flesh. Just hot enough to emphasize the pleasure and tighten the sexual tension already clenching with sharp strikes of sexual intensity at her womb while slickening the inner flesh of her pussy.

"Hmm, that could work for me," he breathed against her neck. "Perhaps trusting me would come easier for you then."

Trusting him? She *had* trusted him, and he'd jumped away from her to rush and shower before he'd even found his release. The fact that he'd brought her back was only due to this freaky hormone thing going on between them, not because he wanted *her*.

Not with the same hunger she needed him.

Ached for him.

Between her thighs, her flesh was swollen, moisture easing from her, preparing her to be pierced by the thick erection she could feel against her outer thigh.

Cupping the curves of her ass and lifting her closer, he had her legs spread and straddling his thighs between one breath and the next. Before she could evade his kiss, his lips were on hers, the spicy heat sinking inside her senses and dragging her kicking and screaming into a chaotic world of pure hunger.

"This has to stop," she whispered as he palmed the cheeks of her rear, lifting her against him until the hard wedge of his erection rubbed against the slick folds of her pussy and the swollen bud of her clit.

It was almost playful, the way he moved her against him, nipping at her lips before taking deep, mind-numbing kisses. Caressing her back, along her sides, he moved his lips over her chin, urging her head back, arching her body as his kisses trailed down her neck.

What was this?

Gripping his forearms, she admitted it was his hands at her back that held her steady. There was no strength in her as his lips moved down her neck. It arched for him as one hand moved along her side until he cupped the swollen curve of her breast. Immediately, he found the tight, highly sensitive nipple. It was peaked, aching with the same nerve-heightened need for touch as her clit was. Hell, as the rest of her body was.

She needed the touch of his callused fingers and hands wherever she could feel them.

Tilting her hips closer to the poker-hot, iron-hard erection spearing up from between his thighs, Gypsy moaned in rising pleasure as his lips moved to the tops of her breasts, his tongue licking over her skin, murmuring his appreciation of her as he blazed a heated, hungry trail to the opposite nipple.

When his lips covered the tight peak, Gypsy felt the sharp, ecstatic pulses of arousal amplifying inside her with a violent surge. It struck from her nipple to her womb, streaked to her pussy, then surrounded her clit with such a deep-seated need for his possession that it bordered pain.

She couldn't keep her hips still. Hell, she didn't want to keep them still. As his lips and tongue worked her nipple into a blazing point of pleasure, she moved against him, hips lifting until the head of his cock was tucked at the weeping entrance of her sex.

"So good," she moaned. How could she have forgotten, between the last time he'd had her and now, how incredibly erotic it was whenever he touched her? Whenever he wanted her?

The sensations were pleasure-pain, they were so sharp and filled with hunger.

"That's it, baby," he crooned at her breast, hard hands moving to grip her hips as she began to bear down on the wide crest of his cock. "Take me, Gypsy, love. Take all of me."

◆　◆　◆

He'd ached for this through the night. Lying beside her, allowing her to sleep, to rest from the incredible release that had swept through her body the day before, Rule had thought he'd go crazy.

Now, he knew he was going crazy.

Feeling her take him an inch at a time when he wanted to lunge inside her was torturous. The fiercely erect flesh was so damned sensitive that all he had to do was think about her touching it and he was ready to fuck. And blaming it all on Mating Heat was impossible. Because the Heat hadn't begun until he'd actually taken her. Until he'd realized on some soul-deep level that he wasn't going to let her go.

Her hips eased up, then bore back down; the slick, hot juices filling the fist-tight depths of her cunt aided the impalement but did nothing to ease the clenched, snug grip she had on him. Her flesh milked the head of his cock, stroked the throbbing shaft and sucked at his dick until he wanted to blow immediately. His balls were drawn so tight with the need to come that he was amazed he was holding back.

Slow and easy she took him. An inch at a time sank inside her, eased back, only to have her take him deeper. With each slow movement of her hips a little cry escaped her lips; the sound filled with her need for him, with the pleasure he was giving her.

And he could feel her pleasure. It wrapped around every sense he possessed until he couldn't tell where her pleasure ended and his own sensations began. He'd never known sex like this. Never known it could be like this. So fucking intimate as the pleasure buried so deep inside emotions he hadn't known he had, until he knew he'd never survive if he lost her.

With each thrust and impalement, each shift of her hips and broken cries that fell from her lips, Rule felt himself slipping deeper into the morass of sensations whipping over his body. Tension began to tighten his muscles as pleasure became an imperative need for release that sent heat streaking to every nerve ending in his body.

Until he couldn't bear it. Until the need to pound inside her, to push them both into the raging ecstasy building inside him, broke the last of the control he possessed.

Muscles bunching, he moved quickly. Without pulling from her, he had her on her back, legs spread, silken arms and legs surrounding him as he began to fuck her with deep, hammering strokes that had them both exploding with a power that caused Rule to snarl with primitive dominance as the overpowering need to grip her neck with his teeth again, to bite and hold her in place, overtook him.

And God, the pleasure.

He was immersed in her.

Her pleasure, her release and his own, in the wild chaos of a sensual storm he couldn't hope to control. In that moment, as the barb extended, became erect and locked him inside her, he realized he was being softened by her. Changed and overtaken by this one small woman with far too many secrets.

And he was all too aware that in too many ways, he was weakened by her.

✦ CHAPTER 23 ✦

It was full noon before Gypsy awoke again, her senses clearer, her anger no longer simmering but fully cemented, and the independent streak that her brother had often declared was a mile wide hardened painfully inside her.

As she opened her eyes and stared around the still-dim bedroom, the narrow shafts of sunlight that spilled from behind her reflected on the wall across from her. They were mocking reminders that the danger of losing everything she cherished was staring her in the face.

Her choices, her ability to live as she chose, her very independence was in danger of being taken away from her. Even in the nine years that she had steadily become one of the Unknown's best contacts, she had never endangered her life or risked her cover. She'd never had to fear her freedom or her independence.

Until now.

Rule had denied her the chance to leave the night before without so much as an explanation or the opportunity to argue her point. She'd seen it in his gaze. He hadn't been willing to hear an argument, his mind was set.

She was going nowhere.

Gypsy was determined to show him differently at the first opportunity.

But first, as much as it offended her pride and sense of fair play, she would have to let him think he'd won. Besides, she needed answers first.

Before she escaped him, she needed to know exactly the effects she would experience once she separated herself from him.

Exactly how factual were the gossip rags where this phenomenon was concerned?

Staring up at the ceiling, with the sheet Rule had pulled over them sometime in the night held snugly over her breasts as the heat of his big body braced her back, she considered exactly how to broach the subject. Because she could feel the stiffness of his erection against her lower back, and the answering ache building between her thighs. And God knew she wanted nothing more than to rub against him like a cat and feel that iron-hard flesh pressing into her and overtaking her. But a woman had to draw the line somewhere.

"Would you like to explain to me exactly what happens there at the end?" Gypsy made certain her tone was calm, controlled.

After all, she didn't do hysteria very well, and learning that the far-fetched stories written in the gossip rags had a chance of being true was definite grounds for slipping into hysteria.

Whether one was into that mode of existence or not.

The arm lying over her waist tightened momentarily as he took a deep breath at her back. "You've read the damned papers," he growled.

"The gossip rags, you mean?" Giving a mocking, desperate little laugh, Gypsy felt her fingers tightening in the sheets. "We call them gossip rags for a reason, Rule. Because the stories in them are supposed to be lies. Remember?"

"For the most part, they are," he admitted, though his tone of voice was anything but relaxed or amused, as it usually was.

"Why don't you just tell me what I can expect," she demanded, still and unyielding against him as she felt adrenaline beginning to gather behind the anger she was determined to keep him from sensing. "Exactly what is truth and what is lie? Because that whole orgy thing, it's not going to work for me."

"There are no damned orgies." His palm flattened at her stomach, stroking over the soft flesh as Gypsy closed her eyes and tried to tell herself that she wasn't going to allow him to distract her.

"Then what exactly is there?" The question was pushed from between her teeth as his fingers found the edge of intimate curls that led to the aching, swollen bundle of nerve endings throbbing below.

"Mating Heat. What you felt as I released inside you is the mating barb. About the size of the end of a man's thumb, it becomes erect beneath the crest of a feline Breed's cock, and not always in the same precise location. According to our scientists, the grip of the mate's vagina determines where it thickens, because its main purpose is to reach that little spot behind your clit, rich with erotic nerve endings." Acceptance filled his tone, surprising her. "And just as the articles suggest, Breeds secrete a hormone from tiny glands in their tongues. Those hormones fill their mate's system, creating an inability to hide or run from the bonds that are being built between them. It increases the arousal as well as the pleasure, and makes it impossible for the couple to be apart for long."

Great. Just wonderful.

"And what happens if they're apart?" she retorted, her thighs tightening as his touch tried to move lower.

As if that pleasure, that temptation weren't enough, his lips pressed to the area he had bitten into the night before, his tongue licking over the little wound with devastating results. With a liquid, brutal pleasure she couldn't fight.

"If they're apart," he whispered, his voice rasping with sensual pleasure as Gypsy felt her thighs weaken, part and give him access to the flesh his fingers were searching for, "then the arousal only increases until it's too painful to endure. Especially for the female mate."

Maybe she was just trying to distract him, she told herself. She was giving him what he wanted so he would keep talking and be completely unaware of her intent to slip from the hotel later.

"That doesn't sound particularly fair," she gasped as his fingers slid past her clit to find the excess dampness building between the plump folds below. "There's no way to make it stop?"

"Only with your mate," he assured her. "A few have managed to bear it longer than most, but the Heat always brings them back together again, forces them to confront whatever's held them apart and find a compromise that works for both of them."

"What if . . ." She gasped as those knowing, experienced fingers parted the slick folds and slid past to rub against the clenched entrance of her pussy.

She wanted his fingers inside her, she thought desperately. Stupid, traitorous body. It was responding to him, her hips shifting, her leg lifting, guided by the broad male palm beneath her knee to rest over his as he moved lower.

"What, baby?" His lips moved against her neck as the wide crest of his cock eased between her thighs and the tip of two powerful male fingers eased inside her—began to rub, to caress as the pleasure began tightening her body further.

"What if there's no compromise?" she whispered, the fear that the threat to her independence could destroy her becoming a hazy thought as his fingers reached farther inside her, filling her, increasing her hunger to be filled.

"There's always a compromise," he promised.

Her lips parted to refute that when his fingers suddenly thrust inside her, sending a shock of spiraling sensation tearing through her senses.

A moan broke past her lips as her hips pressed into the heavy thrust, her head tipping back against his shoulder to give his lips greater access.

"You don't compromise, Rule," she cried out, forcing the words into the open while his fingers began moving, fucking her with deep, even strokes. Her fingers gripped his lower arm as he pushed it beneath her head, bracing her more firmly against him, holding her steady.

"You have no idea, Gypsy," he groaned, his fingers sliding free of her a heartbeat before the head of his cock was pressing into the fiery heat beginning to burn inside her. "Oh baby, you simply have no idea."

A hard thrust of his hips and the throbbing crest lodged inside her, stretching her with exquisite fiery pleasure that bordered pain and lifted her on a rack of torture nearing ecstasy. Each withdrawal and thrust only increased the pleasure as well as the heavy presence inside her. The width of the crest made way for the heavy stalk following as he thrust inside her, slow and progressively deeper.

The rasp of the flared head caressing oversensitive nerve endings and flesh stretched exquisitely tight around him was driving her crazy. Each thrust, each roll of his hips that caressed her inner flesh with the iron-hard crest sent rocketing flares of sharp, internal sensation streaking through her clit before it caused her womb to flex, to clench at the impending explosion she could feel building through her body.

"God, you're so fucking pretty," he groaned, forcing her to lift her lashes and turn her head enough to stare up at him with only hazy awareness.

"So damned pretty, Gypsy, you took my breath away the first time I saw you."

His blue eyes flashed, so brilliant, filled with such an inner fire as the color began to overtake the whites that a distant memory teased at her senses.

It was gone just as quickly, another burning peak of pleasure ratcheting through her pussy and overswollen clit as it stole her breath for a precious heartbeat.

His fingers stroked from her hip to her breasts, testing the weight of first one swollen curve before moving to the other. Lifting the one nearest him, his head lowered, his lips suddenly surrounding the painfully tight peak of a nipple as his hips surged against her, shoving the thick length of his cock inside her with a tight, controlled thrust that caressed that hidden, ultra sensitive spot high inside her pussy.

She heard herself scream at the pleasure, unable to hold the sound back as his hips flexed, shifted, causing the pressure against that internal nerve-laden spot to increase until she was certain she would explode in climax.

His teeth rasped her nipple, as he suckled at it exquisitely while torturing her inner flesh until her hips moved against him, thrusting back. Whimpering, driven to complete pleasure-pierced insanity by the sensations building inside her pussy, Gypsy worked her hips against him as one hand slid unconsciously between her thighs to the swollen bud of her clit.

"That's it, baby," he groaned, his head lifting, as she forced her eyes open enough to follow his gaze to where her fingers were pressing against her clit. "Rub your pretty clit. Let me watch. Let me see you find your pleasure there while I fuck your tight little pussy into coming."

The erotic naughtiness, the dirty words and encouragement stole the last of her common sense. Nothing mattered now but teasing him, urging him to take her faster, harder.

"Fuck me," she begged him, her fingers moving against her clit as desperate pleasure began to shoot through her. "Oh God, Rule. Fuck me harder. Faster."

A snarl echoed around her as his teeth raked against the small bite mark on her neck. Even that sent agonizing pleasure lancing through her system.

"I love . . . it." Oh God, she nearly betrayed herself. "Love this. Like shoving the pleasure to my soul."

He was pounding inside her now, her juices spilling faster, slicker as he suddenly pushed her to her stomach, shoved her thighs apart and came between them without ever completely withdrawing from her.

Hard hands jerked her hips higher, forcing her to pull her knees up, to dig them into the mattress as her clit swelled further between her stroking fingers, pleasure building in the little bud until she was crying out with it.

Or was she crying out for the pleasure pistoning inside her pussy, thrusting hard, fucking fast and deep inside her as she felt the flared crest rake over that hidden trigger inside her pussy one last time.

She exploded.

Her clit imploded from her stroking fingers, shards of racing sensation striking deep inside her vagina, driving through her womb until the pulsating power of the internal eruption of ecstasy overtook her completely.

Shuddering, her body was taken out of her control as she felt his teeth bite into her neck, his cock driving to the very depths of her as that additional erection beneath the head of his cock locked him inside her, and the fiery spill of his seed jetting at the mouth of her womb sent her flying higher.

She was burning. An exploding flame she couldn't hope to control raced through her, licking over every nerve ending she possessed as she jerked beneath him, crying out his name as she felt the barb inside her caressing, pressing inside her.

There was no escaping it.

There was no escaping him.

And as she understood it, there was definitely no escaping Mating Heat.

◆　◆　◆

Rule watched his mate warily, sensing something changing, something hardening inside her. It wasn't a scent, it was a sense, as Jonas had explained it to him. An undefinable feeling whenever the mate was out of sync, or out of sorts with her Breed.

The director had smiled, a curve of his lips at once unfamiliarly softened and terrifying for all the love it held as his gaze had found the sight of his mate while she played with their child.

He understood it now, Rule thought as he urged her into the shower with him so he could wash her hair, wash her body. The need to do such things for her confused the hell out of him. He'd actually laughed in disbelief at the rumor that another Breed mate and benefactor to the Breeds, Seth Lawrence, had bought exquisite handmade, often hand-painted silk panties as well as unique handmade soaps of one-of-a-kind scents from around the world for his mate during the ten years he'd been unable to claim her.

It was said that the scents that Dawn Daniels Lawrence's skin was infused with were so unique that some Breeds had offered him a fortune to disclose who had made them.

Seth had refused. He had a one-of-a-kind mate, he'd declared, and as long as it was in his power, he'd ensure that she had one-of-a-kind scents.

Rule wished he had a one-of-a-kind scent to give her. Something that she could possess that she knew none but he could give her. Something besides that animalistic mating that overtook him each time he touched her.

"You don't have to dry me, Rule." Irritation was blooming in her tone as he grabbed her towel and began drying her sodden hair, watching the curls that filled the silky mass as he dried the water from them.

"Would you stop complaining over every little thing?" he breathed out roughly as the instincts clawing at him in self-disgust refused to relent.

It was obvious the Breed spirit he harbored inside him wasn't happy with him at the moment. But hell, it hadn't been happy with him since the night he'd first glimpsed her nine years before.

Oh yes, he remembered now.

He'd realized how unsettled he was months later, and hadn't tied the restlessness to the young girl being brutalized by those bastard Council Breeds that night. The fact that he'd moved to pull his weapon faster than he had ever done in his life should have warned him, though. If that hadn't warned him, then the fact that he'd fired on the head of the Breed preparing to rape her before being given the order by Jonas should have.

Everything had happened so fast that night, though. All he remembered was seeing those horrified, shock-filled green eyes as the Coyote fell from her a second before the four Coyotes with the bastard had fallen dead as well.

Then Lawe and Jonas had hidden the sight of her from him. Rule had turned and rushed from the cavern. He'd called the Reever ranch for their medic, a female he knew would take care of her. He'd ordered blankets warmed and rushed inside, made the arrangements for her parents, ensured that her brother's body was cared for properly. And he had nearly beaten the Coyote Loki to death before Lawe and several others had pulled him from the Breed. He'd refused to hear the Coyote as he swore he had been the one contacting Jonas that night.

Rule had wanted to kill him. He'd wanted to kill every fucking Coyote bastard there who hadn't kept Mark McQuade alive for his fragile, broken little sister.

Everything that could have helped her or meant anything to her, he had taken care of, and he hadn't even thought to wonder at the impulses that had driven him to take charge in such a way. To ensure that nothing else could hurt her, that no one else could harm her.

When her parents had arrived and had refused to go to the vulnerable, broken child who stood alone in the desert, staring back at them miserably, that animal had nearly rushed to her. Not until Jonas and Lawe had stepped to each side of her—his brother, along with the only man they called a friend at the time—positioning themselves as a protective barrier alongside her, had the animal stood down. At least a bit.

Rule remembered his anger at the parents, his disgust with their hesitancy to rush to her rather than standing at the son's side as though he would suddenly open his eyes and declare the night some joke. It had been no fucking joke. Their son was gone; better to protect and ensure the life of the living child and grieve later, than to leave the living in the cold while trying to warm the dead, he'd thought at the time.

Grimacing at the memory, he finished drying her, then allowed her to move away from him while she combed her fingers through the long tresses of her hair. He'd actually had Lawe purchase him a particular brush when he and Diane had gone out the past evening. One he could use on silky, soft waves without harming the delicate strands of hair.

He'd looked forward to using it once the unbreachable shock of the night before had passed.

He'd longed to go to her last night as she'd lain in their bed alone and silent. The pain of being unable to confront her parents and the truth of what her mother had done had enraged her. Sometimes rage was better slept off, he'd learned over the years. And though the rage was gone, he thought perhaps he'd made a mistake, because something had hardened inside her instead.

"Am I allowed out of my perfect little prison today?" The caustic tone of her voice as she slid her arms into a bra and secured the front clasp had the animal stilling while the man watched her carefully.

He winced at the sudden, sharp pinching sensation that came and went too quickly to be anything but those animal instincts extracting vengeance for causing his mate to feel as though she were a prisoner.

Dammit, he was the man, he was the one in charge, yet he swore he could feel an alternate, detached spirit inside his soul growling out a refutation of that thought.

"You're no prisoner, Gypsy," he told her, glowering silently as those instincts settled marginally inside him.

Fucking animal instincts. If he could wrap his hands around that being's throat and choke the life out of it, then he would do just that for driving him fucking insane.

"I can come and go as I please, then?" The confrontational expression and tone had him tensing at the knowledge that in pissing off the woman, he would be pissing off the animal side of her mate.

Namely him.

Jerking his jeans from the counter, he pushed one foot into the leg before doing likewise with the other and pulling the denim to his hips. He threw her a glare as he sat down on the comfortable stool in the corner and pushed his feet into black wicking socks then, refusing to give her what she was looking for.

At least, as long as he could keep from answering that question.

"I didn't think so." She did likewise, pulling on silky mint green low-rise panties before donning her jeans.

"The scent of the mating is detectable by every Breed with a nose to detect it," he told her warily. "There's no hiding, Gypsy. And your involvement with the Unknown . . ."

"My involvement with who?" She turned on him furiously as she pulled a dark gray T-shirt over her head before staring back at him in outrage.

"You're keeping me locked up here because you think I'm telling some fairy-tale group information about the Breeds?"

His jaw clenched as his lips parted to deliver a scathing retort. A growl rumbled in his chest instead as the words refused to part his lips.

Fucking animal. Son of a bitch, he *was* crazy. The only Breed in existence with an alternate personality that was literally all animal. Wouldn't he just make the list as weirdest Breed ever?

Not exactly where he wanted to see his name highlighted.

"Why not let me know when you're willing to confront me with honesty, mate," he told her as the anger brewing inside him began to simmer.

His cock was becoming erect, and as she turned on him after shooting him a disgusted look and giving him a glimpse of perfectly rounded ass cheeks beneath those snug jeans, the urge to fuck that cute little ass nearly overwhelmed him.

"I've been a hell of a lot more honest with you than you've been with me," she informed him, her face flushing with anger as her arms crossed over her breasts protectively.

He could sense the secrets she kept. At this point, he wasn't smelling a damned thing, he was feeling it. She was his mate and yet she had no idea of the bonds that were beginning to build between them.

Just as he knew the vow she had nearly made as her pussy tightened on his cock. She'd nearly sworn her love. He'd sensed it, felt it, the emotion wrapping around him even as she broke off the words to declare that she loved what he was doing to her instead.

His pretty little liar.

All long hair, big green eyes and raging secrets. Secrets she was going to have to reveal soon, before it was too late for him and Jonas to help her or her parents.

"Listen to me, Gypsy," he growled, moving before she could evade him and gripping her upper arm to hold her to him when she would have turned and flounced off.

Her anger only rose, as did the fury toward him that his instincts began to pour out to him. His mate was pissed at him, and her mate was pissed at him.

He was getting fucking tired of both.

"Listen to what? More of your accusations?" she cried out.

"More of my truths." He tried to soften his tone, something he'd never done with another person in his life. "I can sense your deceptions, mate. Of all the people in the world that you can never lie to, that you can never deceive in any fucking way, I am that person. Do you hear me? Listen to me well, damn you, if you aren't honest with me, then I can't protect you and I can't protect your family. Not without knowing exactly what they face and what I'm protecting them from."

"My family doesn't need your protection." But he could hear the hesitancy, the sudden fear that filled her.

"Gypsy." Releasing her, he raked his fingers through his hair in frustration as he tried one last time. "Sweetheart. Your brother died because he refused to trust those who could help him . . ."

"My brother died because his sister betrayed him." Flat, hard, she spoke the words as though it were a trained response.

"Baby, no." The softness of his voice shocked him as he reached out to touch her cheek, only to have her flinch away from him.

"Go do whatever Breed stuff you do when you're not accusing innocent people of lying to you," she charged, turning away from him, the insulting sense of her complete distrust causing the animal to react before the man could pull back.

He had her against the wall, using his stronger, heavier body to hold her there as she stared up at him in shock.

"I watched my mother lie screaming in inhuman agony as her living body was dissected just hours after her mate's," he snarled in her face, ignoring that flash of horror in her eyes. "Her screams cut into my soul like a blade whose sharp edge I can never escape because I was unable to warn the mate who could have saved her. I was too young, and I was too slow to slip past the guards plotting against them or to sense the packmate, the fucking brother Lawe and I wanted only to protect. One whose loyalty to the Council exceeded his loyalty to his mother. There is nothing, mate, not a fucking thing you can teach me about guilt, dark memories or nightmares. But have no doubt I have much to teach you about fucking loyalty to the only person you know in your heart can help you without betraying you."

Her gaze flickered. For a moment, for the briefest moment he swore she was weakening, that the trust he knew she felt, that he could sense her about to give into, was suddenly jerked back.

Her green eyes hardened, her expression flushing with anger—at herself, at him, at whatever thought or brutal pain ravaged her heart.

"Did you betray your mother?" she asked then, the tears that thickened her voice unbidden, and hated—by them both. "Were your actions the ones that caused her and her mate to die?"

"My inability . . ."

"I'm the brother who betrayed your mother," she retorted furiously then, the agony that raged inside her like her own beast shocking him with its strength. "Do you hear me, Rule? I'm the same as that gutless coward—"

His lips covered hers.

The kiss, filled with fury, with pain, with the need to cut off the agonizing torment of a child made to believe she was a monster, was infused with the hormone that filled the glands beneath his tongue with a suddenness he hadn't heard of.

Anything to hold back the words she would have spilled between them. The knowledge that his mate couldn't differentiate between an innocent girl's actions and a depraved Coyote's use of them.

Tearing his lips from hers, he stared down at her, watching as the tears she should have shed remained locked in her soul and flailed at his like the barbed whips the lab soldiers had used against him when he was just a cub. She didn't shed the tears, but they dripped down her soul, gouging into it and leaving wounds that bled night and day. The sobs she held inside shuddered through her body, causing her to flinch repeatedly in barely perceptible little jerks that tore past her control.

"Say such a thing to me again and I swear to God I'll make sure you regret it," he warned, furious that she believed such a thing. "Never ever, Gypsy, let me believe you are even considering such thoughts inside that far-too-complicated little brain of yours, or the battle you'll have with me is one you never want to face."

Her lips trembled, then hardened.

"Go to hell, Breed," she retorted flatly. "Better yet, get out of my hell and leave me the fuck alone."

Leave her the fuck alone?

His hand moved, a quick reflex action that had him grabbing the curve of her ass and jerking her into the cradle of his thighs.

He'd be damned if she would defy him this way. He'd be damned if she would ever allow another such thought of herself to see the light of day, let alone the dark of a nightmare as long as he lived.

His lips curled over the sharp canines at the side of his mouth, a rumbling growl of dangerous intent sounding in his chest and echoing around them as her eyes widened before her lashes flickered nervously.

He was one second from tearing the clothes from her body and showing her, proving to her exactly why she never wanted to push him to such an extent again. His free hand was only a heartbeat from jerking open her jeans when the vibrating *ping* of the comm device lying on the counter went off with a distinctively coded sound, a warning he knew he couldn't afford to ignore.

"Get away from me," he all but whispered, though the deep animalistic sound of his voice sent a sharp wave of submissive wariness instantly striking at her senses. "Get away from me now, mate, and pray to God that by the time I finish this, I can forget the fact that you're not just trying to destroy us, but you've already by God all but destroyed yourself, and that I will not tolerate."

With that, he jerked away from her, reached out and snatched the link from the counter as he turned for the exit and stalked through it, placing the link competently in his ear and barking out a "What the fuck is going on?" to the Breed unlucky enough to send out the imperative summons.

"The McQuades have just been arrested for bringing another device into the hotel after requesting a private meeting with Jonas," Lawe stated furiously as an enraged snarl could be heard in the background along with raised voices. "This time it was video and audio programmed with an electronic nano-nit. Jonas has just fucking lost his mind. Claws are out, and I need some fucking help here."

Rule slammed the door behind him as he raced from the room, carrying his boots rather than taking time to actually put them on.

A nano-nit was serious.

The tiny, almost-too-small-to-be-seen electronic robot hitchhiked on the back of audio or video devices to the desired location, where it was only activated once the parent device was. It then worked its way from the device to attach itself to an electrical source to power up before following the current and homing in on the specific electrical identifier it was programmed to infiltrate.

A nano-nit was all but impossible to detect, the reason why Jonas had everything that came into the elevators scanned for audio or video before it reached the eighth floor. By doing so, he ensured that the hidden little bugs didn't have the chance to infiltrate the independent wiring and network systems into which all cameras and wireless electronic devices were programmed.

The very attempt to get to the eighth floor with such a device was an infraction of Breed Law. To be caught with a nit was punishable by imprisonment and even, in some cases, death.

And Gypsy's parents had been caught, not just once, but twice, attempting to get a device into Jonas's suite. The second such attempt had included one of the dangerous little nits, which placed Gypsy in a tenuous position, that of being forced to watch her parents arrested, tried and sentenced for breaking Breed Law, for which there were no extenuating circumstances. Or bargaining with Jonas. Either of which, Rule knew, would destroy the fragile trust and love for him that he knew his mate was already fighting.

But it also had the potential to destroy his mate.

CHAPTER 24

Gypsy paced the living area of the suite, biting at a fingernail as a strange, imperative restlessness gripped her. It had been building since Rule's abrupt departure, demanding that she do something.

God, if she only knew what.

Along with the restlessness was an overwhelming sense of dread, and an inner need for him that she realized had haunted her since she'd first seen him two months before. From across the noisy, too-crowded bar their eyes had met, and she'd felt something she hadn't felt for so long that she'd forgotten the lack of it.

Security and warmth.

It had tugged at her senses, urging her to cross the distance, to accept the silent invitation that had filled his too-blue eyes and the savage features of his face. To rest her head against his chest, to let him hold back the nightmares for a while.

Rather than acknowledging the sensation, though, she'd run from it. Just as she was still running from him. Like a frightened child, afraid of the feelings rising inside her and the unfamiliar responsibility it had entailed, she had run.

Just as she was getting ready to run again, she knew.

She knew who and what she was running from, but she couldn't explain who or what she was running to.

"Be brave, Peanut." And her brother had never expected her to be brave. That was what brothers were for, he'd always told her. "Be brave, Peanut..."

And if he couldn't protect her, then—

The thought suddenly vanished as a firm knock interrupted the memory, pulling her quickly from the thoughts that had begun to drag her into the hell of the cavern.

That had never happened outside a nightmare, she thought, dazed as the knock repeated sharply, causing her to flinch at the sound.

Shoving the past back into the darkness where it couldn't destroy her again, Gypsy turned and moved quickly to the door, throwing it open without caring who was on the other side. If it was someone intent on attacking her, then right now they'd have a fight on their hands, she decided.

She stood, blinking in shock at the visitor, though, almost unable to believe who stood there glaring at her.

"Well, at least you're alive," Kandy announced, irritation lacing her voice as she pushed into the room. "And evidently Mom and Dad haven't killed you yet for scaring the life out of them."

Turning, she closed the door, watching as Kandy came to a stop in the middle of the room before staring around with a frown. "Where are they anyway?"

"Who?" Gypsy shook her head, uncertain what to make of her sister's arrival. "What are you doing here?"

"What do you mean who?" Kandy demanded rather than answering her. "Mom and Dad, of course. They came on up to meet with Jonas Wyatt to see why everyone was so certain Commander Breaker had kidnapped you—without your permission, that is—from the bar the other night. Everyone's talking about it, you know? Mom's livid and swears it's going to totally compromise McQuade Consulting." Kandy rolled her eyes at the thought. "They were certain you were being held in chains here. Arrested or being seduced?" Kandy's brows wagged suggestively. "They wouldn't wait on me when Loki stopped me in the lobby to find out why I was there. They came on up while we were talking."

That sense of panic rose sharply inside her now, tightening her chest and filling her with such dread that she could barely breathe.

"I haven't seen Mom and Dad," she told her sister.

Kandy stared at her as though she were suddenly speaking in a foreign language.

"What do you mean, you haven't seen them? They came up the elevator with Thor about . . ." Kandy checked the watch on her wrist. "Hell, almost an hour ago to meet with Wyatt. I was certain you would be there."

Gypsy's gaze swung to the digital clock on the wall across from her. Rule had left nearly an hour ago.

"As a matter of fact, the clock over the elevator read one thirty-three," her sister announced. "I noticed that because Loki said he only had a few minutes to talk before he was due for a meeting at one forty-five. But it was canceled—" Her sister stared around the room again. "Where could they have gone?"

The breath seemed to become trapped in her chest, threatening to smother her as Gypsy suddenly knew exactly where they were.

"No," she whispered, the knowledge that her mother must have done something incredibly stupid again blaring out at her senses, screaming at her to do something, to protect them. "Oh God, no."

Before the words were past her lips she turned, threw open the door as she ignored her sister's startled cry and began racing down the hall, heading for Jonas's suite.

Rule had been called away, the summons evidently imperative enough that he had left a confrontation she knew he'd had no intention of breaking off. He'd been enraged with her, and intent on convincing her of something she knew wasn't true when he'd been called away. At the same time her parents should have been knocking at the door of Rule's suite.

Rounding the corner, she nearly barreled into Loki, surprising the Coyote who had obviously been rushing through the hall himself in the direction of Rule's suite. He reached out for her, his expression startled, and the knowledge that flashed across his face caused her to duck, executing a slide that kept her well out of his reach before she shot back to her feet and sprinted to the end of the next hall.

"Gypsy, no. Wait," he called out, anger vibrating in his voice as she heard Kandy call out his name in confusion.

Adrenaline was racing through her now, dread a close companion as she whipped around the next corner, racing full stride for the Breeds now blocking Jonas's door.

She came to a hard stop, realizing that the seven Breed males had no intention of moving as they had previously whenever she arrived.

"Get out my way, Flint," she ordered the one she knew best, glaring into his dark eyes as he watched her grimly.

"I can't do that, Gypsy." He shook his head, his expression never softening as he kept a careful eye on her. "Just be patient . . ."

"Patient?" she cried out, enraged now, knowing she didn't have time to be patient. "Get the hell out of my way before I move you myself."

How she was going to accomplish that one, she had no idea, but she knew she would sure as hell try if he didn't let her through.

◆   ◆   ◆

The nano-nit technology was ingenious, Rule thought as he surveyed the device the McQuades had attempted to bring in, inspecting it from beneath the microscope set within a secure, impenetrable shell just for such dangerous electronics or minute robotic devices.

The nano-nit was attached to a microscopic line leading to a nano-reader pad inside the shell. Access to the technology was through a set of ports protected by sealed latex that adhered to the user's hands as they entered and ensured that an air-free, no-exit environment surrounded the nit and the reader.

"Storage capacity exceeds previous known standards," he murmured as he finally managed to crack the encryption set on the nano-nit's technology. That security wasn't really strong. The nit could bypass almost all known security measures, but it couldn't prevent access to its own programming. "Programming consists of activation upon a remote signal, whereby it would detach from the host device and make its way to the nearest electrical source before boring inside and making its way to the designated receiver signal to begin storing audio and video. In twelve hours it would then travel along the electrical current to the next floor, to the nearest device capable of transmitting, including satellite or the lesser used cellular phones."

Straightening from the microscope's electronic eye, he faced Jonas; Lawe; the Prime Alpha of packs and prides, Callan Lyons; the Lupine of the Wolf packs, Wolfe Gunnar; and the Coye of the Coyote packs, Del Rey Delgado, as well as one of the strongest pack leaders, Dash Sinclair, who had arrived late the night before for meetings scheduled that week concerning the new Bureau division in Window Rock.

The presence of the Breed hierarchy wasn't a good sign for the McQuades, who were still being held in a secure room lacking any electronics, digital or otherwise, or electrical access. Blackout, as it was referred to, was standard in all hotel conference rooms since news of the nano-nit had been announced several years before.

So far, there was no encryption or security that had been invented that could keep even the weakest nano-nit from accessing secured files or even network systems. If the nit managed to get in place, then the system was completely compromised with no way to destroy or even track the tiny bot once it was inside.

Only the director's paranoia and his habit of placing the strongest audio and video detecting technology in place outside secured areas had allowed the nit to be found.

For all its advanced ability to access a system, the nit was weakened by the fact that it could only be attached to certain devices. The simpler the device, the easier it was for the nit to detach and obey its programming without becoming confused by the programming already in place in the host device it rode in on. The only way to find the nano-nit was to detect the host; then, by using the digital microscope and attaching a nano-reader, it could be detected. The expense in technology and manpower to scan each and every device that could be used to host the nano would be astronomical for most companies.

Thankfully, the Breeds were a hell of a lot more experienced than any company and had a nearly unlimited source of ready, expert manpower.

Each and every Breed was taught nano-technology before they reached their teens. Council minds had created it, and now the Breeds were working to make it obsolete.

Jonas had gone primal upon the realization of what the McQuades had attempted to bring into his suite. His claws had yet to retract from beneath his fingernails; the tips of the razor-sharp bonelike extensions were still bloodied from having broken through the thin flesh that healed rapidly once they retracted.

The silver of his eyes swirled and massed like living mercury while the pupil seemed to almost blend in with the color of his eyes. Eyes that bored into Rule's demandingly, refusing to allow him to back down from the confrontation they both knew was coming.

A confrontation with not just the Breed who had stood at his back no matter the battle, but also the mate Rule refused to turn his back on.

"I won't let this pass," Jonas stated; the message he was sending Rule was clear. Gypsy's parents would be charged with Breed Law. "They will be punished for attempting to betray the people that they're well aware saved their daughter from a fate no child should have to suffer. Every Breed in the area has known she has personal favor with me for the past nine years, and they've treated her accordingly. Protected her accordingly. This act by them was unconscionable."

And that would destroy Gypsy in ways Rule knew she would never recover from.

"Gypsy's suffered enough, Jonas," he stated quietly, knowing there wasn't a chance in hell that the argument was going to hold any weight with the other Breed.

For once, his animalistic instincts were holding back, poised just as the man was, and waiting to see the danger his mate faced rather than letting rage overshadow what logic might be able to save.

"And Amber hasn't?" The primal rasp of Jonas's voice assured everyone listening that the man and the beast were in perfect accord at the moment in this particular Breed. "What of my mate, Rule? What of the child she's forced to watch suffer each day, wondering how much more her tiny body can take? What would you risk? Who would you risk, to save your child?"

He would risk everything but his mate, even his honor, to save their child, and Rule knew it.

Amber might not be Jonas's biological child, but that didn't matter to the director. His bond with that child was as strong as any that Rule had sensed between a Breed male and his own babe.

Rule couldn't fight Jonas's argument.

Gypsy had suffered, but her suffering, all but emotional, had ended that night nine years before, after the Breeds had poured into the area.

Amber's and Rachel's continued with little hope that it would end in anything but the horrifying death Phillip Brandenmore had suffered seven months before.

"Let the parents go." Dane spoke up then, his voice low, the demand firm as the South African accent seemed to deepen. "Ban them from all Breed facilities and ban all Breeds from interacting with the family or their businesses." His gaze met Rule's. "As well as any Breed mates, or their daughter. Sever all connection to them, and that would contain the threat they represent."

Jonas snarled at the suggestion. "You believe that cutting them off from their daughter will convince them to tell us anything?" Fury tightened his expression. "Hell, you weren't there the night their son was killed and their daughter nearly raped. They stared at her as though they didn't know her while trying to warm their son's hands. She stood in the fucking cold by herself, Dane, the scent of her pain and the rejection she felt running so deep it was enough to make me want to cry for her. She's damned sure not cried for herself since, and I highly doubt they shed a fucking tear for her."

Jonas turned away from his half brother as Dane's fist clenched atop the table where he sat, a grimace pulling at his features while Jonas stalked to the heavily reinforced windows at the side of the room.

"I swore to her she would always be protected by the Breeds if her parents didn't want her," he sighed. "That she would always be safe with me." Running the claw-tipped fingers around the back of his neck, Jonas breathed out wearily. "Then I left and never looked back. I didn't check up on her, I didn't send anyone out to watch over her. And I should have." He turned back to them, his expression heavy. "As much as I regret their actions, though, I'm not responsible for her parents' betrayal of her, then or now." His voice hardened. "And I won't be responsible for releasing them and giving them the chance to destroy the Breeds." His gaze locked on Rule once again. "Or a friend, at a later date."

Rule had always believed that the responsibility Jonas carried for the Breed community was one the director carried, perhaps not easily, but without regret. In this moment, he knew beyond a shadow of a doubt that the regret lay just as heavily upon him as the responsibility did. It was that he accepted both, knowing it was the only way to ensure the survival of the Breeds.

"But you want me to stand aside and let you destroy my mate now?" Rule demanded, wondering if he would ever be able to handle the portion of that responsibility that he had accepted as division director. "If you convict her parents, Jonas, you'll destroy her."

"I'll crucify them," Jonas snapped in ready agreement, his canines flashing in a promise of retribution. "If they can't or won't tell me who gave them that device, then I will make damned certain they're punished for it. If I don't, then I'm giving every son of a bitch with a grudge against the Breeds permission to use any of our mates' families against us. And that I won't do, Rule. Even for a friend. Even for your friendship."

Jonas was known to make concessions for his enforcers, especially those who gave their loyalty to him, that he would never make for another living being outside his mate. He'd always said there were few lines he wouldn't cross for them.

Evidently, Jonas had finally found a line.

"Rule, he's right." Lawe spoke from the other side of the room, where he stood with his own mate, his senses reaching out to Rule, urging him to open, to allow the twin bond Rule had denied for so many months to merge with his. It was a demand Rule continued to deny. "If we don't move now to show our determination to protect ourselves, then we're giving future enemies the ammunition they need to escape justice later."

Breed Law was like a living, breathing entity with the potential to grow, or to wither, with each decision the Breeds made regarding it.

"Unfortunately, even I have to agree with Jonas," Callan sighed, his amber gaze holding a wealth of compassion as he sought out Rule's. "If Jonas relents here, then any mate whose family members strike against us has precedence to get away with it unscathed later if it goes to trial. Just as with human law, we're setting the strength or weaknesses of our own mandates with each action we take, just as we're setting the strength of our honor and the example we make to our people if we attempt to subjugate the laws we set up ourselves."

"That's a complete crock." Dane leaned forward, his green eyes flashing furiously as he faced the group. "No one knows but those of us in this room, and your enforcer Thor, that anything is even amiss. By admitting to it to anyone, the McQuades would be signing their own death warrants. There's no sense in destroying a young woman who has, from your accounts, Jonas, done everything she could to ensure the success of the Breed communities and the Breeds by working with this sect of warriors you're so certain can lead you to Gideon. Show your willingness to stand by the loyalty she's given by attempting to rectify this in a reasonable manner, and perhaps it would build enough trust that Rule could convince her to give him the information she may hold."

At this moment, for this meeting, Dane was a direct link to his father, the first Leo, who was overseeing the meeting via the comm link Dane wore with a specially designed additional video monitor attached to the audio wand. And the Leo's opinion was never discounted.

Often argued, rarely obeyed, but never discounted.

Jonas glared at his brother before turning back to Rule. "Would it work?"

The question was in no way an agreement, but it was a sign of consideration. And for that alone, Rule refused to lie to him. He owed Jonas far more than just the truth to this question.

"At this time?" Rule breathed out heavily as he gripped the back of the chair that sat in front of him. "No. She's loyal to them, believes implicitly in them. I can't even get her to admit she works for them, let alone give you what you need to identify one of them."

Jonas turned back to Dane. "Any other suggestions, Junior?" he questioned him mockingly.

"Arrogant little fuck," Dane muttered as he sat back in his chair heavily. "You'll be the death of me, you know."

God only knew what their father was muttering. Both father and legitimate son had their issues with Jonas. And it was well known that he had his issues with them as well.

Jonas only glared at him for a moment before turning back to the room.

A chill of foreboding raced down Rule's back as the director's gaze hardened and turned icy, and he knew what was coming.

Just as he knew that the pain it would cause his mate was more than he could allow her to face.

"No one here regrets this more than I," Jonas stated as he turned to the alphas who were listening silently, considering each argument and its merits. "As director of the Bureau of Breed Affairs, gentlemen, I'll need your signatures on both the arrest warrant as well as the—"

"I'll stand in the McQuades' stead." The decision sliced at his soul, and Rule knew, if accepted, the decision would ultimately destroy him. It would separate him from his mate, his brother, and the freedom he'd risked his life to attain. It would all be taken from him and he'd serve the rest of his life once again confined to a cell.

It was a decision the man was willing to make.

It was a decision the animal accepted with a sense of quiet resignation.

Breed Law was a complicated, honor-driven set of mandates created to adapt and strengthen the Breed community as a whole. But it was written by compassionate men who believed in the inner strength and honor of the Breeds it was made to protect. It was also written to protect what they considered the very heart of the community as a whole. Their mates and their children. And the fact that there were times when certain circumstances could arise that would threaten their mates or their children within Breed Law. For those eventualities a Breed could purchase a onetime pass for whatever the mate would have to face. A pass that would forever imprison him and ban him from any Breed associations.

Shock held the room silent for long moments. Never had a Breed requested Self-Warrant, or even suggested requesting it for anyone. That one was now doing it, not for his mate, but to ensure that his mate did not face the pain of her parents' actions, was unthinkable.

"The hell you will." Lawe surged forward, suddenly enraged as his mate gasped, gripping his arm and being nearly dragged behind him before Lawe came to a hard stop. "I won't allow it, by God, you will not do this."

"You have no say in it," Rule informed him, though he never once took his gaze from Jonas's. "If the McQuades refuse or don't have the information that will exonerate them, and if Gypsy refuses to give it, then I demand Self-Warrant. I'll take their punishment as my own."

"Why?" Lawe roared out, enraged now, his eyes burning as Rule met his gaze calmly. "For God's sake, Rule, tell me why you would give your life for those fucking bastards."

"She's my mate," Rule sighed heavily. "The burden she carries each day where her brother's death is concerned is destroying her a little more every year, Lawe. It eats away at her soul like acid. If she lost her parents to Breed Law, she would never be able to live with the guilt of it. I'd lose her anyway. At least this way, she has a chance . . ."

"No," Lawe snarled, trying to break his mate's grip to rush to his brother, to try to knock the sense back into him that Mating Heat seemed to have knocked out of him. "Goddammit, Rule, I won't accept—"

"There's no one else I can trust to look after her, Lawe," he stated heavily, knowing the burden his brother would carry with the request he was making. "No one else I could ever make see what I see in Gypsy, but you."

"I won't do it," Lawe snarled, enraged. "There's not a chance in hell."

Sorrow surged through Rule as he opened a small part of himself to the emanations of the bond swirling around him. He gave his brother but a few small seconds to glimpse what had lived inside him since the moment he'd met Gypsy's eyes across that crowded bar.

The aching sorrow for the pain he sensed inside her, but also the depth of the pain he sensed that gouged at her tender soul. The nightmares the animal inside him sought to ease for his mate, and the love he'd felt for her since the night his animal instincts had bonded with her, nine years before.

The sound that broke from Lawe's throat was a roar of pure rage, shocking everyone but Rule. There was a reason he hadn't allowed his brother in for the past two months. A reason he'd kept that shield firmly in place. Because his mate's pain, her nightmares and her inability to accept that she deserved every ounce of the pure, steel-core devotion he felt for her was gouging those same wounds into his spirit as well.

Gypsy didn't love him, not as he loved her. The potential for it was there, he believed. Given a bit more time, he could have helped her heal enough of her inner self that she would have accepted his love for her, and accepted that she could love in return. But now, the chances of that time ever coming were diminishing by the second.

Jonas didn't speak for long seconds. Then he strode stiffly to the monitors on the wall and activated the link.

"Yes, Director?" Thor stepped to the video console immediately.

"Bring them out," Jonas snapped.

What the hell was he up to?

Less than a minute later, Hansel and Greta McQuade stepped from the blacked-out room into the videoconferencing module.

Greta had been weeping, while Hansel stood resolutely beside her.

"You admitted to knowingly bringing a stealth device into a secured Breed location, is this true?" Jonas snapped.

"We did," Hansel answered for both of them.

· C H A P T E R   2 5 ·

"My patience is at a fucking end, Flint," she informed the Breed furiously. "Those are my parents in there and I'll be damned if I'm going to allow Jonas Wyatt or Rule Breaker to browbeat them into admitting to something they may not have had a choice in."

A frown marred Flint's brow as his surprise gleamed in his eyes for the barest second. "Is that what they do, Gypsy? Strange, I've always known both Jonas, as well as Rule, to be highly unlikely to browbeat anyone, especially where a mate is concerned. Jonas has bent over backward to accommodate every Breed Enforcer on his teams and their mates. And Rule is one of his most trusted commanders; I can't see him doing anything less with his own mate. Or her parents."

Shame threatened to suck the fury from her, but nothing could penetrate the cold hard core of fear tearing her guts to shreds.

"If they're in trouble . . ." Her breathing hitched. "Please, Flint, let me see them. Let me help them," she whispered, aware of Loki and Kandy coming in behind her. "They're my parents."

"Are they?" he asked, gently, perhaps too gently. "I've seen very little proof of that, Gypsy. But if you'll give me two minutes I'll contact Assistant Director Brannigan and see if he can't get in to talk to Jonas. Because this suite is on total lockdown. The only way to get through any of us is to kill us. Can you do that?"

She hadn't cried in nine years. The agony trapped inside her hadn't had a release in so long that Gypsy had forgotten what the moisture in her eyes should feel like.

Until she had to blink it back.

She looked over his shoulder to the door, knowing she wasn't getting in there, even if she did manage to kill every Breed blocking it. "You don't understand."

"I've known you a long time, Gypsy," he stated, that soft, compassionate tone tearing at her, reminding her of how many times Rule had spoken to her with the same gentleness, that same understanding, that she had made herself ignore. "And you know what? I've seen Kandy's parents rush to her side many times. I've yet to see them rush to your side once. Even when I know for a fact that you needed them."

That didn't matter. Kandy had needed them, she had deserved them. What had Gypsy deserved after leading Mark to his death? Besides, she had never asked her parents to come to her, had she?

"Just get me in there, Flint," she demanded, her voice so hoarse, so filled with dread that she barely recognized it.

"What is he talking about, Gypsy? Gypsy, what's going on?" Kandy whispered behind her, fear trembling in her tone. "What's happened to Mom and Dad?"

Gypsy's fist clenched at her sides. She didn't need Flint or Rule to tell her what had happened. She knew her parents. Or rather, she knew her mother. Greta McQuade had gotten away with slipping the device in before, she believed. She would have been convinced she could do so again.

God, why hadn't she gone last night when Rule had refused to allow her to leave alone? If she had confronted him, if she had demanded it, he would have taken her, she realized. She knew Rule, almost as well as she knew many of the other Breeds. But she had slept with Rule, and she knew things about him that a woman only knew about the man she chose as her lover.

Stepping to the side of the door as the other six Breeds covered the panel, she watched as he touched the comm link at his ear and flipped down the small wand to rest at the side of his cheek.

"Yes, sir, Mr. and Mrs. McQuade's daughters are at the door. Gypsy requests access to ascertain the charges being brought against her parents and to assure herself of their well-being."

God no.

Oh God, if they charged her parents with Breed Law, there would be no fixing the damage it would make to their lives.

"Gypsy, what is he talking about?" Kandy cried out, though her voice was low, from behind her. "What charges?"

When she didn't answer, her sister grabbed her arm firmly, sending a rush of almost violent pain stabbing at her flesh before she hurriedly jerked back, turning to face the young woman she had always tried to protect.

"What is he talking about?" her sister demanded, tears bright and threatening to fall from her eyes as the Coyote behind her, Loki, stood with his back to the wall, his head lowered as he apparently stared at the tips of his dusty, worn boots.

For a second, she could swear she had met him before his arrival in Window Rock two months before. Something about his shaggy, dark blond hair kept tugging at her memory before she was forced to focus her attention on her sister instead.

"It's a long story, Kandy," she muttered, swiping her fingers through her unbound hair, and glanced back at Flint.

She wanted to hear what he was saying, but her sister refused to wait.

"Then start talking." Younger, but by no means less determined, her sister stared back at her furiously, the tears in her eyes threatening to fall at any minute.

"He knows." She nodded to Loki. "That's why he distracted you and held you back when you arrived with Mom and Dad. Isn't it, Loki? You already suspected what they were going to do. Why didn't you tell Kandy before she warned me that they were here?"

He looked up at her through the generous length of gold-tipped lashes, his features impassive, his dark gray eyes flat and deliberately cool.

"How was I supposed to know, Gypsy? I intended to take Kandy out to lunch when your parents arrived with her, concerned about the rumors that Rule had kidnapped you from that bar. They had already requested the meeting with Jonas after they were called and assured of your safety. Assured you would contact them later. They wouldn't wait for Kandy and me to talk a minute; they didn't even acknowledge that she had stopped to speak to me. They just stalked to the elevators and demanded to see the director," he told her quietly, his eyes shifting with such a slight movement to the Breeds behind her that she doubted they even knew he'd done so. When they came back to her, there was a warning in them before he then allowed the shift to move in Kandy's direction.

The message was clear. Drop the subject or Kandy could become involved as well.

He'd deliberately delayed Kandy, there was no doubt about it, just in case her parents were stupid enough to pull the same stunt they had pulled the last time they had arrived at the hotel to speak with Jonas.

"Gypsy." Flint drew her attention as he stepped from his position against the far wall, his gaze solemn as she felt her throat tighten apprehensively.

Shoving her hands into the pockets of her jeans and hunching her shoulders protectively against whatever bad news he might be delivering, she faced him anxiously.

"Assistant Director Brannigan is on his way up," he informed her, watching her warily now. "Now listen to me, he's not Jonas. Jonas knows you. He feels protective toward you, and that's allowed you to get away with a hell of a lot since he arrived here, things Brannigan's not going to tolerate."

It was more than clear that he was worried as Gypsy frowned, glaring back at him. "What the hell are you trying to say, Flint?" Her hands came out of her pockets, crossed over her breasts.

She watched him militantly, suddenly angry at the implication that she didn't know how to be polite.

"I believe," a familiar, imposing voice spoke before Flint could answer her, causing her to whirl around in surprise, "that you're a bit rude, Ms. McQuade, unless it suits you to be polite. Which, as I understand it, it rarely does."

Mr. Freaky from the bar.

Just what she needed, another smart-ass Breed.

His smile was all teeth and curved canines.

And a Coyote to boot. Just what the hell she needed. Other than certain ones, she did not get along with Coyotes very well.

"Loki, could you please escort Ms. McQuade the younger to your suite until I contact you?" It might have been phrased as a request, but it was clearly an order.

Loki gave a sharp nod as he straightened, his gaze meeting the frozen, Celtic green gaze of the assistant director warily before he turned to Kandy and extended his hand to her.

"Gypsy, please tell me what's going on," Kandy whispered tearfully, breaking Gypsy's heart. "I'm scared."

I want to go home," she whispered as Mark stared back at her, his eyes filled with sorrow. "I'm scared, Mark."

Don't cry. Be brave, Peanut, *he mouthed, his gaze boring into hers, and she knew he was trying to tell her something. Something she didn't understand.* "Don't cry. Be brave, Peanut."

"Ms. McQuade? If you're going to come with me, then now is the time." Brannigan's tone hardened in demand.

"I promise I'll explain everything later, Kandy," she swore. "Go with Loki, I'll be there soon. I swear."

She turned back to Brannigan, staring up at him directly, refusing to quail beneath the icy regard as he watched her knowingly.

"Neither Jonas nor your parents are in his suite," he told her then as he turned and started down the hall. "Come with me. Jonas is in one of the conference rooms on another floor, while your parents are in the one next to him. I believe you might recognize the title they gave it. The blackout room."

She swore that she felt as though she were going to pass out. A wave of sickening realization swept over her as a cold sweat suddenly popped out on her forehead and a sense of unreality threatened to blanket her entirely.

Shaking it off wasn't easy.

Reaching out, she steadied herself as she followed him by bracing her palm against the wall as she walked, certain she didn't want to fall in this Breed's presence.

He would instantly take advantage of the sign of weakness.

He didn't even glance behind him as he led the way to the private elevator in the next hall and stepped inside, waving her in.

Gypsy moved into the narrow cubicle, waiting as he stepped inside with her, remaining silent as the doors closed behind them. The elevator didn't begin moving immediately, though.

First, a strange hum filled the area as a dim, white light began moving over both of them.

Her eyes closed for a second in acceptance. When she forced them back open, he was watching her, his arms resting comfortably at his side.

This would take forever, she thought fatalistically. The scanner was no doubt one of the new ones her contact had warned her about weeks before the Breeds arrived. Designed to pick up any anomalies whatsoever.

"I have never betrayed the Breeds," she whispered. "And I would never have aided anyone else in doing so."

"But you'll do everything you can to protect your parents, no matter the actions they've taken? Correct?" The clinical, considering gleam in his gaze had her stomach tightening in dread.

What did he expect her to say? "If there's any way possible."

He nodded to that. "I think that's perhaps the hardest part of this job in some ways, from enforcers on up to Jonas's position. Understanding that loyalty to parents when we don't even have foster parents as a guidepost, siblings or children. But we do try our best to take that into consideration when needed."

Gypsy held his gaze, knowing he could read the fear rising inside her clearly. "Just tell me what I need to do. Don't play with me."

His lips quirked, his eyes darkening assessingly.

"And you would do whatever you have to?" he asked, his voice low, warning.

Gypsy steeled herself for the coming battle with her own conscience. "I will do whatever I have to do, Mr. Brannigan."

"Even if it means sacrificing your mate?" He tilted his head to the side as he leaned against the side of the elevator. "The one man, perhaps the only person in this world, who would be willing to give his life for you?"

The elevator began a slow descent as the scanners continued their work.

"That's enough." She forced the order past lips that were suddenly numb from the accusation.

He nodded slowly. "Tell me, have you heard much of Breed Law?"

"Some," she admitted, suddenly wary of the question. "Why?"

"Have you heard of Self-Warrant?" Something seemed to flicker in his gaze at the question.

Gypsy shook her head slowly. "I haven't."

"It's a part of Breed mating law," he admitted. "Perhaps you haven't. I believe those mandates are kept within secure Breed hearings if needed."

"Then why ask?"

"Self-Warrant is a onetime get-out-of-jail-free card that a Breed can use for his mate, or child, should one of them break Breed Law seriously enough that the sentence they face is more than the Breed believes is bearable. It can also be used in other situations. Such as a mate's parents facing an enraged director of the Bureau of Breed Affairs who's considering using the fullest extent of Breed Law against them for the crimes they've committed."

"I don't understand," she whispered, but she was very much afraid she did. "What does this have to do with me?"

His brow lifted lazily. "Listen and you'll know what it has to do with you. To ensure that the human doesn't suffer the full effects of Mating Heat, she would be taken to her Breed monthly. It would be enough to keep both of them sane, barely—though the female has options with the hormonal treatments our scientists and doctors have come up with that the male does not. Other than that, the Breed is locked in a cell similar to that of the labs he was created in, because the need for freedom would soon make him enraged. As long as he is calm, he can have his mate once a month. But for the rest of his life, other than those few short hours, he speaks to no one. No letters from home. No television, no weight room, library or computer privileges," he sneered. "Breeds don't suffer idiocy well. And if another Breed willingly gives up his life for the protection of his mate, to serve such a sentence for parents who obviously have no love for his mate to begin with, then why should we show him mercy? It would teach others that came after him the foolhardiness of such a decision."

"What are you trying to say, damn you?" She snapped, tired of this game. "What has Rule done?"

Oh God, he wouldn't do that. He wouldn't sacrifice himself in such a way, would he?

"It's what your parents have done, Ms. McQuade," he snarled. "And what that Breed is willing to do to save you the pain of their judgment and punishment. Under Breed Law, any human or Breed attempting to bring a nano-nit device into any area marked as Breed Secure invites punishment by death under Breed Law. What would Rule do to save you the pain of watching your parents die for attempting to threaten the infant child of the director of Breed Affairs when they brought in a nit programmed to activate, and record, upon the sound of a child's innocent voice?"

No. No, her parents would not do that.

But they had. She knew her mother, and she knew her mother would do anything if Kandy were threatened, to protect her. And everyone knew Kandy was her parents' weakness.

What would Rule do?

She stared up at the Breed in horror, watching his green eyes go from frozen to fiery in a heartbeat before they once again iced over as though the heated fire of rage had never touched them.

"What would your parents do, if they believed you would face that punishment rather than your mate?" he asked then.

The elevator doors slid open into a conference room filled with Breeds. Across from her, Rule stood as a wide flat screen monitor showed her parents, amplified her mother's voice and the pain-filled accusation that opened Gypsy's soul like a scalpel and left her emotions, the anger, fear and self-rapacious guilt, to flood her system like a tidal wave that destroyed everything in its wake.

"Mrs. McQuade, did you not admit to bringing a stealth device into—"

"I did," Greta cried out painfully. "I told you I did."

"And if I told you that your daughter will be punished—for the rest of her days, she will know a hell unlike anything you could imagine in payment for your crimes unless you divulge the name of the person or persons who aided you in this—would you then give us the information we require to prosecute them instead?"

"What? What are you saying?" Hansel shook his head, obviously fighting to understand the implications of what Jonas was saying.

"I am saying, Mr. McQuade, that should your daughter accept a statute of Breed Law that allows her to bear your punishment for your crimes, would you willingly allow her to do so? Would you allow her to suffer, in pain, in isolation, for the rest of her life to protect whoever set you on this course of action? Or would you give us the answers to the questions that were submitted to you when you were first detained for attempting to bring that damnable device into what is effectively my damned home and risking not just my life, but my wife's and my child's?" he demanded, the rage building in his voice with each word.

"No . . . you can't do that," Hansel whispered in horror and disbelief.

"She hasn't been our daughter since the night she helped those bastards kill my son," Greta sobbed, her expression twisting in agony as each Breed watched her in shell-shocked silence. "My daughter died with him that night."

"No, Greta." Hansel stared at his wife in horror as she voiced the rage she carried toward a child who had played no part in the horror she had suffered as well.

"You know it's the truth," Greta sobbed, all but hysterical. "All that mattered then was the next party, and that's all that matters to her now. The next party, the next wild drunken night and trampy two-bit Breed she can fuck. That's how she honors the brother who died because of her stupidity." Her eyes suddenly shot past Jonas, horror filling her face as Hansel McQuade's followed. Her father's eyes suddenly filled with tears as they met Gypsy's through the two-way video monitor.

She felt frozen. Locked into place as all eyes turned to her, staring at her in varying degrees of pity.

"Fuck!" someone whispered, a male voice, low, a hiss of raw fury a second before Rule roared out in rage, lifted an object from the conference table in front of him and hurled it at the screen.

It shattered, throwing shards of glass outward as Jonas ducked, and those nearest turned their heads quickly to avoid the sharp projectiles.

Something stung her forehead, her cheek, but she wasn't certain what.

The sickening realization that her parents believed the act didn't surprise her; she had been damned good at her job over the years. But to have them voice it to these men who respected her enough to see through her party-girl act destroyed her. To know that they might suspect or even privately blame her was one thing, but to have her mother accuse her so virulently with such disgust and lack of warmth, she had to admit, laid her soul bare.

That was her mother.

The woman who had raised her . . .

No, her parents hadn't raised her, she finally admitted.

Mark had.

They'd been busy building their business, or playing with Kandy, the girly-girl of the two sisters who liked to dress up, and didn't get dirty and didn't beg to go hunting with her beloved brother.

It had been Mark who had taught her how to ride her bike, to roller skate, to hunt, and to race dirt bikes over the desert. He'd taught her how to spy while making it a game, how to be quiet, how to slip out of the house and how to pick a lock.

He had been teaching her how to know what he was thinking with just a look . . .

Her eyes met Rule's as she felt that paralyzing fear she'd felt nine years before, the first time she'd seen his eyes go feral like that. All blue with no whites, the pupil retracting with rage.

He'd been there then, she realized, her eyes locked with the naked rage and pain in the brilliant, too-sharp blue of his eyes. With the same look in that oddly colored gaze, the same wild fury she could see there now.

And the same warning.

The same warning that had been in Mark's eyes just before he had died.

"*Don't cry. Be brave, Peanut.*" *His lips moved slowly, making certain she knew what he wanted her to see, staring at her, his gaze locked on hers, intent, warning. A message she couldn't read no matter how hard she tried. "Don't cry. Be brave, Peanut.*"

She was rarely called Peanut, she realized in that second, and never by Mark. He had never given her pet names. She was his Gypsy Rum, baby sister or baby girl. Never, ever had he called her Peanut.

And baby sisters didn't have to be brave, he'd told her over and over again, that was a big brother's job. He could be brave for both of them, and she could cry all she needed to.

And still, she couldn't cry. She was brave, foolhardy even. She had taken on her brother's work, protected her sister as she had been told over and over again that Mark would have wanted her to.

Mark died for you . . . How many times had that accusation been leveled at her in the form of a chastisement?

It wasn't your fault, Gypsy, they knew Mark's weakness . . .

She was his sister, but everyone had remarked as she grew older how Mark had always treated her more as his child than a sister.

"I'm supposed to be brave," she whispered, nine years of unshed agonizing pain scraping over her throat.

Rule shook his head slowly as a tormented grimace tightened his face. "You've been brave enough for all of us, for far too many years."

Slashing, agonizing, the wave of pain that swept through her, jerked her head to the side as she closed her eyes against the stone-cold reality of choices she couldn't control, nearly had her losing control of that inner scream of denial she wanted to let free.

When her eyes opened, it was to meet the tormented features of Jonas Wyatt's expression. The pain he shared with her, she imagined. Choices and decisions that had perhaps not gone as planned, lives that were lost because he hadn't been Superman that day. She could see it all in his face.

The director who had fought for more than ten years to build Breed awareness and ensure the survival of his people. The friend who had watched over the Breeds under his command and who grieved as no one but his mate could understand when he lost one.

And the father.

The father forced to stand by and watch as his child possibly died in front of his eyes.

These Breeds together had saved her life. Jonas, Lawe, her mate Rule, Flint and perhaps even Loki. She now knew he had been there that night. They had been there, and without them she wouldn't have lived. Mark's sacrifice, no matter how undeserving she was, would have been in vain, just as her mother believed.

"As his mate, I refuse to accept his demand for Self-Warrant and ask that you do the same." The words left her lips before she was even aware she intended to say them. "The crime isn't his, and the punishment would be not only undeserving but also lacking in gratitude."

Her mother would never understand Rule's sacrifice. But Gypsy did. He wasn't making the sacrifice for them, but for her. He was doing what everyone had imagined Mark had done. Giving his life for her.

"Dammit, Gypsy," Rule growled as she swore she heard Lawe mutter, "Thank God."

"And," she continued. "I request leniency for the crime committed by my parents until an explanation is given and possible exoneration based upon circumstance is heard by the Breed Ruling Cabinet."

Jonas's eyes widened. She had just given herself away and she knew it. She shouldn't have known about this law, any more than she had known about the one Brannigan had informed her of.

Jonas nodded slowly as she watched Rule moving from the corner of her eyes, prowling, stalking closer to her as though she would bolt at any second.

And God knew, she wanted nothing more than to bolt.

She wanted to sink into the pit of pain and rage that she'd held back for nine years, but first she had to finish what she'd just started.

"Agreed, Ms. McQuade." It was the Prime Alpha, Callan Lyons, who accepted her request.

"Agreed," Jonas repeated.

"And I request their release and a gag placed on any announcement of their crimes until that hearing can be held, with an offer of information in exchange for such and a promise to ensure that they arrive promptly at the hearing to answer for their crimes should exoneration not be made after they're questioned."

"I'm not much of a liar," she whispered, remembering her brother laughing at how easily she gave herself away. "It's better if you just make certain no one knows what you're doing; then they don't have questions you can't answer, right?"

"Stop this," Rule snarled furiously as she edged away from him, the intent in his gaze assuring her that he would stop her now if he could. Stop her, until he learned what she had to exchange before anyone could have a chance to hold her to it.

"I won't let you destroy yourself for me." Her gaze blurred from the tears that filled her eyes, Gypsy pressed her clenched fists into her stomach, nearly heaving with the pain tearing through her. "I won't be the cause of it. Never again, Rule."

He snarled furiously as Lawe suddenly caught hold of his arm, pulling him to a stop before he could reach her and quickly whispering in his ear.

She turned back to Jonas quickly. "I don't know the identity of my contact," she stated, trying to breathe past the tightness of her chest. "But not very long ago, I saw the two men he met with outside my apartment. Give me forty-eight hours, Jonas, and I swear if you don't have what you're seeking to save your daughter, then I'll give you the identity of those two men and you can ask them yourself."

"No." The fury in Rule's voice surprised her, causing her to jerk in protest as fear began to surge inside her again at the sight of Jonas shaking his head.

Oh God, she was sure he would take the offer. Certain she could save her parents another way.

"Do you actually believe I saved your life nine years ago to watch you throw it away by meeting with only God knows who and possibly getting both yourself and your mate killed?" Jonas snarled then, allowing the blood, and the breath, to rush back to her head in a dizzying wave. "I believe I've had enough experience with headstrong mates and their stubborn-assed Breed males to know for a certain fact that a mess like that is nothing I want a part of this year, thank you very much. Think again, Whisper."

She knew that code name she was given was a very bad idea.

She shook her head desperately. "All I have to do is send a message." She was giving that message now, and she and Dane Vanderale both knew it. "Give me forty-eight hours. I won't leave Rule's suite, and you can fill the damned place with Breeds if that's what you want. But I swear to you, Jonas, one way or the other, you'll have what answers I can give you when that time is up. Please," she whispered, knowing she was losing her grip on the tears that had been building for so many years. "They're still my parents. And I still love . . . both of them." Her breathing hitched as the regret slamming through her system nearly stole her breath and weakened her knees with the uncertainty of what he would do now. "Jonas, please, they're still my parents."

She didn't dare glance at Dane or at Dog where he sat near the South African. And she sure had no intention of meeting Rule's eyes as he stood stock-still by his brother, Lawe. If she did, she would give them all away and she knew it. The second she did, Rule would know it. He knew her too well, she realized.

And knowing both Dane and Dog as well as their reputations, they would find a way to ensure that Jonas was satisfied without once sacrificing their own identities.

And she needed to do this without sacrificing the promise she had made to the man who had trusted her brother so implicitly that he had given a fifteen-year-old on a fast track to death's door a reason to live.

But more importantly, she had to do it without placing the burden of her parents' punishments on the chance she was being given to finally have a life of her own. A life outside the guilt, outside the lies and outside the traitorous acts of a man who had attempted to destroy it to begin with.

The same man who had betrayed her brother nine years ago and used her to ensure his death.

CHAPTER 26

LOBO REEVER'S ESTATE
THAT SAME NIGHT

"I know who you are," the Breed hanging from the wall, his toes barely touching the floor, hissed with what he must have thought was an intimidating sound.

Gideon, Graeme to those at the Reever estate, smiled. It meant playtime. And he sorely did enjoy playtime.

He ignored the Coyote for the moment, laying out a few tools he would need later. A few pliers of differing sizes and uses, a heavy hammer, ball gag—sometimes the bastards just didn't stop screaming.

He was searching for a particular knife he'd lent Khi—Khileen as others called her—Lobo's stepdaughter, during the interrogation of the Coyote's partner two weeks before, when the satellite phone he carried at his hip vibrated insistently.

Pulling the phone from the holster, he stared at the number and grimaced in irritation. He really wasn't in the mood to deal with this right now, but damn if he wasn't fucking obligated.

Finding his mate might have started the process of returning his sanity, but a few individuals had been instrumental in completing the process and making certain he found his way to Lobo Reever's ranch with enough credentials and references to ensure he was hired on the estate.

"Yeah?" He answered the call, hoping it wouldn't take long. A useless hope in most cases where this hybrid was concerned.

"The jig is up, old chap." Amused and inherently irritating, that foreign accent cloaked in a lazy drawl never failed to raise his hackles.

This time, they didn't just rise, they started doing a little jig on the back of his neck.

"What jig?" he growled, though he had a feeling he knew exactly what the "jig" was.

"Contact Jonas," he was ordered, the voice firming with the demand. "Or we're all going to be in damned hot water, with more Breeds after our asses than we know what to do with. And I'm sincerely not in the mood to have to explain getting caught to my sire."

Graeme snorted at the order. "Let me guess, you managed to fuck this up before I could finish saving that kid's life? Why doesn't that surprise me, you little prick?"

Why didn't that surprise him?

This wasn't the first time he'd worked with the bastard, and though the hybrid was usually damned competent, there were times, highly inconvenient times, when he had a habit of throwing a monkey in the works and letting it play hell with the plan.

Graeme always thought it better to just shoot the fucking monkey, but what the hell did he know? He was just the Breed who managed to hide right under everyone's nose. And how did he accomplish that, he asked with silent sarcasm. Let's see, *he stayed the fuck out everyone else's business maybe?*

"When's the next injection due and how many before we're finished?" Hell, now the accent had managed to completely disappear; that didn't bode really well for him. That meant he could possibly get sacrificed as a useful but regrettably required casualty. And that wasn't a part Graeme had any intention of playing.

"Final injection is due within the next eighteen hours." And he was damned glad it was the final one. Hearing that baby's pain-filled cries and the patient, unwavering love and pain in her mother's voice was taking a toll on his hard-won sanity.

"We have forty-eight hours," he was told imperiously. "Get Jonas the information he needs or my partner and I are history here. Someone witnessed a meeting we had with our contact in the Unknown. If you don't give up the secrets, my friend, we're all screwed."

A snarl escaped before he could control it. Dragging his hand over the dance of nerves being played out over the back of his neck, Graeme checked the mirror he kept hanging on the wall next to his work area.

Fuck. Fuck. Was that a shadow of a stripe coming across his face? He was going to kill the little bastard on the other end of the call before it was over with.

"You're the one who was caught," he reminded the other man coldly. "Unlike you, I'm not into the damned games and machinations you and your brother so enjoy. I keep my nose out of everyone else's business and get along damned fine. If I contact Jonas before that final injection, there's no way in hell I'll get in there to finish it. And I'm not quite so willing to sacrifice that child's life for yours, asshole."

"Finish it, then contact him," he was ordered. "But have it done in the required amount of time, Graeme. Because if our witness identifies me and our partner, then we'll give up the goods on you to save our own asses. Never doubt it."

"So take care of your fucking narc," he grumped, rolling his eyes and catching sight of the prisoner he'd dragged into the Reever cells less than an hour ago. "I have things to do. Dealing with Wyatt isn't one of those things."

"Then make it one of your things. Our narc is Whisper. Exactly how do you expect me to take care of that one?"

Son of a bitch.

Pinching the bridge of his nose, he swore he could feel the stripes that once marred the flesh of his face beginning to shade his skin again as fury rose inside him. He couldn't touch Whisper and they both knew it. Hell, he didn't just owe her his life, he owed her the life of his mate. Whisper was the child who had overheard the plot to kill Judd, Honor, and Fawn before the Unknown had managed to hide their identities. Had it not been for her contacting the man her deceased brother had worked with, then Fawn would have died. And Gideon—Graeme—would never have found his sanity.

He'd kill for her, but he'd never consider killing her.

The bastard on the other end of the call was another story, though.

"I'm going to take this one out of your hide, asshole," Graeme warned him.

"Stand in line." The suggestion was amused and filled with a confidence that his safety was assured.

Graeme wasn't so certain about that.

"You actually have forty-six hours," he was told then. "I expect to hear the roars of rage long before that deadline is actually up."

Yeah, he just bet the bastard did.

Disconnecting the call, he turned to the soldier staring back at him malevolently, wondering how pissed Lobo would get if he just beat the shit out of the bastard instead of wrapping him up nice and pretty for Lobo's stepdaughter.

She'd gotten to him, Graeme admitted. The little toddler slowly becoming a Breed. Once he'd explained it all to her in a way she could understand, she had warmed to him. She knew it was going to hurt at first, bad enough that she wouldn't be able to stop crying maybe. That she would feel really bad, but once it was over, she would be her daddy's little girl for sure.

The first injection Brandenmore had given the baby had begun the process of changing her DNA. Almost overnight her ability to understand and to reason began rising exponentially. If one knew how to communicate with the child, then seeing the world through her eyes, through her observations, almost made a Breed believe in miracles.

Now, four injections later, the last and by far the most painful was coming. What Brandenmore had done should have destroyed the child in the same manner in which he had died himself. What no one had known, but Graeme had found in the blood and tissue samples Phillip Brandenmore had taken that night, was that Amber would soon have been diagnosed with the same type of leukemia that had nearly killed Honor Roberts.

Had the scientists begun injections in Honor sooner, then the pain of reversing it would have been much lower, closer to the levels Amber was experiencing.

But hearing that tiny child cry, seeing the pain in her eyes as he'd returned for each follow-up injection, was killing him.

He believed himself to be a monster. What did that make the scientists who had created and tortured the Breeds for so long?

"Got problems, *Gideon*?" The name that fell so easily from the Coyote's lips had Graeme turning slowly, the monster that existed within him making its presence known.

Graeme felt the burn of his flesh, the primal response that ignited a genetic code and flashed the dark stripes across his face, his hips, alongside his left leg.

As quickly as he lost control, he snagged it back, holding on with a desperate grip before it could escape forevermore as it had before.

The Coyote saw it, though. His eyes widened, he swallowed tightly and an instant later Graeme was in his face, canines bared, his eyes picking up hues of color, differences in body temperature and the fear the Breed had been fighting to hide as claws gripped his neck, exerting just enough pressure to pierce the tough hide and threaten the large artery in his neck as the sound that rumbled from his throat echoed in the caverns like a lost nightmare.

"Say that name again," Graeme suggested, "even think it, and we'll see how easy it will be to skin you." With the other hand he used a razored nail to lay open the thin layer of skin and slice between it and red meat.

He knew what it felt like. He carried his own scars from the scalpels the scientists had wielded.

"Then I'll dissect you as they did the fine Gideon. Living. Screaming. Your bowels bloodied as the waste of it seeps from your body like liquid terror and you piss yourself from the pain. And that's just the beginning," he hissed, feeling his eyes begin to redden. "Within seconds you try to beg for mercy, but the pain is such that no words can form, your brain no longer recognizes the need for speech, the need to rationalize—it only knows one thing. The agony, the horror of it and the inability to move. The stark realization that you can't tighten a muscle, can't jerk a limb. You can't even control your own heartbeat as they reach in and touch it, slicing into your brain with such a brutal punch of agony as they do so that those animal genetics of yours tuck their tails and start howling for death."

A second later he scented the wash of the Coyote soldier's urine as it began seeping from his body.

Fuck, and here he thought he had a soldier of better mettle than the others. The scent dragged him back from where he'd slipped once again, though. It jerked the sanity back to his mind, the logic and ability to think, to reason flooding back into his senses.

"Don't test me," he growled, stepping back from the obviously terrified Coyote Breed. Casting him a sneer, he asked in disgust, "You bastards used to have more iron in your spines. What did we do? Kill all the crazy ones?"

He was starting to think it was possible.

◆　◆　◆

This was a complication.

Dane inhaled the sweet, black cherry taste of the slender cigar and considered his next move.

It wasn't that he enjoyed this particular game, and God knew he didn't. It was that he knew his brother far too well, and their parents were certain at the time that there were no alternatives.

Dane had even suggested to Jonas that if the message went out to Gideon and Judd that the injections rather than the code itself were needed, one or even both would help. Both Jonas and Rachel had instantly rejected such an action, though.

And Ely, the Breeds' doctor, wasn't yet in a place where her confidence could match Jonas's will as it had once done. That had left Dane to do the dirty work, as it usually did.

He didn't care to get his hands dirty, but if Gideon, or Graeme as he was called now, didn't give Jonas what he wanted within forty-eight hours, then Dane could kiss his entire American family and friends good-the-fuck-bye, because Rule's little mate would tattle on him like a five-year-old.

"Remind me to stay the fuck out of your little games from here on out." Dog sidled next to him, struck a match and lit the tip of his own cigar. "I'd heard conspiring with you could get dangerous. Strange, never heard of you getting caught before, though."

Dane threw him a careless, confident smile. "I've got this, my friend," he drawled with far more assurance than he felt, he admitted. "All will be well."

"Let's hope Leo's ready to welcome me home when Jonas puts out that execution order on me," the other Breed sighed in response. "I've been getting rather bored with America anyway."

Dane almost snorted at that one. Dog? Bored? He rather doubted it. Dog lived for the games he was able to play within the Breed societies here.

Like all the Leo's protégés, Dog was a master manipulator and a calculating son of a bitch in the bargain. So much so that when Leo realized Dog was in America working at freeing the Breeds and not just helping them to set up their societies, but encouraging it in a fashion, he'd been livid and dared the Coyote to return.

Leo was still a bit upset over that one.

The patriarch worried incessantly about the safety of the American branch of the family, and still swore that the world simply wasn't ready for Mating Heat, and keeping it a secret much longer would be impossible.

Dane shuddered to consider what his father would do if he ever learned that his son, his legitimate heir, had been bankrolling the Coyote's little venture at the time. He often wondered if Leo, as he often threatened, would actually disinherit him.

He was afraid his father just might do so.

"You worry too much, Dog," Dane informed him absently as he drew on the cigar and considered the night thoughtfully. "You should relax a bit."

"This is why we were never friends, Dane," Dog reminded him with that ever-present mockery, "Hell, this is why I just stayed the fuck away from you. You cause havoc no matter where you go."

Of course he did, that was his job, Dane thought as his gaze narrowed on a flash of long auburn hair and a particular turn of the head.

When the female turned back to him, the face was wrong, the slender body too soft, without the play of well-honed feminine muscles beneath her flesh.

Would he ever stop searching for her, he wondered a bit somberly. Each time he was even near the area he would watch, wait, certain at some point that he would catch a glimpse of her.

Yet he never did.

He prayed he never would.

Letting her go had been the hardest thing he'd ever done in his life. Allowing her to have the mate she longed for, the life she had dreamed of, had shattered his heart even though her happiness was all he'd ever asked for.

Sadly, he'd forgotten to include himself in the wish.

He breathed in slowly, heavily.

"We were never friends because we truly never knew each other," he retorted to the Breed's earlier statement. "Father was smart enough to ensure that one of us was always gone whenever the other was there."

The Coyote had come to the compound ragged, filthy and suffering from dehydration and juvenile primal fever. Dane had been in London at the time overseeing several of the Leo's properties, but he'd heard of the bedraggled Coyote youth, more wild than trained, who had gone in search of the fabled compound of the first Leo at the tender age of six.

"Leo's going to have both of us killed if he finds out about this one, Dane," Dog assured him.

Dane shook his head. "He'll regret it. He'll hate the need for the deception, but he's as aware as we are that the child would have died without the assurance we gave Gideon of protection if he would aid the child. We never specified how he was to do so."

Dog grunted at that.

"What now?"

"Now, we wait," Dane informed him, crossing his arms over his chest as he leaned against the rough stone of the outer wall and continued to watch the guests of the hotel arrive and depart.

"You do that a lot," Dog observed.

"What? Wait?" Dane grinned.

He did rather do that a lot.

"No, tense whenever you see a particular color and style of hair," Dog pointed out just as Dane tensed further, cursing silently as the black military-reinforced SUV pulled slowly beneath the hotel awning.

Several Breeds sat in the front; behind them, he knew the small family.

He waited, hungry for the sight of her. Watching as first Lance Jacobs stepped from the SUV before lifting the toddler into his arms, then helping his mate, his treasured wife, from the vehicle.

Jacobs made her a good mate, though, he admitted. And that boy, he was a combination of both. The child who had finally tamed Death. Auburn hair, a little long and a bit shaggy. Loose jeans and a blue T-shirt. He looked like his father, thankfully, though the boy had his mother's eyes.

Then she stepped out.

God help him, how beautiful she had become over the past years. Still regally graceful, as exquisitely beautiful and more dangerous and . . . His throat tightened, his chest aching at the sight of her rounded tummy beneath the pretty gold silk blouse she wore with her jeans.

Pregnant.

Once again, she was with child, and just as before, it gave her a glow to her features that made her incandescent. Made his chest swell with such emotion that once again he wondered if hybrid Breeds had the ability to find their mates, or if the natural age retardation once they reached adulthood also signaled that they, like their human counterparts, risked losing the very hearts that could come to mean so much to them?

Just as he had lost this heart.

"Harmony Lancaster," Dog murmured. "Son of a bitch, what's she doing here?"

"Amber," Dane whispered as he felt his stomach pitch with the pleasure of hearing her laughter. "She became very close to Amber the last time she and her family were in Sanctuary."

"There are too many high-ranking Breeds here, Dane," Dog protested then. "Someone's going to become a target. Her mate's already taken two bullets. I wouldn't imagine he'd survive very many more."

The fucking bastard was healthy as a horse, Dane thought furiously. As though having nearly met his maker twice had only strengthened his resolve to ensure that his mate and children were never left unprotected.

They would never be unprotected, though, Dane knew as he watched the two dark-colored vehicles pulling in behind the SUV. The six hard-eyed, steel-cold Breeds who exited the vehicles and stood watchfully in place were her permanent shields.

Hers and her mate's.

They were rushed into the hotel as Dane watched, dipping his head as she seemed to pause for a moment, looking behind her as the guards surrounded her and her mate urged her inside.

And Dog was right. There were far too many upper-hierarchy Breeds here and one more important to him than all the others.

"I heard the rumors," Dog stated then. "But until now, I never believed them."

"And what rumors would those be?" Stilling the anger that threatened to bloom inside him wasn't easy.

"The rumors that you used to be in love with her."

Dane straightened slowly. "That will teach you to listen to rumors."

Tossing the cigar into the narrow disposal unit, he strode quickly away from the Coyote and the hotel, heading to the parking lot and the vehicle he kept parked there.

He didn't "used to be" anything, he thought furiously as he shoved his hands into the pockets of his slacks and let the darkness enfold him.

He loved her then, he loved her now, and he feared he would always love her even more in the future.

She was his weakness, and he didn't dare allow anyone to learn that secret.

Not again.

· CHAPTER 27 ·

Rule would have missed it if Lawe hadn't forced him to stop, forced him to use his senses and the knowledge he'd gained over the months where his incredible little mate was concerned. And Lawe wouldn't have known if Cassie, God bless her heart, hadn't contacted him just before Rhyzan had allowed Gypsy to overhear the cruel, destructive words that had spewed from her mother's lips.

As Gypsy had stood still, her gaze locked on the shattered screen, the soul of the woman he realized was more than just his soul ruptured in such agonizing knowledge that Rule wanted to howl with fury. Riding quick on its heels was something far more dangerous, more destructive than her pain, though. The link he hadn't known he'd established within the stubborn, independent little hellion snapped quietly, so naturally going into effect that if Lawe hadn't forced him to wait for it, he might not have realized it was there until too late.

And he would have missed perhaps the second most important moment of not just his life, but also Gypsy's.

Gypsy had realized something far more than her mother's belief that the daughter had been the cause of the son's death.

She had realized something far more dangerous, to herself.

Turning down the hall to their suite nearly an hour later, Rule watched with narrowed eyes as Lawe stood outside his door with several other Breeds.

He could feel Gypsy tensing, uncertainty rising within her as Lawe nodded to the nearest enforcer. The Wolf stepped to the door, unlocked it quickly and pushed it open.

"I need to talk to Kandy," Gypsy protested, though only halfheartedly, he realized as he dragged her into the room.

The door closed behind them.

"To tell her good-bye?" Using his hold on her wrist, he swung her into his embrace, one hand going to the back of her neck to ensure that his gaze met hers as she stared up at him in surprise.

And in an undercurrent of nervous suspicion.

"Good-bye?" Bravado suddenly gleamed in her eyes. "Why would I need to tell her good-bye?"

"What did you remember, Gypsy, that has you steeling yourself to die?" he asked, rather than answering her question. "Why did I suddenly sense the fifteen-year-old child you once were, filled with such guilt and self-hate, suddenly still, before she winked away as though she had never existed? Did she finally realize that what happened that night wasn't her fault?" His head lowered, his lips pulling back from his teeth furiously. "Did she finally figure out that the same person might have betrayed her and her brother both?"

◆　◆　◆

How had he known? How could he know?

Gypsy stared back at the Breed whose presence in her life had changed so many things, too many things too fast; she felt a part of her soul that lay so undefended, so raw and bleeding since the moment she realized who and what had taken a child's only security, fill with something so much stronger, so much more intuitive than anything she had ever known.

Suddenly everything was more intense, more intent.

Each sound, each scent, the brush of air across her flesh, the heat of her mate's body next to hers, the feel of him, inside her spirit, where none should exist but herself.

Yet Rule was there. A comfort. A strength that grounded her as nothing had ever grounded her before.

She couldn't tear her gaze from him.

Gypsy felt her breathing slowly even, felt the heartbeat that she hadn't known had been racing with fear suddenly slow and calm.

"Lawe and I survived because of a bond no one knew we had," he growled, satisfaction glittering in his eyes as that presence inside her refused to vacate. "Because we could strengthen each other. Because we could open ourselves, allow each other in, and whether the strength we needed was physical or psychological, we could provide it. Until he mated. Until I realized he was building a much stronger, much more intuitive bond with the woman he called his mate."

She shook her head, emotions rioting through her as she realized there was nothing she could hide from this man, this Breed. There was nothing she could do to hide from him, and nothing she could do to protect him.

She couldn't push him out. She couldn't hold on to the fear, the driving fury or the hunger for vengeance. She couldn't shut that inner, emotional door on the Breed who had stood by her side since the night she had stared across a crowded bar into his eyes . . .

"Far longer than that," he revealed as her eyes widened in disbelief. "I've been by your side, Gypsy, since you were fifteen years old. If not I, then later, Cullen Maverick. Or should I say, the Bengal Judd."

He knew what she had suspected? That Cullen Maverick was the Breed Jonas searched so desperately for?

Gypsy shook her head, her breathing roughening. "No . . ."

"Your contact is the Bengal Judd, Gypsy," he told her quietly, his expression filled with such emotion that she had no idea how to combat it. "I may not have realized I was your mate, but the instincts inside me, that animal that ensures I never completely fuck up, knew. It knew, connived and conspired within my subconscious, until I did exactly what I had to do to always watch over what belonged to me. Including conspiring with a Breed who would become wanted by every agency, every Council team, every fucking scientist in the world, and even the one man I owed every iota of loyalty to, Jonas Wyatt. I conspired to the point that I ordered him to take the bargain of working with him to you, on the condition that no other man touch you. That you have no lovers, no one to stand between you and your mate when the time came for me to claim what was mine. And later, when Jonas began searching for that Breed, I hid my knowledge of this from even my own brother. Trusting. Believing he had sent everything he had to Jonas. Knowing, without him, you would have drifted away from this world within a year of Mark's death."

He was the reason that demand had been made of her?

She could feel adrenaline pumping into her system—disbelief, amazement, it was all there, yet her heart wasn't racing, and she couldn't feel betrayal. She couldn't feel it, because she was just as entrenched in his heart as he was in hers now. Feeling him.

Breathing him.

"I was a part of you before I ever caught your attention that night," he promised her, his free hand moving to cup the side of her face, his thumb brushing against her lips. "I've always been here, Gypsy. Just a heartbeat away from you. More damned scared of what I was feeling than you could imagine, because losing you would have destroyed even the animal that lurks beneath the skin. The animal that fought with every heartbeat, with every breath, to ensure your protection every second after the night you lost what was most dear to your heart. Because you, mate, are most dear to my heart."

She had to blink back her tears.

Gypsy couldn't believe she was on the verge of shedding tears.

Her breathing hitched, a sob tearing from her chest as his head lowered, his lips touching hers.

"Don't try to push me out, Gypsy. Don't take that from me. Don't take what completes me or allow a knowledge you refuse to share to destroy the only bond I've ever allowed myself other than that which connects me to my twin."

His lips took hers then. Entrenched inside her spirit as he was, not just giving pleasure, but sharing his own. It felt like liquid nitrogen shot straight to the demand already heating in the depths of her pussy.

Her juices began trickling from her core, dampening the inner muscles before spilling the moisture to the swollen outer folds.

His lips moved over hers, his tongue sinking past them, filling her senses with the taste of chocolate and peppermint and a hunger she couldn't deny herself. One she couldn't deny him.

Before she could stop them, her hands were buried in his hair, the battle still raging inside her senses to hold on to him, to push him from her, to ensure that nothing risked him. Especially the ghost of the past that she knew she had to face alone.

The kiss, the hunger pouring through her was suddenly absent as his head jerked back. A snarl sounded from his chest, causing her eyes to widen as her lashes jerked open.

"You can't hide from me, mate, not with a secret as important as your life." The sound of his voice was animalistic. More animal than man, and with more primal intent than she had ever heard in it before. "You'll learn, beginning now. You will never attempt something so foolhardy, ever, Gypsy."

The next kiss locked her soul to his, she swore it did. He burrowed inside her, held her to him, opening her to emotions, to needs, to hungers she had never known existed inside her. That she had never known she even ached for the lack of.

Holding to him, she was only dimly aware of her clothes being all but torn from her. In some cases, seams ripped. A few buttons popped and rolled to the floor.

By the time Gypsy found herself in the bedroom with him, a trail of clothing—hers as well as his—lay behind them.

Naked, the muscular heat of his body wrapped around her as the taste of his kiss intoxicated, overwhelmed and bound her in ways she was certain she would protest later.

And she loved it.

She should hate the loss of control.

She should fight the hold he was securing within her. She would have, except it was the first time in nine years that she had felt really, fundamentally secure in something other than grief.

"God help me," he groaned, tearing his lips from hers, spreading nipping kisses, the sharp edges of his canines rasping against her neck as she tilted her head to give him easier access.

Shivers worked over her flesh, icy heat striking at her nerve endings before flames began to lick between her thighs. Her clit ached, throbbing in time to the blood pumping through her veins, racing with a hungry excitement that only increased the erotic flow of her juices and the need. A need that sensitized her flesh, that only increased the hold she hadn't realized he had on her.

Hunger poured through her.

His hunger for her.

Hers for him.

God, where was the line between his senses and hers, what he felt, what she felt?

She couldn't find it, everything seemed to merge, to blend seamlessly until the pleasure of it was a racking chaos of sensation that she had no hope of escaping.

Demanding and hot, his lips covered a nipple as he carried her from the floor. Lifting her knees to his hips as his erection became trapped between their bodies drove a whimpering moan from her lips. The heavily veined shaft rubbed against her clit, driving her to distraction, making her crazy now to have him take her, to fill her. To experience the pleasure she could feel emanating from him, into her and from her into him.

Blending sensations, a mix of desperate need that invaded her senses, invaded her body until she was ready to fly apart in pleasure as his tongue rasped her nipple a second before a growl of hunger vibrated against her flesh.

Gypsy gripped his hips tighter, lifting herself to him as the broad shaft of his cock rubbed against her clit. That wasn't the pressure she wanted, dammit. She wanted him inside her. She was desperate to drive that broad crest between the plump, slick folds of her pussy.

"Oh, it won't be near so easy," Rule growled. "I'll be damned if I'll let you off so easily."

Let her off? He was killing her with need.

Lifting her from him despite her attempts to stay right where she was, he turned her, pushing her to the bed even as she struggled against him, determined to get the upper hand. A surge of dominance suddenly rushed from him, into her, pulling free a dark, powerful need to just submit, to lift her ass to him and let him do whatever the hell he wanted. If he would just make her come.

Her eyes flared open.

Submit?

A second later she found herself on her stomach, his larger body pressing her to the sheets. Gypsy felt her eyes widen, impressions, sensations, a dark demand drawing a shocked gasp from her lips.

"Oh yes, baby, you know exactly what's coming now, don't you?" he crooned before nipping her shoulder erotically. "Before you ever consider taking such action again, you'll damned sure reconsider it first. I'll ensure it before you ever leave this bed."

His hand smoothed over the curve of her ass, callused and heated, a rasping caress that sent tingles of awareness flooding her senses, her juices flooding her vagina.

"I didn't do anything, Rule," she protested, desperation or was it pure anticipation engulfing her senses.

Anger, a hint of male trepidation, almost fear, slipped into her senses as she felt the wide, bulbous crest of his cock press between her thighs, parting the slick, swollen folds of her pussy and pressing to the entrance. Sliding through the heavy layer of dew collected there, slickening, preparing to take her as a rumbled half-animal, half-male sound of pleasure shocked her senses.

And she was helpless against him. God, she'd never felt this helpless, this completely dominated, completely secure and immersed in pleasure as she did now.

"What are you doing to me?" Fisting her fingers in the blanket beneath her, she couldn't help but lift to him, even as she knew exactly what was coming next.

She knew, because she could sense him, feel him, anticipate each move, yet she was helpless to counter any of it. Hell no, all she could do was lift her ass, shift her hips and try to force him deeper inside her.

His fingers parted the curves of her ass, a callused thumb finding that forbidden, far-too-sensitive entrance hidden between the rounded flesh.

"Claiming you." Guttural, intent, the tone was a primal growl that sent shivers racing along her spine. "Claiming what's mine, all the way to your soul."

He wasn't just claiming her, though. It was far more than claiming. He was dominating her in a way that only a being as intensely protective, as fully primal as a male Breed could be, could claim a woman who had denied the sensual, erotic hungers that plagued her. A woman who had fought far too long for herself and wanted nothing more than to be taken, to submit, for once in her life, to simply exist for the man controlling her senses.

"This won't work," she panted, fighting for breath, fighting to separate his hunger from hers, his needs from hers. To find a line, a boundary that would divide the link he was establishing within her soul.

"Think it won't?" A heavy press of his hips and his cock head breached her vagina further, separating sensitive tissue and clenched muscles as a cry of pure pleasure escaped her lips. "Let's see if we can't make it work, mate."

His hands smoothed along her flanks before the caress was gone. Moving over her, he pressed deeper inside her, the smooth, short strokes of his cock creating a passage for the heavy width of his flesh as the heated stretch of her tissue sent pleasure-pain striking at a deepening well of hunger.

Hard, muscled, his larger body stretched over hers for an instant as he pushed deeper, deeper, filling her, taking her an inch at a time. One burning, lightning-sharp sensation at a time, until he was buried fully inside her.

Seated to the hilt, the taut sac of his testicles pressing into her clit, Rule gave no concession, took no mercy in the erotic combat playing out between them now. The more she tried to sever that steadily evolving link he'd made with her soul, the more firmly entrenched it became.

"Think of this, Gypsy." His lips seared the tender flesh at the point between neck and shoulder where he'd marked her the night before. "Remember this. If you ever. Ever attempt to steal from me the mate I'll kill to protect. The mate I'll betray all others to protect. Remember what the hell you're stealing from both of us."

Straightening behind her, she felt him reach for something, knew what he was doing, knew how he would imprint himself in her soul and still, she couldn't stop him. His touch returned between the narrow cleft of her rear, his thumb, slick now with lubrication, pressed firmly against the tightly clenched entrance there. Rubbing, pressing, exciting nerve endings she'd never known could be so erotically sensitive, he began preparing her.

Without conscious volition, without any attempt to accept and with every intention of rejecting, still, she felt the tightly puckered entrance ease and allow the broad tip of his thumb to enter her slowly.

Gypsy was helpless against the cries that escaped her throat. Helpless against the smooth, stretching burn that parted the snug opening and began stretching it, caressing inside, fueling a hunger she shouldn't know, shouldn't feel.

His hips shifted, the wide head of his cock shifting and caressing inside her pussy with such resolute sensual destruction that she nearly orgasmed for him in that second.

That diabolical thumb pressed deeper inside her, pulled back, then slid in again. He took her in a way she couldn't fight, neither mentally nor emotionally, and that emotional edge was going to destroy her.

Gypsy could feel it rising inside her, a wash of so many emotions—

"No. Please, Rule." She jerked against him as she felt it coming, felt the breaks in the barriers she'd built over the years as the connection to him began to tighten, to strengthen.

Her head shook as she pressed it into the pillow, her fingers clenching tighter, a band of sensation beginning to tighten in her breast.

"I have you, Gypsy," he crooned behind her, that wicked, wicked thumb easing back as she felt his cock stroking her internally in a way that had her breath catching in near ecstasy.

A second later, his fingers returned instead.

Parting her buttocks, she felt one ease inside her, stretching her again, filling her as more of the lubrication slicked his way.

He repeated the penetration. Pulling back completely, he returned seconds later, another layer of the slick gel coating her inner, untouched flesh as she panted beneath him. But this time, it wasn't just one finger, but two. Parting them, stretching the entrance and internal muscles of her anus further, he blazed a path of complete surrender through her senses.

She should tell him no. That was all she had to do.

She could do it, she told herself desperately.

Instead, her hips lifted as his cock pulled free of her, a cry breaking from her throat that shocked her. A sound of such wild hunger, of such need that she couldn't make sense of it.

What she could make sense of was the fact that once this was finished, he would own her.

Her breath caught, fear edging at the boundary of pleasure . . .

"Oh God. Rule." She cried out his name as that wide crest of his cock pressed against the tender entrance he'd prepared so carefully.

"That's it, baby, so sweet and hot," he groaned as virgin flesh began parting, stretching with such incredible heat that Gypsy found herself trembling in anticipation as the snug, tightly stretched entrance rippled at the intensity of sensation. "So fucking mine." His teeth were at her shoulder, raking the little mark he'd left there, scraping it with his teeth. "Feel me, Gypsy. Feel me, inside all of you."

He *was* inside all of her.

A scream tore from her throat.

Sensation rushed through her like a firestorm of rich, thick lava. She flooded with not just her pleasure, but his. Bound by not just the velvet emotion he was wrapping around her, but also the tightly woven threads that led from him to her. From her to him.

"Rule, please . . ." she cried out, her voice hoarse as she shuddered at each sensation. The wide, brutal heat of his cock sinking in where she'd never imagined she'd allow a man to take her sent her senses spinning.

It was just as sensual, just as exciting as she heard it could be, with none of the feelings of degradation or repulsive control she'd feared it could hold.

What it held was her submission, and it was complete.

That realization swept over her as the heavy length pushed deeper, the blunt head of his erection easing that tighter, more sensitive ring of muscles deep inside her anus wide enough to take him fully. As the head popped past the last barrier, he buried himself completely inside the tight channel to the hilt before pausing, before letting her *know* what he had done.

"Rule." She couldn't scream, she couldn't cry.

The sound was rough, the sob that hitched her breath something she hadn't heard from herself in so many years.

And she was terribly certain she might become scared. There was something about being impaled in such a way, taken with such intimacy that was shattering something inside her.

"I have you, Gypsy." His lips pressed to that mark and pleasure clenched every muscle further, strained her already ragged defenses. "You held yourself for nine years, baby. Every day, every dark lonely night that I was too fucking stubborn to claim you." He licked the little wound then and she felt the muscles gripping him suddenly tighten with the wave of sensation that rushed through her senses. "I'm here now, baby. You don't have to be brave by yourself anymore, Gypsy."

Brave?

She jerked in his arms, crying out as she felt the final wall between them beginning to fall. His hips moved with easy, powerful movements as he fucked her with such elemental eroticism that it was impossible to fight.

The feel of the broad length of his cock impaling her anus, shuttling back and forth across nerve endings never before stroked in such a way, inflamed her senses.

"I think I don't want this." Her fingers clenched tighter on the blankets beneath her as he began moving, small, shallow thrusts that began to heighten each sensation in the heated, oversensitive flesh to the point she had to fight to remember what it was she might not want.

"Sure?" His voice was a croon, heavy, indolent with wicked, sensual intent and primal demand as his thrusts began to lengthen, to increase. "Are you sure you don't just want this, baby? Are you sure both of us don't fucking need it?"

His teeth tightened on the mark, his tongue stroking over it, easing any fear, heightening the pleasure, the erotic need pulsing through her.

Following his lead now, her hips lifted to him as he pulled her to her knees, straightening behind her once again, his hands gripping her hips, holding her steady as he began thrusting harder, faster inside her.

Every deep, stretching thrust spilled wave after wave of not just pleasure, but something more, something darker, something so intense, so hot and completely all-consuming that she knew she was lost.

"God yes, Gypsy," he growled behind her, each stroke pushing her closer, shafting inside her with a heavy intent that Gypsy knew would shatter her.

There was no fighting it.

It was blazing through her senses, taking her, laying waste to trepidation, to fear, to anything but the knowledge that never again would she face the night alone.

"You're mine." His lips were at her ear, his voice darker now, deeper as the animal that ruled so many of his senses surged to the surface. "Do you hear me, damn you? Fucking mine."

And she felt it. The animal, the beast that lurked inside him, that marked her, determined to imprint itself just as deeply inside her as the man had.

Dark. Prone to savagery but controlled by a fierce, ever-deepening honor that guided it within the man. Primitive and primal and he was claiming her.

Her eyes shot open.

Experienced, knowing fingers pushed inside the weeping depths of her pussy, fucking inside her and filling her with more than just the pleasure. More than just the alternate stretching heat of his thrusts between her thighs even as his cock laid claim to her rear.

The added sensations were too much. Too many.

It was too much heat, too many waves of striking, ecstatic bolts of hyperpleasure being hurled through her.

Before Gypsy could counter them, before she could balance herself, she was suddenly flung into the heart of a flame so intense, so rapturous that she swore she felt the brand it left on her soul.

◆　◆　◆

He couldn't hold on much longer.

Rule clenched his teeth as the sweet clench and burn surrounding his cock began to ripple as shudders began racking the delicate body beneath him.

It wasn't just the physical pleasure, this link his instincts had established with his mate with such suddenness. It was an intensity of pleasure. A knowledge of it. A certainty that though the mating took the choice from her hands, still, that choice had been made before it happened.

It was being inside her, buried in the heated depths of her rear, his fingers stroking and caressing the snug tissue of her pussy as the pad of his palm pressed into her swollen, hypersensitive clit.

It was feeling her explode as her breath caught and a brilliant wash of incredible, engulfing heat blazed through her senses and into his.

Her pleasure merged with his. It became a double-edged sword of such pleasure, such desperate ecstasy, that he wondered if he could possibly survive.

White hot, a surge of energy raced up his spine; as it hit his brain a storm of intense, brilliant sensation began to wash over his body. He had seconds. Another thrust, two . . .

A brutal snarl tore from his lips as he felt the barb extend, bringing his thrusts to an instant halt as the first ejaculation shot from the depths of his balls. Where the thinner, but no less intense ejaculation from the barb originated from, he wasn't certain. What he was certain of was the pure, undiluted ecstasy of feeling his pleasure riding so close on the heels of hers, even as he felt her knowledge of it and the sensations of his pleasure engulfing her.

A brutal, never-ending circle of rapture.

He'd never heard of it existing with another couple before. To his knowledge, no others had attained this link with their mate.

A mating so deep, so never-ending, that as the final pulses of his release shuddered through his body and she relaxed beneath him, Rule felt his senses sink deeper inside hers.

And felt the wispy tendrils of knowledge as it crept from her subconscious, seeking the warmth of the animalistic senses that were now a part of her.

A vision formed in his mind. A fact, a history, a betrayal so deep, so resolute Rule knew that before the night ended, he would do what he'd ached to do nine years before. Tonight, he would shed the blood of a man, to defend a child whose brother had died to protect her.

The same man who had bought her brother's death.

Frightened, uncertain, that hidden part of his mate touched his senses as he felt her drift into sleep. It reached out to him, and still locked to her, buried deep inside her, he felt the tears she still held inside, felt the pain, the rage, and the ragged uncertainties that filled that dark corner of her soul.

"Don't cry. Be brave, Peanut," Mark's voice whispered through her mind, as it did each time she tried to sleep, tried to escape the guilt that had plagued her for so long.

He was trying to give her a message that had been unable to penetrate the shocked, terrified senses of a fifteen-year-old child.

He'd always told her that her tears healed all her wounds. He'd told her she didn't have to be brave all the time, that was what big brothers were for. And he had hated the pet name, Peanut, that his best friend had given her.

It was the only clue he had to give her.

Jason had betrayed them.

"I have you, Gypsy," Rule whispered against her ear then. "You can cry now, baby. You don't have to be brave alone anymore. Never again, sweetheart. You'll never be alone again."

CHAPTER 28

Kandy wasn't waiting on her as Gypsy assumed she would be the next morning as she was taken from the hotel to the secured base where her parents were being held until Gypsy's forty-eight hours were up.

So far, neither Dane Vanderale nor Dog had come forward, but with a weary heart she knew it no longer mattered. Rule would take care of the situation before the time was up.

Inhaling slowly, deeply, she stepped into the surprisingly comfortable rooms they were waiting in. The sitting room was tastefully appointed with a private bathroom and small bedroom off the side.

Her mother sat alone on the sofa, while her father stood at the small window on the far left side of the room that looked out onto the desert.

There were no security cameras, no electronic security period in the building she had been taken to. Old-fashioned locks and radios were used, though the weapons the Breeds carried were anything but old-fashioned.

Her mother looked up as the doors closed, her tear-swollen face still appearing far younger than her years while her green eyes were dark with grief.

"Gypsy." It was her father who moved quickly to her, stopping a second before touching her, his gaze suddenly frantic as he stared down at her. "Mr. Wyatt said we couldn't touch you," he said hoarsely, the hand that had dropped to his side lifting, then falling helplessly before he raked both hands through his hair. "I haven't hugged you in so long, have I, baby girl?"

Baby girl. That was what Mark had called her. It was what her parents had called the tiny, delicate little bundle they'd named Kandy Sweet.

Gypsy felt her throat tighten, the tears she could feel building in the ragged depths of her soul threatening to spill at any moment.

She swallowed tightly as a hard, single shake of her head did nothing to dispel the emotions tearing her apart.

"Jonas will release you sometime tomorrow," she stated, unable to answer the question. "There's a gag order on the crime you're being held for until you can be questioned regarding the reasons for trying to betray the Breeds—"

"They've always meant more to you than anyone else did." Her mother's tone was hoarse, tears and anger filling her voice as she rose shakily to her feet.

"That's enough, Greta," Hans demanded, turning to her, his expression tortured. "For God's sake, let this go."

"When you were five and the Breeds revealed themselves, you cried for them and told Mark all you wanted was for someone to save them. Until then, Mark hadn't involved himself in hacking, or in trying to save anyone. He was a good boy who loved his family . . ."

"Mark still loved his family," Gypsy stated, her heart breaking, burning in pain as the accusation deepened in her mother's eyes.

"For God's sake, he acted as though you were his child," her mother cried painfully as her father turned and paced away, a grimace contorting his face. "From the moment you were born. He even diapered and bathed you."

"Because otherwise she cried in constant pain because her diaper wasn't changed often enough, or stank of urine because she wasn't bathed regularly," her father finally bit out, turning back to the room as Gypsy's gaze swung back to him in surprise. "We were too busy building a business that went nowhere and running a store that was no more than a fucking joke."

Anger filled his tone as tears fell down her mother's face once again.

"That isn't true," her mother sobbed.

"God, Greta, it *is* true. Mark was barely ten when Gypsy was born, and within months he was the one caring for her, because we were too damned busy or too damned drunk," he assured her with such loving gentleness that Gypsy had to turn away from the sight of it or lose control of the tears she was barely holding in check. "By the time Gypsy was fifteen, neither of us even knew who or what our child was becoming, except that she was Mark's. And Mark made certain we didn't forget it if we tried to step in."

"No . . ." Greta fought to disagree, the pain that filled her expression so great that the hollow grief in her eyes was almost alive.

"For God's sake, admit it."

Gypsy flinched at the anger in her father's voice as it rose in response to the continued denial.

Greta lowered herself back to the couch, shaking her head as she lifted shaking hands to cover her tear-drenched face.

"Wyatt told us that night what happened," he said furiously, moving to the couch to stand over her mother, his rare display of anger shocking Gypsy. "If Gypsy had been home that night she would have died as well, and you know it. Just as Mark would have . . ."

"If she hadn't made him hack those bastards, then it wouldn't have happened." Her mother came off the couch, rage engulfing her as she pointed a shaking finger at her daughter and faced her husband in blind grief. "She made him do it."

"I'm starting to wonder if your parents weren't right where your mental abilities are concerned," he accused her roughly. "Because God as my witness, Greta, we both know even now that there wasn't a force on this Earth that would have convinced him to do something he didn't want to do. And that's the same lesson he taught the child he raised. He raised her, and he did a damned fine job doing so, because from what I've heard, she's done nothing but honor him since his death."

"You're as blind to her as Mark was," Greta cried out as Gypsy watched the anger now flowing between her parents.

"And you're still just as blind to the fact that you've always blamed an innocent child for the fact that Mark had far more of a life than the one we forced upon him when he took her to raise."

She'd never seen such displays from them, but as she watched them, she realized the tension she'd always felt around them might not have been just the anger her mother felt at Mark's death but perhaps their anger with each other as well.

"The person who betrayed Mark is at fault, no one else," Gypsy interceded during the apparent lull in the argument. "Mark lived the life he wanted to live, even I know that.

"I was too irresponsible." Her father shoved his hands into the pockets of his cargo shorts before pacing to the window once again. "Too damned stupid to be the father I should have been." He shook his head as he turned his back on them. "And your mother was no better. She simply refuses to accept it."

Her mother's breathing hitched on a sob as she sat down once again, staring at the floor.

"Where's Kandy?" Greta whispered a second later, her head lifting to stare back at Gypsy miserably. "I kept trying to keep ahead of her at the hotel so she wouldn't be in the elevator with us, just in case we were caught. She didn't know about the device. You can't punish her."

"I'm not punishing anyone, Mom," she breathed out painfully, aching for the parents she'd never had, and the ones that had never existed. "I thought Kandy would be here, but she must have decided to wait."

"She decided she can't face either of us," Hans sighed, his back still turned to them. "And I don't blame her. I don't blame either of you."

Weary acceptance stooped his shoulders as Greta covered her face with her hands once again and lost the battle with her sobs.

He turned back, glanced at his wife heavily, then stared back at Gypsy. "What will happen to your mother, Gypsy?"

He loved her, Gypsy knew. Loved her mother until nothing or no one else mattered. Or had mattered.

"As I said, you'll be released soon, by tomorrow afternoon, though mentioning this to anyone will see you very publicly arrested and formal charges filed." She pushed her hands into the back pockets of her jeans. "Don't say anything, pretend it never happened, and if we're extremely lucky, perhaps I can make it all go away."

"You?" Her mother questioned her, voice rough and filled with doubt. "How can you do anything?"

"The same way I managed to get you released pending a review by the Breed Ruling Cabinet of the charges and a decision made regarding whether justice would be best served by killing my parents for breaking Breed Law or convincing them to cooperate by turning over the person who gave you a nit equipped with a technology more advanced than any they've seen so far," she informed the other woman, realizing that the bond she'd always ached for with her mother had never been there.

She'd indeed become an orphan when her brother had died.

"And you were able to do this how? A good-time party girl. How did you make the Breeds owe you so much that they would do that for you?" Her mother's disbelief in her ability to do anything but party was apparent.

"I guess party girls have their uses," she sighed, resigned to the fact that her mother would never accept the truth.

Why hadn't she seen any of this over the years? she wondered. Hell, she hadn't even heard rumors to suggest the woman her mother truly was beneath her quiet, generous façade. Or perhaps it really was just her elder daughter she so hated.

"Thank you, Gypsy," her father said softly, the regret and, surprisingly, a father's love, echoing in his voice. "Even I saw the rapport you've developed with them. And I meant what I said earlier, Mark would have been incredibly proud of the woman he raised."

"Give them what they need, Dad," she all but begged him. "Please. Don't let this happen to you."

He gave her mother a weary look then. "I didn't even know she had the damned thing," he said softly. "Only she can answer that, and she won't even tell me."

Because she believed she'd found the closest she could get to the son she had lost, Gypsy thought sadly.

Maybe, she thought. If it just hadn't taken her nine years to figure out what he had been trying to tell her.

"We need to call Jason," her mother said then. "He'll have to make some decisions regarding the company. Perhaps Kandy can handle the Breed account . . ."

"Mother, you know that account is gone now," Gypsy sighed as she fought to push back the fury at the sound of Jason's name. "The contract you signed became null and void the second you brought that first device into Jonas's suite. Surely you realize that?"

The look her mother shot her was one of resentment and anger.

"How do we handle losing the contract if we can't say anything?" Hansel asked then, confused, wary. "What do we do, Gypsy?"

"They can't afford to take that contract," her mother burst out then, her expression becoming calculating, conniving. "There's more to this than merely helping us because of her." She flung a hand in Gypsy's direction. "She's lying and we all know it."

Guilt, anger and grief had destroyed her mother, Gypsy thought sadly, wondering if there was any way to repair the damage Jason Harte had inflicted when he betrayed his best friend.

Hansel McQuade ignored his wife's declaration but continued to stare back at Gypsy.

"Jonas will discuss everything with you before you're released," she promised, tired, drained by the knowledge that nothing could ever convince her mother that there had been no way to save her only son once his best friend had learned his secrets.

"Gypsy," her father sighed, the regret, the desperation in his gaze breaking her heart.

She shook her head at whatever he would have said.

"I need to know who she was working with, Dad." She didn't bother asking her mother. There was far too much anger there. And she needed to hear it. She needed to hear his name.

"He doesn't know," her mother bit out then, furious. "I never told him. And I won't tell you."

"You've already lost a son," Gypsy stated, the chill building inside her unrelenting now. "Dad will be convicted beside you. He'll die with you. Is that what you really want?"

Greta's eyes widened as tears began to fall once again, sobs shaking her shoulders. "If you had just stayed home," her mother cried brokenly. "Mark called Jason that night. He told him he had to find you. You didn't even tell Mark you were leaving as you were supposed to. Jason told us all about it, Gypsy." Greta's strangled scream was accompanied by an accusing finger pointing to her with shaky determination. "Jason told us how you were responsible."

Gypsy shook her head, fury building, tearing at her.

"Mark knew where I was going," she snapped back at her mother, furious now. "I would have never left without telling him, Mother. Never. He knew of the only party in the desert that night, and he knew I had wanted to go. Just as he knew that if he yelled at me and ordered me not to go without discussing it with me, I would sneak out and go anyway." Gypsy had to swallow past the hatred burning inside her now. The need to kill. To destroy Jason as she had been destroyed. "Mark knew me. He raised me. Just as Jason knew you." She couldn't hold back the contempt in her voice now. "Knew you so well that he knew he could lie to you and you'd never even face me with it," Gypsy cried out. "You couldn't even face me with his lies. You let me rip myself apart day after day for nine years and never told me . . ."

She turned away, fighting to breathe, to find that place in her heart where she would always remember, *they were her parents!*

"I have to go," she finally whispered, the realization that Jason had destroyed more than he probably ever knew burning through her mind.

"Gypsy, I'm so sorry," her father whispered, and the sorrow he felt filled his eyes, his expression. "Tell Mr. Wyatt we'll do whatever he needs." He glanced at her mother before turning back to her. "We'll tell him everything he needs to know."

He watched her with such resignation and regret that her heart broke for him.

"I wish . . ." Her voice broke, taking precious moments to find her control once again. "I wish I could have stopped this from happening."

"You can't stop what you're unaware of, sweetheart. The blame doesn't lie with you, it lies with me." His voice was heavy with regret, with pain and a resignation born of the knowledge that some things could never be fixed.

She nodded shortly, turned and moved to the door.

"Gypsy?" Her mother's voice had her pausing, her fingers on the door-knob, though she didn't turn back. "Stay away from Kandy, don't destroy her too."

"God, Greta." Shock filled her father's voice now.

She didn't wait to hear more. Pulling the door open, she stepped out, closed it behind her, then stood as still as stone to pull in a ragged breath.

"Mark adored you, Whisper."

Her head jerked up, her gaze meeting the emerald depths of Dane Van-derale's quiet, compassionate one as he leaned against the far wall, his arms crossed over his broad chest negligently.

"I know he did." She nodded before glancing around, realizing that the Breed guarding the door had quietly disappeared.

"I have in my possession a video taken from your home the night your brother died," he told her as she blinked back at him. "He was actually on the phone with me that night as I ordered forces to his location. As Jonas told you, the Breeds were unaware of his location. Until he learned you were in danger. He called me just before you left the house and told me how he intended to get you to Lobo Reever's ranch by speaking so cruelly to you. I advised him to take you and run instead, but he was far too certain he would be unable to protect you long enough for my forces to reach you."

One shock after another, Gypsy thought. Would she be able to bear many more surprises?

"Why didn't you tell me?" she asked him, unaware that the words were even a thought. "Why didn't anyone tell me?"

Breathing in deeply, he lowered his head for long moments, the tension she'd never seen around this man shimmering in the air for but a moment before he once again became the lazy slouch he pretended to be.

"Would it have made a difference?" His gaze lifted to hers quickly, no doubt catching her answer before she was aware of it herself.

"He was my brother . . ."

"He told me once he was the father he'd always imagined he would be," he broke in, his tone soft, gentle as a reminiscent smile tugged at his lips. "He told me of the young girl he'd taken as a babe, bathed and powdered her, comforted and held her when he was but a child himself. Ten, I believe."

She nodded. "He was ten when I was born."

"And he took one look at the tiny scrap you were and cherished you from that first look," he told her. "We talked many times. I may not have known where he was, or who he was exactly, but I knew many things about him."

"Did you know who had betrayed him?"

Had this man allowed Jason to live after Mark had died?

A flame lit in his eyes then, only to disappear a second later. But she saw it, the rage that flared for that briefest moment.

"Had I known who betrayed Mark McQuade, I promise you that I, Dog, and Cullen Maverick would have torn him apart, piece by bloody piece." The South African accent deepened, thickened with the fury he didn't bother to hide now. "There would have been no hole, no crevice he could have hidden within, Gypsy. I swear this to you."

She nodded.

"Tell me who it was."

She almost answered. At the last second, the words locked in her throat as determination tightened inside her, overwhelming her.

"He's mine," she swore flatly. "He owes me far more than he owes you."

Dane's eyes narrowed on her, the green flickering eerily as she stared back at him, her fingers curling at her sides as she fought to rein in the pulsing fury, the lancing pain . . .

Suddenly, the sweeping emotions threatening her control calmed, eased, and she felt Rule.

God, she felt him. Right there in her heart, wrapping himself around her, somehow aware of the struggle playing out within her soul.

Dane's lips twitched as though aware of what was occurring. Could he know, she wondered? "He won't let you go alone. You know that, don't you, Gypsy? Vengeance will be diluted by a mate who will refuse to allow you to kill. One who will push you back and shed that blood himself."

"How do you think this will convince me to let you shed it instead, Dane?" Quizzically, she watched him, seeing the calculation, the gentle manipulations the Breed used as others would use a weapon. Efficiently, unmercifully.

"I was merely hoping." He shrugged.

"Strangely," she told him, "I really don't give a fuck who cuts his throat, as long as someone does. And as long as they wait until I get the answers I want. Then I don't care how he's sent to hell."

"Understandable," he agreed before breathing in deeply and straightening against the wall. "Do me a favor, dear, don't tell anyone but your mate I was here, if you don't mind. I rather enjoy my American family, and learning who you saw the night your contact met with Dog and me could endanger our slowly merging bonds." His grin was mocking. Too mocking.

"None of my business, Dane," she promised him. "As long as Jonas gets what he wants and my parents walk away from this, then it's really none of my business."

"And they deserve to walk away?" he asked as she turned to leave.

Gypsy lowered her head, all too aware of the fact that she'd linked her fingers in front of herself nervously.

"They don't deserve it," she answered honestly. "But no one was hurt,

Dane. No harm was done. And I don't think I could survive seeing them punished when I should have known what was happening. When I should have remembered what Mark was trying to tell me."

If she had, then she would never have spent nine years believing in a guilt she hadn't owned. And maybe, just maybe, her mother wouldn't have ended up hating her.

With that, she turned and moved along the short hall to the main room of the facility where her parents were being held. There, Lawe and Diane waited along with half a dozen Breeds to escort her back to the hotel.

"Ready?" Lawe came to his feet, his expression concerned.

"I'm ready." She nodded before turning to Diane. "Has my sister been found?"

"She's still at the hotel." Diane nodded. "She's refusing to see them."

Gypsy understood that one. She wished she had stayed at the hotel herself now.

"Has anyone contacted Jonas yet?" she asked Lawe then, knowing Dane had been there for a reason.

Lawe grimaced. "Sorry, Gypsy, not yet. Are you sure they will?"

She nodded shortly, remembering the look in Dane's eyes as she turned away from him.

He was a calculating son of a bitch, she suspected, but his compassion, the empathy she sensed he felt and his love for not just his species, but also the family he spoke of, had been like a flame refusing to be quenched.

"They will," she stated resolutely. "Someone will. They can't afford not to." Then, squaring her shoulders, she moved for the door. "I need to leave now, there are things I have to do."

She had to see a man about a betrayal and the blood he owed her. But first, she had to find the man stroking her senses from a distance that should have made such a thing impossible.

The Breed who owned her heart.

◆　◆　◆

Rule stepped into Jonas's suite, finding the director instantly where he stood, staring through the tall windows onto the desert below.

"I should fucking kill you." The animalistic growl in Jonas's voice should have filled him with wariness. It was a sign, a signal that Jonas could be making a trip to a hungry volcano very soon.

He wasn't a fit meal for Madame Lava, though, Rule assured himself as he stared at the stiff set of the other Breed's shoulders.

"You have all the information he has, Jonas," Rule assured him. "I'm certain of it. There's nothing the Unknown, or the Bengal Judd has, that can help Amber or the Bureau."

"And you know this as a fact, how?" Jonas turned then, the pupils of his eyes obliterated by the dark, stormy swirls of color flickering there.

Freaky as shit, Rule had always thought, but he was used to it.

"I made sure of it," he reminded the director. "It's all in my report. Nine years' worth of notes as well as everything Judd stole from those labs. He was never a threat or a link back to Gideon. He was a tool, nothing more. He drew Gideon here but you and I both know that Judd can't force Gideon to show himself. If Gideon wanted him dead, then no doubt, he'd be dead."

Aristocratic nostrils flared as Jonas's features seemed to tighten further. Rule couldn't detect any emotion, tension or intent in the Breed. It was rare that Jonas let anything free with anyone except his mate and his child.

"Do you know what Gideon was in those labs?" Jonas asked then.

"A guinea pig?" Rule had a feeling he was not far from the actual answer, though.

Jonas inclined his head in agreement. "Of sorts," he revealed before stepping forward and moving to his desk.

Not that the danger was past, Rule knew better than that. The animal Jonas was lurked far too close to the skin.

Moving to the comfortable desk chair, Jonas took a seat and stared up at him for long moments before nodding to the chair across from him.

Rule sat down slowly.

"Gideon, like many Breeds actually, was simply exceptional in his creation. What made Gideon unique, though, was the fact that rather than living up to his killer genetics, his mind took a far different route."

Jonas paused, his lips pursing for long moments before he relaxed back in the chair and turned slowly to stare back at the windows. Rule glanced that way, wondering what drew the director's attention.

"Do you feel him watching?" Jonas asked quietly then.

"Gideon?" Rule asked.

The Breed nodded. "He watches, waits, and I suspect he listens as well." Turning back, Jonas glared back at Rule. "He wants Judd bad, Rule. He thinks Judd took something that belongs to him. He would draw him out."

Rule shook his head. "Gideon's been here for a while now, Jonas. If he wanted Judd, then he would have had him. Now what are you trying to decide to tell me where Gideon is concerned?"

Jonas's expression never changed. "Gideon's genetics held a single ancestor known for his exceptional intelligence and driving curiosity in the world of science. It was Gideon who helped on each phase of the Brandenmore serum. He knows the code, the formulas, the encryption, and I suspect that if he wanted to, and likely he has, he could re-create it exactly from memory alone."

Rule sat back, surprised. "This isn't in his file."

Disgust flickered in Jonas's gaze. "Is that information I would allow free, Rule?"

"No, it isn't," Rule agreed. "But information I should have known. With the game you're playing with Gideon, sending me against him without that information was stupid."

Jonas's brows lifted. "Do you think I wanted you to bring him in?"

Rule nearly chuckled. "No, Jonas, whatever game you're playing has nothing to do with capturing Gideon. So why not tell me what you are after?"

"My daughter's life." Jonas straightened in his chair. "Nothing more, Rule, nothing less."

And that was such a lie Rule swore he could nearly catch the scent of it. But he merely nodded. He had a feeling he knew what Jonas was after and if he was right, then the game the director was playing would be far more reaching than anyone imagined.

"I want Stygian to take two teams and head to the safe house we set up for his mate. I then want two teams to take Claire to the one we set up for her as well. I want it taken care of tonight."

"Very well." Rule nodded. "But tell me, when Gideon makes the move you're after, Jonas, how will you ensure he survives?"

Jonas's lips twitched. "Who says I mean for him to survive?"

Jonas suspected Gideon had ears into this room, which meant honesty wasn't something he wanted at the moment. Damned good thing, Rule thought, because he had a feeling the chance of this backfiring on Jonas was growing by the day.

"I'll take care of it," Rule assured him.

Jonas was silent for long moments then, staring back at Rule, assessing, narrow eyed.

"You knew who Cullen was all along," he said.

"So did you, Jonas," Rule sighed. "And we both know you did."

Jonas's lips quirked. "Dane believes he's hiding it from me, and Dog is so amused by the whole venture he nearly cackles whenever we're all together. If the situation weren't so fucking imperative where Amber's life is concerned, I'd just tell them exactly how little they're hiding."

But it was imperative. For all the game playing and maneuverings, Rule knew Jonas took it more seriously than anything else he'd ever faced.

"The team you sent out for Jason Harte," Rule asked. "Have they returned?"

Storms flickered in Jonas's eyes. "Not yet. We're still searching for him. When Gypsy returns, bring her to me and we'll see if we can figure out where he's gone."

He would have known Gypsy's mother would be caught, and he would have expected Gypsy or Kandy to come to him, Rule realized. When neither had, no doubt he had run. Now, he would have to be found.

And no doubt Jonas was somehow using that bastard too. He wondered if Jonas ever became confused concerning who was involved in which of his little games.

As he started to straighten, a blaring, shrieking alarm pierced the room; it was the hotel.

Swinging his gaze to Jonas, he watched the second the Breed realized where it was coming from and swore Jonas paled.

"Amber." The growl was an animal's roar of fury.

They moved at once.

Rule's weapon cleared his holster as he slammed his body into the door, taking it to the floor, knowing Jonas would cover him as his weapon swept the room.

Amber's room.

Rule didn't dare fire his weapon as he found the target, no more than Jonas could.

"Da, ba' ki'y," Amber chortled as Gideon held her close to his chest, her tiny body appearing more delicate than normal against the broad chest.

Primal stripes darkened the Breed's face like fire-scorched scars. Dark blond hair fell across his brow, the unusual dark strands of golden brown threading through it like a tiger's stripes.

"Gideon." The tension in Jonas's voice was unmistakable now. "Where is my mate?"

Gideon's gaze flickered to the corner of the room, where Rachel was slumped against the wall, her wealth of dark red hair lying over her face.

"She's alive, and unharmed," Gideon drawled as Jonas rushed to her, never taking his eyes from the Bengal as Rule became aware of more than a dozen Breed Enforcers suddenly filling the area behind him. They were breathing down his neck, all eyes on Gideon as the Bengal flicked them an amused glance over Rule's shoulder.

"Let the baby go, Gideon," Rule ordered softly as Amber played with the long strands of the Breed's hair as her delightful baby talk seemed directed at Gideon.

"Amber and I are excellent buddies, aren't we, sprite?" Gideon spoke with an icy chill as Amber giggled back at him.

"Ba' ki'y," she seemed to accuse him as Rule tried to make sense of what she was actually saying and why she seemed so amused.

If he didn't know better he would swear she was calling Gideon "bad kitty" each time he spoke in that merciless tone.

Rule eased to his knee, all too aware of Gideon moving slowly closer to the open balcony door, Amber held securely before him, protecting him as nothing or no one else could have.

"Let her go, Gideon." The animal's snarl was in the director's voice now, animalistic fury pounding in waves of tension through the room.

"Da?" Amber swung around quickly in concern, her bright eyes going between her father and Gideon. "Gi gi, ba' ki'y." There was a slight suggestion of an explanation in her tone.

Rule searched for the link to his brother, found it immediately and drew on it. Instantly, Lawe was there, not in spirit, but in strength, animal senses and intuition.

Gideon's gaze swung to him instantly as he stepped to the opened door, his gaze narrowing as though he could sense that bond.

"Interesting," he murmured as though he too could sense what Rule was doing and how he was doing it.

That intuition, the animal senses that were strong to begin with, were suddenly off the scale, and what Rule sensed was far more than he bet Gideon understood.

This wasn't the insane creature the Breeds had faced before. There was no insanity here. Cunning, intelligence, determination and . . .

Son of a bitch, that striped bastard held such affection for Amber that Rule nearly reeled from the knowledge of it.

Gideon shook his head and sighed before turning back to Jonas. "She'll be ill for a few more months," he told the director matter-of-factly. "She hasn't been slipping away from you, Director, merely slipping away from the human moorings she once held. Once Brandenmore injected her, he began changing things within her. To ensure her future health, to ensure her life, I took it upon myself to complete what he started."

The backs of his fingers brushed against the little girl's face.

"You did what?" That was fear in Jonas's voice, Rule thought.

Gideon's lips quirked. "You see such secrets, such forms as to make a man believe he's lost his mind. What you didn't see, couldn't yet see, was the fact that this sweet child was dying before Brandenmore touched her."

"He's lying," Rachel gasped weakly. "It's a trick, Jonas."

Gideon glanced at her sympathetically before turning back to the director. "The file is in her crib. Brandenmore's codes, encryptions and formulas for this particular serum. The same serum both Honor and the other were given." Demonic fury flickered momentarily in his gaze as Amber laid her small head against his chest and jabbered something softly.

"Yes, sprite, Gi-gi is fine," he promised gently, almost smiling back at Jonas. "A treasure you have here, Jonas," he stated then. "A very unique one. Get the files to Ely. The serum that will complete her recovery is contained there as well. As we both know, she's not fully recovered from her ordeal. You'll learn why in the papers I left."

"You're not leaving," Jonas snarled.

Gideon chuckled. "It was a great game we've been playing, my friend, and perhaps one day soon, we can sit down and discuss it, but that day is not today."

"The hell it isn't," Jonas retorted furiously.

Rule knew the instant the Bengal decided the discussion was at an end. And exactly how he intended to end it.

"Catch."

Amber flew from his arms as Gideon jumped through the open balcony doors to the two-man stealth copter that suddenly flew past.

Just that fast he was gone.

Just that fast, both Jonas and Rule missed the tiny child flying through the room as she giggled gleefully.

She wasn't flung into the wall. She didn't fall to the floor.

Rule watched in amazement as she was suddenly suspended from the ceiling, the nearly invisible lines holding her aloft a familiar sensation for the child, if he wasn't mistaken.

"How?" Jonas whispered as both he and Rachel watched as their child bounced happily in the air. "How the hell did he pull this off?"

Rule looked from the baby, to Jonas, then back again.

He cleared his throat.

"Do you think he's related to Dane?" he asked then, knowing Jonas wouldn't miss the backhanded insult.

Was the director related to Gideon?

Hell, Rule was beginning think Jonas and Gideon didn't share just genetics, but parents if it weren't for the fact that he was a Bengal rather than a Lion.

The growl that left Jonas's throat had him wincing.

"Maybe not," Rule lied, though he was now convinced it was highly likely.

CHAPTER 29

Gypsy knew the second the Dragoon had increased speed and begun racing for the hotel that something was wrong. No more than a heartbeat later she felt something shift inside her own senses. A door opening so swiftly inside her that she had no idea how to close it or what to do with it.

"Go with it, Gypsy," Lawe suddenly ordered as the Dragoon roared along the highway. "Rule's in trouble."

Rule was in trouble?

In danger?

She focused on that link, ignoring the doorway that had opened into Lawe's senses and concentrating totally on Rule's instead.

What was she supposed to do? How was she supposed to do it?

Centering her attention on him, she remembered how he said he could borrow from Lawe's strength, but was he trying to borrow from her?

It sure as hell wasn't her patience because she was going to kick his ass for making her wait to find out what was going on.

Eyes closed, she felt a glimmer of amusement touch her mind as Rule became so firmly entrenched inside her soul that she swore she could feel steel bolts anchoring him to her.

Mental strength, she realized. If he wanted stubbornness, she had that in spades.

Was that a chuckle echoing through her head without sound? Oh God, she was so going to kill him for this.

"Interesting." She heard the voice, felt Gideon's name whisper through her mind. A second later she knew what was going on and felt her heart nearly stop in dread at the knowledge that the insanity Rule had described as Gideon held Rachel's baby in his arms.

She couldn't "see" what was happening. It was impressions, a sense of Breeds filling the suite, Gideon's amusement and Jonas's fury. And a second of complete terror at the knowledge that Gideon had tossed the child free of him as he jumped from the opened balcony door, over the railing to a two-person jet-copter obviously there to retrieve him.

Lobo Reever had a jet-copter. It was the only one in the area, she thought. At least, the only one she knew of. Except for the one the Navajo Covert Law Enforcement Agency owned.

The link between them immediately shut down as Gypsy blinked in surprise.

"Son of a bitch," Lawe hissed through his teeth, his gaze meeting hers in the rearview mirror for the briefest second. "Tell me, Gypsy, just how many fucking secrets is my brother hiding from me?"

Uh-oh. She had a feeling Lawe just might be one up on the fact that Rule had been hiding Judd for the past nine years or so.

Bad Rule.

"He's your brother," she scoffed, glaring back at him. "Take that up with him."

His gaze shot to hers through the mirror once again, the suspicious disbelief glittering brilliantly in the lighter blue hue.

"You know, Gypsy," he pointed out, his tone rougher, frustrated as he turned his attention back to the road, "I'd be careful. Even as his mate, you'll learn you're not exempt from Rule's manipulations."

"I could have sworn I heard the same thing said to Rachel at some point concerning Jonas, just in the past weeks," she mused, turning her attention out the window of the Dragoon once again.

For a moment, her thoughts had been distracted from her parents, their crime, and the decision she faced concerning her brother's betrayer.

Eight years before, she'd shot a Council informer that the Unknown had been certain had betrayed her brother. He'd deserved to die for other crimes against both Breeds and the Navajo, but knowing he had been the wrong one cut at her.

The man who betrayed Mark deserved to hurt. He deserved to feel the same hell Mark had felt, knowing that his sister would be raped and killed and even the chance to help her was denied him. The fact that she had been rescued at the last moment hadn't helped Mark. It didn't salve her fury now.

Years of distrust made sense now. She'd been so angry as she'd watched her parents allow him to take Mark's place. He tried to be a brother to Mark's sisters, he'd married Mark's fiancée, he'd taken over Mark's company.

He'd thought he could live Mark's life.

Her nails bit into her palms as she realized they'd curled into fists, prepared to inflict whatever damage possible.

Damn him.

She wanted to slip away now. She wanted to find him, wanted to tear his throat out herself.

The only thing stopping her was the knowledge that he had disappeared, just as she'd known he would. The Breed team sent to find him that morning had reported that he couldn't be found either at his home or at his office.

Where would he go? she wondered. Where would Jason hide?

Eyes narrowed, she scanned the desert as it rushed by, going over old haunts Mark had once shown her, remembering bits and pieces of her childhood that she'd refused to allow herself to remember before.

As she did, she could "feel" Rule. As though the very fact that she was considering where he could be, where to find him, how to make him pay, had alerted Rule to her not-so-hidden desire to kill him herself.

She almost smiled as she felt him. Geez, it was the strangest damned feeling. He would just be there, like the caress of a breeze, but in her mind. She really wasn't certain if she liked it or not.

One thing was for damned sure, though, she thought on a sudden sigh; there would be no going after Jason by herself, and there wasn't a chance in hell Rule would allow her to kill him herself as Cullen had. And she wondered if anything else would exorcise the ghosts of her past?

◆　◆　◆

Did she love him?

Had she just accepted the mating, nothing more?

Standing in the lobby of the hotel as he leaned against one of the stately pillars that supported the atrium, Rule crossed his arms over his chest and glared at the doors as he waited for Lawe to roll into the courtyard with his mate. Allowing her to make that trip without him had been hell.

He'd been a part of her in one form or the other since her final surrender to him the night before. Exploding like the fourth of July and crying out his name, she had opened every part of herself to the link he had forged within her soul. And still, he was damned if he could sense whether that love was there.

"Damn creatures," Dane murmured as he sidled up beside him. "I can tell by your glare, fixated into space, that the lovely Gypsy McQuade is no doubt driving you to distraction."

"You got back fast enough," Rule grumbled. "How?"

Dane chuckled. "Father ensures that I have the fastest, most technologically advanced vehicles possible whenever I'm out of his sight. He's somehow convinced himself it lessens the danger I may find myself in."

"Or just gets you there faster?" Rule grunted. "Tell me, Dane, was that your technologically advanced personal jet-copter that Gideon caught a ride on earlier?"

"I was wondering if there was a way I could take credit for that one," the Breed sighed morosely. "Unfortunately, it wasn't to be. And the black-hearted bastard is refusing to answer my calls."

"Well, go figure." What the hell did the fucking hybrid expect? He was dealing with a psycho, not just another manipulating, calculating Breed as he usually did.

"Gideon was nearly dead when I found him." Dane's voice lowered as he too leaned a shoulder against the pillar. "Nearly emaciated to the point of death, so savage Father feared he would have to have him caged. And the Leo does not keep cages on any of his estates, you know."

Rule flicked him a look.

His dark blond brows were lowered, his green gaze distant as though his look into the past wasn't a pleasant one.

"The secrets he knows," Dane whispered. "So much intelligence, Rule. Insights into Breed physiology unlike anything you could even guess. The few months he was healing in South America after we found him, Mother was in scientific heaven just from his ramblings."

"And once he healed?" Rule asked.

Dane inhaled heavily. "One night he was fevered and rambling about a transfusion and why it had driven him insane, speaking of the creature pacing, lurking and breaking free. Mother left the audio recorder on and went to check on another of the unfortunate Breeds we were attempting to coax back to health. When she returned, the recorder had been turned off, part of it obviously erased, and Gideon had simply vanished through a steel door or concrete walls. We're really not certain how, because strangely, the recording from the camera trained on him was destroyed for nearly an hour up to the moment Mother returned." Dane chuckled. "Smart-ass fucker had taken a moment to get into the camera and hack the programming from within the device itself. Though how he fuzzed the equipment before doing so eludes me."

"What are you up to here, Dane?" Rule asked when the explanation finished. "Why not just go to Jonas, tell him you could acquire what he needed and allow Ely to continue the injections?"

"Jonas would have never allowed it," Dane told him, his tone suddenly weary. "At the most, he would have injected them himself to take the responsibility from Ely's steadily weakening shoulders, and only Gideon truly understood what he was doing. It was far better to maneuver my baby brother rather than watching that sweet child, or Jonas and Rachel, being destroyed from the inside out should something go wrong."

Rule stared outside the main doors for long moments once again, his eyes narrowed against the glare of the sun as it spread across the glistening lobby floors.

"Callan so resembles Father that there are times I find an edge of jealousy rising inside me," Dane said, his voice filled with amused self-disgust. "And such pride the Leo has in him, despite their differences. But if one knew the Leo as only Mother and I do, then they would see the pain he suffers each time Jonas is about. The guilt and self-recrimination, the unspeakable nightmares that have haunted him for years where one of his children is concerned. And this was before we learned of the reports he'd acquired that Jonas's maternal genetics were from Mother rather than Madame LaRue, as we had believed. Since he learned that piece of information, his anger at himself often worries Mother."

"Leo doesn't seem to be the type to stress over past mistakes," Rule offered. "Or children who were created rather than conceived by him."

"Ah, but how little all but I and Mother know him," Dane retorted mockingly. "Father suffers for past mistakes, decisions that resulted in less than the situations he anticipated, and the children who carried his genetics. His pride in Callan is absolute. But his pride in Jonas is ever growing, my friend. A pride that demands that Jonas acknowledge that choices are often made with a knowledge of the outcome and its tragedy, but they are never made without regret and without grief."

"Jonas understands that." Hell, of all people, Jonas knew that better than anyone Rule could think of. "Leo has amends to make, Dane. Many of them."

"Jonas resents Leo for leaving him in the labs when he feels he could have gotten him out."

Rule shook his head, staring back at the other man in surprise. "Is that what he thinks?"

"That's what Jonas states. Often." Dane's look sharpened.

"No, Dane." Rule was the one to breathe out roughly now. "It wasn't that Leo left him in the labs. It was that Leo left Harmony there. That Harmony suffered as long as she did and that he was forced to turn on her to ensure her survival. He will never forgive the Leo for the price he paid when he lost his sister's love. A condition that continues, even now."

Silence stretched between them now. For the first time since he'd known him, Rule watched as Dane appeared saddened. No manipulation. No calculation. Just unaccountably saddened.

"It would seem, then, both Jonas and I have a particular grudge against our father," he finally said softly before turning and spearing him with a sharp, fierce look. "Take that as a lesson, my friend. Don't wait for your mate to declare her love. Don't wait for her to realize her love. Give of yourself first if you must. Perhaps when you do so, she'll realize what she's refusing to allow herself to see for fear of losing once again that which sustains her."

Rule narrowed his eyes back at the hybrid as Dane turned and moved away from him, heading back to the bank of elevators, his shoulders not as straight, his head not thrown back as arrogantly as normal.

He knew Dane had feelings for Jonas's sister Harmony, just as he knew damned good and well Harmony's love for her mate, Lance Jacobs, was absolute. A mate she had been given a chance to find through Dane's and Jonas's machinations, separately, though no less effectively.

He almost smiled.

He could smell the true affection and sense of loss and regret Dane felt, but the love . . . no, it wasn't love. It had been close. Perhaps the closest Dane had ever come, or ever would come. The man jumped across continents like other men traveled across town. The chances of finding his mate, or of finding love, wasn't going to be high.

Rule had a feeling when and if it happened, though, Dane would be thanking his father for whatever hand he'd had in taking Harmony from his son's life rather than resenting it.

Straightening as the Dragoon shot in beneath the hotel awning, Rule strode quickly to the doors, Dane's comment running through his mind.

Let her know how he felt. Let her feel it, he thought. Maybe, just maybe, she'd realize she didn't have to hide her tender heart from him. Nor her fears.

He had her back, and he was about to prove it.

Dane wasn't the only one to whom Gideon owed a favor or two.

◆　◆　◆

The heavy iron door slammed closed with enough force that the cavern itself seemed to shudder from the impact.

A roar ripped through the underground space, sinking into stone before echoing back, only to be followed by another.

A glass beaker shattered against the doors, spilling a dark liquid that instantly turned to mist and filled the area with a hint of sandalwood and a male genetic scent that would have fooled any Breed living but the one who had made it.

"Motherfuckers." The roar was nearly incoherent as the animal lent its voice to the explicit curse.

Another beaker shattered, this time, the scent evocative of desert nights with a hint of a rose. Poison should smell sweet, he'd always claimed.

His head tipped back, his lips curled back from his teeth, and this time the roar all but shook the rafters and might have actually caused dust to rain down from the cavern's roof.

"Oh really, Graeme, what the hell did you think would happen?" Khileen propped her hands on her hips and watched the primal Bengal with a healthy dose of amused wariness. "Did you really believe you had us fooled? That we weren't very well aware of exactly where the Bengal Gideon was hiding?"

Propped against the curve of the far entrance, she tilted her head and let a smile curl at her lips when he swung around to her, his head lowering, his amber eyes morphing to the most incredible green color.

It really was too bad she couldn't stand another man's touch, she thought regretfully, because Gideon was no doubt hell in bed. He was simply too much male, too much animal, not to be.

"Leave." The order was ground out with the hoarse snarl that only an animal could have made.

She crossed her arms over her breasts and narrowed her gaze back at him. "No. We simply have to discuss this. Because I know what you're going to do . . ." She gasped as she suddenly found herself face-to-face with the primal stripes and glittering, bloodthirsty gaze of a Bengal tiger staring back at her from the man's face.

"Now." The rumbled, deep-throated growl almost had her obeying.

"The show is quite impressive," she promised him with an air of boredom. "But if I leave, then you'll just pack up and disappear, and I can't allow you to do so. It's simply not in your best interests, nor is it in mine. So pull back that very savage, very impressive creature you're trying to set free and let's discuss this, shall we?"

Astonishment glittered in his eyes as they widened. A second later his hands shot up, clawed fingers raking through his hair as a truly horrid-sounding growling snarl erupted from his parted lips as he turned away from her.

She grimaced at the sight and sound of it. "Lobo does that rather often, you know. Is it just me?"

Tiberian had once done so as well, when he had been there. Before her life had gone to hell in a handbasket and he'd begun chasing the bitch who had destroyed them all.

"You are certifiable," he snapped, turning back to her. "No wonder Tiberian left. He's likely running for his life."

"No doubt." She nodded slowly, silently agreeing with him.

No doubt that was exactly what Tiberian was doing, in a way.

"Fuck!" A glass bowl shattered on the other side of the room as she lifted her brow at the rage inherent in the destruction.

"Really, Graeme-Gideon?" Her brows lifted in amusement. "It's not so bad," she chided him. "It's not as though we turned you in or anything. No one knows you're here."

"You have got to be the craziest fucking female I have ever laid my eyes on," he yelled at her, turning back to stare at her in amazement. "Fucking insane, Khileen."

She had to laugh at that. "You haven't met my good friend Claire yet," she told him. "So sweet she'd give you a toothache until she dons this racy black little skin suit she wears whenever she tracks rogue Coyotes in the desert. It's really quite amusing."

He stilled, his head swinging back to her. "Who?"

"Claire Martinez." A sudden thought struck her. "Oh, do tell me the two of you haven't been after the same rogue? Let me guess, she beat you to him?" She had to laugh at that. "She's exquisitely well trained, you know. I wish I were half as vicious as she can be when she's tracking them. I love watching the show."

Something glittered savagely in his eyes.

Oh dear, perhaps it wasn't a joke to the surly feline. Well now, just imagine that.

He lifted the side of his lip in an insulting little sneer before turning away from her. "No female outtracks me, Khileen, and you know it."

"I can't outtrack you," she admitted with a light laugh. "But trust me, Claire has mad tracking skills. I'm very proud of her. If the Unknown actually existed, then I would say she's their next candidate as a warrior."

"I'm leaving." His stride became determined as he began moving for the exit leading to the mountains beyond.

That fast?

"No explanation?" she questioned him sharply. "Well, isn't that a fine thank-you for all the trouble we've gone through to hide your cute little ass here."

He swung around again, the clawed fingers curling as though he wanted nothing better than to claw for blood.

"Hide my ass?" he snarled again. "Like fuck, little girl. I was hiding myself just fucking fine when your *daddy*"—he sneered the word—"decided he needed a little side work done, with his baby brother out chasing your momma and all after she so conveniently faked her death."

Her eyes narrowed. "Watch it, Gideon," she warned him quietly. "I owe you several debts, but none of those debts give you leave to treat me so disrespectfully. Because never have I treated you with less than utter respect."

And he couldn't deny it.

"What the fuck do you and your damned family want from me?" he roared back at her, muscles bunching, shifting dangerously beneath the fine white shirt and fawn breeches he wore.

He was truly an exceptional male, though she knew one more so . . . She cut that thought off quickly.

"Your friendship," she answered sincerely, stilling the anger that could have risen inside her, reminding herself that friends were something Gideon, the Breed who now called himself Graeme, had very few of. "You owe many debts; consider the request Rule made merely the absolution of one of those debts. The request isn't too onerous, and you gain a favor from the Breed slated to become the division director of the Western Division of the Bureau of Breed Affairs." She gave a little laugh. "Say that three times quickly. I dare you."

He glared at her rather than sharing her amusement as he once would have.

Straightening, she dropped her arms, tucked her fingers into the pockets of her riding breeches and faced him squarely.

"Fine, Rule would owe both of us a favor then. You for taking care of this matter for him, and for allowing him and his mate to be a part of it. He would owe me for ensuring there was a safe place to have the matter dealt with, and that no other eyes or ears are aware of the event. I may have need of that favor in the future."

"When your mate is brought up on charges of violating his agreement with the Bureau when he covered up his brother's crimes, you mean?" he sneered. "Really, Khileen, do you think this favor is that big? Big enough to save the man you—"

"Don't." She kept her voice soft, firm, though the well of pain that rose in her chest was like a brutal white-hot poker searing her soul. "Don't make us enemies. You're only angry because I realized your secret and was smart enough to follow you and ensure your escape."

"I had my escape covered, little girl," he bit out. "And I'm angry because you made me break the promise I gave your mate to ensure you stayed out of danger. You are fucking danger waiting to happen in capital fucking letters."

"And the vulgarity so does not become you," she sighed. "Now, back to the original question. Yes, this favor will garner quite a large amount of brownie points with the division director. I promise you that. After all, he contacted you, didn't he? Jonas isn't here demanding you show your-self." She fanned her arms to indicate the estate as a whole as well as Lobo Reever's home. "You're simply in a snide mood because you know this last injection will make the child cry for you and you won't be able to go to her. I understand that. And I did tell you once that if you ever needed help in your ventures, I would be there to aid you as well, didn't I?"

He blinked back at her.

He turned from her, looked over his shoulder in disbelief, then raked his fingers through his hair again before stalking to her favorite recliner, the one he hadn't returned to the storage room, then threw himself in it, sprawling out with such disrespectful slouchiness that she could only shake her head at him.

"You amaze me," he said, his voice a bit more normal now. "Absolutely-fucking-amaze me, Khi."

At least he was calling her Khi again.

"Why, thank you, Graeme." She smiled back at him with all the charm her mother had beaten into her when she was younger. "I'm rather proud of my ability to do this to such a strikingly intelligent man, you know."

He blinked back at her again before narrowing his eyes, that brilliant light green color gleaming back at her with a hint, a promise of retribution if she wasn't extremely careful.

She didn't do careful really well, though.

"Call him," he growled. "Put your ass on the line with mine if you're so fucking sure of him. Call him, tell him he'll find the coordinates buried in the programming of the nano-nit currently attached to his e-pad. Time will be at thirty minutes before the time Mark McQuade was killed. If he doesn't know the exact time, he can ask his mate. I'm certain she remembers."

She nodded slowly. "That doesn't give you much time."

Gideon shrugged, breathed out roughly, rose to his feet, shifted his shoulders restlessly, then stalked over to a secured metal door on the other side of the room.

Khileen followed, curious when he stared back at her as though impatient with her lack of haste.

Swinging the door open, he allowed her to stare inside the darkened room, tiny to the point of claustrophobic, and holding a single bound, gagged and blindfolded male. The same male Rule Breaker was searching for.

Lifting his hand and crooking his finger in a "come here" signal, he then led the way to the bank of security monitors on the other side of the room, flipped one on and surprised her yet again.

"The wife?" she glanced up at Gideon's gaze questioningly. "Why kill the wife?"

"Kill her?" Gideon smiled. "Honey, I'm not going to kill her. I'm going to let her hear the bastard's confession when he starts spilling his guts. Now make that fucking call before I do what I was going to do when I arrived. Kill the bastard, release the wife outside town and get the hell out of Dodge."

She had to laugh at that. "And leave the mate you're obviously well aware exists close by?" she asked softly.

He stilled. Not a muscle moved, and even the pulse at his neck seemed to still.

She smiled gently. "I told you, I'm no fool. But neither am I your enemy. Think about it, think very very closely, and you'll realize, Graeme, I'm probably the dearest friend you'll ever hope to have."

With that, she turned and walked slowly away from him, showing him her back, giving him the chance to take her out if that was what he wanted to do.

Hell, he'd be doing her a favor if he did.

CHAPTER 30

FOUR HOURS LATER

The cavern was dark, shadowed. It had obviously been used for more than simply holding one gutless bastard beneath the glare of an uncovered bulb. It worked for that, though. Very well actually.

Gypsy stepped toward the light slowly, aware of Rule, Lawe and Diane at her back, ensuring her protection.

Was it the same, she wondered, not bothering to censor her thoughts as she felt Rule's presence inside her. Was it the same as the hunt, the heady rush of adrenaline once he would have been caught?

He wouldn't have run.

No, she thought as a whisper of certainty touched her mind. He wouldn't have run. He would have lied. He would have turned to Thea and her parents and they would have believed him, no doubt.

"That's far enough." The voice came from the darkness, drawing her to a hard stop as her gaze jerked to the darkness behind the light.

Gideon.

"He's not at his most presentable." The voice was amused and filled with disgust, the primal rasp of sound had Jason Harte flinching, a whimper leaving his throat as the scent of urine became decidedly stronger.

A heavy sigh sounded from the disembodied voice a second before broad fingers curved over his shoulders. Where his nails should have been, strong, sharp claws stained with dried blood extended instead.

"He doesn't hold his water very well," Gideon drawled then. "I remem-

ber when we were in the labs fighting for the fucking Council. The bastards they sent us up against didn't piss themselves so easily, did they,
Commander?"

"No, they didn't," Rule agreed as Gypsy felt the heavy weight of sorrow, remnants of remembered fury and pain echoing from him as she tried
to find a way to comfort him as he did her.

She reached for him with her hand, feeling his fingers enclose hers as
she continued to stare at the terrified Jason.

His brown eyes were bloodshot, pupils enlarged with terror. The tanned
flesh of his face was strikingly pale, the once immaculate shirt and slacks
hanging on his frame, torn, smeared with dirt and blood.

"Mark was brave when he died," she whispered, seeing none of
that quality in the friend he'd so trusted. "He wasn't afraid for himself, just
for me."

She remembered that. Remembered the pain and regret, the sorrow and
how his gaze had been so heavy with the lack of hope.

The hand on his shoulder moved.

Another whimper left Jason's throat, filtering through the gag tied across
his lips just before it was released.

"Gypsy?" Frantic, terrified, he searched the shadows where she stood.
"God, Gypsy, honey, what are you doing here?"

He tried so hard to seem sincere, confused. He wasn't confused, not in
the least.

"Mark always told me to cry when I needed to," she mused, feeling a
heavy, dark fury filling her. "He said it would heal my heart. He said I didn't
have to be brave, that was what big brothers were for. And he never gave
me nicknames. But you always laughed at me. Told me to be a big girl when
you caught me crying over something. You always jeered at me because you
said I wasn't brave. And I fucking hated being called Peanut," she spat out
at him. "It's over, Jason. I remembered what Mark was trying to tell me
when he told me to be brave, not to cry, and called me Peanut. But even
more, I remember what I saw when I watched Grody whisper the name of
the friend who betrayed him in his ear. The pain." It tore through her, ripping at her soul. "He loved you like a brother."

Jason's nostrils flared as he stared back at her, despite the darkness
surrounding her. His gaze searched the darkness for some sign of weakness,

for a way out. She recognized that look. The look of guilt, calculation and pure fear.

"Gypsy, you're wrong—"

"Save it," Rule snapped. "She's not alone, Harte, and the stink of your lies makes me want to rip your throat out myself."

"Gypsy, please . . ." Jason cried, only to whimper as that claw-tipped hand landed on his shoulder again.

"I have a better idea," Gideon rasped, amused despite the anger she could feel pulsing from him. "You want the truth, but this man will never give you such a thing without a little help. And with men like this, they never give such things willingly."

"No," Jason whispered, shuddering, whimpering as the claws bit into his shoulder.

Blood seeped into the shirt from the points where the sharpened nails bit into his flesh.

Gypsy inhaled, fury beating at the edges of her brain despite the shield she felt Rule throwing between her senses and the ragged, raging emotions clawing at it.

"Stop," she whispered to him. "Don't make me hide from it."

"Gypsy, you don't have to hurt like this," he growled, the sound powerful, commanding.

"Me and my emotions are old friends, Rule," she told him then. "I've waited nine years for this moment. I don't want to lose a single emotion, a single second of it."

Lawe murmured something to him, and though the shield was suddenly gone, she felt Rule with her more strongly than ever.

She could handle that, though. It kept her moored, kept the agonizing rage from poisoning every particle of her being as a low, enraged cry parted her lips.

"Dammit, Gypsy, I loved Mark like a brother . . ."

Grody leaned to Mark, but his gaze was on her as he whispered the words. She watched his lips, saw the words form and her gaze jerked to her brother's eyes.

Resigned sorrow and rage had filled her brother's eyes.

"When Grody whispered the name of the friend who'd betrayed him, Mark had one last minute to tell me something in a way that if Grody were to have mercy, he'd never know what Mark told me. 'Be brave. Don't cry, Peanut,'" she spat back at him. "You miserable bastard. Only you ever told me that. Only you."

His jaw clenched, fury gleaming in his gaze as his lip curled in disgust. "He treated you like you were his fucking child . . ."

"He treated you like a fucking brother," she charged furiously. "You had him killed, Jason. You tried to steal his family, you stole his fiancée, were you really that jealous of him?"

"You're crazy," he yelled back at her. "I tried to help your family . . ."

"He's lying," Gideon stated with an air of boredom. "I have a wonderful little drug that will ensure he tells you the truth, though."

"You fucker!" Jason screamed, spittle flying from his lips as the Breed chuckled behind him.

"Tell her the truth or I give you the drug. It will make you certifiably insane, but we'll get the truth. And it is rather painful. Agonizing, from what I remember myself. You choose."

"Fuck you."

"I'd rather not. You stink of piss."

Jason dropped his head.

"I can be merciful, Mr. Harte," Gideon said softly. "Especially when I really have no desire to compound one tender young woman's nightmares. But I'm also rather selfish. I want the truth, as does she. However bad it hurts her, or you, I'll get it."

Gypsy took a step forward. "Why did you betray him, Jason?"

He shook his head, his breath hitching as Gideon growled.

"I was working with the Council," he whispered. "The Genetics Council. I was one of their spies in the Nation, had helped them identify several breeders with certain traits they were looking for, along with one of the Nation's leaders. Mark was getting too close to me, but he was also getting very close to identifying the more important political contact within the Nation. I planted the video and audio devices at his workstations because you couldn't put shit on that fucking computer of his without him knowing. When I saw him hacking into another spy's cell phone records, I knew it was just a matter of time."

"You knew what he was doing? That he was hacking the Council's records and hadn't turned him in before that?" she scoffed.

"God, Gypsy, he was my fucking friend," he cried, his voice torn now, ragged. "I loved him like a brother. But he would have found out I was working with them. He would have learned things I couldn't afford for anyone to learn." He was crying now. It made her sick to see his tears, to see what she knew had to be false sincerity.

"You didn't love Mark," she whispered. "Mark benefited you, nothing more."

"No." He shook his head, his expression creased with pain now. "I did love him, Gypsy. But I loved my father, my life, and I loved Thea." He inhaled raggedly. "My father worked with them as well, that's how I ended up working for them. Dad was the one who chose Morningstar Martinez to be taken by them as well as several other young girls from other parts of the Nation. He and whoever his friend was within the Navajo Tribal Council." His head lowered again, tears dripping to the urine stain on his pants. "I was assigned to gather information on any Breeds coming into the Nation. Just before he hacked into that covert agency officer's cell phone files, Mark was tracking two teenage girls and two Bengals being slipped in by the Unknown. He worked with them a lot. Once I learned that, I knew I would have to keep an eye on him, so I set the audio and video at the two places I knew he worked most often."

"How did you know who he was helping?" She had to grip Rule's hand with all her strength to hold back, to keep from killing him now, before she ever learned the full truth.

"When I found out Mark was hacking Council files," he said roughly. "The Council was searching for a hacker and had heard rumors of the Unknown. They were searching for him for years." His head jerked back up. "I knew for over two years what he was doing and I never breathed a word of it," he cried out. "Not once, Gypsy."

"Grody's orders were to kill both of us." The tears didn't faze her. He was going to die. As Gideon said, it was just a matter of how.

"I knew how close he was to you," he said roughly, his head still lowered. "I didn't know what you knew, and I couldn't risk you suspecting it was me. When the Council sent out the order to take him, you weren't included in it, even though I told them how close the two of you were. You weren't considered a threat. I called Grody myself and gave the order."

"Then you moved right in, took over his life, his company, his parents and his fiancée," she laughed mockingly. "Was it worth it, Jason? Did you get what you wanted?"

He shook his head. "She never forgot him. She never loved me like she loved Mark."

There wasn't even a second of warning. Between one heartbeat and the next she went from holding herself back from killing him to being pulled backward, sheltered by Rule's hard body as a gunshot rang out.

"Fuck!" Gideon cursed.

Lights flared, low, but dissipating many of the shadows as Gypsy struggled to gain enough purchase beneath Rule's body and the recliner he'd taken shelter behind.

"Thea?" she whispered, shocked. "Let me go, Rule."

Diane was moving toward the other woman as she stood still, silent, the handgun now held loosely in her hands as she stared at the man she'd married seven years before.

Rule let her rise slowly, holding on to her until Diane gripped the weapon and slid it slowly from Thea's hand.

"Thea." Gypsy rushed to the woman her brother had loved so deeply that he'd begun to try pulling back from the shadowy group he'd worked with.

"Thea?" she whispered again as the delicate blonde lifted her head, violet eyes staring back at her dully.

"The night Mark died," Thea whispered. "I was attacked outside my dorm room."

"I know." Gypsy frowned back at her, hearing the ragged pain still echoing in her voice.

"I was carrying Mark's baby." Tears spilled from her eyes then, running in rivulets down her face as a cry tore past her lips. "I miscarried. I lost our baby and I always knew." Thea's fists clenched and pressed into her stomach as her expression collapsed in agony. "I knew whoever killed Mark sent someone to hurt me too." Her gaze swung to where Jason sat limply in the chair he was tied to, the front of his shirt now soaked with blood from the bullet that had torn into his heart. "I knew, and I swore, if the chance came, I'd kill him." Hatred filled her tone now. Her eyes were so dark they looked bruised, shattered. "He's betrayed everything I've believed in my whole life and destroyed everyone I loved. If I could kill him again, I would."

She wrapped her arms around the woman she'd always regretted had never been her sister-in-law and held her. Rule moved behind Thea, staring back at her, compassion, somber regret and a question in his eyes.

"It's over," she whispered, not just for Thea, but for Rule as well. "The monster's dead now. It's over."

With that, Rule gave a sharp nod, and as Gypsy and Diane eased Thea to the lone recliner in the room, he and Lawe began the work of disposing of Jason's body.

Gideon stood silently, watchfully.

Waiting.

Thank you, she mouthed silently, wondering if he would understand the gift he had given her in ensuring she wasn't forced to battle Rule for the confrontation she'd been given with Jason.

He nodded once, his gaze returning to Rule and Lawe.

"Give us a hand, dammit," Rule commanded him. "We need to have his body dumped—"

"Leave it," Gideon growled, and she swore the stripes across his face weren't as dark as they had been when she'd gotten her first glimpse of him. "I know what to do. Get these women the hell out of here and I'll take care of it. Just get the scent of their pain the fuck away from me."

Turning, he stalked to the far end of the cavern, crossed his arms over his chest and waited.

"Let's go," Rule decided, obviously more than willing to take him up on his offer. "I've had enough of that bastard's stink for the night."

Lawe lifted Thea into his arms as he and Diane moved toward the entrance of the cavern. Rule's arm went around Gypsy, pulling her to his side and following quickly.

Jonas could never know about this, she knew. It was the deal Rule had made with the devil nine years before, the first time he betrayed his friend when he'd identified the Bengal Judd and struck a bargain. What was one more, he'd breathed out roughly after Gideon's message had come through hours before. After all, the files the Bengal had left Jonas had given them everything they needed to ensure Amber's health. She would live. Something she wouldn't have done if it hadn't been for Brandenmore.

Who could have known Amber had been only weeks away from being diagnosed with the same virulent leukemia that had nearly killed one of the young women Jonas had searched for, Honor Roberts?

But Brandenmore had taken the proof of it. Vials of blood he'd taken from the baby before giving her that first injection held the proof. Blood samples Gideon had left with the files, along with records of his own tests on it.

Her age, the disease and a small chromosome Gideon had identified and notated, and an observation he'd left that it needed to be studied, were the reasons the serum hadn't killed the baby but would kill an adult every time.

The reason why Amber was slowly becoming a Breed as well.

◆   ◆   ◆

Speeding away from the cavern and back to the hotel, she sat still, silent, a restlessness gripping her now that it was over. A restlessness she had no idea how to identify. She'd never felt it before. Never known it existed.

But it burned in her chest, wrapped around her heart, and urged her to . . .

She stared into the desert, closed her eyes and wondered how in the hell she was possibly going to be able to do it.

· CHAPTER 31 ·

Genetics were a bitch, especially Breed genetics.

Rule sat in the shadows of the bar that night, tapping his fingers against the small round table where he sat and grimacing at the low growl rumbling in his throat.

Gypsy was with her family again. Her parents, and then her sister, she'd stated. She had decisions to make. He had a feeling those decisions affected him more than she was letting on.

She was his fucking mate. What the hell was the problem here? It wasn't like there was divorce. She couldn't run and never see him again.

And she wanted him. The sweet smell of her pussy had tempted him to convince her to wait to deal with her family. The heat building in her, in him, tempted him to claim what was his and just fucking tell her how it was going to be.

That wouldn't work with Gypsy, though, he thought with a sigh. Order her, and she'd do the exact opposite. In those precious moments he'd spent buried so deep inside her soul that there was no beginning, no end between them, he'd learned quite a bit about his stubborn, determined mate.

He'd learned enough to know that the distance she'd put between them could only mean one of two things. Either she was deciding how to accept a future with him, or she was deciding how to throw him out of her life.

He realized he was growling again, that low dangerous rumble building in his chest.

Son-of-a-bitch Lion genes. The bastard inside him was pissed and wouldn't just let it go any more than Rule was willing to let his mate go. Unfortunately, the beast inside him was snapping at the man Rule was, enraged with him for giving their mate the time she needed.

He almost rolled his eyes at the thought. As though they were fucking separate entities or something.

The irritation building in the animal sent an overwhelming urge inside Rule to pace, to satisfy the clawing restlessness.

To find Gypsy.

To fill their kiss with the taste of peppermint and chocolate that the mating hormone seemed infused with—no wonder he hadn't recognized the minute amount that had slipped from the glands as he chased her.

His lip lifted, a snarl almost sounding in his throat again.

Damn you, settle the fuck down.

Directing the fierce order to the animal crouched and ready to spring, he was on the verge of snarling himself.

Don't even think about it.

That involuntary, muted growl rumbled in his chest as his instincts snapped at him again, like sharp teeth raking his mind.

He could feel each instinct as though it were an alternate personality, sharing with him the irritation and restlessness burning inside it.

He'd never bothered to ask other Breeds if they could sense their animal in such a way. Hell, he wasn't sure he'd get the answer he wanted to hear, and in this case, he wasn't sure he wanted to accept any other answer.

Intelligent. Cunning. Sometimes enraged. Always restless.

Where Gypsy was concerned, just damned pissed and eager to get back to her.

The animal was ready to pace at this point, or fight. A fight would feel damned good. Fists bunched and slamming into flesh, enraged roars echoing around him.

Hell. The fight would just alleviate the burning aggravation of being locked out of his mate's senses. How the fuck had she managed to do that anyway?

Rubbing his tongue against his teeth to ease the irritation in the small, swollen glands, Rule grimaced as he realized he was only torturing himself.

After all, each time the glands were stroked, more of the mating hormone spilled.

Hormonal Mating Glands.

He wanted to snort at the title as he slouched back in his seat once again and lifted the beer in front of him to his lips. Tilting the bottle, he relished the chill bite of bitterness as it raced over his taste buds, wishing its effects would sedate the animal that suddenly wanted to snarl in displeasure.

What the hell do you think you want? he thought with a snap of anger, wondering at his own sanity as he attempted to push back the irritated presence.

A growl rumbled in his chest, bringing an immediate scowl to his face as he glared into the dimly lit bar he'd entered about four beers ago.

Go back to sleep, why don'tcha? he ordered the creature. *That's what you fucking get for playing "Jonas" games with me for nine fucking years.*

Manipulating, calculating sons of bitches. It bit his ass to imagine a creature smart enough to fucking hide what it was doing in his subconscious from him. As though the animal genetics were separate. What the fuck was up with that?

He looked at the beer. How many had he had again?

One too many, he was starting to believe.

Another rumble burred just beneath his breath.

A sound of irritation and impatience.

Shut the fuck up before I go hunt those pills Merc took so he wouldn't have to deal with this shit!

For years, Mercury Warrant, one of their most primal Lion Breeds, had been forced to take daily medication to hold back the last phase of Breed insanity known as feral fever.

Those drugs had kept his animal instincts in check in such a way that it was like putting the animal inside him into a deep, cold sleep.

He almost gave a rather insane bark of laughter as the highly advanced Lion genetics suddenly stilled as though surprised by the threat. He had the sudden, vague impression of the animal lurking inside him sitting back on its haunches and glaring at him uncertainly, as though debating whether he would actually carry out the threat.

"There you go," he gritted out, taking another lengthy drink of the cold beer before breathing out heavily.

The reaction might be a little too weird to suit him, but at least the beast seemed willing to sit back rather than aggravate the shit out of him.

Hell, he shouldn't be here drinking. He should be with his mate. Touching her. Loving her. Doing as he'd intended and whispering his love to her, giving her the chance to realize that was what she felt for him as well.

He knew she did. He'd felt it on the way back to the hotel earlier that night. Like a pulse of heat she'd lost control of, burning through his heart, his soul, for the slightest second.

Just enough to make him hungry, greedy for more.

His chest clenched, and the animal jumped forward again as though to take complete advantage of the slight weakness.

Back the fuck off!

Nostrils flaring, tensing, he restrained the inner animal forcibly as he wondered if he should attempt to learn the cause of the genetics suddenly rising inside him.

But doing that would require scheduling a session with Dr. Morrey, the Lion Breed physiological specialist and Jonas's little medical spy. And he didn't trust her so well after she'd attempted to destroy Mercury.

Admittedly, she'd been drugged and not exactly working with a fully operational hamster wheel there, but still. It had happened. Rule was pretty sure he didn't want to have to experience it himself.

As he finished off the beer and placed the bottle to the side with the other four empty bottles, his gaze was drawn to the Breed entering the establishment.

Lawe didn't join him for a drink anymore, as he used to.

That mating bullshit, Rule thought angrily, as he had the vaguest impression of the Lion inside him snapping back at him angrily.

Go to sleep, prick.

Lawe's blue eyes were narrowed on him, his expression thoughtful.

Catching the bartender's eye, Rule gave a short little nod to indicate another order of the whiskey shots and beer he'd been drinking. Lawe pulled out a chair, sitting down before catching the bartender's gaze as well and pointing to the four empty bottles Rule had set behind the shot glasses to indicate the beer he wanted.

Turning back to him, Lawe propped his arms on the table, leaning forward intently as Rule remained slouched back with all apparent laziness.

The laziness was an illusion. The animal inside him was growling, snarling, snapping furiously because he refused to seek out his mate. Refused to demand, to beg, whatever it took to ensure she didn't walk away.

She's mated to us, he reminded the creature absently. *She can't walk away.*

As stubborn as she was . . .

Fuck. Another growl sounded, this one more dangerous than the one before.

Lawe lifted a brow mockingly. "Rule, have you considered the fact that there's a high probability, as far as I'm concerned, considering your penchant for these little games you play, that you could be related to Jonas?"

Was he serious?

Rule glared back at his brother resentfully.

"Go to hell," he grumbled, wondering seriously if Mercury had any of those instinct sedatives he'd once taken left in his possession.

Just that quickly his instincts settled back, making him wonder seriously if the animal genes weren't somehow trying to detach into a separate personality.

♦ ♦ ♦

Lawe scratched the side of his jaw, still watching his brother closely.

"What's going on, Rule?" he asked quietly. "Why are you here rather than with your mate?"

Rule shook his head slowly before running his fingers through his hair in a gesture of irritation. "I needed a drink."

Had he? Lawe watched him closely, still sensing that closed door to his brother's thoughts.

"I can't even sense when you're lying to me anymore," Lawe stated, pausing as the waiter brought their drinks.

Rule went for the whiskey first, tossing it back with a grimace and clench of his teeth as the fiery burn seared his insides.

Lawe's gaze narrowed, following his hand as he placed the shot glass next to the four others sitting in front of the four bottles of beer he'd already consumed.

"What the hell makes you think I'm lying?" Rule snorted as though the statement were nowhere close to the truth.

"Gut instinct?" Lawe suggested. "I know you, Rule. You shut me out of your mind the minute you realized I'd found my mate. I appreciate the time it gave me to build boundaries around Diane, but I'd done that within weeks. You still won't let me in, though. Why have you shut yourself off from me, Rule?" He finally asked the question Rule had to have known was coming.

Picking up the beer, Rule took several long, hard drinks before letting the bottle thump heavily back to the table.

Lawe's gaze moved from the bottle, then back to Rule as he eased forward slowly, his tall, broad body moving in until his position was the same as Lawe's. Arms folded on the table, leaning forward intently.

"Do you know why I closed that bond, Lawe?" Rule growled, the sound so animalistic, so filled with some unnamed emotion that Lawe nearly flinched.

"I've asked," Lawe reminded him. "You've refused to tell me."

"Would you enjoy knowing I sense your lust and hunger for your mate? Or that I sense your pleasure in her when you take her?"

Lawe straightened, barely holding back the shock and instinctive snarl of rejection that rose to his lips.

The chuckle that came from Rule was deep, dark, a mocking reminder that sometimes Lawe had suspected the link they'd established could possibly go deeper than he had thought where Rule was concerned.

"Don't worry, brother," Rule leaned back, a mocking curl to his lips that Lawe had never known his brother to turn on him. "That prick-assed Lion inside me made sure we didn't spy on you. Besides, he was too busy pestering me with excuses to make trips out here to check up on my own mate."

Lawe blinked back at Rule as he picked up his beer and finished it in one long drink.

Rule hadn't been with him on that mission to track down the sister of Jonas's mate. Lawe had gone in with Mercury, Dog and several other Bureau Enforcers to find Diane.

The second he'd caught the scent of the lone prisoner shackled in a dark, damp cell, he had known she was his mate. He'd known she was hurt, he had scented her tears. A second before his instincts, enraged by the affront of his mate's tears, her pain, had been overcome with rage, he remembered that link snapping in place.

They rarely fought separately. He and Rule had always known that fighting together made them stronger. Lawe hadn't known their link could reach across such distance until that moment, though. His brother's strength had been his in that second. His control, his ability to restrain all emotion, to push back any weakness, had infused Lawe.

He'd felt Rule's animal then as well. It had centered his own, holding it back with steely purpose as Lawe managed to lead his team in to rescue the woman whose scent wrapped around his soul and opened his heart.

The second, the very moment he'd had Diane in the heli-jet and the danger to her significantly decreased, the bond he hadn't known was in effect the entirety of their lives was suddenly gone.

He'd known it was there when they faced danger, when their instincts reached out and combined, creating the fearsome warriors they had become. But until that moment, he hadn't realized that he and Rule had never been completely separate entities.

Until the moment he had felt a total and complete isolation.

A breath later, that isolation had been infused with the knowledge and the scent of his mate, though. He'd been so amazed by it, so taken aback by the warrior his woman was and his inability to control the animal's need to protect her, that he'd forgotten the only breath of time that he'd felt the total darkness, the total aloneness within his memories, his torments.

That aloneness his brother had known since that moment.

The curse that sizzled from him had Rule staring back at him with a distance Lawe no longer resented.

How could he even apologize? To say he was sorry would be more a lie than any he had ever spoken, because it would mean telling his mate he was sorry for the understandings, the love, the complete togetherness they had found together.

"There's nothing to feel sorry for," Rule stated absently as he gestured to the bartender again.

Lawe stared at the five shot glasses, five beer bottles that stood empty on the table at Rule's elbow again and realized he hadn't spoken those words aloud.

Strengthening the shields around his thoughts, he wondered just how strong that link with his brother really was. And suddenly, he wasn't so surprised that Rule had learned so well to maneuver others so easily.

"You've had enough," Lawe finally told him, realizing Rule seemed determined to drink himself into a fighting drunk.

Not a good thing.

What the hell was going on here?

"Not yet, I haven't," Rule sighed. "I'm still conscious."

◆　◆　◆

It wasn't the bleak darkness that filled him that had him drinking. It wasn't anger or resentment; he even understood why Gypsy needed this time with her family first.

Sort of, anyway.

It was that damned Lion driving him insane. He could feel his instincts—fuck instincts—he could feel the Lion snapping at him furiously, demanding that he go to Gypsy now. That he force this whole "do you love me?" issue.

It was sickening. He'd be damned if he would do it. He wasn't going to beg her for shit.

He frowned thoughtfully. Hell, maybe he was just going crazy.

More than one Lion Breed had gone feral after escaping the Genetics Council's labs. It wasn't unheard of for any Breed to slip into the feral rages and never return. Was that what was happening to him now?

Except mated Breeds didn't go feral.

There wasn't a single instance of mated Breeds slipping into feral fever. As though the mating itself stabilized the creature's rage.

"Return to your mate, brother," Rule sighed wearily as the bartender set the whiskey and beer in front of him.

"It's not safe here," Lawe sighed. "If you're going to drink yourself to a stupor, then I'll stay with you until you're ready to return to the hotel."

Rule shook his head. "Not returning yet. If I don't get a little bit drunker, then I might embarrass myself."

He'd be damned if he was going to beg her to love him. He had some pride. He had some self-control.

He lifted the shot, tossed it back, and thought with a measure of comfort that the bite of the alcohol wasn't nearly as fierce this time.

Staring back at his brother, Rule was amused to see the concern in Lawe's eyes. No doubt, at the first opportunity—he snickered at the two Breeds that entered the bar. Ah well, perhaps he'd been smart enough to call in reinforcements before entering.

He turned his gaze back to his brother broodingly.

"Babysitters?" he asked.

Lawe shrugged, the gesture dismissive. "I assume they're here for a drink."

Were they now?

Loki—that lying fucking Coyote and his master Dog—or was Jonas the master of both? Some days he wondered which Breed knew his own path and which Breed was merely content to allow Jonas to guide him.

He grinned at the two Coyotes. "How you two have managed to escape Jonas's matchmaking is what I want to know."

Dog's brow arched with a measure of polite indulgence before glancing at Lawe. "Drunk already, is he?"

"He's getting there," Rule assured the three of them.

Lawe grunted at that, spearing a look in Dog's direction as they seemed to share some unspoken message.

Placing the glass to his side, Rule lifted the beer to his lips, and once again, when he lowered it, barely half of the brew remained.

"I believe the reason your brother came looking for you"—Loki was the one to speak, the graveled tone of his voice always making Rule wonder what torture the Council scientists had devised to destroy his voice in such a way—"was to drag you back to our esteemed director for debriefing."

"I turned in my report." He frowned, but the statement forestalled the next order.

Why wait between each drink? Why the hell was he getting slowly drunk when he could do so in a few hours, rather than one drink per hour?

Efficiency, he reminded himself, beginning to lift his hand to indicate more when Loki's hand was suddenly securing his wrist.

The animal reacted, existing far too close to the skin at the moment; the affront became an insult of unimagined proportion. Before any knew his intent, he lashed out with his right arm, his fingers curled into a fist of iron that plowed into Loki's face before the Coyote could avoid it.

He didn't even have a second to enjoy the surprise that immediately transformed the Coyote's face before he was thrown back, chair and all—Rule couldn't help but laugh at the sight—and went flying backward.

Rule slapped his thigh, laughing so hard that he admitted he just might be a bit drunk after all.

Looking at Lawe and Dog, the complete shock on their faces, the widening of their eyes as their heads jerked from the sight of Loki sprawled out on the floor to Rule's laughter, had him laughing harder.

Until the animalistic snarl sounding through the room suddenly slammed into him.

He didn't go flying.

Rule shook the sudden scattered lights from his vision before turning his head, very slowly, and loosing the animal snapping at his senses.

"Fuck. Rule. You struck first." Lawe was suddenly between them, directing a glare at Dog. "Contain your man."

"Contain my man?" He pulled a slim cigar from the leather vest he wore, his smile tight as he inserted it between his lips and retrieved a set of matches from another pocket.

They all watched as though fascinated as he lit the tobacco. Until Rule looked over Lawe's shoulder to see Loki, his lips drawn back from the curved fangs, his eyes lit with an inner fire that was frankly freaky.

Rule had to laugh at the sight.

Then Loki grabbed Lawe and tossed him out of the way before his brother could anticipate the move and compensate. Thrown off balance, he landed on his ass, snarling. "Fuck it. Kill his ass, Rule."

His senses opened. Hell no, he didn't fight fair. His brother's mate wasn't here right now and neither was his own, and he was drunk. He might need a little extra—

It was all he could do not to laugh as his left fist went for Loki's face, struck and threw the Coyote into his commander. The cigar went one way and Dog went the other with a snarl . . .

"Hell yeah," he whooped. "Let's get it on."

CHAPTER 32

Gypsy stared at the sight of her bruised, banged, freshly showered lover . . . mate, she amended, and had to hold back a smile as she watched him sleep.

Bullying him into the shower hadn't been as hard as she had anticipated. Of course, she'd had to put up with groping hands trying to pull her in with him. Thankfully, her full-grown Lion Breed male had simply been too damned drunk to really put much strength into it.

Come morning, his eye was going to be horribly swollen, and his lip was split. He swore Loki had cracked a rib, while Dog must have punctured his lung with a fist.

Lawe was still laughing like a loon when he and Jonas dumped Rule inside the suite and glared at her as though it was all her fault.

And maybe it was.

She'd felt the horrible aloneness circling her as she dealt with her family and her own emotions. It was only for a few hours, she'd told herself, and then she intended to fix it.

She hadn't intended for him to get all drunk and rowdy while he waited, but that was exactly what he had done. Though Lawe assured her Dog and Loki looked worse.

Thinking of Loki brought her sister to mind. Kandy had listened as Gypsy had explained Mark's death, and her father had explained, or tried to explain, their mother.

When it was over, Kandy had just shaken her head, turned and left her parents' home. When Gypsy had left as well and looked over to the apartments, she realized that the black heavy-duty pickup that had been parked just down the street wasn't there any longer.

Loki had been all but staying with her sister for weeks and Gypsy hadn't realized it. Until now.

What had happened that the Coyote Breed was no longer taking up space in one of the few parking spots on the back street, or in her sister's apartment?

She would have asked, but as she started down the walk Kandy had left again. Moving quickly to her own truck, she had sped from the parking lot before turning and heading into town.

Now, well after midnight, Gypsy sat next to her drunken, abused mate and couldn't help but let a small grin tug at her lips. The entire time she'd been with her sister and parents she'd felt him, just beyond the shield she'd placed around her thoughts.

Rule hadn't seemed to be as autocratic, as dominant as she was learning he could be. Still, he'd respected the shield, even if he had gotten drunk and apparently started a fight with Loki and Dog instead.

"Silly Lion," she murmured softly, her heart softening as slowly she allowed her senses to meet his once again. "Did you really think I wouldn't be back?"

The man might be staggered from drink, but the Lion, those animalistic senses that guided so much of him, was there. She could almost imagine the exhausted, morose creature as he lay with his head on his paws and stared back at her dejectedly.

Running her hand caressingly along her mate's chest, she found herself completely unable to be angry with him. She'd learned so many things in the space of such a short time. More importantly, though, she'd learned how this Breed who'd sworn to run the moment he sensed his mate had been checking on her since the night Mark had been killed. The trips he had made to New Mexico. The years and favors amassed in an attempt to ensure that no matter what might happen to him, she was always taken care of.

Her quiet, often witty, too-intense Breed had given Jonas a run for his money when it had come to the games played to ensure her protection, and what happiness she could have found.

Warmth curled against her senses, a weary sort of nudging, as though he were leaning against a door, barely open, knocking softly.

"I saw you across a crowded bar and our eyes met," she whispered as she let her fingers stroke down his still-damp hair. "Neon blue, shadowed but warm. You drew me in. You warmed me. Confused me. Made me want, made me ache and made me sigh." With her fingertips she caressed the line of his shoulder where his hair ended. "I dreamed of you that night and every night after. I looked for you wherever I went. I held the image of you close to me, no matter who I met. And I ached. Until I felt your embrace." Her fingers trailed along his chest. "The warmth of you, the taste of you, the pleasure of being possessed by you." His heart was racing.

Gypsy restrained her smile. Perhaps he was a little more aware than she was giving him credit for.

"I should have told you." Her hand paused at the edge of the sheet just below his ribs. "How each time I saw you, I saw your eyes, I saw the Breed that saved me that night. Each time I saw you, I loved you a little more. Loved you deeper. I loved you truer."

She lifted her eyes to his to see the gleam of that rich, heated blue staring at her beneath lashes that dipped with drowsy arousal.

Her hand slid beneath the sheet and found flesh hardened with hunger and throbbing beneath her fingertips.

His jaw bunched as she ran her palm down the thick shaft to the tightly bunched spheres of his testicles, where she cupped gently.

"You shut me out," he accused her, his voice heavy, husky.

"I had to think, Rule," she chided him. "There will be times I have to think, times I'll have to sort my emotions for myself before I express them. If you get drunk and fight every time, then Dog and Loki are going to start protesting."

He grunted. "Fuck that. Next time, I'll find a human to pound on. They don't hit nearly as hard. Dog punctured a lung, Gypsy." He affected a wounded-hero look that almost broke her resolve not to laugh at him. "And Loki cracked a rib. I know he did."

"Poor little Lion," she sighed, brushing the sheet aside as she lowered her head to a nasty bruise forming just below one side of his broad chest. "Would it help if I kiss it better?"

She blew a light kiss over the bruise.

"You keep kissing and I'll let you know," he suggested with affected pain. "I'm certain it will eventually."

A hint of certainty nudged at her senses. The bruising was tremendous, but Breeds didn't feel pain as their human cousins did. The faker—the pain might have been bad for an hour or so, but she doubted it would be more than a twinge no matter what he was doing.

He stretched lazily against her, the fingers of one broad hand threading into her hair to press her lips closer to the abused flesh.

"I could need a lot of those kisses," he rasped, the deep, rough sound of his voice adding to the heat building beneath her own flesh and between her thighs.

She licked over the bruise, feeling his big body tighten, flex at the sensation.

"A lot?" she asked breathlessly. "It could take a while. I'm sure you're tired."

"Yeah, I should be," he groaned. "But I'll try to make sure I stay awake for it. Just to make certain you get each bruise."

She couldn't help the light laughter that escaped.

"I love you, Gypsy Rum. For so long, I've loved you."

The words had her pausing, blinking back tears and lifting her gaze to meet the somber, deepening emotion filling his.

"You should have told me." Lifting to him, she let her lips settle gently against his, careful of the flesh a heavy fist had split. "You should have let me love you, Rule."

The long length of her dark hair fell over her shoulders, shrouding them in an intimate cocoon as he stared up at her, drawing her to him, his lips parting.

Chocolate and peppermint filled her senses, heated spice and the sweetness of a love that knew more than selfishness, more than greed. A love that had watched, waited, and when the life she had chosen was no longer what she wanted, he was there.

That knowledge seeped into her, not from the man, but from what she was beginning to call the animal that tempered the man.

"Yeah," he breathed. "Because had I known what you were to me, I would have played hell having to wait until you were eighteen. Greedy. Impatient and selfish. I'd have taken everything I could and begged you to like it."

Their lips came together again, her tongue rubbing against his, the addictive taste of him infusing her senses further until they came up for air.

"You would have run." She continued the sensual debate in which, as words were spoken, emotions awakened and knowledge whispered into both of them.

"Think?" He nipped at her lips. "I was there the night you turned eighteen, Gypsy. Standing at the back of the crowd, watching, aching for you as you showed off your new leather pants and those sinfully high-heeled boots you wore. And all I could see was the aloneness that surrounded you and how I ached to replace it with a hunger for my touch, my kiss."

His lips slanted over hers as she gasped in pleasure, in surprise.

His lips stole reason, stole objection if there had been any. As his hands held her to him, one buried in her hair, the other gripping her waist as his tongue pierced her lips, penetrated her mouth and spilled more of the rich taste to her senses. Over and over again, as though he were fucking her mouth . . .

The image of him doing just that dragged a shattered groan from both of them.

She tore her lips from him, raining kisses down the tough line of his jaw, the surprisingly sensitive plane of his chest and along the tight abdomen where the throbbing crest of his cock waited impatiently.

Oh God, she was hungry for him.

Following his guiding hands in her hair as she moved between his thighs, Gypsy found herself becoming lost in the pleasures and fantasies that filled his mind as she touched him.

When her tongue licked over the blunt head of his cock and the wild, dark taste of his pre-cum exploded against her taste buds, the fantasy was obliterated, though. Shockingly, gentle hunger, protective greed and an overwhelming need circled her own emotions. As though he were wrapping his senses around hers, ensuring that she never feared allowing them free. He alone knew them. And he would never mistake the vulnerable sexuality she hid inside her soul for weakness.

As though that knowledge were all that was needed to release the hungry woman inside her, Gypsy felt it escape. Everything she had held back over the years, everything she had denied herself.

Her lips parted, her mouth sinking over the head of his erection, feeling it penetrate her lips as they both cried out in pleasure.

His pleasure whipping around her. Hers meeting and merging with it. Like a storm that threatened to never end.

Sucking at the blunt head as it thrust back and forth between her lips, Gypsy gave herself to the flames licking around her, inside her. She tongued the sensitive little spot beneath the head that throbbed a little harder, felt a little hotter. There, where the male mating barb released, locking him into her.

Her pussy clenched in hunger then, slick heat spilling to the swollen folds and distended bud of her clit as she pressed her thighs tight together and sucked him deeper into the depths of her mouth.

As she held him as deep as possible, her tongue rippling against the sensitive flesh beneath the head now, her lashes drifted open, her gaze meeting his.

"God, that's good," he groaned, panted. "Fuck, Gypsy, your mouth is so good. Sucking me so good."

Strong fingers clenched in her hair again, tugging at the strands as she began moving her mouth over him, meeting each upward thrust of his hips as he fucked into her mouth.

"Ah, fuck, yeah," he growled. "Tongue it just like that, baby. Damn, it's so good. So hot and so good."

Holding the base of the shaft with one hand, she stroked the rest of it to where her fingers met her lips. Her head bobbed up and down, her tongue licking, stroking, making them both crazy as desires met, married and swirled around them as one incredibly fierce need to please, to pleasure, to explode.

Strong thighs were taut, hard, like silk over iron as they flexed next to her shoulders. Controlled and fierce, her Breed growled, almost purred and cursed as the pleasure heated and the feel of moisture trickling from her vagina to the outer folds pulled a helpless moan from her.

Rising until her lips covered just the sensitive head to where the barb throbbed beneath his flesh, she sucked him tighter. Curling her tongue around it, licking, flicking against the narrow slit where the taste of his pre-cum tempted her, Gypsy teased and tempted the animal growling beneath her.

When he took her—when he came behind her, gripped her hips and surged inside her without pausing—she would be branded by the pleasure-pain of it.

She let the image of it fill her head, the remembered sensations torturing both of them as she felt his cock tighten, thicken further. He was fucking her lips with hard, short lunges, the head of his cock filling her mouth, rasping against her tongue as he groaned as though in agony.

"Enough."

Before she could stop him he had her on her back, his lips moving to her nipples. If she had thought to torture his cock head with her mouth, then he did more than think to torture her nipples with his.

Sucking one between his lips, he tightened the wet suction, drawing on her as a slightly rough rasp of his tongue sent one hard flash of exquisite pleasure striking at her womb, at the too-sensitive bud of her clit.

His fingers slid down her abdomen as his teeth rasped the little button of her nipple. His hand cupped her pussy, fingers curling inward to find the clenched entrance to the hungry inner flesh.

Two broad male fingers sank inside the saturated flesh, immediately flooding her senses with fiery pleasure, stretching, agonizing need as he pushed into the depths of her, his wrist turning, fingers reaching high inside her to find that place just beneath her clit.

Gypsy's eyes flared open.

"Rule, please," she cried out as he began spreading kisses from her nipples to her stomach, lower, moving between her thighs as his fingers stroked, rubbed and held her poised on the edge of rapture.

"Oh God, let me come," she cried out, her fingers clenching in the blankets beneath her as she strained toward him. "Rule, please . . . Oh God, don't stop."

The penetration pulled back, eased.

Gripping her hips with both hands now, he lifted them, his head lowering.

A wail of hungry need left her lips as he pushed his tongue inside her instead. The hint of a sandpapery roughness licking inside her, pushing into her, thrusting through the slick, tightened tissue was like agony. Like the most exquisite pleasure she'd ever known.

He ate her decadently, licking at her juices, growling in hunger as the impression of senses becoming immersed in her taste, in her need, slipped through her mind.

He fucked her pussy with his tongue as though he'd craved the taste of her forever. And maybe he had. Years of fantasy were drifting through his mind and he made no attempt to hide them from her. And this had been one of his favorites. Lifting her to him, licking her like a favored treat to his starving tongue.

Over and over he thrust into the needy channel, filling it with his tongue, her juices clinging to his lips each time he drew back, his gaze locked with hers.

Holding her thighs apart with his broad forearms, he kept her opened to him, wicked and hungry.

And he let her watch.

Let her watch as he pulled back, her juices clinging between her folds and his lips like nectar. Each inward stroke of his tongue came with the flickering licks inside her as he tasted her. Devoured her.

And Gypsy was certain she couldn't survive. Her clit was throbbing almost painfully, the need for sensation, the need to come, to explode driving her insane.

God, she needed. Needed him.

Pulling back, his stroking tongue moved higher, his fingers returning, pushing inside her as his lips surrounded the little bud of her clit and burned her senses with his hunger, with her need.

Impaling the heated depths of her pussy, his fingers parted the sensitive flesh there, scissored and stroked, stretching her, spilling more of her juices as she lifted to him, desperate now to escape into the chaotic pleasure awaiting her.

His tongue curled around her clit, sucked it into the heat of his mouth, worked his mouth around it, rubbed at it with his tongue, growled, the sound rumbling with vibrations of sensual greed and striking at a trigger she hadn't known her sensuality possessed.

She exploded.

Crying out, bearing down on his fingers a second before she dissolved around the penetrating pleasure, Gypsy felt herself flying apart at the seams.

She didn't exist anymore, not physically.

She was pleasure. Nothing but an erotic star going supernova in Rule's arms.

Her hips jerked against the suckling pressure of his lips around her clit and she exploded there a second later. The alternate explosions ruptured through her senses, throwing her higher, taking her further into a world where nothing but sensation ruled her now.

The fierce explosions were still sending aftershocks racing through her when he came to his knees, lifted her hips to him and watched, oh God he watched, as the head of his cock began pushing into the clenched entrance it sought.

She felt every molecule of sensation.

The heat. The stretch of flesh thicker than the fingers he'd pushed inside her to prepare her. The hard throb of the crest, the power in the iron-hard shaft.

"That's it, baby," he growled, sweat easing down his chest in thin rivulets as his eyes darkened, glowed brighter. "Take me just like that. All tight and slick, with all those pretty juices clinging to me as that tight pussy sucks me right in."

Another cry slipped free of her lips as she realized she was being pulled straight into the steady climb to another orgasm before the first one was finished tossing her through the sensual storm that had possessed her.

"Rule." One hand gripped one of his wrists as the other tore at the blankets beneath her. "Just do it. Oh God, I don't know if I can stand this."

Pleasure was a racking, torturous ecstasy as he took her slowly. So slowly, letting her feel every inch of his cock ease inside her, parting her with the wide, blunt head, staking claim, branding her inner flesh with erotic heat.

"That snug little cunt sucks at me like a hungry mouth," he groaned, the explicit words more involuntary, an expression and extension of his pleasure more than anything else. "Fuck yeah, suck me right in, baby. Tighten that hungry pussy around me."

A half growl, half snarl left his chest as she did just that involuntarily to the sound of the sexy order.

"Dream of this." He pushed in deeper, his hips flexing, driving his erection inside her another inch, pulling back, sinking in again as she began to writhe beneath him.

It was so good.

It was too good.

She didn't know if she could survive it. If she could survive the coming explosion.

"Rule!" She tried to scream out for him as he suddenly powered inside her.

Taking her in a single, deep stroke, burying his cock balls-deep inside the tight inner shudders of her pussy as sensation began to pulse, to throb inside her senses as she felt her orgasm building.

"God, I feel your pleasure," he groaned as she stared back at him in dazed, nearly uncomprehending hunger. "It surrounds me, Gypsy. Strokes me."

As his did her.

Pulling back, he drove inside her again, but this time, he didn't pause. He pushed his arm beneath her hips, lifted her hips and began fucking her with a hunger torn out of his control.

If he'd sensed her pleasure, she swore she had to feel his. The ultra tight, rippling flesh gripping him, stroking him as he sank to the very depths, his cock head burying itself in giving flesh, as if the blunt crest had buried itself in liquid lightning.

Pleasure struck at the sensitive crest, wrapped around the shaft, stroked and flicked and licked with electric pleasure that only built with each inward stroke until he was shafting inside her harder, the pleasure climbing, taking her, sealing her to him, until it suddenly pierced both their senses with blow after blow of such ecstasy that Gypsy wondered if they would survive it.

Her pussy tightened further around him, flexing and rippling as the first hard jet of his release pulsed inside her. Then that swelling extended from his shaft, just beneath the head of his cock. It became quickly erect, tucking in that narrow crevice behind her clit and increasing the sensation, the brutal pleasure with bolt after bolt of sensation even as the pulse of his release ejaculated inside her.

When it was over, his weight partly collapsed upon her, the rest boneless against the bed, exhaustion seeped through her. Through every muscle, every bone and cell, until it came to a shadowed, hidden part of her soul.

But Rule knew it was there. When he had found it, why he hadn't tried to force it open, she wasn't certain.

An impression of gentle chastisement touched her senses then.

No, he would never force it from her.

He would never take it from her.

It was hers to give as nothing else ever could be.

It was more precious than her love, more dear to him than her laughter or her smiles, she realized.

Gypsy tentatively released the final shield she'd built years ago between herself and anyone who threatened to touch her heart.

But Rule had done more than threaten to touch it. He owned it. He owned every part of her, even this fragile, so very vulnerable part of her soul.

For the first time in nine years, Gypsy gave her trust.

Completely. Willingly and without hesitation she bound herself to her Breed, both man and inner beast.

He found the energy to lift his head, to brush his lips against hers, then meet her gaze.

They didn't have to speak.

They could feel.

They didn't have to make vows.

It was all there already.

In that link that would never have existed if man hadn't thought he could create life, if the Almighty hadn't taken those creations and made them his own.

A link that gave her Breed full access, heart and soul.

But gave Gypsy complete, endearing love, dedication and an assurance, even if tomorrow didn't come, right now, here in his arms, she was finally complete.

"She was the child we did not believe we would be blessed with." Orrin Martinez sat with his two sons and their families. Their wives and children.

President of the Navajo Nation, Ray Running Wolf Martinez; his wife, Maria; and daughter, Claire. Orrin's younger son and legal advisor, the widowed Terran Martinez, and his two daughters, Isabelle and Chelsea. Behind Isabelle stood her mate, the Coyote Breed negotiator, Malachi Morgan. Sitting just behind Orrin and to his side was the Navajo Nation Headquarters head of security, Audi Johnson. Behind him stood his wife, Jane, and their daughter, Liza Johnson, as well as Liza's Wolf Breed mate, Stygian Black.

The entire family of Orrin Martinez as well as his lawyer faced two Lion Breeds and their mates, who had been summoned by the head of the chiefs of the Six Tribes to answer the question of their declaration of kinship to the Martinez family.

Rule sure hoped Isabelle had a little thankfulness in her heart after the secret he'd revealed for her. To save her father from a rash decision that would have destroyed her, based on another's lies, Rule had admitted to Terran that Malachi had never been in the labs where his baby sister, Morningstar Martinez, had been held captive for so many years before she was murdered beneath the cruel scalpel of the scientists that worked there.

Rule and Lawe had been in those labs, and they knew Malachi hadn't been there. They were the children of Morningstar, and whoever had come in contact with her during those years, they had known of it.

Rule and Lawe sat in front of the wide desk of the head of the chiefs of the Six Tribes, facing the family Orrin claimed. They were part of this family by blood, separated from them by intent.

As Orrin was one of the chiefs of the Six Tribes, his position on the Nation Council was assured. His opinion was highly respected. Orrin was well known for his honesty, his integrity. His son Ray had gained the vote as president of the Nation mainly because of his father's backing. But Orrin was also known just as well for his missing daughter and his determined search for her until twelve years past, when the Breeds had *officially* notified him of her death.

"Her mother, Aliva," Orrin continued, "died of grief two months after we received news that she had died." He shook his head, his voice thickening. "I, Ray, and especially Terran, we followed every lead, searched every place on this Earth we could search and we could not find our precious Star. The grief was more than her mother could bear."

It was all Rule could do not to sneer. The only thing that held the curl of disgust from his lips was confusion. Confusion because Orrin knew he had received all the information he had needed to find his *precious Star*, and he had ignored it. Yet the old man sat across from him, his face weathered and lined, his black eyes filled with tears that were blinked back quickly, and his scent one of honesty.

For his mate, for his Gypsy, he waited and listened. Feeling her hand on his shoulder, her silent support at his side, he did as he'd promised and listened with an open mind.

Orrin Martinez was one of the few whose scent was untainted by more deceit than truth, and Rule was damned if he knew how the old man did it.

He listened silently, his gaze drawn to the DNA results Orrin had demanded and now held in his gnarled hand. That hand shook, trembling so hard the chief finally laid it as well as the papers on the desk. Propping his elbow on the arm of the chair he sat in, Orrin bent his arm and covered his lips with his hand to hide the slight, supposedly uncontrollable tremor there.

He was lying, Rule knew he was lying, but he was damned if he could smell the scent of it. That shouldn't be possible.

He and Lawe both had risked not just their lives, but the lives of their younger brother and sister to send the proof of Morningstar's existence, her location and the fate she would soon face were she not rescued quickly.

And no one had come for her.

She and her Coyote mate, Elder, had died in an agony worse than any Rule could envision.

He stared at Orrin now, the long, thick gray braids that fell over the front of his shoulders, a traditional style that the Navajo males rarely used now. The appearance of tradition would have been comforting if Rule didn't know the man he was facing. If he wasn't well aware how the Martinez family had turned their backs on his and Lawe's mother while pretending to search so desperately for her.

It sickened him.

"This report states there were four children." Orrin's head lifted then, his gaze moving to Rule rather than Lawe, the older twin by several minutes.

Rule was slouched back in his chair, one booted foot propped on his knee, his black uniform pants still smeared with dirt along one side. Unlike Lawe, who had changed into fresh jeans and a white shirt that his mate, Diane, had waiting for him when they came in from yet another search in the desert for the Coyote teams amassing there.

Diane stood with Lawe, as Gypsy stood with Rule. The women stood between them, silent, listening, a steady strength for their mates.

Lawe sighed as though weary when Rule refused to answer the question concerning that younger brother and sister.

"There were four children." Lawe finally spoke. "Before fertilization, the DNA of the sperm and ova used were mutated with the Lion DNA. Using the same patriarchal samples, years later, the scientists mutated those with Cheetah and Coyote DNA. The Coyote DNA was that of the one called Elder, the head of their security forces who died with her. Our brother and sister were taken from the labs and moved only days after Morningstar's and Elder's deaths."

"Why were they moved?" Orrin asked, his gaze going once again in Rule's direction.

Not once did anyone ask why a Coyote was murdered with Morningstar. And Rule had no intention of answering any of the questions directed at him.

"They wouldn't stop crying." Lawe finally answered that one as well.

Rule remembered far too well those hours and days after Morningstar's screams had been silenced. The quiet, inconsolable sobs of the two youths refused to be silenced.

"What do you mean? They wouldn't stop crying?" Orrin tuned to Lawe, obviously tiring of his game and his attempt to force Rule to answer his questions.

At that point, Rule was damned sick of the charade, though. He leaned forward, dropping his foot to the floor, his gaze locked on the old man.

"Rule," Lawe muttered warningly.

Beside him, Gypsy tensed, her fingers caressing his shoulder where they lay.

"Have you watched the documentaries?" he asked the chief coolly.

"Rule." Malachi, the Coyote Breed that Terran Martinez's daughter Isabelle had mated, moved as though to step forward, or to protest.

Orrin's hand jerked up in a gesture of silence.

"Let him speak," he bit out, anger heating his expression as Rule's gaze locked with his.

"When we cried, when we showed emotion we were taught from birth not to show, then at that age, there were three options." He held up three fingers as Lawe growled his name once more. "They use that Breed as 'prey' in a hunt for the older Breeds, usually Breeds at their home lab. Those raised with them, to test the older littermates' savagery and lack of loyalty to their own." He lowered his little finger, leaving his ring and middle fingers raised.

"Dammit, Rule," Lawe bit out, his warning strengthened with an underlying growl.

Rule smiled, cold, hard, and continued. "They can transfer the Breed to another lab for research, or if they're considered worth rehabilitating, then they're retrained." His ring finger went down, leaving only the insult of the middle finger lifted in unconcern. "Or they're just taken out and shot like a rabid animal of no worth." He took his good old easy time lowering his middle finger.

For a moment, a surge of agony filled the room. Male and female pain alike whipped around them. But in that second of uncontrollable emotion, there was also the briefest sense of smug satisfaction.

Someone here knew the truth, knew Morningstar's fate and the horror of how she had died.

"You are a disrespectful little bastard," Orrin snapped out painfully.

"And you're a coldhearted son of a bitch to sit here before your family and pretend you knew nothing of your daughter's fate or the children she left behind when you were the one who ignored the plea we sent to *you!*" He stabbed his finger in the old man's direction. "To ignore the knowledge that she would die were she not rescued." Rule came furiously to his feet with a snarl as his mate's concern reached out to him, wrapped around him. "You received the file, the maps, the pictures, all of it, nearly two weeks before the scientists dissected the living bodies of both *your daughter and the Breed who gave his life to try to save her.* And yes, old man," he sneered. "Her youngest cried. Sobs that would not be silenced, and for that, they were in all likelihood killed as well."

He was furious, enraged. Slapping his hands down on the desk as he leaned forward, nearly staggering beneath the shock rippling through the room, he snarled into Orrin's pale face. "Now, what else would you like to fucking know?"

"Rule, this isn't helping," Gypsy whispered, and he could smell her tears, feel them along the link he shared with her. A pain she felt for his suffering, for the fears that still haunted him.

Moving to the opposite side, Gypsy pressed her forehead against his back, letting him know she was there and the strength of her love open to him if he needed it.

"Rule, enough!" Lawe surged to his feet, his hand landing firmly on Rule's shoulder, but rather than pulling him back, his fingers gripped it for a long second in shared pain, and in warning. "Enough, brother." He leaned closer. "Sense what I sense."

Rule pulled back. His senses merged with his brother's, something that rarely happened now that they both had their mates.

The shock was horrifying. It rolled and built, pulled from the hearts and souls of those who had loved Morningstar.

All but one, and that one wasn't Orrin.

Rule focused on each, finally following Lawe's gaze to the son standing still and silent behind his father, between the wife and daughter there to support him.

"How horrible," Ray whispered, as though they expected a reaction from him.

A Coyote growl rumbled through the room, followed by a Wolf's, as both Malachi and Stygian began sensing what Rule and Lawe had already tracked.

"You stink of a lie, President Martinez." Malachi turned slowly to face the other man with icy suspicion.

"No . . ." Orrin came quickly to his feet, disbelief surging from him as he stared at his son.

"We have proof the package was sent, and proof that it was signed for," Lawe stated, facing Ray as the president stared back at him with all the cunning deceit of the most depraved mind. "By Orrin Martinez."

"No . . ." Orrin whispered, shaking with such strength that he seemed to shudder. "I saw no package. I saw no proof that my precious daughter lived."

Ray's eyes flicked between the four Breeds facing him. "I signed for nothing . . ."

"Do not lie." Malachi, closest to him, caught the scent first. "Already I smell the stink of your deception, Ray, and it goes deep. What betrayal have you given the father you owe for your life and for your freedoms?"

"There were pictures of her children," Lawe stated softly. "Especially of the girl. The baby. She was only five. She was the one Morningstar called her precious Little Bit, because she was so tiny."

Orrin appeared to stumble, pain resonating from him as he stared back at Ray in shock.

"What have you done, Ray?" he whispered. "She was your sister. She loved you as she loved no other."

"There's proof someone of the Nation was supplying the Genetics Council with the names of Navajo girls whose family line showed a strong psychic connection," Lawe stated softly.

Rule could feel a part of his soul bleeding. He had treated this old man with disgust and disrespect, despite the truth that resonated even in his scent, because of the deception of the son.

"Morningstar cried for her brother." Rule couldn't hold back the rumble of the animal's growl. "From the time we were babes she would cry for her Ray," he sneered. "She would vow that her brother, so strong and loving, was coming for her. And all that time, it was the brother she so loved who destroyed her."

Ray stood, staring back at them all with icy disdain, refusing to speak.

"One of our own was selling our girls to the evil of those labs?" Orrin whispered painfully. "No. Ray. Tell them you did not do this horrible thing. Tell them."

"You know I wouldn't, Father." Sincerity filled his expression despite the coolness in his voice. "Star was my sister. I loved her . . ."

No Breed refuted the words, but the stench of the lie had all four losing control of the dangerous, predatory growls that rumbled in their chests.

"He's lying." It was Terran who spoke up, tears escaping his eyes as his daughters moved to surround him. "I came to him with the proof of my suspicions that someone within Window Rock was working with the Genetics Council since before Star was taken. He took the file I'd been putting together for decades and later swore it had been stolen. As though I'm so stupid as to not keep a backup." Fists clenched and rage poured from him. "You bastard. You bastard. We could have saved her. We could have brought her home."

Malachi and Stygian both jumped for Terran as he moved to grab his brother, murder firing in his eyes as the scent of vengeance began to pour from him. Like a sweet-smelling acid, it burned at the senses and the knowledge that given the chance, Terran would indeed kill him.

Even Ray's daughter, Claire, and wife, Maria, had stepped back from him, staring at him in horror.

Sneering at his brother, Ray straightened his jacket with a jerk. "I'll be damned if I have to stand here and listen to this." Turning to his wife and daughter, he snapped, "We're leaving."

Gripping his wife's arm and pulling her behind him, he was halfway to the door before he realized Claire hadn't followed.

Pausing, he glared back at his daughter to spit furiously, "Now, Claire."

Terran reached out for the girl who stood alone, tears whispering down her pale cheeks, her arms wrapped around her chest as though to hold back her pain.

Pulling her to him, between his own daughters and the protection of the Breed who stood with them, he sheltered her as Rule and Lawe had heard he always protected her.

"She's always come to me to escape the cruelty you pretended was so misunderstood," he stated, his voice heavy with pain. "She'll stay with me now."

Terran held her as she buried her face against his chest, her thin shoulders shaking with her silent sobs.

"And she'll regret it." A retaliatory sneer curled Ray's lips before he turned to Audi, Jane, Liza and the Breed who now stood with them. "They'll both regret it," he promised, his voice soft.

"Don't do it, Ray." Audi glared back at him. "Don't compound the horror of what you've already done."

As Audi spoke, Maria Martinez jerked from her husband's grip, quickly avoiding his attempt to grab her again as she stumbled against the back of Rule's chair.

Before either Rule or Lawe could steady her, Diane was there. Placing herself between the larger, broader Ray Martinez and his petite wife, icy contempt filling her eyes, she stared back at the Navajo president with a jeering smile.

"Touch her," Diane whispered, "and I'll take immense satisfaction in castrating you."

"You'll all regret it," Ray promised, his gaze slicing to Audi. "You especially."

With the final warning, he turned and stalked from the chief's office.

"Dog, keep an eye on President Martinez." Lawe activated the clip at his ear as the door slammed behind the other man. "If he leaves the building, I want to know where he goes. Lock jamming on all communication devices he attempts to use and inform me immediately if he attempts to contact any Council sources."

"Affirmative." Dog's reply came back immediately.

Breathing out heavily, Rule turned back to the Martinez family, his gaze going to the man who could have been his grandfather. If he had been born a man rather than a Breed.

Orrin sat down slowly, his gaze meeting Rule's, those endless dark eyes filled with nearly forty years of misery.

"You came to this office when first you arrived and spoke to my son, to request the help of the Navajo Nation in finding a rogue," Orrin whispered, shaking his head. "In your eyes I saw a carefully veiled contempt, and I agreed with Ray's suggestion that nothing good could come of help-ing you."

"He convinced us all, Grandfather," Audi spoke then, the title Orrin had given him use of when he was but a boy slipping from him as he stared at the old man in regret.

There was love here now, Rule thought. The tendrils of deceit and mal-ice that he hadn't been able to pinpoint finally identified. Now, only love and aching regret remained.

Orrin nodded slowly, still holding Rule's gaze.

"I have ached for the day that if the children of my daughter existed, they would come to her family. That they would reach out and allow us to extend to them all the love we felt for our precious Star, and more besides." A tear slipped past his cheek. "I would pray that the day would come that you would extend me your hand, grandson, and grant me the chance to show you the truth of my words."

Rule glanced at Lawe, knowing his brother had hoped this would be the greeting they received when they first arrived.

Lawe nodded slowly. Rule turned to him and slowly extended his hand. "I look forward to knowing you, sir."

To that, Orrin smiled sadly. "Ah, my daughter's son, I look forward to knowing my grandson." He turned to Lawe then, took his hand and whis-pered, "Both my grandsons, as well as the women they so love."

Orrin turned to his family then. "Liza, could you, Chelsea, Claire and Isabelle step into the outer office with your and Claire's mothers?" Audi Johnson asked heavily as he slowly moved his arm from where he'd held his wife to his side.

"Come on, girls," Jane Johnson ordered, holding her arms out to Claire as Terran released her. "Let's let them talk."

"About us?" Isabelle rolled her eyes, but kissed her father's damp cheek and did as Audi asked.

When the room had cleared of all but the Martinez men, Audi Johnson, Lawe's mate, and the four Breeds, Orrin clasped his hands on the desk and breathed out shakily.

"Audi, you must tell them all that you know," he ordered, lifting his gaze to meet his grandson's. "Then I will tell them of a ritual that was enacted on two young women whose souls were already passing, and lay to sleep the souls of two young women who would have died otherwise. Perhaps then, they will know how to protect these children who are so much a part of our hearts, no matter their names, no matter from where they came. They are ours now, and we will not give them up, our children, especially our daughters, without a fight."

✦ B R E E D   T E R M S ✦

Breeds: Creatures of genetic engineering both before and after conception, with the genetics of the predators of the Earth such as the lion, tiger, wolf, coyote and even the eagle added to the human sperm and ova. They were created to become a super army and the new lab rats for scientific experimentation.

The Genetics Council: A group of twelve shadowy figures who funded the labs and research into bio-engineering and genetic mutation to create a living being of both human and animal DNA, though references to the Genetics Council also refer to affiliated political, military and Breed individuals and groups.

Rogue Breeds: Breeds who have declared no known loyalties and exist as mercenaries following the highest bidder.

Council Breeds: Breeds whose loyalties are still with the scientists and soldiers who created and trained them. Unwilling or unable for whatever reason to break the conditioning instilled in them from birth. Mostly Coyote Breeds whose human genetics are far more dominant than in most Breeds.

Council Soldiers: Mostly human, though sometimes Breeds, soldiers who willingly give their loyalty to the Council because of their ideals or belief in the project and their belief that Breeds lack true humanity.

Bureau of Breed Affairs: Created to oversee the growing Breed population and to ensure that the mandates of Breed Law are fully upheld by law enforcement agencies, the courts and the Breed communities. The Bureau oversees all funds that are paid by the United States as well as other countries whose political leaders were involved with the Genetics Council or any labs in their countries. They also investigate species discrimination and hate crimes against Breeds and track down scientists, trainers and lab directors who have escaped Breed justice.

Director of the Bureau of Breed Affairs: The position has been held for the past ten years by Jonas Wyatt, a conniving, calculating and manipulating Lion Breed who ensures that Breed Law is upheld and all Breeds given a chance to be free to find mates who will ensure future generations of the Breed species.

Breed Ruling Cabinet: Composed of an equal number of Feline, Wolf and Coyote Breeds as well as human political leaders. It governs and enforces the mandates of Breed Law and oversees Breed Law where the separate Breed communities are concerned.

Purists and Supremacists and Their Various Groups: Groups of individuals who for reasons of religion, fear or just personal feelings believe that the Breeds are not human, but no more than puppets created in man's image. They're determined to destroy first the Breeds' public standing, then their lives. They dream of a world where Breed genetics have no hope, no chance and no threat of ever infecting the human population.

Their species discrimination against the Breeds includes but is not confined to the following: capturing Breeds and Breed-mated couples for further scientific study of how to weaken them or create a drug that will prevent the conception of hybrid children; guerrilla attacks against Breeds and Breed facilities; public outcries and protests against Breeds, Breed-funded and -hosted events and/or charities; bombings of Breed offices, attempts to kill key Breed political figures and general harassment whenever possible.

Nano-nit: A tiny microscopic robotic device that can be attached to a video or audio bug. Once in the proper location, it can be activated remotely, when it then detaches and finds the closest electrical source, where it will burrow inside and then follow the current to a designated electrical impulse for cameras, computers, televisions or any audio/video or computerized component, and then begins uploading specifically programmed information. Once the internal hard drive is filled, the nit then detaches and follows the electrical currents once again, to a point away from the original location, where it then finds a device, any device capable of Internet or uploading capabilities, and then transmits the information to a location that cannot be determined unless the nit is found during the upload process, after initial activation.

Named a nano-nit because of its size and similarity to the parasitic louse egg, or nit.

There is no known security to detect a nit specifically, and once activated, it's impossible to find, detect or exterminate. To find out, the host device must first be detected, then placed in a static-free, airtight shell, where a nit reader is plugged into the host device. The nit is then activated and makes its way from the host to search for an electrical source. It moves then to the nit reader's signature using the attached nit cord, which is an open-ended electrical cord that simulates the source the nit requires. Once there, a tiny probe locks the nit in place, allowing the reader to decode the programming and determine its original commands.

Nits have very little encryption. Because of their size and the requirements for upload space, programming is confined to what to upload and where to dump.

Because of their specific technology, a host device can be only an audio or video transmitter or bug. The nit is unable to function independently when attached to any other device.

Mating Heat: A chemical, biological, pheromonal reaction between a Breed and the male or female Breed or human that nature and emotion have selected as their one mate. Believed to be able to only mate once—though as Breed scientists have noted concerning other anomalies within the Breeds, nature is playing with the rules of the Breed species. To this point, general information on Mating Heat has been contained. Tabloids and gossip columns write about it, but no proof has been found to verify the rumor of it. Yet.

Mating Heat Symptoms: (Breed) A swelling of the small glands beneath the tongue and a taste, often different from Breed to Breed, which could be spicy, sweet, or a combination of both. Heightened arousal. The need to touch and be touched by the mate often. A heightened need for sex that results in a sensitivity to each touch and release that heightens the pleasure as well.

(Mate) An almost addictive need for the taste of the mating hormone secreted from the glands beneath the Breed's tongue. A sensitivity along the body and heightened need for sex that can become extremely painful for the female, whether human or Breed. Heightened emotions, an inability to refrain from touching or needing to be touched by the other.

Desert Dragoon: A vehicle built with independent suspension to traverse the rough, rocky and often uneven terrains of the desert. Built wide, for power rather than speed, blocky and capable of ramming through obstacles and carrying mounted weapons. Equipped with stealth technology, real-time GPS, satellite communications and laser- and bullet-resistant force fields that operate for short periods of time and act as theft deterrents.

Breed Ruling Cabinet: A cabinet of six high-ranking Breeds of each species and six humans of prominence and/or power who makes decisions for the Breed community as a whole.

Breed Law: The laws that govern every legal, contractual, criminal or enterprise endeavor involving any Breed or Breed affiliate, including but not limited to wives, children, siblings, parents, lovers, intended spouses, or the same of mates involved, and how the various governments of participating countries must deal with them.

Law of Self-Warrant: Any Breed can, one time only, accept punishment or death for any criminal act that would cause their mate, child, parent or other associated relative to face a punishment the Breed believes would cause his mate or child more harm than the loss of the Breed would cause.

Hybrid/Breed Hybrid: A child concieved naturally of a mated couple or of a Breed-human couple, whether mated or through artificial insemination.